PRINCES GATE

A DCI FRANK MERLIN NOVEL

ABOUT THE AUTHOR

Mark Ellis is a thriller writer from Swansea, and a former barrister and entrepreneur.

Mark grew up under the shadow of his parents' experience of the Second World War. His father served in the wartime navy and died a young man. His mother told him stories of watching the heavy bombardment of Swansea from the safe vantage point of a hill in Llanelli, and of attending tea dances in wartime London under the bombs and doodlebugs.

In consequence Mark has always been fascinated by WW2 and in particular the Home Front and the fact that while the nation was engaged in a heroic endeavour, crime flourished. Murder, robbery, theft and rape were rife and the Blitz provided scope for widespread looting.

This was an intriguing, harsh and cruel world. This is the world of DCI Frank Merlin.

Mark Ellis is also the author of *Stalin's Gold*, the second title in the DCI Frank Merlin series, and a member of the Crime Writers' Association.

He now lives in London with his family.

PRINCES GATE

A DCI FRANK MERLIN NOVEL

MARK ELLIS

LONDON
WALL
PUBLISHING

To Mair Ellis

First published in hardback, paperback and eBook in the UK in 2011 by
Matador, an imprint of Troubador Publishing Ltd

This edition published in 2015 by
London Wall Publishing Ltd (LWP)

A CIP catalogue record for this book is
available from the British Library.

PB ISBN 978-0-9929943-8-9
EB ISBN 978-0-9932917-0-8

1 3 5 7 9 10 8 6 4 2

Print and production managed by
Jellyfish Solutions Ltd

MIX
Paper from
responsible sources
FSC® C013604

London Wall Publishing Ltd (LWP)
24 Chiswell Street, London EC1Y 4YX

ACKNOWLEDGEMENTS

I would particularly like to thank Jon Thurley and Patricia Preece for their extensive advice on this book. My mother and my good friends Keith Ross, David Deane and Ian James read early drafts of the manuscript and gave me useful comments and encouragement, while John Collis helpfully cast his professional eye over my work. Kate Ellis helped with the choice of cover and, together with Victoria, Claudia and my family and many friends, provided strong support. Audrey Manning coped heroically with the typing of the manuscript's many drafts. I thank them all. Finally, I am grateful to Rachel Hudson and Fiona Marsh at London Wall Publishing who have helped with the production of this book.

PROLOGUE

London – January 1940

It was lunchtime and the Lyons Tea House was doing a lively trade as usual. A pungent fug of cigarette smoke, stewing vegetables and body odour hung above the crowded, clattering tables of a restaurant whose drab decor accorded well with the general dowdiness of its customers. Just after one o'clock, on what was a particularly chilly winter's day, a sudden burst of colour enlivened the scene as a pretty young woman, her flowing, golden hair capped by a bright red beret, hurried through the entrance and looked into the room, big blue eyes darting around anxiously.

"Is there an upstairs here? I'm meeting someone, you see, and I can't see him."

The busty, peroxide blonde waitress nodded brusquely towards the back of the room.

"The way up's over there, love."

Muttering her thanks, the young woman began to make her way through the press of tables. She ignored a leering young soldier who pursed his lips theatrically into a kiss, to the amusement of his colleagues, and reached the foot of the stairs. Then she saw her luncheon companion leaning back casually at a small, out-of-the-way table reading a newspaper. Her heart sank. He had caught her unawares that morning when he had bounced up from nowhere, flashing his perfect teeth as she sat miserably at her desk, and she'd said yes without thinking. Now there he was, his paper set aside, grinning and waving to her. She put her head down and pushed her way past the tables with their prattling customers and headed, with dread, to join him.

When he had calmed down, after paying the bill, he suggested a walk in the park and she told him to go to hell.

"Suit yourself, then."

An icy gust cut into her face and she shuddered as she watched him stride jauntily away. He had had the gall to suggest a re-run. When she'd refused he had lost his temper and made threats. The meat pie, which he'd ordered for her, churned in her stomach. Tears, which had been building below the surface throughout the meal, began to trickle down her cheeks.

A grizzled old man, rolling himself a cigarette at his pitch outside the tube station, paused to watch her as she turned and ran down the street. He took a couple of puffs and resumed his patter. "Mr Chamberlain's speech to the House. New rationing regulations. More German atrocities in Poland. Read all about it!"

* * *

The blackout was particularly dense and all-enveloping that night. The man hunched his shoulders as he leaned into the biting wind whistling down the invisible Mall. He wore a mackintosh which hung to within an inch of the ground and a homburg hat one size too small. In his right hand he carried a heavy, old black briefcase. In his left, where his arthritis was playing him up tonight, he carried an umbrella. He turned a corner and made his way slowly across Horse Guards Parade. A distant searchlight provided the faintest glimmer of background light. No matter. For once he had remembered his torch, which he held in the same hand as his briefcase. The beam led him over the road into the park, then on into Birdcage Walk. Cars drove past sporadically, groping their way through the treacly darkness with blinkered headlights. His teeth were chattering, but soon he would reach the station. It was a straightforward journey from there.

The annoying meeting he had just concluded at the Ministry replayed in his mind. Why wouldn't they listen to him, those pinstriped idiots. Ach! Why did he bother? He could feel his blood pressure rising. "Count to twenty. Be calm. Count to twenty." That's what his friend Spinoza had always said to him when he could see the temper flaring. He was too old to have such a short temper. He started counting. He had reached the end of his second twenty when he stumbled on a crooked flagstone and the torch and the briefcase fell to the ground. The torch rolled to the edge of the pavement and its light dimmed as it settled against the briefcase. As he bent down he heard an engine revving in the distance. He grasped the torch and stood up, feeling his knees creak, then bent again for the briefcase. The engine sound grew louder and louder, before all at once there was a high-pitched screech of brakes and he felt a massive thump on his shoulder. A searing pain scorched his spine and he fell forward into the gutter. Briefly he heard doors bang and the sound of footsteps. Then nothing.

* * *

The pigeons squawked and fluttered their wings in irritation as the two men hurried across Trafalgar Square before crossing over to the Strand. They turned right past the station and headed towards the Embankment. The drunks and tramps sleeping under the arches made little complaint as the men nimbly picked their way through them. The Wiseman brothers, still known to many down the Commercial Road as "The Knockout Twins" in memory of their youthful prowess in the ring, had found some easy pickings down here before Christmas. It was dangerous, of course, with Scotland Yard so close at hand and the roaming river defence searchlights to watch out for, but they had been working Kensington and Mayfair for the past couple of weeks with surprisingly little success and had agreed easily on a change of scene.

They were both over six feet but Stan was the burlier of the two. He led Sid across the road and leaned over the river wall.

The searchlight beams were concentrating on the City and the east, and their chosen patch was dark enough.

"Hush. There's someone."

The sound of steps and muffled laughter came to them from fifty, perhaps a hundred, yards away. A man and a woman. Stan squeezed his brother's arm. "Let's do it."

Keeping their heads down they slipped silently along the pavement. A half-moon dipped in and out of the clouds above. A few yards ahead a match was struck. They could see the glow of cigarettes. The couple had stopped under a tree and were looking out over the river.

"I'll take the man, you do her." Stan whispered.

He found the cosh in his pocket as he ran towards the couple. His arm flashed through the night air. The man fell heavily to the ground as Sid put his arm round the woman's shoulder and clamped one hand on her mouth. His other hand held a knife with which he stroked her neck. "Keep your mouth shut darling and everything will be alright."

The woman squirmed and he nicked her. The clouds parted and he could see the thin scarlet trickle on her pale skin. She became still.

Stan knelt down beside the unconscious man and, in business-like fashion, went through his pockets. A thick wallet, several notes and coins and a pocket watch emerged. He chuckled as he rose to his feet, pulled the woman's handbag from her hands and looked inside. "Our lucky night" – he removed more notes and coins, a compact and a cigarette lighter – "and look at this." A pearl necklace was roughly torn from her, as were her rings and bracelets. Stan stuffed his own pockets and Sid's with the takings. The man on the ground was breathing heavily and clouds of steam rose into the frozen air about him.

"A big one, isn't he? Good job I caught him proper." Stan turned his attention again to the woman. He unbuttoned her coat and ran his hands over the smooth fabric of her dress. "This one's quite a sweetheart. Perhaps we've got time for a bit of fun before we go. Her boyfriend's going to be in the land of nod for a while. Let's…"

The sound of a car's brakes screeching nearby interrupted him. He thought he could see a car up towards the bridge. The moon came out of the clouds again and now he could see figures at the side of the car. There was a flash of red and then of white. He could hear a man's voice shouting and a woman's responding. Then a man's voice again. Was it the same man or another? He couldn't tell and he couldn't make out any words. A woman's voice started again, a strained and anxious voice. Sighing, he turned back to his female victim and stroked her cheek. "Better not push our luck, eh, dear? You'd have enjoyed it, though." He patted her bottom. "Let's hop it."

Sid released his grip on the woman, pulled back his fist and hit her hard in the stomach. As she slipped to the ground they ran off as fast as they could, their pockets jangling with their takings. They didn't stop until they reached the gardens in front of the Savoy. They fell onto a bench and, when they'd recovered their breath, they could hear nothing except the light snoring of a tramp in the bushes behind.

CHAPTER 1

Monday January 22nd 1940

Patches of snow covered the riverbank and small ice floes drifted along in the river. The sky was a brilliant blue and the Colonel wished he'd brought along his old military goggles to shield his eyes from the glare. His next-door neighbour, Thompson, a city broker, had told him over a friendly sherry the night before that his office colleagues were running a book on it proving the coldest winter of the century. The freezing weather meant that his regular morning walk had been brisker than usual and, by his reckoning, as he approached Barnes Bridge he was probably ten minutes ahead of schedule.

The ugly metal latticework of the bridge sparkled in the sun as he strode along the river path, thinking happily of the bacon and eggs awaiting him at home. When he was almost under the bridge, a large boat chugged by creating a wake, which flowed rapidly towards the shore. It was high tide and, before he had time to take evasive action, several waves splashed over the bank and onto his best tweed trousers. Swearing loudly he turned to wave his walking stick uselessly at the boat, a working barge heading up river. He bent down to mop his trouser legs with a handkerchief. As he rose stiffly, having made little improvement to the sodden state of his turn-ups, his eyes roved over the flotsam gently pushing up against the riverbank. There was the usual mixture of empty tin-cans, beer bottles, newspapers, wrapping paper, sticks and branches. However, in an area of water near the bridge, at the point where the sharp glare of the daylight became subsumed in the dark shadow of the bridge, the Colonel's attention was caught by an object which, because of the intermittent dazzle, appeared as if caught in the flashing beam of a semaphore light.

He reached out with his stick and poked the whitish object a few times but couldn't get it to move towards him. Edging closer to the water's edge, he was grasping a stanchion of the bridge for support when he heard the engine of another boat. He scrambled back up the bank and watched a small cruiser pass under the bridge on the far side of the river. There were no waves to worry about this time and his gaze returned to the floating object. His heart pounded as he realised with horror that he was looking at a human hand, attached to a body which was slowly rising to the surface. He took a couple of very deep breaths. The body appeared to be female and clothed in pale pink underwear, but he didn't have the stomach for close analysis. The empty eye socket was enough for him. He took another deep breath and headed for the police station, which was just a short distance up the road.

* * *

Detective Chief Inspector Frank Merlin stared angrily out of his window at the barrage balloon drifting aimlessly above the London County Council headquarters. He had timed his discussion with Assistant Commissioner Gatehouse badly. As he had entered his boss's office he should have realised that something was amiss from the deep red tinge of the A.C.'s cheeks.

"May I have a few words with you, sir?"

"Yes, but 'a few' means 'a few' and be sharp about it."

"I wondered if you'd given any further thought to my request of the other day?"

"Request? What request? Oh, you mean your request to leave me in the lurch and enlist?"

"Er – yes sir. I would like to volunteer to join up as we discussed."

"Merlin, I have just come from a deeply unpleasant meeting with the Commissioner and the Home Secretary. Sir John may appear in public to have the animation of an elderly Scots

Presbyterian undertaker, but I can tell you that in private he has a little more vim about him. I have just been berated for over an hour on the numerous failings of the part of the Metropolitan Police under my command.

"Sir John Anderson tells me that while our nation currently stands at perhaps its greatest ever peril, he would sleep better at night if we, or rather I, would get off my backside and get a grip on, in no particular order of importance, Irish republican bombers, pilfering dockers and factory workers, Mosleyite fifth columnists and the numerous ruffians and thieves taking advantage of the blackout, not to mention the rocketing accident statistics caused by the murderous driving habits of most after-dark drivers. This I am required to do when I have already lost, or am about to lose, large numbers of my brightest youngsters to the forces, and several of my best senior people have been seconded to the Government for security purposes. At this moment you, probably the finest detective I have, having already done a good bit for King and Country in the last show, want to bugger off and get your head blown off with the British Expeditionary Force."

"But sir …"

"No. The answer is no. Your country and, more specifically, *I* need you here and that's final. Don't think I don't appreciate the sentiments but if all my best officers disappear, chaos will ensue – and chaos, Frank, is worth a hundred divisions to Herr Hitler. Just think of it that way. Anything else?"

"No, sir."

Merlin fumbled in his jacket pocket for the packet of Fisherman's Friends. He had become strangely addicted to these powerful menthol lozenges over the past year. As he took his fix his eyes refocused on his reflection in the glass of the windowpane. A lock of jet-black hair hung over his forehead. He needed a haircut. His dark green eyes stared back at him. His hand rose to his cheek. A few more creases there. Eight years to go till he was fifty. His father had been an old man at that age. Still, he didn't look so bad. He had a long, narrow, rather elegant nose and a full mouth. His laughter lines remained despite his recent tribulations. There was no fat on his face and he had the same collar size as when he was eighteen. He had a trim, lean figure on which his suits hung well, as Alice had often remarked.

Behind him in the reflection, he could see the office which had become his second home. He'd had it since his promotion just over three years ago – that would be just six months after he got married. There was the solid oak desk he'd picked up for nothing on the Portobello Road to replace the rickety Scotland Yard standard issue. The desk was always swamped with papers. Tidiness had never been his strong point. His comfortable battered leather chair sat behind the desk, facing two less comfortable companions on the other side. In the corner was a small table and another chair mostly used by his trusty Sergeant – someone else whose military ambitions had been thwarted, though for different reasons. When he'd moved into the office, the walls had been a dreary green colour and he'd insisted, to the irritation of the A.C., on having them repainted off-white. On the wall facing the window was a large-scale map of London, beside an ornate cuckoo clock acquired on a fraud goose-chase in Switzerland a couple of years earlier. Behind him was a picture of a 1924 police football team, featuring a blurry picture of him at the back right-hand corner. On the wall facing his desk were two Van Gogh prints – he loved the post-Impressionists and the mad Dutchman most of all. He had a print of a Goya painting too – a firing squad in action somewhere in Spain, or was it Mexico? He'd never found out. This was to the left of the office door which, half-paned with frosted glass, was in turn to the left of the London map. The floor was linoleum but he'd put down a couple of intricately patterned red Persian rugs to liven things up a little – again modestly-priced acquisitions from the Portobello Road.

He shook his head and looked down at the lunchtime throng trudging through the snow and ice beneath him. Time for a walk to clear his head, he thought.

Turning out of the Yard on to the Embankment, he made for Parliament Square. It was as cold as he could remember and the Thames was frozen over in several places. His navy overcoat was getting a bit threadbare and the wind shearing off the river hit him like a knife as he rounded the corner at Westminster Bridge. He needed a new overcoat really, and some new suits, shirts and shoes would not go amiss. He'd been quite fussy and proud about his clothes and appearance for most of his adult life, but since his wife's death he'd let himself go a little in that department – well, no, if he was being honest, he'd let himself go a lot. His brother's wife Beatrice had nagged him about this and other things, and had recently started making small contributions of her own. Fortunately she had good taste.

The news posters outside the tube station had moved on from the most recent parliamentary cause célèbre, the forced resignation of the War Minister, Hore-Belisha, and were now focusing on Russia's invasion of Finland. "Russians press forward. Finnish resistance fighting fiercely." Merlin smiled to himself as he thought of his good friend, Jack Stewart, staunch socialist and supporter of the Soviet experiment. He looked forward to hearing him tie himself in knots trying to justify Stalin's motives for the attack on the hapless Finns.

After a quick circuit of Parliament Square, he had got most of the A.C.'s bile out of his system and he stepped into Tony's Café for a hot drink.

★ ★ ★

Frank Merlin had been born Francisco Diego Merino, the eldest of three children, in the Limehouse district of East London, in September 1897. His father, Javier Merino, a shepherd's son from Northern Spain, had managed to escape a life of backbreaking rural poverty by making his way, at seventeen, to the bustling port of Corunna and going to sea. After twelve years of circling the globe on merchant vessels small and large, he had tired of the seaman's life and had dropped anchor in the port of London. After a brief unhappy period when he had to scratch his living on the streets as a dancer and singer of romantic ballads, his dark good looks had caught the discerning eye of Agnes Cutler, daughter of Alfred Cutler, the proprietor of Limehouse's largest chandlery store. Javier was personable and good with figures and his wife, as Agnes swiftly became, soon ensured that he was installed as her father's right-hand man. In due course, on his father-in-law's retirement, Javier became general manager of the store. Three children had arrived in quick succession – Francisco, Carlos and Maria. Shortly after his daughter was born, Javier, finally tired of the laboured efforts of his friends, neighbours and customers to pronounce his name properly, and Anglicised it. He became Harry, while for good measure his sons became Frank and Charlie, and his daughter Mary. A short time afterwards, Alfred decided to make his son-in-law his full partner and Javier took this opportunity to lose the Spanish surname as well. It reminded him of those damned sheep he'd had to chase around those arid, rocky, Spanish crags back when he was young. An intelligent, self-educated and well-read man, he had always loved the Arthurian legends. So Javier Merino became Harry Merlin, and Cutlers Chandlery became Cutler and Merlin's Limehouse Chandlery Emporium.

* * *

Merlin was stirring his tea when a tall, burly young man with a mop of fair hair pushed through the door. The sight of his right-hand man always raised his spirits, and he couldn't restrain a smile as Sergeant Sam Bridges lolloped clumsily in. He swiftly checked himself though, and feigned irritation. "'See the conquering hero comes, sound the trumpets, beat the drums' Huh! So much for my little moment of peace."

"Sorry sir, but something's happened in Barnes."

The Chief Inspector sighed loudly and put down his spoon.

"That's a turn-up for the book then. Normally nothing ever happens there, excepting the final gasps of the Boat Race that is. What's up?"

The Sergeant scratched a cheek. "A body, sir. They want us to go round there straight away."

"By 'they', I suppose you mean the not-very-competent local constabulary?"

"Inspector Venables called me. Thought it looked suspicious and we might want to take a look. He might be wrong but remember you gave him a hard time about that Martins case in Richmond when he didn't get us involved at the outset. I suppose he's just being cautious."

Merlin grunted and sipped his drink.

"The body's female and young, so far as they can tell. Fished her out of the river. Not a pretty sight apparently."

"Never are, are they? Can't one of my inspectors handle it?"

"They're all out on cases, sir. We're the only ones available and…"

"Alright, alright. Have you got a car outside?"

On the journey, Merlin carefully examined his Sergeant's face as he concentrated on the road. Bridges' ruddy features had resumed their customary happy-go-lucky cast and the shadow that had darkened them recently seemed to have disappeared. He appeared to be back to his normal self, but Merlin wasn't completely sure. The rejection had been humiliating for him, reinforcing the insecurities of a miserable childhood which Dr Michaels at Barnardos and, more recently, his new wife had done so much to help him overcome. Despite all the traumas of his upbringing he had turned out to be a bright, diligent, kind young man. Now the Army Board had made him feel a freak again. Perhaps it was a freakish thing to have six toes on one foot, but did it really make him unfit for military service? Of course now that Merlin had suffered his own rejection, he could not help but feel relieved that Bridges would continue by his side. But he'd have to keep a close eye on him.

A band of policemen were milling around at the river's edge when they pulled up. A haze of tobacco smoke shimmered in the icy air above them. Merlin saw Venables' hairless head jerking up and down in animated discussion with his colleagues and pushed past the small crowd of onlookers on the towpath.

Hector Venables was a large, ungainly man, whose prominent Adam's apple jumped around his neck as if it had a life of its own. "There you are, Frank. I don't quite know what to make of this one."

"Now there's a surprise," Merlin muttered to himself under his breath.

Venables shook his head before leading the way under the bridge. A constable carefully pulled back the top of a white tarpaulin. Merlin tasted something unpleasant at the back of his throat. The woman's left eye was closed and the other was missing. Her lips had contorted in death into a quizzical smile. Venables bent down to pull the tarpaulin completely off. The woman's petticoat had ridden up her body and the policemen stared down uncomfortably at the grey-white flesh of the woman's legs and her pink underwear. Merlin's eyes slowly travelled from the large bruise on her right thigh to the livid mark poking out from beneath soggy strands of fair hair on her forehead.

Venables scratched his nose thoughtfully. "Not so pretty now but she might have been a bit of a looker."

Merlin tried unsuccessfully to imagine the living face.

"Quite a young thing too, Frank."

They heard steps echoing under the bridge.

"Here's the sawbones."

A portly, elderly gentleman in a battered deerstalker approached and nodded his greeting. After a cursory examination, Dr Sisson made a few notes, paused to take a pinch of snuff, then spoke in a high staccato voice. "I'll take her away now if that's convenient and I'll give you my detailed views tomorrow morning."

"What do you think, Doc? What about the eye. Think it's …?"

The doctor clucked his tongue at Venables.

"No premature inspired guesses, gentlemen. I'll do the work and then I'll let you know."

He threw the tarpaulin back over the body which two constables then carried carefully into the police ambulance parked nearby. The waiting crowd jostled for a view and there was a collective sigh when an arm slipped out from under the cover, as it disappeared into the back of the vehicle. The ambulance drove off and the murmuring onlookers gradually dispersed.

"Who found the body, Hector?"

"Colonel Trenchard. Local man." Venables nodded towards a riverside bench a few yards beyond the bridge, where the old man had been waiting with increasing impatience. They strolled over to him and Merlin made his introductions.

"Just tell us as simply as you can what happened, sir."

"I was taking my morning constitutional, as always, down to the brewery and back. Done it pretty much every morning for the last fifteen years since I packed it in with the regiment. Leave at 0730 and back to Mrs Trenchard at 0900 on the dot. Never late, sir. Never. Until today that is."

"And Mrs Trenchard would be where?"

"We have a place near Hammersmith Bridge on this side of the river. Lived there for years with the wife. Since the last nasty business in fact. Bought the house in 'nineteen. Got a great bargain. Bought it from this French chap. He thought he'd done very well on it but I've…"

"So you walk every morning from Hammersmith down to the Watney's brewery in Mortlake and back, is that correct?"

"That's it. This morning I set out at the usual time. Bloody freezing morning. It's going to be the coldest January for years apparently. My neighbour…"

"Just stick to the walk please, Colonel."

"Right-ho. Sorry. Anyway, got down to the brewery in

good time. Then on my way back encountered this dreadful sight. Poor dear!"

The Colonel's eyes watered and he produced a purple handkerchief into which he blew noisily. "Awful sight. I wasn't sure what it was at first. A boat passed by and drenched me. I was trying to dry myself when I noticed something. Thought it was a piece of wood. Her hand that is, which is all I could see at first. Then the rest of her came to the surface. Seen worse sights at Ypres, but still…"

"Could the body have come from the boat, sir?"

"Well, do you know, I don't know, Sergeant. I suppose it might have. There was a lot of splashing, when the waves hit the bank and when they hit me. I didn't notice what turned out to be the body until after the boat had passed, so it's possible."

"What kind of boat was it?"

"Just a normal old river barge. Didn't really get a good look as I was attending to my soaking trousers. Couple of fellows on the back of the boat but I couldn't really describe them. Think there was a flag, now was it blue or blue and white? Blue and white I think."

"Did you see anyone else around?"

"No. Another boat passed a little later on the other side. I was the only one on the towpath straight after I found her. I walked along to the local police station over there. First person I saw was the bobby at the desk. I told him what I'd found and after that there's just been a lot of bloody tedious waiting around."

"Sorry about that, sir. I think we can get you off home now. Just give the Sergeant here your address."

The old man rose stiffly. "Best of luck catching the bugger who did it, gentlemen. Anything else I can do, just call. I may be getting on a little but I've still got all my faculties, you know!"

* * *

The girl hurried across the Gloucester Road in the fading

10

winter afternoon light, dodging crawling lorries and taxis struggling to make their way through the gloom. She was carrying a basketful of small cakes and biscuits which she had bought at the little bakery around the corner. She turned down a side-street and was soon back at the staff entrance of the large house in Princes Gate. The Ambassador was away in America, but there was still plenty of work to do. She'd been at her typewriter all day and was glad when Miss Edgar had allowed her to go on this small shopping errand.

A modest celebration was to take place. Miss Edgar, who was in charge of the administration of the Ambassador's residence, had given permission for a tea party for one of the Ambassador's chauffeurs, whose twenty-first birthday it was. Below stairs of course, but as Kathleen Donovan saw it, it was very decent of Miss Edgar, who was forbidding to look at but had a kind heart. She'd even contributed to the pot Kathleen had collected from among the other secretaries, butlers, maids and chauffeurs. The birthday boy was Johnny Morgan, a dark, attractive young Welshman. Nearly all the girls in the residence had a soft spot for him. Even Miss Edgar treated him with a trifle more indulgence than she offered elsewhere. He was also a favourite of the Ambassador, for whom he had been working for the past year.

She skipped down the creaking staircase and joined a group of some twenty people in the small parlour next to the kitchen. "Here are the cakes, everybody."

"Thank you, dear," said a tall, bespectacled woman wearing her hair coiled in a tight bun. "Please set them down on the table. Now come along everyone. Tuck in. Come on, Johnny Morgan, make the most of your birthday. Your next one could be in uniform and I don't mean the one in which you drive Mr Kennedy."

"Don't say that, Miss Edgar. I'm sure it'll all be over this time next year." Morgan's smile expanded into a broad grin. "The Ambassador says that Mr Chamberlain will have to agree a truce with Mr Hitler and there'll be no real fighting as everyone will realise we haven't got a hope in hell on the battlefield."

"That's enough of that. Just because it's your birthday doesn't mean you're at liberty to repeat the Ambassador's private thoughts. Everyone here will kindly forget those remarks. I am sure whatever Mr Kennedy said was not intended in a defeatist way."

Several of those present smiled to themselves. The Ambassador's defeatist views were well known within the residence and embassy and outside. Indeed, at that very moment, Mr Kennedy was back in America doing his best to ensure that his President did not commit national resources to such a hopeless case as Britain.

Kathleen's green eyes lingered on Morgan's face. Although she knew that he was a milkman's son from a small mining village outside Swansea, his high cheekbones and chiselled features gave him an aristocratic air, or so it seemed to her. She was a looker herself, with silky red hair, striking green eyes and a warm, welcoming mouth. Her old friends at home in Kerry called her Maureen because of her resemblance to the Hollywood film star Maureen O'Hara. A more recent friend in the Ambassador's residence, Joan, another pool typist, had made similar comparisons. She laughed along with the teasing and compliments, but, looking intently at herself in the mirror in her digs, she worried that her face was too bland, plain even. She had never had a boyfriend and was nervous in male company. Johnny Morgan was nice to her, though, and she didn't feel quite so shy with him. He was nice to all the girls, to Dora, Virginia, to Joan... Looking around suddenly, she wondered where Joan was and asked Miss Edgar.

"No idea, dear. She didn't turn up for work on Friday, nor today, and I've had no message about her being ill. I'm a little annoyed as there's a backlog of work for her. Mr Norton has a pile of reports he wants typed to be sent to the Ambassador."

"Do you know, Johnny?"

"What?"

"Where Joan is. I thought she'd be here to celebrate your birthday."

"Maybe she's not well or something."

"Didn't you see her for lunch on Thursday? How was she then?" Priestley, one of the other Embassy drivers, joined them.

Morgan fumbled in his pocket for a cigarette. "Not me, Bill. I haven't seen Joan for a week or so." He turned towards the main door. "Sorry. This tea is running through me like nobody's business. Back in a minute."

Henrietta, an upstairs maid, lifted her pert nose. "I suppose that's the vulgar behaviour you must expect in wartime when the best service jobs are going to miners up from the valleys."

"I expect it's nothing. A cold perhaps or some small problem at home," said Priestley, who was a small, pale man with buck-teeth. "Funny though. I could have sworn I saw the two of them going into the café round the corner on Thursday." He greedily demolished a teacake. "My missus keeps on at me to get some spectacles but I don't think there's really a need. Probably saw him with another of his floozies." Kathleen blushed. "Well we all know what Johnny's like, don't we?" Priestley wiped his mouth on his sleeve. "Anyway, I don't think it's right for a chauffeur to wear glasses, do you? Don't think the Ambassador would like it either."

Morgan returned and flashed a winning smile in Kathleen's direction. "Fancy a drink after?"

"I don't know. I was going to try and get home early and…"

"And what? Don't be a spoilsport. Just a quiet one. To properly celebrate my birthday. What do you say?"

"Alright then. Just a quick shandy." Morgan patted her shoulder and she felt a warm tingle run down her back. The mystery of Joan's whereabouts faded from her mind.

CHAPTER 2

Merlin awoke in his Chelsea lodgings with a groan. His mouth was as dry as the Sahara Desert. He sat up in his bed, pulled back the heavy grey curtains and looked out of the window. He was living in a pleasant part of town but he couldn't say his view was that wonderful. He could see the backs of two terraces of houses, separated by a row of tiny gardens. In the distance he could see the steeple of a church covered in scaffolding. Problems with the roof apparently. Turning inwards he gazed blearily at his small bed-sit. The Bush radio he'd spent a couple of guineas on at Christmas sat heavily on his bedside table. He had an old red armchair that needed re-covering next to the table and not much else. A dark brown wardrobe and chest of drawers stood by the washbasin opposite the door. Another Van Gogh print, the one of the starry night, hung out of alignment next to the mirror above the sink. His battered old record player sat on the floor by the window. There was little comparison with his and Alice's cosy quarters in their old Fulham house.

He rose, walked over to the basin, straightened the Van Gogh, and bent to drink copiously from the tap. He had sold that house as quickly as he could after Alice's death. The agent had told him he could have got a much better price if he'd just been a little more patient. But Merlin hadn't wanted to be patient. He'd also sold most of the household effects at knock-down prices, needing desperately to get shot of everything as quickly as he could. Alice's death had been so sudden. The house was full of her – the ornaments, the furniture, the pictures, the china, the air – everything vibrated with her personality, her beauty, her spirit. He couldn't bear it. Jack

Stewart had been a brick. He'd found the agent. He'd found the people to dispose of the household effects. After the funeral, he'd put his friend up for a while at his little flat in Pimlico. And when Merlin had insisted on not being a burden any longer, Stewart had found the bed-sitting room off the King's Road in which Merlin now shivered.

He had wanted something simple and central. He had the money now, after Alice's death, to afford something better. He could have bought another house in Fulham or a nice flat in Chelsea. But these lodgings were fine for the moment. He was, in many ways, a solitary man, but he liked the sound of human activity in the house. His landlords were good people. Dr Hewlett was a retired GP, a genial, white-haired man, seldom seen without his pipe and with a penchant for malt whisky and lengthy discussions about the merits or failings of the Surrey cricket team. Mrs Hewlett was a bubbly little Northerner, who chided her husband over the polluting impact of his pipe-smoking but shared his drinking and sporting tastes. In many ways they had the same sort of down-to-earth teasing relationship that he'd had in his marriage.

He splashed the freezing water over his face. It had been a mistake to meet up with Jack Stewart. He'd never been much of a drinker before Alice died – an occasional pink gin perhaps or a glass of red wine. Stewart had encouraged him to drown his sorrow with beer and plenty of it. He had now acquired the taste and was, he knew, drinking too much. This was hard to avoid if your principal, indeed only, drinking companion was someone like Stewart who could, and often did, put six or seven pints away without batting an eyelid. This his friend had done last night at The Surprise. Apparently, he'd been on continuous AFS duty for seventy-two hours, during which time Merlin presumed he hadn't drunk any alcohol. But then again, since the anticipated airborne arrival of the barbarian hordes had yet to materialise and the Auxiliary Fire Service had little to do but organise sandbagging and practice running up and down their fire towers, what was to stop the firemen dropping into the pub for a few drinks every once in a while? Stewart's duties certainly didn't inhibit his scope for pulling girls, as he had elaborated on at length last night after the apologia for Marshal Stalin had been duly delivered. In any event they had drunk a bucketful and Merlin couldn't remember whether at any stage they'd taken any food to soak up at least some of the alcohol. He thought not.

* * *

There was nothing at the Yard to cheer him up and his hangover, if anything, seemed to be getting worse, despite the consumption of three head-clearing mints.

"I think you could do with a nice cup of tea, sir," said Detective Sergeant Bridges, with what seemed an offensive level of cheerfulness. Merlin grunted and Bridges took this to be an affirmative response. The first thing that he saw on his desk was a memo from the A.C.

I would appreciate, at your earliest convenience, reports on progress on the following items:
The Barnes Incident
The Birdcage Walk hit and run of a week ago, and Johnson's progress thereon.
Verey's progress with the East India Dock investigation.
The forthcoming McGillvray IRA terrorist trial.
The review of our fingerprinting methodology requested several weeks ago.

There are a number of other outstanding items as you know but I regard an update on the above as the most pressing.

"Very kind of you to be so accommodating," Merlin said to himself.

"Beg pardon, sir?" Bridges deposited a steaming cup of tea on Merlin's desk.

"Nothing, nothing. Thanks, Sergeant. Let's hope this does me some good."

Merlin parked the memo under the paperweight on the

right of his desk. The paperweight, a bronze replica of the Eiffel Tower, had been a souvenir from his last holiday with Alice before she died. Paris in June 1938 – what a time they had had. He pinched himself hard. At the beginning of the month he'd made a New Year's resolution to avoid wallowing in the past. He was determined to keep it. There was no room for any more self-pity either. He pinched himself again.

"Any news on Barnes?" It had been forty-eight hours since the girl's body had been discovered and they still hadn't received Dr Sisson's report, promised for the day before.

"I've put another call in this morning, sir, but Venables said the doctor had been called out to a road accident in Richmond and that his assistant had no news."

Merlin slammed his right hand down on the desk a little harder than he'd intended and winced. "What the hell does he think he's playing at? Idiota!"

Bridges, acknowledging one of the few Spanish pejoratives of his boss which he understood, shook his head sadly and sucked in his breath.

"Did you ask Venables whether he had anything to add to his own completely unenlightening report?"

"He doesn't."

"Huh! Any interesting missing person reports?"

"Nothing that really matches in yesterday's batch but I'm expecting last night's reports to be sent to me in the next hour."

"And what about that boat?"

"I'm working on it."

"Very well. Be sure to chase that police doctor during the morning, won't you?" He closed his eyes briefly and sighed. "Now perhaps you can ask Peter Johnson and Verey to come up and update me on their cases. Oh, and Sergeant?"

"Sir?"

"Could you have a look in the medicine box and see if there's anything in there for my headache?"

Arthur Norton straightened his bow tie and applied the last touches of oil to his hair. Wearing his new Savile Row evening wear, he preened in front of the full-length Venetian mirror in his entrance hall. To the casual observer, Norton's features might appear acceptably regular, though a little spoiled by a weak chin and a puffiness which bore witness to the liveliness of his social life. To Arthur Norton, however, the face which stared back at him was one of which he was inordinately proud. His looks, he thought, especially with the recent addition of a little dignified salt and pepper in his hair, were even improving with age. He wondered briefly whether now was the time to remove the moustache which he had added to complement the portrait a year or so ago. "No," he murmured, remembering the young debutante who had commented favourably on it the other night. His figure wasn't so bad either, though his waistline had expanded a little since his arrival in England.

He stepped into the living room and poured himself a large Scotch. He still felt the need for a little Dutch courage before entering the social fray. So unlike his friend and patron, the Ambassador, who had for many years maintained a fantastically complicated private life against a background of expanding family obligations and buccaneering business dealings, yet had little need for alcoholic stimulation. Norton didn't think he'd ever seen the Ambassador take more than one alcoholic drink in an evening of entertainment, and more often than not he'd seen him drinking only water or a soda. Women were Joe Kennedy's alcohol, and he didn't need the hard stuff to put lead in his pencil.

Norton stepped into the pitch-black Mayfair street below his flat and set out on the short walk to his evening's destination. It was twenty-to-eight and he was due on the hour. As he walked around the corner into Hill Street, he heard steps. He had forgotten his torch and swore at himself.

He hurried across the road. Street attacks had multiplied tenfold since the introduction of the blackout. The steps behind him picked up their pace and he began to run.

"Mr Norton!"

Norton recognised the voice and stopped.

"It's me, sir."

Norton caught his breath and turned to face his pursuer.

"Goddam it, what do you want? I'm in danger of being late for a very important dinner."

Not for the first time, Johnny Morgan sniggered to himself at Norton's strange way of speaking. 'New England Lockjaw', he heard someone call it when discussing the Ambassador. For some reason the Ambassador's version of the accent was much easier on the ear than Norton's braying nasal twang.

"Come on Morgan, spit it out or get on your horse. I have no time to waste."

"It's about the arrangements, sir."

"What arrangements?"

"You know. With the girls. Those arrangements. I need…"

A loud bang sounded from nearby and Norton jumped.

"Only a car exhaust, sir."

"Look, I can't talk now. Let's have a word tomorrow."

"When?"

"I'll meet you in that pub just around the corner from the embassy – no, then again, let's meet a little further afield. St. James's Park, at the entrance nearest The Ritz. Say at about midday. You can get away then, can't you? With the Ambassador away you can't have much to do at the moment."

"Yes, sir. I'll get away somehow."

"Very well. So, good night."

"There's one thing that can't wait."

"What, Goddamit?"

"The money, sir."

"We can discuss that tomorrow."

"No, sir. I need some now. I want what's due. You know the amount." Morgan's voice now had a steely edge.

Norton paused for a second before reaching into his trouser pocket. "Lucky for you I'm carrying some cash."

"I knew a fine gentleman like yourself would be carrying cash on a night out on the town, sir. Better watch out for ruffians, though. Plenty of them about in the blackout."

Norton handed over some notes then hurried away towards Berkeley Square, while Morgan turned into The Running Footman to check that he hadn't been short-changed.

Norton's destination was an imposing house at the end of a side-street behind Claridges. It was a large Georgian property fronted by a fountain, in which various pop-eyed sea-creatures spouted water over a gang of winged cherubs. A uniformed flunkey let him in to a brightly-lit marbled hall, where a pretty woman with a coquettish smile broke off from her conversation with a very tall but stooped elderly man.

"Lady Pelham. A pleasure to see you again. Thank you for having me."

"The pleasure is all ours, Mr Norton. Reginald, say hello to Mr Norton, you remember, from the American Embassy."

"Welcome, welcome. Jolly nice to see you again." Lord Pelham inclined his shining cranium, which was completely bald save for a fringe of white hairs that stuck out untidily over the back of his neck. Norton guessed that he had a good thirty years on his wife, a striking woman with film-star looks, whose clinging pale-blue evening dress stunningly highlighted the shapely contours which lay beneath. Norton eyed his hostess' diamond-bedecked décolletage appreciatively and wondered whether his lordship was able to take full advantage of his luck in having such an engaging partner.

Reginald Pelham had been a Cabinet Minister long ago. One of his ancestors had been a side-kick of the warrior Duke of Marlborough and had secured rich pickings from this relationship. His lordship had a fabulous stately pile in Oxfordshire, where Norton had recently been a guest at a most enjoyable weekend party. Pelham had only recently married, after many years as a bachelor. An ambitious as well as an attractive woman, Diana Pelham, making good use of her husband's wealth and position and her own not insignificant connections, had embarked on a campaign to establish herself as a leading society hostess.

"Come, Mr Norton. Won't you join the rest of our party? We are a small gathering tonight but I believe you will find the company stimulating." Lord Pelham nodded in the direction of a door just behind him. Norton followed his hosts into a large wood-panelled room, where he was immediately offered a champagne cocktail by a waiter. "Let me introduce you to our other guests."

Glancing quickly around the room he recognised some faces from his Oxfordshire weekend. Lady Pelham guided him towards two men standing by the fireplace. "I believe you know Major St. John…"

"Norton, hello, hello. And how's that fine Ambassador of yours keeping?" Major Edward St. John was a stocky, white-haired man, whose bright red nose bore testament to his close affinity with fine wines and spirits. He was a Tory member of Parliament whom Norton knew to be a prominent Chamberlain supporter.

"He's in the pink, I believe, Major. Still in America but due back next month."

"Mr Pemberton. Good to see you again."

Vivian Pemberton, a slight, elegant man whose face appeared to portray a permanent look of mild amusement, was smoking a pungent cigarette through a long silver cigarette holder. He looked back through a haze of smoke. "Likewise, Norton."

"I saw one of your plays last week. The one at the St. James' Theatre. Knockout stuff. Are you working on another now?"

Pemberton took a long draw on his cigarette. "I'm afraid the Ministry of Information have me working on some more serious stuff at present. An awful bore, I'm afraid, but as everyone keeps saying, there is a war on."

The three ladies who had been chatting over their drinks at the other end of the room joined them.

"My wife Madeleine, Mr Norton."

Norton shook the hand of Mrs St. John, a small mousy creature who smiled weakly at him. The elder of the other two ladies raised her eyebrows at him and held out her hand.

"And this is Lady Celia Dorchester, and her niece, Nancy Swinton."

Norton kissed Lady Dorchester's raised hand. Her niece held her hand out at a lower level and he shook it. Supposedly Lady Dorchester had been a famous beauty in her day but it was difficult to discern the traces of her youthful charms through the layers of fat now enveloping her face. Miss Swinton was a tall, healthy, rather gangly-looking girl. Not really his type on first impression – too natural looking a beauty for his taste.

"Norton is a close associate of the American Ambassador, ladies." St. John drained his cocktail and signalled for another.

"Yes, yes, we know that, don't we, Nancy? I am a great admirer of Mr Kennedy. A man of such energy."

Lady Dorchester nodded her head for emphasis and her jowls shuddered. Norton was considering whether Lady Dorchester had been numbered in her youth among the long list of Kennedy conquests, when a servant announced from the end of the room that dinner was to be served.

As the guests proceeded into the dining room, a loud rap was heard at the front door.

"I think that's our late arrival." Diana Pelham stepped back into the hall.

Norton had just found his name card between Nancy Swinton and his hostess, when she returned.

"I think you all know Freddie Douglas, don't you? The fastest rising star in the Foreign Office, at least that's what Edward Halifax told me the other day."

Douglas, a slender, good-looking young man with oiled black hair and deep-set dark, wary eyes, smiled apologetically. "I don't know about that, Diana."

"False modesty, Freddie. Come on now. Sit down here by me."

Douglas sat down on Lady Pelham's other side. He was wearing an immaculate, dark pin-striped suit, unlike the rest of the men around the table.

"Sorry about the kit. Everything's so busy at the office, I didn't have time to get home to change. You're such a sweetie, Diana, I thought you'd tolerate my failings in etiquette." Lady Pelham gave him a dazzling smile as he paused to look around the table and exchange greetings.

"Arthur. How are you? Enjoyed the other night. I need to chat to you about a couple of things. We'll speak later."

Douglas tapped his nose meaningfully and sat back in his chair. "Sorry, Diana. Very rude of me, conversing over your head. My profuse apologies."

"Don't worry, dear. Ah, here's the wine. Now I'd like your opinion on this. Our new butler found it the other day in St. James'. Tell me what you think."

Norton didn't hear Douglas' opinion on the wine but as far as he was concerned, it was as fine a Puligny Montrachet as he'd ever tasted, and that was saying something.

"And so, Mr Norton, do you like living in England?"

"Well, yes I do, Miss Swinton. Of course, I think I'd have to say I'd like it even more in different circumstances."

"Indeed. Different circumstances. How I long for different circumstances. For the purposes of tonight, let us assume different circumstances and talk about pleasant things. I am tired of talking about the war. My aunt can talk about little else. Are you keen on country pursuits?"

Pretending to a far greater affinity with horses and guns than was strictly accurate, Norton enjoyed his chat with Nancy Swinton. She might be an ungainly sort of girl but on further acquaintance she had a sweet nature and a certain sort of charm. Perhaps his first impression was wrong?

Inevitably, to Miss Swinton's disappointment and a little to his, the talk of the table at large soon turned to the war and they were not allowed to stay out of it.

"And what do you think, Norton?" The robust colour of St. John's nose had now extended to the rest of his face.

"Sorry, I didn't catch what you said."

"I was saying that this war is a stupid mistake. It's not Herr Hitler that we should be fighting. It's the communists and socialists we need to worry about. We should be working with Hitler, not against him. What do you say?"

"I don't think that would be the Roosevelt administration's line at present."

"Oh come on, Mr Norton. I've heard Mr Kennedy say much the same thing as I've just said."

"The Ambassador does have some strong views on Stalin, I have to admit."

"Strong views indeed. Look. I've met Herr Hitler several times. So he's a strong man and has done some things we don't like. But my God, sir, we can and should do business with him. Isn't that so, Douglas?"

Douglas finished his glass of the inspiring Chateau Lafitte, which had accompanied the roast lamb, and set down his napkin.

"As you know, Major, government policy at present is to work with all our might in assisting our French and other allies in Continental Europe in maintaining at least the status quo for the present, while we go about the serious business of rearmament. It is of course legitimate to question whether that will remain government policy. I, and I think I can say many of my colleagues at all levels of departmental responsibility, would certainly concede that there is an argument that instead of confronting Herr Hitler, perhaps we should consider reaching some sort of accommodation with him. Might Herr Hitler, if allowed to expand and consolidate his power in Continental Europe, be content to leave us and our Empire alone?"

"Exactly, my boy. And I am certain he would take that view. Then perhaps we can join forces against Stalin and his red hordes."

Reginald Pelham cleared his throat loudly. "Gentlemen. May I advise care. Some might say this conversation was verging on the treasonous."

St. John's hand banged down on the table. "With respect, my friend, it would be treason to waste this country's resources on an unnecessary and futile battle against Hitler's formidable armies. We should recognise reality."

Lady Dorchester nodded her head vigorously. "Absolutely. Nancy and I couldn't agree more."

Norton could sense Nancy squirming on the seat to his right.

"I'm afraid, aunt, you'll have to speak for yourself there. I can't believe that any sensible person would wish to be friends with Hitler. What about his cruelty, the lack of liberty, the fanatical hatred. Look at the way the Jews have been treated. Mr Churchill says that…"

"Oh for goodness sake, Miss Swinton. Don't talk about that warmongering charlatan. Look, Hitler dragged his country out of the mire. He had to have a firm hand. He had to deal firmly with agitators, socialists, communists, many of whom were Jewish. You can't make an omelette without breaking eggs you know. I'm sure Mr Chamberlain has the right perspective and will follow the sensible path. Eh, Douglas?"

Douglas nodded at the Major and wiped his mouth with his napkin.

"Perhaps that's enough of politics for now, eh, Diana, at least until the port arrives. And so, Vivian, what's new in your world?"

"Oh my dears. It's so tiresome. Last spring I made up a little party with the Oliviers and some other friends to go to Vienna and we were going to repeat the experience again this spring but," he sighed, "another casualty of war I suppose. And anyway, Larry and Vivien are stuck in Hollywood. It's all just so ghastly!"

CHAPTER 3

Tuesday January 30th

Merlin finished the bun and pulled his chair a little closer to Tony's electric fire. The paper had a story about volunteers joining up to help the Finns. This irritated him, prohibited as he was from contributing directly to the war effort by the A.C.'s injunctions. His irritation was compounded by his failure to make any meaningful progress with the Barnes case. Bridges had put in a lot of tedious spadework in identifying the flag of the boat seen by Colonel Trenchard and then tracking the boat down to a waterman's boatyard in the Pool of London. It turned out that the boat owners had been employing casual labour on the boat that day, having unluckily lost their full-time crew of three all in one go to the call-up in the first week of January. They had names for that day's replacement crew, who had been carrying a small load of agricultural equipment up the Thames to Maidenhead, but no addresses. The boatmen had been paid cash-in-hand at the end of the day's work and had not been seen since.

All this effort by Bridges proved to be wasted when, five days after the discovery of the body, they finally received Dr Sisson's report. The doctor estimated that the body had been in the water for at least three days. The boat line of enquiry had been dropped and Bridges muttered something rude about to which orifice the good doctor's snuff might be applied in future.

The report did confirm, as expected, that they were dealing with a murder case. The gruesome absence of an eye had nothing to do with the girl's death but was down to a scavenging fish. Death had been caused by a blow to the head and, in Sisson's view, had certainly occurred before the body's immersion in the water, as the lungs were empty. So the next question to resolve was the identity of the victim.

They ploughed unsuccessfully through all vaguely applicable missing persons reports. Looking for missing persons in London had become a nightmare since the war started. The evacuation had relocated thousands of women and children to the countryside. Some had settled down in their new homes but many had quickly given up on the delights of rural life and returned to the city. These movements back and forth inevitably complicated police enquiries considerably.

They looked into a few likely prospects, only to find that the girls reported missing had escaped their families to live with boyfriends in or out of London or, in one case, to work in a brothel.

Things were not going well on other fronts either. Johnson was still struggling to make a breakthrough on the hit and run he was investigating. Little progress was being made with the dockers investigation. The preparation for the IRA trial was tedious and time-consuming and Merlin just couldn't bring himself to get moving on the fingerprint report. Meanwhile, crime was a moving target, and new cases were coming in all the time to their undermanned and overworked office.

Merlin left a couple of coins on the counter and headed out into the cold. The river in front of the Yard was now almost completely solid. He remembered reading somewhere about winter fairs held on the frozen Thames in the sixteenth or seventeenth century. He'd like to see that but somehow doubted that Londoners would be in the mood for such jollity this winter.

Back at the Yard, Bridges caught up with him as he reached the top of the stairs. "We've had a break – I think we've found the Barnes girl, sir."

Merlin pushed through the door into his office, threw off his coat and fell heavily into his chair. "What have you got?"

"Joan Harris. A Miss Edgar who works for the American Ambassador reported her missing yesterday. Apparently she hadn't turned up at work for over a week. Miss Edgar, who is her boss, thought it was odd as she was a very reliable girl. Said she didn't report it straight away as she assumed there must be some good explanation."

"That's strange. If she was so reliable, I'd have thought it would be a matter of immediate concern that she hadn't turned up. How do we know she's our girl?" Merlin picked irritably at a loose thread on his jacket.

"Just to finish the story, sir – apparently the girl lived on her own in lodgings in Hammersmith. Her family live in Gloucestershire and Miss Edgar thought there might have been some problem at home which required her to go back there at short notice. Something like one of her brothers being called up and her wanting to see him off, or such like. In any event, apparently one of her brothers turned up at the Ambassador's home the day before yesterday looking for her. He told Miss Edgar that Miss Harris hadn't been home to Gloucestershire since October. They hadn't even seen her at Christmas as they had expected. In the light of that, Miss Edgar sent one of the embassy chauffeurs around with the brother to the girl's lodgings. Her landlady said she hadn't seen her for over a week and complained of being owed rent. Not a sympathetic sort, I understand."

Having resolved the problem with his jacket, Merlin turned his attention to the tie which he had knotted too tightly. "So we know this girl is missing but how do we know that she's the Barnes girl?"

"Well, the description from her brother generally fits. She was missing from almost exactly the same time as our girl was killed. She's not one of these evacuees about whom no one has a clear picture. She was a good worker with a good job and no apparent reason to go missing."

Merlin gave a small sigh of relief as he finally managed to loosen his neckwear. "She might have had a boyfriend to be with and that's why she didn't go home for Christmas and now she's decided to run off with him. Still, it's worth checking out. Let's see if the brother can identify her. I suppose the body's still in the Central Morgue?"

"Yes, sir."

"Where's the brother now?"

"One of the staff has taken him for a drink near the Ambassador's house in Kensington – to calm his nerves."

Merlin ran his hand through his hair.

"Better tell them we're on our way."

Driving past Horse Guards Parade and into Trafalgar Square, they passed a team of police and firemen making further adjustments to the sandbagging. At the top of his column, a saviour from a previous time of danger stared out into the distance, scanning for any sign of invading Nazis.

We could do with Nelson now, thought Merlin, and better throw in Marlborough, Henry V and Richard The Lionheart for good measure. He sighed. Well, we haven't got them but let's hope to God that the current batch of military leaders turn out better than the duffers of the last war. If we have the equivalent of Haig and Co again we won't stand a chance. Of course, no one had really tested the German army yet – they'd had a very easy time of it, although the Poles had done their best with their brave but doomed cavalry brigades. Perhaps the Boche wouldn't turn out to be as good as they were cracked up to be. One could only hope.

As for the politicians, he couldn't see Chamberlain being the man to inspire the nation. Who could? Halifax? He had been a prominent appeaser. Attlee? Too dull. Many people felt Churchill could be the man but his whole career so far had been one of bombast and unreliability. Merlin personally had a lot of time for Winston, who had been right all along about Hitler, as he had kept on reminding his sceptical brother, Charlie. Rolling these thoughts over in his mind, he leaned back in his seat as they made their way rapidly through the sparse traffic on the Mall, on up Constitution Hill to Hyde Park Corner and then through to Kensington.

The Ambassador's house was a lofty, imposing building within an elegant terrace of mansions facing Hyde Park. It was a short drive from the Embassy itself, which covered one side of Grosvenor Square. As they arrived at the residence, Merlin saw two men on the pavement engaged in what appeared to be a heated argument. One of the raised voices had a Welsh lilt.

"You didn't get it done, did you?" The older man waved his finger in front of the Welshman's face.

"Look, I'll get what you want, just as I always do. It just didn't work out this time, that's all."

"But you promised me…"

The men became aware that they had an audience.

"Morning, gentlemen. Is there some sort of problem?"

"No. No problem. Can I help you?" said the Welshman.

"This is the American Ambassador's residence, isn't it? We're police officers here to see Miss Edgar."

"Oh yes. You're here about poor Joan. I'm Johnny Morgan, one of the Ambassador's chauffeurs. I have been looking after Joan's brother."

Bridges turned to the second man.

"Mr Harris?"

"Of course not. I am an embassy official and I have an urgent appointment for which I am already late." The man turned on his heels and walked away hurriedly before hailing a passing cab.

"Unusual accent he's got, sir?"

Morgan chimed in. "He's a Boston Yankee, sir. Same as the Ambassador, Mr Kennedy."

Merlin followed the chauffeur up the steps.

"I didn't catch his name, Mr Morgan."

"Norton. Arthur Norton."

"Embassy bigwig is he?"

"He's an assistant to the Ambassador."

"Is he? So where is Mr Harris?"

"He's in the lobby, sir. Seems pretty cut up, not surprisingly. I think Miss Edgar is with him."

The three men walked through the Ambassador's front door into a richly-furnished entrance hall. Portraits of previous Ambassadors, interspersed with landscapes or cityscapes of prominent American locations covered the walls. Large, ornate chandeliers hung down from the high ceiling. Four heavily-cushioned sofas lay to the right of the doorway. On one of these sat a prim-looking, middle-aged woman. Next to her was a young man, whose long and greasy hair hung down untidily as he leaned forward with his head in his hands. He wore a crumpled blue mackintosh which reached down to his shiny black, patent leather shoes.

"Come on now. Let's perk up. It may yet all be a dreadful mistake."

"No, it ain't. I know it ain't. Summin' terrible has happened to our Joanie. I know it. She wouldn've missed Christmas wiv'us for all the tea in China."

"Now, now. We know that Joan was fine at Christmas as we saw her at work after Christmas, so Christmas has got nothing to do with it."

"Issa sign of sumfin'. Sign that trouble was brewing. I knows it. Not like her at all not to come home."

Miss Edgar rose to greet the approaching policeman. Merlin doffed the smart brown trilby his sister-in-law had given him for Christmas and made his introductions.

"Philippa Edgar, Chief Inspector. I'm in charge of the administration of the Ambassador's residence. This is Mr Joseph Harris, Joan's brother. I am afraid he's not in the best of shape." She glared at Morgan who was hovering by the door. "Of course he would have been in a better condition had someone not decided to take him to the public house and pour several whiskies down his throat."

"Thought he'd be better for it, mam. He wasn't in much different shape before the drinks as he is now."

"Mr Harris is clearly not much of a drinking man and you have not helped the situation."

Harris lurched unsteadily to his feet. "W'as appen'd to her? We told 'er not to come up to London. Should'a stayed at home with us. But not her, with 'er fancy elocution lessons and 'er sectarial training. No, she wanted to come up 'ere. Fat good it's done 'er."

He subsided back onto the sofa.

"I think perhaps before we talk to Mr Harris and take him, to er…" Merlin lowered his voice "view the girl, it might be wise to give him a cup of coffee."

"I'll see to that now."

"And perhaps, while that's being done, you and I could have a little chat."

"Of course. Give me a moment and then I'll join you in my office. It's on the first floor. Morgan will show you the way."

They followed the chauffeur up the richly-carpeted grand staircase and then down a wide corridor. Opposite a large print of San Francisco before the great earthquake, they were ushered into a snug room with blue patterned wallpaper and a roaring fire.

"Sit yourselves down, gentlemen," said Morgan. "If you need me, I'll be down in the garage."

Merlin looked out of the window at the picture-postcard view of a white and frosty Hyde Park. In the distance a lively pair of energetic dogs scurried up and down the icy steps of the Albert Memorial.

Their hostess arrived and seated herself behind a small desk near the fire. "An awful business. I do hope there's some mistake."

"Of course."

There was a knock at the door and a striking, young, red-headed girl poked her head through the door. "Do you need anything, Miss Edgar?"

"I'm not sure Kathleen. Do you want anything to drink gentlemen?" The policemen declined and the girl disappeared, oblivious to their appreciative glances.

Merlin cleared his throat. "I'd just like to get an idea of what sort of girl Joan is, Miss Edgar."

"A pleasant but ordinary girl, Chief Inspector."

"Sociable? Does she have many friends? Girlfriends, boyfriends?"

"She is a young, twenty-year-old girl up from the country. She appeared to be friendly and sociable. I am not aware of any boyfriends but I can't keep tabs on the Ambassador's staff once they leave the building."

"Does she have any particular friends amongst the staff?"

"I suppose she is friendly with Kathleen, whom you saw a moment ago, and some of the other girls."

"Is she a pretty girl?"

"In a common sort of way, I suppose." Miss Edgar glanced quickly at her own profile in a mirror facing her desk.

"What is her job exactly?"

"The Embassy has a pool of typists of which she is one. The Ambassador does a lot of his work here in the residence and likes to have a few girls based here rather than at the Embassy. As I'm in overall charge here, I keep an eye on them. There are usually three or four girls based here at any one time. Joan is one, Kathleen is another. When they're not required for pure secretarial work I use them for various errands. I like to keep everyone busy. Of course, the girls continue to support the rest of the pool at the Embassy as and when required." A car horn sounded noisily in the street outside.

"Is Miss Harris a good worker?"

Miss Edgar carefully examined her fingernails. "She is a very proficient typist. Probably the quickest and most accurate in the pool."

"Do her typing duties cover all levels of communication?"

"What do you mean?"

"Does she see top-secret documents?"

"All the Ambassador's personal staff naturally have security clearance from the US government but I can't see how that…" A fly landed on the desk and Miss Edgar paused to brush it away. "But, yes. Yes is the answer to your question."

"How long has Joan worked here, Miss?"

"About eighteen months, Sergeant. She joined us in the middle of 'thirty-eight, just after the Ambassador had arrived."

"Any problems with her during this period?"

"None that I can particularly recall. She is very good at her job, keeps good time – at least she did up till now – and has a pleasing personality, although naturally she is a little, how shall I put it, er, gauche."

Bridges cast a puzzled look at his boss. "Miss Edgar means naïve, Sergeant, a little unsophisticated. Does Miss Harris work particularly closely with any of the Ambassador's staff?"

"As I say, she is a member of a pool. Because of her efficiency, of course, some staff request her services in particular." Miss Edgar leaned back in her chair and removed her spectacles. "On the day she went missing, for example, I remember Mr Norton getting into a real tizzy because he had some reports to get typed up and he wanted Joan to do them. Had a bit of a tantrum in fact, but he's often doing that. Mr Norton, Mr Zarb, the Ambassador himself – they all had a preference for Joan because she was so quick and made few mistakes, if any."

"I believe we met Mr Norton at the door. He has a senior position here, does he?"

"Well he doesn't really have a formal position, not in diplomatic terms that is. He is a special aide to the Ambassador. Mr Kennedy brought him over to England from Boston when he took up his post in 1938. I understand Mr Norton performed important work for Mr Kennedy in some of his commercial ventures in the United States."

"I see." Merlin looked at his watch and then at Bridges. "I wonder if Mr Harris is in any better shape by now. You have been most helpful. Naturally, we shall have other questions for you and your staff if unfortunately it is indeed Miss Harris in the morgue. Would you mind if we took Morgan along as a second party to confirm the identification? He would be able to do that, wouldn't he?"

"Certainly. No, I have no objection."

* * *

The steady metronomic tick of the clock in the corner seemed to compound the slow passage of time. Lord Halifax had begun the meeting with his senior civil servants over three hours ago. The long minutes and hours had been monopolised by his droning voice as he analysed the situation in France and in Europe generally, and complained vehemently about the short-sightedness of several of his Cabinet colleagues. Douglas had managed to make a few pithy interjections, which seemed to meet with the approval of his boss. His office-mate, and junior, Edward Fraser, had also made some telling contributions, much to Douglas' irritation. Now Fraser was speaking again, tentatively quoting Halifax's arch-enemy, Winston Churchill. His Lordship's face darkened and Douglas smiled to himself.

"I'd be most grateful, Mr Fraser, if you refrained from repeating that gentlemen's words to me. I have little regard for Mr Churchill, as you know. He is a dangerous man who would lead us into oblivion if he ever got the chance."

"But, sir, I think…" Halifax raised his withered left arm and glared at Fraser, who subsided back into his chair.

Douglas licked his lips and felt his stomach rumble. He was looking forward to his lunch at The Ritz, although his expected company was not up to much. Nevertheless when duty called, he obliged, and duty certainly did now call, as Halifax had explained to him in the private meeting which had preceded this one. He and Fraser had been cultivating the rather odd American chap he was meeting for some time, on Halifax's instructions. Now he had been given the task of taking matters just a little further.

At last Halifax wrapped up the meeting. As he went out of the door he gave Douglas one of his wintry smiles. "How's that charming fiancée of yours doing, Freddie? Hope you've found some time to see her."

"Unfortunately not, sir. Her father's keeping her out of London at the moment. A little nervous of bombs I'm afraid."

"Ah. A pity for you, my dear fellow." Halifax disappeared through the door.

"A pity, eh? What do you know, you old cripple?" Douglas muttered under his breath.

"What was that, Freddie?"

"Nothing, Edward. Nothing at all. Must be off. Important lunch. Tell you all about it later."

* * *

Norton was flustered. Morgan was full of bullshit, the policemen had irritated him and he was going to be late. He snapped a command at the driver and the taxi lurched off into the traffic. Ten minutes later they drew up outside The Ritz Hotel and Norton fumbled some change into the taxi-driver's hands and ran up the stairs. After searching the lobby bar and enquiring at the restaurant, he realised that he had arrived earlier than his lunch companion and so relaxed a little. He was shown to his table and ordered a dry Martini. Looking around him he saw that the room was almost full. In a far corner he recognised Nancy Swinton, who was looking smart in a navy-blue outfit. She was lunching with an older man with a shock of flowing white hair. His face was partially obscured but seemed familiar. Nancy had seen him and returned his smile, and Norton was on the point of wandering over to exchange a few words when his host arrived.

"Arthur. Sorry I am late. I got stuck in a frightfully boring F.O. meeting with his lordship and only just managed to extricate myself."

"No need for apologies. I was a little late myself."

A waiter rushed to help Douglas into his seat.

"Entertaining evening at the Pelhams, wasn't it, Freddie?"

"Indeed, and I enjoyed the after-dinner fun as well." Douglas winked then noticed Norton's empty glass.

"A dry sherry please, Pierre. And another of whatever my friend's having." Douglas surveyed the room to see which of the great and good were lunching today, catching the eyes of several diners and acknowledging them with cheerful nods. In one case he stood up and bowed. "The Marquis of Londonderry. Fine man. Very sound on our current difficult situation."

He sat down and continued his scrutiny of the other diners. "Isn't that the charming Nancy Swinton who was with us the other night? Looks a picture. Lucky Lloyd George. The old man's still got some steam in him, eh?"

"Ah, that's who it is." Norton knew that Britain's former prime minister had been very keen on the opposite sex throughout his long career but surely he wasn't at it still?

"Only joking, Arthur. I think LG is a long-standing friend of Nancy's family, so I'm sure their lunch is perfectly innocent. In any case, I believe that the goat in him has finally been put out to pasture. Well this is grand, is it not? The Ritz in all its glory and the menu and wine list as good as always. You can hardly tell there's a war on, can you, with everyone here in their luncheon finery?"

"Good of you to invite me when you must be very busy."

"Busy, yes. But, you know, it's funny – even in this mad situation, most of the senior officials still maintain their pre-war practice of starting the working day at 10.30am or 11.00am. Amazing, isn't it? I tend to get in to my office around 9.00am and am regarded as something of, how do you Yanks say it, an oddball?"

"You surprise me. I know the Ambassador always makes a very early start, but he's exceptional even in the American context."

"A human dynamo from what I hear."

The waiter arrived with menus and the men carefully assessed their options. Eventually both chose the roast beef and Douglas suggested a bottle of Brouilly as accompaniment.

"Lightly chilled please, Pierre, as usual."

Over lunch they discussed various acquaintances they had in common and exchanged idle gossip about their respective organisations. Douglas told a few amusing and indiscreet stories about his superiors at the F.O. while Norton ran through a few war stories, much diluted and edited, from his commercial experiences with the Ambassador.

Afterwards, they found a quiet corner in the lounge and ordered coffee and cigars. "Care for a brandy, Arthur?"

"Sure, but isn't it getting late for you? Aren't you needed back at the office?"

"Not really. Work can be done in or out of the office and enjoyable as this lunch has been, there is an element of associated business."

"Oh. How so?"

"I mentioned the other evening that I needed to talk to you about something. You are a man of influence with the Ambassador and my friends and I at the F.O. are keen to see him continue with his fine work."

"I'm happy to do anything I can. What is it that particularly interests you?"

Douglas leaned forward. "As we all know, he has been a strong supporter of Mr Chamberlain since his arrival in 1938."

"He admires the Prime Minister enormously."

"And he has been a strong proponent of peace, of, er, using all efforts possible to reach a negotiated settlement of some sort with Germany."

"So he has and it's cost him some too. He's always had his enemies here and I'd say in some way they've had the upper hand in recent months. But more important to the Ambassador, his views have led to some poor publicity back in the USA, and he's very unhappy about that."

"I can quite understand." Douglas took a long pull from

his cigar. "Wonderful cigars. Of course, if this war continues to develop we won't be able to get them through the German blockades. And plenty more besides. There will be massive shortages, more rationing. It will be very unpleasant and that's even without taking account of the bombing."

"I can't see it happening. Surely everyone will see some common sense and come to a settlement. I don't think the common man here really gives a fig about Hitler's designs on the countries of Eastern Europe, provided Britain and its Empire are unaffected."

"Quite. And as I was saying the other night, we are sure that Hitler will be quite happy to guarantee not to interfere with us and the Empire provided we allow him some breathing space in the East." Moving his chair forward, Douglas drew to within inches of Norton's face. "Confidentially, as your Ambassador probably knows, we are continuing to get feelers from Germany to confirm this. A deal can no doubt be struck. Perhaps we'd have to give up a few small colonies but who cares if we avoid the disaster of war?"

"You know we can agree on that. The Ambassador, as you are well aware, is adamantly against a US entrance into the war and without American help, if Germany chooses to target all its military power against Britain, I wouldn't give a cent for your chances."

"Precisely. Now you mentioned a moment ago that the Ambassador was unhappy with some of the bad press he's been getting back home."

"Yes, although he's still got plenty of supporters in the press as well."

"Beneficiaries of the famous Kennedy largesse, no doubt."

"No, that's not the case. The Ambassador does not…"

"Hold your horses, my friend. Just my little joke." Douglas re-lit his cigar. "Am I right in thinking that Mr Kennedy has ambitious domestic political aspirations?"

"I don't know about that."

"Come on, Arthur. Don't be coy. We've seen the American

press speculation. Mr Kennedy would like to take on Mr Roosevelt and become America's first Catholic President."

"So some think, although I'm not really at liberty to discuss his plans."

Douglas' lips moved to form a thin smile. "Very well. All I'd like to say is that I and several of my colleagues at the F.O. fully support the Ambassador's outlook. I'm talking here about colleagues at the highest level, Arthur. We'd like him to know that many in the government, indeed in the country, still value his forceful expression of this outlook, and his influence in bolstering American isolationism. If he has presidential aspirations, we applaud and support them. Some of my superiors are unfortunately inclining to the views of the warmongers amongst us, Churchill et al. However, I believe our views will prevail and that by the end of the year we shall have an international settlement. Who knows, maybe that settlement will be presided over by President Kennedy! At the F.O. I have access to a good deal of very interesting information. If certain political ambitions do in fact exist, some of it may be of use, if you get my drift. I know that the Ambassador's access to inside information has been considerably restricted of late, since his views have become, let's say, less popular with some elements of the government."

Norton drained his brandy glass. "So, Freddie, in plain English you're saying that you support the Ambassador's views and are keen to see him continue to promote them. In this context, you may be in a position to give him some pieces of information which could be of political use to him. Have I got the drift?"

"Bingo, Arthur. And with you as the essential link. Indeed, it may also be that circumstances arise to offer the Ambassador the opportunity to be very directly involved in bringing about a peaceful resolution to the political situation. Of course he has his influence with the current incumbent of the White House to exert and then imagine the possibilities ahead of an election – Joe Kennedy, master diplomat and peacemaker.

What about that, eh? In fact, there's something – well we shouldn't discuss it here. I'd like to introduce you to someone. Perhaps, if you're free tomorrow night…"

"I will make myself free."

"Good. An interesting person. I'll call you later to make arrangements."

The two men were now alone save for an elderly couple playing cards in a far corner. Nancy and her retired goat had long since departed.

"One more for the road, Arthur?"

"Sure. We can drink to Anglo-American cooperation."

"To that and… well, why not, to the Thirty-Second President of the United States, Mr Joseph P. Kennedy."

* * *

"Morning, guvnor."

A bearded man in a stained white coat greeted them and led Merlin and his two companions through the swing doors into a small, white-tiled room. In its centre, harshly illuminated by a flickering bright central light, was a trolley bearing an object covered in a sheet. They all stood for a moment at its foot, the only sound apart from their breathing the steady drip of a tap in a basin in the corner. A strong smell of chemicals pervaded the room and for a moment Merlin thought he would need to sneeze. The silence was broken by a whimper from Joseph Harris. "Is that 'er then?"

Merlin nodded to the attendant who pulled back the sheet.

The head and upper part of the pale, lifeless body was revealed and raised a collective sigh from the visitors before Harris cried out, "Oh God! That's our girl. My beautiful sis'. What have they done to you, Joanie?" Tears began to stream down Harris' unshaven cheeks.

"You're sure?"

Harris wiped his nose with his coat sleeve and nodded. "Look. There's her little mole there on her shoulder." He reached out to touch the small brown mark and stroked it tenderly. When he withdrew his hand he balled it into a fist. "I'll get the bastard who did this. I'll swing for 'im I will."

"There'll be no need to do that. We'll find the culprit, I promise you. Sergeant, send Morgan in will you?"

Bridges gently pulled Harris away from his sister and through the door.

Morgan's jauntiness disappeared when he saw the trolley.

"Her brother's certain it's Joan but I thought you'd better have a look anyway. Do you recognise her?"

Morgan shook his head. "I, I don't know for sure." His breath caught as he reached his hand out to the dead girl and then withdrew it sharply without touching.

"Mr Harris recognised this mole. Do you...?"

Morgan continued shaking his head. "Never seen her back, naked like, so I don't..."

Morgan's face now had a sallow tinge and Merlin saw that his hands were trembling.

"Very well, no doubt we can get someone else in the family to confirm the identification if we have to."

Out in the corridor, Joseph Harris was being sick. Bridges had a comforting hand on his shoulder, while with his other hand he tried to manoeuvre a bucket into the line of fire. They waited in embarrassment for him to finish. The morgue attendant produced a glass of water which Harris knocked to the floor. "Don' want no bloody water. Don' wan' nothin' but fer you people to leave me alone. No 'uman dignity in there, is there? Jus' a slab of meat. Poor lil' Joanie."

* * *

He'd seen plenty of dead bodies of course. Plenty of messy ones too. In the Somme he'd seen scores of men blown to smithereens by shells or shot to pieces. One of his best mates had had his head blown off right next to him. One second Archie was shaking his head with laughter at some awful joke

Merlin had made and the next he had no head to shake. He'd seen all sorts of death in his years as a policeman – men and women strangled, knifed, poisoned, battered to death. From the physical viewpoint, as bodies went, Joan Harris' wasn't too awful – the ravages of a few days in the river, some bruises and now of course the stitched-up incisions of a pathologist. Even so, it never got any easier, and the young ones were the most upsetting, however damaged. Most upsetting of all, of course, was Alice's. She'd lost weight but in fact she hadn't looked that bad at the end. A good-looking corpse, if there was such a thing.

Merlin shook his head, slapped his left hand with his right and refocused on his plate. He gazed unenthusiastically at his meat and veg. His appetite had disappeared. The Sergeant, however, seemed to have had few difficulties with his steak and kidney pudding and was now polishing off a large piece of treacle tart, oblivious to his boss's self-flagellation. Merlin took a deep breath.

"So what do we know about this poor woman, Joan Harris? A nice, cheerful, country girl, betters herself by taking a secretarial course and elocution lessons. Escapes a poor country family. Obtains what, for her, must have been a very exciting job with the American Ambassador, which she gets just after Mr Kennedy takes up his post in, er, when was that?"

"March nineteen thirty-eight, sir."

"Right. And despite her humble background, she turns out to be a star turn of a secretary. A Paganini of the typewriter in fact."

"Paga – who sir?"

"A virtuoso violinist, Sam. Never mind. Anyway, she lives in what I guess are modest lodgings in Hammersmith."

"Yes, sir." Bridges finished off the last piece of tart and sighed with satisfaction.

"She's sociable. She's pretty 'in a common sort of way', as Miss Edgar puts it. I'd be surprised if she didn't have a boyfriend or boyfriends. Being good at her job, senior Embassy officials request her specifically for typing work, and she's fully cleared in security terms, so will no doubt have seen a lot of confidential stuff."

"Think there's a security angle here?"

"The girl must have had access to some very interesting information. Information that people might pay a lot of money for, or information that people might be very unhappy to see revealed."

The bear-like owner of the café moseyed up to the table. "I might have to charge you two gentlemen rent, the amount of time you're spending in my place. You need anything else, no?"

Tony bent to mop the table, brushing remnants of the day's food into Bridges' lap.

"Hey!"

"Sorry, Mr Sam. I give you two teas on the house. Is alright?"

"Another time, thanks."

Merlin started to make notes. "Johnny Morgan. He should be useful. Bit of a ladies' man, I should think. He could help us as regards Joan Harris' love life, as could her friend Kathleen Donovan. We'll need to interview all Miss Harris' colleagues in the typing pool and any other work friends we identify. Also the people she worked for."

"All of them?"

"Let's make it simpler for ourselves to begin with and just identify the ones who particularly requested her services. That Norton chap for a start. He seemed a little fishy to me. Get the other names from Miss Edgar."

"Right, sir."

"If you make a start with the interviews, I'd like to go and take a look at where Miss Harris lived and speak to her landlady. Did you get her name?"

"Mrs Bowen." Bridges handed over a piece of paper on which he had written Joan's address.

Merlin rose, picked up his hat and set it at a rakish angle.

"Off you go then. I'm going to pop back to the Yard first to check on a few other things. Then I'll head to Hammersmith and after that join you at Princes Gate."

* * *

"Chief Inspector?"

Merlin recognised the A.C.'s bark on the telephone.

"Yes, sir."

"Could you come up to my office straight away?"

After a moment's consideration, he supposed that he could.

He trudged up the stairs. At her station by the A.C.'s door, his ancient secretary raised her pencil-black eyebrows as she bashed away on her typewriter.

"You're looking as beautiful as ever today, Miss S. The A.C. asked to see me."

"Better not keep him waiting then." Miss Stimpson's beady eyes glinted. "He hasn't had any lunch today and I suspect you'll do nicely."

Assistant Commissioner Gatehouse stood, arms behind his back, gazing out at the river. He was wearing his normal uniform of dark jacket, striped trousers, wing-collar and one of his abundant collection of sombre ties. Merlin was relieved to see that no unpleasant red blotches decorated the A.C.'s cheeks as they had on the occasion of their last interview. Initial signs indicated that he might be in a moderately good mood.

"I gather you've made some progress on the Barnes case." Merlin wondered at the speed of the Yard grapevine.

"We've identified the girl. An employee of the American Ambassador."

"Any suspects yet?"

Merlin thought of answering "Of course not, you idiot, we only identified the girl an hour or so ago," but good sense prevailed. "No, sir. We are just about to undertake interviews of friends and staff."

"Better go careful on the staff side, Chief Inspector. Don't want to upset our American friends at this delicate period."

"How do you mean? I've got to investigate the girl's work and social relationships at the Embassy."

The Assistant Commissioner stretched his arms before sitting in an uncomfortable-looking armchair by the window. He waved his hand at another chair which Merlin took. His eye was caught by a new photograph on the A.C.'s desk. A nice-looking girl with long blonde hair. "Of course you have, Frank. All I mean is go carefully. We don't want any diplomatic incidents, so to speak."

"That's hardly likely. The Ambassador is currently back in the United States, and I don't believe he is expected to return for some time. I am investigating an employee of pretty low standing in the Ambassador's entourage, and I can't really see any chance of a diplomatic incident. Of course, however unlikely it appears at the outset, there may be some security aspect in the case and I shall naturally be cautious in my approach to such areas."

"That's all I meant, Frank." The A.C.'s mouth opened in an approximation of a smile, revealing a set of mottled brown teeth. "We have to remember that the attitude of the American government to Great Britain, and its potential to provide assistance to us in this damned war, is of crucial importance. However unlikely it may be, we don't want the murder of an insignificant girl to queer the pitch in any way, do we?"

Merlin couldn't help visibly bridling at this.

"Insignificant, sir? Are you saying you don't want me to properly investigate the murders of 'insignificant' people while the war's on?"

The A.C.'s cheeks flushed. "You know that's not what I meant. Just go carefully, that's all."

Merlin counted silently to ten.

"Very well. If you don't mind my asking, what is the current view in government circles of the American Ambassador?"

"Just what you'd expect. The honoured representative of our greatest ally. A man to be respected."

"Really? Is that still appropriate when we know he's been an arch-appeaser and tells all and sundry that Britain hasn't got a hope in hell in this war?"

"I can't really get into that, Chief Inspector. If you're asking me what the government thinks of Mr Kennedy, may I remind you that Mr Neville Chamberlain is still the head of the government, and that Mr Chamberlain was the architect of what some people call the appeasement policy and what others call the pragmatic policy in dealings with Germany. This same Mr Chamberlain has been on pretty chummy terms with Mr Kennedy since his arrival in 'thirty-eight. Anyway, what the devil has this got to do with your case?"

"Probably nothing sir. I just wanted to know a little more about the lie of the land at the Embassy. Best to know the lie of the land, I think, when you're trying to avoid diplomatic incidents."

The A.C. produced another sickly smile and got to his feet. "Very well. Any word on how Johnson's getting on, by the way? This chap who was run over was some sort of scientific adviser. The War Office have been on, worrying about there being some sort of foul play."

"I haven't seen Johnson for a couple of days. When I get a chance I'll try and get a full progress report. Now I have to get on with my investigation. Will that be all?"

The A.C. grunted. As Merlin passed Miss Stimpson he gave her what he intended to be an enigmatic smile.

* * *

Having heard that there was some traffic hold-up on the Cromwell Road, Merlin crossed to the south bank of the river. Traffic was sparse and he reached Hammersmith Bridge in less than half-an-hour. He stopped for a moment on the bridge and got out of the car. The river was still iced over in many parts.

Some river traffic was edging its way with difficulty through the baby icebergs. A gaily-painted river barge glided down the centre of the river and he wondered whether the unidentified boatmen who had been on the river when Joan Harris' body was found were at work today. He stared up at the gloomy overcast sky and the barrage balloons hovering above the bridge. The A.C.'s approach to the case worried him. What did it matter that Joan was 'insignificant'? So the case might cause the A.C. political problems if it proved embarrassing in some way for the US embassy. So what? He didn't give a damn for the defeatist Kennedy, or indeed for that stuffed-shirt Chamberlain, whom Hitler had comprehensively hoodwinked. Nothing should stand in the way of a murder investigation, however lowly the victim. No doubt Joan's fate would seem unimportant in the greater scheme of things whenever the Luftwaffe got round to bombing London, but that was nothing to him. It was his job to seek out the truth behind her death, regardless.

He tossed a stone into the river and rubbed his hands. Come on, he said to himself. Let's get on with it.

Joan Harris' lodgings were in a terraced house in a dingy road just off King Street. Merlin parked his car on the kerb and banged the knocker which, much smoothed from use, appeared to have originally taken the form of a cat's head. Eventually the door slowly opened to the accompaniment of a ferocious bout of coughing.

The woman was large. She wore a shabby dress on which he could see several stains, some of which were yellow and seemed of recent origin. Her large breasts, seemingly unsupported in any way, sagged towards her knees. A frizzy grey down covered most of the lower half of her face, while her obviously dyed hair was tagged up in curlers. Piercing the beard on the lower half of her face was a red gash of a mouth, from which an almost spent cigarette sagged and which eventually exchanged coughs for words. "Cat got your tongue?" the apparition growled. "Come on, state your business, I haven't got all day and I'm in the middle of my tea."

"Detective Chief Inspector Merlin, madam. I'm here to investigate the death of your lodger, Joan Harris."

"Oh, dead is she? When her brother and the copper came she was only missing. You found her quickly then. Will her brother be paying me the arrears of rent?" The landlady took one final puff of her cigarette, looking at it with more emotion than she apparently felt for Joan Harris, and threw the stub onto the pavement.

"I am sure something will be worked out Mrs – er – Bowen, isn't it?"

"Yeh. So what now? I'd better get on and clear her stuff out."

"I'd prefer it if you didn't do that for the moment."

"Why not? Got to get someone else into the room. Can't hang around. Perhaps you think I'm made of money?" Mrs Bowen attempted to fold her arms under her imposing bosom but, failing in that endeavour, she raised her right arm and leant against the doorpost. Merlin stepped back as her breasts rose and swung in his direction.

"May I come in?"

Mrs Bowen's expression softened slightly as she appraised her visitor. "Oh, alright then. I'm always a sucker for a handsome face. Suppose you want to poke around her room?"

"Thank you."

Stepping into the hallway he had a view of the main living room to his left and was surprised to see a very tidy interior. Mrs Bowen appeared to compensate for her personal slovenliness with a keen attention to her housekeeping.

"Mind if I finish my egg and chips? You can have a cuppa if you want." Mrs Bowen shuffled towards the kitchen at the end of the hall corridor.

"No thanks. Where is Miss Harris' room?"

"It's the door facing the stairs on the first floor. Don't make a mess, please."

The room was large, larger in fact than his own in Chelsea. He idly thought he could do with a bit of extra space. Then again, Hammersmith was a bit further out than he liked, he didn't quite fancy the change in landladies, and he wasn't so keen on a room recently inhabited by a dead girl.

A single bed lay against the wall to his right. On the far side of the bed, next to the room's one window, stood a large wardrobe. On the near side, next to a washbasin, was a chest of drawers. The walls of the room were covered with a yellow lacquered wallpaper on which a small cast of Victorian figures posed in various hunting tableaux. Clashing somewhat with this decor, a faded pink armchair sat in front of the bed and to the side of an ornate Victorian fireplace.

He put on his gloves. A range of ladies toiletries covered the washbasin and two shelves above it. It seemed to him that there was quite an amount for a young girl of limited means. Alice had never been a great one for make-up, perfumes or nail varnish. A dab of lipstick and a splash of eau-de-cologne had been all she wanted. He carefully went through the clothing in the chest, trying not to feel like a pervert when he rummaged through the underwear. He found nothing of interest. Moving to the other side of the bed, he opened the wardrobe and found a colourful selection of dresses and skirts. His eye was caught in particular by a long silvery evening dress.

A wave of sorrow passed over him, superseded swiftly by a surge of anger. A young life full of possibilities snuffed out meaninglessly. He sat down and took out his notebook. "Clothing, etc. seems to me of high quality – too high quality for secretary up from country – ditto perfumes, etc." He went over to the fireplace. On the mantelpiece was a black and white photograph of a working-class family. Merlin recognised Joan's brother in the picture, which also featured a sour-faced woman, a similarly miserable man, three young children of indeterminate sex, and a pretty teenage girl. He picked up the photograph and scanned Joan's blurred features. She had indeed been a looker. The eyes were large and doe-like.

Her flowing fair hair fell prettily on her shoulders and her full lips were parted in a winsome smile. Despite being dressed as shabbily as the rest of her family, she seemed a cut above.

Merlin slipped the photograph into his inside pocket. Further along the mantelpiece were a group of china puppies and kittens, a small clock and a neat pile of books. At the top was an Everyman edition of *Pride and Prejudice*. Beneath was a battered copy of *A Tale of Two Cities* and beneath that a bright new edition of *Huckleberry Finn*.

He riffled through the pages of the Austen and then the Dickens. Nothing unusual revealed itself. *Huckleberry Finn*'s glossy wrapper portrayed a very blue Mississippi on a sunny day, with a river steamer making its happy way between the river banks. When he opened this book he noticed a spidery inscription on the flyleaf.

"To J. Hope you enjoy it as much as I do. Good luck with everything. Your friend J."

He looked at the back of the book to see if there were any other written inscriptions but found none. He flipped through the pages as before. A small object fell to the floor, and he knelt to pick it up.

It was a blue matchbox. On the cover was a silhouette in white of a curvy female figure holding out a cigarette in a cigarette holder and a name – 'The Blue Angel'.

Merlin knew most of the nightclubs in London from the time, a couple of years before, when he'd had several major gangland cases. Investigating these had involved much trawling around clubland – smart dining clubs, cabarets, spielers, clip-joints, seedy drinking clubs and clubs which were brothels in all but name. Despite 'The Blue Angel' sounding familiar, he could not recall it.

When he went back down the stairs, Mrs Bowen was hovering in the hallway. She had taken her curlers out and appeared to have made some effort to improve her appearance, although the yellow stains remained. "Finished?"

"Yes, thanks. Could I have a few words with you about Miss Harris?"

"Alright, but I'm sure I've got little to tell you. Come in here." Mrs Bowen opened the door of her living room. He followed her and sat down on a comfortable settee in the middle of the room.

The landlady relit the new cigarette dangling in her mouth and sat down opposite him.

"What sort of a girl was Joan?"

"I don't really know. Kept herself to herself. She was polite – I'll give her that."

"Did she have any friends to visit?"

"One of her girlfriends from work came around a few times. Don't know her name. Pretty thing with red hair."

"Any men?"

"None. Rule of the house. No male callers. I won't have any funny business." Mrs Bowen primly pursed her lips.

So your other lodgers are female?"

"Yes they are. I've got two other lady lodgers."

"Who are they?"

"Don't think they'd welcome me talking about them. Very private people."

"I would be grateful for their names."

Mrs Bowen took a long draw on her cigarette. "Miss Simpson and Miss Foster. They're friends. Old ladies. Been here about four months – since just after the war started."

"Are they here now?"

"They went away. Visiting friends in the country. Wiltshire or Gloucestershire I think. Back today or tomorrow I believe."

"Could you let them know that I or one of my officers will need to speak to them when they return?" He wrote down the names in his notebook. "Did Miss Harris ever stay out at night?"

The landlady pursed her lips again. "I have rules in my own house, but I can't have rules outside, can I? I lock and bolt the door at 10.30 at night. If any of my lodgers are later than that they have to make other arrangements."

"Did she miss 'lock-up' many times?"

"Didn't keep count. A few times certainly. She was away for a few weekends as well. Visiting her family, I think."

"She had some nice clothes in her room."

Mrs Bowen's heavily lipsticked mouth opened into something between a leer and a smile. "Pretty stuff she had. Saw her in her shiny evening dress more than once."

"Did you ever see anyone pick her up?"

"Told you, Inspector. No male callers."

"I just wondered whether she ever had someone waiting outside. A car perhaps?"

"Not that I noticed. And I don't make it my business to spy on my lodgers. Did see her get into a taxi once though. Thought that was a bit flash for a girl like her." Mrs Bowen vigorously stubbed her cigarette out in a silver ashtray on the table in front of her. She leaned back in her chair and attempted unsuccessfully to cross her legs, displaying a considerable expanse of white flesh in the process. Merlin decided he'd got enough information for the moment.

"Time to get back to the Yard, I think. Thanks for your help."

Mrs Bowen rose to her feet. She smiled and fluttered her eyelids. "Are you sure I can't offer you something? Something a little stronger than tea. Sherry perhaps?"

Merlin smiled regretfully and hurried out into the street.

* * *

She sat hunched up over a corner table weeping. From the beginning of the war pubs had seemed to be standing room only every night but this evening was an exception. A couple of AFS officers propped up the bar. In the opposite corner of the lounge, three old ladies sat silently together, slowly sipping their port-and-lemons. A couple of tables away two well-dressed older men, breaking their journeys home from the office, exchanged quiet words under their bowler hats. Johnny Morgan returned with the drinks. "Come on, Kathleen. Get this down your neck. It'll make you feel better."

She removed a small handkerchief from her bag and blew her nose on it as delicately as she could. The tears stopped momentarily. "It's so awful. Who could have done such a thing?"

"Some madman, I suppose." Morgan's nose disappeared into his pint glass.

"Who would have wanted to kill someone so kind and lovely?"

After fidgeting with her handkerchief for a moment, the tears began again.

All eyes were on her. Morgan put his arm around her shoulders. "Close friend died you know. Girl's a bit upset – as you'd expect." The ladies in the far corner nodded sympathetically. The two office workers raised their hats and mumbled a few indistinguishable words, while the AFS officers turned away, uninterested.

"Drink your drink. It'll make you feel better."

She reached for her gin and sipped it carefully. Her tears stopped. Morgan reached into his jacket for a packet of cigarettes and waved it in front of her. "Yes please, Johnny."

Morgan lit up the two cigarettes in a flamboyant style he'd seen in a recent Bette Davies picture and passed one over. "Did you see that policeman then, sweetheart?"

"Yes, I did."

"What did he ask you?"

"Oh, this and that. He asked me what Joan was like, who her friends were, did we go out together and so on."

"And what did you tell him?"

"That she was a lovely, friendly girl who was good at her job. That she and I used to go out together sometimes, to the pictures and so on. He asked whether she had any boyfriends."

Morgan blew a smoke ring which slowly disintegrated above them. "And what did you say to that?"

"I said none that I knew." She took another sip of her drink and then looked up sheepishly at Morgan. "Do you know if she had a boyfriend?"

"Me? No. Why should I?"

"Just wondering. I know that she occasionally went out on the town in the West End with someone or other but she was always very secretive about it. Perhaps she mentioned something to you. You know, like on the Thursday before she disappeared."

Morgan clenched his teeth. "I didn't go for lunch with her that day."

"But Mr Priestley said…"

"He's a blind old fart. You didn't tell the police anything like that?"

"No. But you did see her outside the office from time to time didn't you? I saw you together in the park once."

"A lot of us see each other outside the office from time to time. Nothing in that is there? Anyway, she wanted to ask my advice once or twice."

"Advice about what?"

"Nothing important. She didn't like her lodgings and she asked me if I could help her find a new place."

"Funny, she didn't mention that to me. And I know some lodgings going quite cheap round the corner."

He drained his glass and got to his feet. "Fancy another drink?"

"I don't think so."

"Come on. It'll do you good."

"Alright then, but…?"

"What?"

"You're telling the truth – Joan wasn't anything to you was she?

"Of course not." He bent down and gave her a quick hug. "I'll go and get those drinks."

* * *

Merlin leaned back in his chair and planted both his feet on the desk. He felt exhausted. It had been a long day. After his trip to Hammersmith he had joined Bridges at Princes Gate for the interviews of embassy staff. It was past eight by the time they got back to the Yard.

"So what do you make of all that, Sergeant?"

"You learned more about Joan Harris at her lodgings than we did from all our interviews."

Merlin scratched his neck where his shirt collar was particularly stiff.

"Pretty unhelpful bunch weren't they? Apart from that Irish girl, no one admits to having had more than a work relationship – and none of the men acknowledged the slightest interest in her, which is a little hard to believe. You couldn't tell from the mortuary slab but I found a photograph of her in her lodgings and she was a very pretty girl. Here, look."

Bridges took the photograph and whistled.

"Almost as pretty as my Iris."

Merlin smiled. He, together with everyone else in CID, was well aware of the extent of his Sergeant's besottedness with his wife of three months.

"I missed Morgan. Did he have anything interesting to say?"

"Not really. Said Miss Harris was a nice, quiet girl. Said he passed the time of day with her. That was about it."

"Confident sort of chap, Morgan, for such a young man in his position. What's his background?"

Bridges searched through his notebook. "Up to London from South Wales about eighteen months ago. Says an uncle of his living here helped him to get his driving licence and then a friend of his uncle's gave him an introduction to the Embassy. He was then given a junior chauffeur's job and has been doing that for about a year."

The Sergeant's attention was drawn to a hole in one of Merlin's shoes. He knew all about holes in shoes did Sam Bridges, and it pained him to see his boss's in that state. The man desperately needed a woman's attention, as Iris kept on telling him.

"His background needs a bit more looking into."

Bridges rubbed wearily at his right eye.

"Will do, sir, but do you mind if I get off home now? Iris said she'd be cooking something special for me tonight."

Merlin wondered sceptically to what heights Iris' culinary skills might rise then reproved himself for his meanness. "No, of course. You get on home and enjoy what remains of the evening. We've got a few more people to interview tomorrow, haven't we?"

"A couple of the junior staff were out of the office and we couldn't get to see some of the more senior people. Here's the list."

"Thanks. Goodnight, Sam. Enjoy your meal."

Several of the names listed meant nothing to Merlin but he recognised some of the senior people. Bridges had put down the Ambassador and his family for form's sake, but the A.C. would probably have kittens if he got on the phone to Kennedy in Boston or wherever he was. Mr Zarb, the First Secretary, remained to be seen. And Arthur Norton's name was there. A couple of Morgan's chauffeur colleagues had also been unavailable for today's interviews.

His stomach ached with hunger. Lunch, of course, had been a washout and he was starving now. Perhaps he'd stop off for a pie and mash in Victoria, or maybe fish and chips. A brief glance at the photograph of his wife, which he kept in the top drawer of his desk, gave him a different ache in the pit of his stomach. He pinched himself before heading down the stairs and out into the freezing night.

* * *

The sharp disc of the full moon shone down, brightly lighting their way. She leaned against his shoulder as he struggled with the stiff lock on the street door. Eventually the door gave and he pulled her up the small flight of stairs. Another lock had to be negotiated but he managed this more easily. Morgan flicked on a light and she saw a bed-sitting room larger and more expensively furnished than her own. "God, it's cold in here, isn't it?" He struck a match and lit the gas fire.

"This is a nice place. How did you manage…"

He shrugged then pulled her roughly towards him.

"No, Johnny. I really shouldn't be here. I must be getting back home. It's very late and I need to be back at work early tomorrow as Miss Edgar has a pile of things for me to do." She pulled away.

"Come on, Kathleen. Don't be boring. I've got a bottle of whisky here that someone gave me. Let's have a nightcap."

She sat down in the room's one armchair, while Morgan stretched out at length on the bed. She had already drunk more than she'd ever drunk before. Was it four or five gin-and-its? Four, she thought, but were they singles or doubles? She felt giddy and her head was pounding.

Morgan rose from the bed and pulled a bottle of whisky and glasses down from a shelf. "Here you are. Take a swig of this. Best Scottish malt whisky. Macallan it's called. It's very smooth. You'll love it."

The amber liquid gleamed in the low lamplight as he poured out two glasses.

"No, really, Johnny. I've had too much to drink. I don't like whisky anyway."

He held out a glass. As she continued to refuse it he lurched forward, tripped and sent the drinks flying.

"Look what you've done, you stupid man."

Morgan displayed a lopsided grin as he raised himself up from the floor. "Not to worry, sweetheart. I'll clean it up for you." He moved to a basin by the side of the bed and ran water over a flannel. Kathleen stood in the other corner of the room patting herself down.

"This is my best dress, Johnny Morgan, and look what you've done to it now. It's ruined."

"No it isn't. Don't worry." He brought the sopping flannel over and started mopping at the stains.

"Give me that. I'll do the mopping, thank you."

"Oh come on, let me help you, Kathleen. There's a spot right there." He raised his hand to cover her right breast.

"What are you…?"

"And there's another spot." His other hand moved to her left breast.

"You cheeky boy. Leave me alone." Her attempts to sound righteously indignant faltered as she noticed that there was something quite pleasant about the way Morgan's hands were moving.

"That's nice, isn't it? You've got a beautiful body, you know, sweetheart." His left hand slid down and stroked her lower back before moving below.

"Stop it. Stop it." His right hand turned her face towards his and he kissed her lips hard. She struggled to pull away.

"Johnny. This isn't fair. I've had too much to drink. I've not done this sort of thing before."

"Don't worry. I have. Leave it to me. I know what I'm doing." He kissed her again on the lips and then bent, kissing her breasts through the fabric of her dress. His hands moved to her legs and lifted the hem of her dress slowly up to her waist.

"Don't hurt me, Johnny."

"I won't. Trust me."

* * *

As the nearby church clock chimed, he got out of the bed and lit a cigarette. Muffled sobbing sounds came from the pillow in which Kathleen's face was buried. He went to the window and half opened it. The moon still shone down brightly on the mews. Across the way he thought he saw a moving shadow. A moment later he heard the sound of a dustbin rolling on the ground. He threw the remains of his cigarette out of the window and got back into the bed.

"There, there, sweetheart. It always hurts a bit the first time. You'll enjoy it more second time round."

He took a glass from the sink, ran the tap and dropped something in it. "Here you are. Have a little Eno's liver salts. This'll make you feel better."

* * *

Merlin decided to walk home. He hadn't had a good long walk since before Christmas. When he was younger he had been a keen soccer man, turning out regularly for one of the police teams. He hadn't been a bad player. There had even been some talk of him playing professionally. Scouts from Fulham, Chelsea and the Arsenal had come to watch him. He had been a dashing inside left with a strong right-footed shot and a good head. There had been some overtures from the Chelsea and Arsenal scouts. Requests had been made several times for him to play in trials but he had declined. He hadn't been able to see much future in it and, though he liked football, the police was his first love. So he passed on the chance. He'd never regretted it but after giving up playing in his thirties he had come to miss the feeling of wellbeing which came with the high level of fitness he'd had to maintain. When he got married he took up tennis, which was a sport Alice had played since her youth, and he enjoyed the game. That had helped him keep in shape but since Alice's death he hadn't picked up a racquet. His lean figure these days owed little to exercise and much to nervous stress and missing too many meals.

Tonight would see another missed meal as, by the time he had reached the end of Birdcage Walk and mulled over his morning visit to the morgue, his yen for a pie and mash or anything else had vanished.

He looked up at the Palace. He knew that the sentries were standing out in the cold beyond the sandbags in the courtyard, but although it was a clear night he couldn't see them. There was no sign of life, although he knew the King and Queen were in residence. The full moon shone and the stars sparkled brilliantly in a still bomberless sky. Gloomy lines from a Robert Louis Stevenson poem came suddenly to his mind: "Under the wide and starry sky, dig the grave and let me lie". He shivered.

The quickest way home from the Palace was through Victoria, Eaton Square and Sloane Square. The pavements here had been cleared of most of the ice and snow. He decided to extend his exercise and take a roundabout route home. He walked up Constitution Hill to Hyde Park Corner. Then instead of going down the Brompton Road past Harrods he headed towards Kensington. The odd blinkered car drove by. A couple of drunks weaved their way past him, almost knocking him over.

It was nearly chucking out time and he realised that he was very thirsty. Alcohol didn't appeal but a glass of lemonade would be nice. He just had time to grab a drink before the pubs closed.

He was near Princes Gate and knew a nice little place around the corner. As he was entering, a young couple, much the worse for wear, fell giggling out of the swing doors. Merlin stood back to let them pass before making his way to the bar. "Have I time for a lemonade?"

The burly young barman looked at the clock above the spirit bottles. "Alright sir, but make it quick."

Something suddenly troubled him. He hadn't really looked at the couple who had passed him at the door but he felt there was something familiar about them. He had caught a quick glimpse of a dark male face and an abundance of red hair. Of course, he thought. We're just around the corner from the Ambassador's residence. Johnny Morgan and a girl. Probably that nice Irish girl. He turned and pushed through the pub doors.

"Hey. Your drink's here, guvnor."

Merlin looked to his left and right in the darkness. The

bright moonshine gave him a glimpse of someone disappearing around a corner. He went back into the pub and tossed a coin to the barman. "Sorry. Something's come up." He turned and walked briskly after the couple. He was probably wasting his time but a capacity for idle curiosity was no handicap for a policeman.

He saw them as he took the first left turning. They were leaning against a wall thirty yards or so ahead and he could hear murmurings of mild resistance from the girl as the man kissed her.

The couple moved off and he followed them until they suddenly disappeared from view. Merlin kept going and found a short alleyway leading off the street. He heard muffled footsteps and followed. He found himself in a cobbled mews street which appeared to be a cul-de-sac. A door nearby closed. He walked slowly down the street and halted opposite where he thought that door was. A light above briefly flashed before the window was covered by the blackout curtains.

He stood outside gradually feeling more and more uncomfortable. I'm a policeman, he thought, not a moral enforcer, nor a Peeping Tom. He waited for a quarter of an hour and was about to leave when he heard a cry from above.

Soon after he heard footsteps approaching down the alleyway. He was leaning against a garage door opposite the house. A few yards away there was a recessed doorway into which he moved. The footsteps stopped close by but he could not see the new arrival. He could now hear the sound of laughter from above.

Time passed. After another fifteen minutes, Merlin heard the sound of a window opening and he could see the small pinprick light of a cigarette being waved in the window frame above. A dustbin near the alleyway entrance fell noisily to the ground and he saw a shadow move. His heart jumped as something touched his leg. The something began to purr and rubbed itself back and forth against his leg. He held his breath and tried to nudge the cat away gently with his foot.

While he was attempting this, a blaze of light hit the mews as Morgan's front door opened. He saw someone of medium height wearing a long overcoat and a hat move quickly through it. Two male voices acknowledged each other with grunts and the door closed.

Merlin fell exhausted into his bed with numb feet and tingling fingers. He had waited another half-hour outside the flat, hoping for the late visitor to depart so that he could follow and identify him. No one had emerged and he had considered whether the visitor might be a flatmate without a key – but then why had he waited so long outside? Something didn't add up but the cold had got to him and he had packed it in. He reached out to switch on the radio and attempted to find one of the continental stations. He always found it easier to go to sleep to music. The other night he'd found a French station playing the songs of Charles Trenet and Tino Rossi. Alice and he had seen them both at the Lido on their Parisian trip and had loved them. He had been particularly enthusiastic. Perhaps a little of his Latin blood coming out? His father had sung Spanish lullabies to him when he was little. Some of the tunes still lingered in his head. Javier Merino had had a beautiful tenor voice. He wasn't aware of any popular Spanish singers in the same category as Trenet and Rossi. Not much to sing about in Spain in recent years of course. There was an Argentinean chap, what was his name? Gardel, that was it. Carlos Gardel, a tango singer. He wasn't bad at all. He'd have to go and see if he could find some of his records. He twiddled on the radio some more but couldn't find anything good. It didn't matter as within seconds he was asleep.

CHAPTER 4

Bridges arrived outside Princes Gate a few seconds after his boss, who greeted him with a concerned look.

"You're looking a little peaky, Sergeant. Are you alright?"

"I'm not feeling great, to be honest."

"What's up?"

Bridges took a deep breath of the morning's freezing air and rubbed his stomach.

"Might have been something I ate."

"Weren't you having a special meal last night?"

"Yes – it was a little, er, exotic."

Merlin raised an eyebrow.

"The thing is, her old dad, he spent a long time in India in the army. Got keen on the local food. Curry and so on. He taught Iris a few recipes and she tried one last night. Very nice it was too, but I'm afraid it was rather spicy."

"How's Iris?"

"She's right as rain. A cast-iron stomach, she has."

"Better get her to stick to plain English fare from now on. Or if she wants to try some foreign stuff, I can give her a few wholesome and safe Spanish recipes."

"Sir."

Bridges took in another lungful of air and followed his boss up the stairs.

The reception hall smelt wonderful. Vases of freshly-cut flowers had been scattered about the place. He'd had a girlfriend years ago who had been passionate about flowers and he had learned much from her. She had written learned articles for magazines about her favourites. She had been particularly interested in orchids. There were no orchids as far as Merlin could see, but pansies, primroses and several other winter varieties he couldn't name.

"Take in some of this wonderful scent, Sam. Should help clear the system."

"I'm surprised you can smell anything, sir, with all those lethal mints you eat.

"Very funny, Sergeant."

Miss Edgar appeared from behind the staircase and hurried up to them.

"There you are, Chief Inspector. Enjoying the flowers I see. I thought I needed to do something to cheer the place up. Everyone is so affected by poor Joan's…" She dabbed a handkerchief to her nose then pulled herself together. "Come along. I'll put you in my office again."

They followed her up the stairs. On the way they met Kathleen Donovan hurrying down, her arms piled high with files. As they stepped aside for her she tripped and fell, spilling papers everywhere. She jumped to her feet before they had a chance to help her, and ran down to the lobby in tears.

"I don't know what's the matter with that girl this morning. I know she's upset about Joan but so are we all. I'll be back in a second."

Miss Edgar went back down and they made their own way to her room.

"Poor girl. Perhaps she had a dodgy meal last night too."

"Drink in her case rather than food, Sergeant."

"You seem to be speaking from knowledge."

"I'll tell you about it later. Here's our first interview."

A smartly-dressed male figure hovered at the door to Miss Edgar's office. He didn't look happy.

"Come on in, Mr Norton. I believe we've met before. I'm Detective Chief Inspector Merlin and this is Detective Sergeant Bridges."

Arthur Norton ignored Merlin's extended hand. "You realise that it is an impertinence to request this interview. I am an accredited US diplomat and have no obligation to speak to you. It is highly inconvenient and I am only here because Miss Edgar, whom I respect, made a particular request that I do so."

"Well, thank you very much indeed for agreeing to speak to us. I apologise if this interview is in any way inconvenient. I doubt very much that we shall detain you long. We are just asking a few simple questions of the staff here…"

"Staff, Inspector? I would hardly call myself staff. I am one of the Ambassador's key aides. A senior diplomat in my own right." Norton's squeaky twang reverberated around the small room.

"Didn't mean to cause offence, sir. All I was saying was that we have a small number of straightforward questions to ask and then you can be on your way. Would you like to remove your overcoat before we begin – or are you comfortable as you are?"

"As you assure me, Inspector, that this is likely to be a brief interview, I think I'll keep my coat on. Please proceed." Norton sat down heavily in the indicated chair.

"As you know, an Embassy employee, Miss Joan Harris, has died in unfortunate circumstances. We'd just like to know about any dealings you may have had with the lady?"

"I hardly knew the girl, Inspector. She did a little typing for me. That's all."

Norton identified a few flecks of dirt on his otherwise immaculate grey trousers, and picked at the offending areas with his forefinger.

"She was a very good typist, I understand."

"She was competent, Inspector. Nothing to brag about, though, I'd have thought."

"I understand that you preferred her to do your typing."

Satisfied with his trousers, Norton looked up and faced the policemen directly for the first time. "I probably used her more because most of the others are incompetent."

"What sort of things would she type for you?"

"My reports, of course, and occasional correspondence."

"Would there be anything particularly confidential in those reports, sir?"

Norton snorted derisively. "Of course there was confidential stuff in there. All of my reports are confidential."

"And what exactly are your reports about?"

"Are you off your head? You can't expect me to tell you that."

Merlin bit his lip. Before his marriage he'd been known for having a short fuse. Alice had worked hard to cure him of it and since her passing he'd resolved to live up to her standards in this regard. He felt that Norton was going to test this resolution severely. "I am not attempting to pry into state secrets, Mr Norton. I am simply attempting to pursue one potential line of enquiry with regard to Miss Harris' death, that being whether her possession, through her work, of confidential information might in some way have had a bearing on her murder. Can you assist me in any way on this point?"

Norton crossed his legs and yawned. "I am retained by the Ambassador for a number of purposes, one of which is to be his eyes and ears among London society. I report to him on a regular basis details of my encounters with, and observations on, leading figures in British life. I do this, primarily, you understand, in order to contribute to his evaluation of British morale and to the development of political trends. While he is resident, of course, my reports are merely supplementary to his own wider experience of political and social developments. While he is away consulting our government, as at present, I would pride myself that my reports are of great importance." Norton paused to remove a cigarette from a silver case and to light up. "No doubt my reports contain much that might interest other people. That being said, I can't conceive of a poor mite like Miss Harris being able to understand the content of the reports to such an extent that her safety might in any way be put at risk. Now, if that's all you want to know I take it we are finished and that I may take my leave of you."

He rose to his feet.

"Just a couple more questions, if you please. Did you ever see Miss Harris socially?"

Norton sat back down with a petulant grunt. "What in heavens would I be doing seeing Miss Harris socially?"

"Pretty girl wasn't she, sir?"

Norton pursed his lips. "You are sorely mistaken, Sergeant, if you are suggesting that I had any kind of relationship with this girl."

"Miss Harris was a natural beauty, I'd say. It is not unheard of for men of the most exalted position to have affairs with their secretaries, particularly pretty ones, so the Sergeant's question is not out of order. You have given us a clear answer for which I thank you."

"I'll be damned if I don't complain to your superiors, Merlin."

"I wouldn't do that if I were you. We wouldn't want your highly valuable time 'encountering leading figures in British life' to be sullied by the requirements of the Metropolitan Police complaints process."

Norton scowled across the desk and got to his feet once more. "I take it I may leave now?" Merlin nodded but as Norton went through the door he had an afterthought.

"Sir?"

"Goddamit! What now?"

"A man like you, out and about amongst London society, would know most of the fashionable clubs and nightclubs in town, would he not?"

Norton's features relaxed a little. "I am sure I know most of the best places."

"Do you know a club called 'The Blue Angel' by any chance?"

Norton studied the ceiling. "The Blue Angel – sounds familiar. It's a film, isn't it, with Marlene Dietrich? A sleazy nightclub in Berlin I think. I can't say I know of one in London. Sorry I can't help you there."

"That's alright. I'll find it one way or another. I am something of an expert on sleazy clubs – sleazy people as well for that matter."

Norton sneered before making his departure. They listened to his steps clattering down the corridor.

"Quite a charmer."

"Indeed, Sergeant. 'Culo pomposo', as my father would have said."

Bridges returned a bemused look.

"Pompous arse, Sam."

"I think I might have ruder words, sir. Think he's got anything to do with this?"

"Probably not, although it's tempting to think the worst of a man like that."

Merlin sucked on a lozenge and breathed eucalyptus fumes on his colleague as he smoothed out the list of the day's interviewees that had been left for him on the desk.

"You were going to tell me about Kathleen Donovan, sir."

"So I was." Merlin related as succinctly as he could the story of his adventures of the previous night.

"If my stomach wasn't already turning of its own accord, it would be now. Poor girl. Do you think it bears on the case?"

"Perhaps. Morgan likes girls. They like him. Joan Harris was pretty."

"He says Joan was never a girlfriend. Says he hardly knew her."

"We'll just have to find out if he's telling the truth."

There was a knock at the door, followed by the diffident entrance of a little man in a chauffeur's uniform. Merlin looked at his list. "Mr Priestley. Come on in."

* * *

Johnny Morgan made his way carefully down the steep unlit stairs. Snow showers had turned to sleet in the Soho streets outside. At the bottom he looked to his right. There was a faint light at the end of the corridor and he made his way in that direction. Arriving at a door, slightly ajar, he pushed against it gently. A dull glow emanated from a single hanging bulb. He saw a desk around which were three unoccupied chairs. From the other side of the room he could hear rhythmic breathing. Slumped in an armchair was a very fat man whose huge bald head lolled forward on to a barrel chest. A few greasy strands of hair hung down to one side like ivy creepers.

Morgan nudged the man, who responded with a grunt.

"Come on, Uncle. Wake up. It's early."

From another corner of the room, Morgan heard a snort. A second dozing man materialised.

"Christ, come on, Uncle. Shake a leg."

Eventually the large mound of flesh beneath his hands began to move of its own accord. "Wassat? Jimmy? Who's there?"

The other figure rose from its chair, moved forward in the murk and swore as it stumbled on something.

"It's me, Uncle. No need to panic. It's me, Johnny".

His uncle's piggy eyes gradually obtained focus. "What the hell are you playing at?"

"Not playing at anything, Uncle. Just came to pay you a visit. Didn't realise that seven o'clock was your bedtime."

"You little bugger." The voice retained elements of its Welsh origins but was predominantly cockney, reflecting the forty years or so of life that Maurice Owen, known to all as Morrie, had spent in the metropolis.

Morrie lifted a small object from his lap and threw it at the prostrate figure on the floor. "And you, Jimmy. You useless bugger. You're meant to be on the lookout for me, aren't you? Not bloody sleeping in a corner while I take my evening nap. Don't know why I bother to employ you. Get up off your arse and make yourself useful for once. Turn on the corner lamp so I can see what I'm doing."

Jimmy Reardon raised himself stiffly from the floor and moved back towards his own chair. The gloom lifted as he turned on the lamp, and the full squalor of Morrie Owen's office was revealed.

"And you can give me back my account book, thank you."

Reardon, a bent, haggard-looking man with greying hair, dark bags beneath his eyes and a large wart on his cheek, picked up a black book from the floor and passed it back to his boss.

"And now I'll have a nice little chat with my idiot nephew here. Off you go." Owen struggled to his feet and waddled over to the desk. It was strewn with papers and the remains of his fish and chips supper.

Turning to a dingy mirror behind the desk, Owen dabbed his fingers to his tongue and moistened his eyes. He lifted the cats-licks hanging down from his head and laid them carefully across the giant dome of his skull. He applied further moisture from his fingers on to the hairs in an effort to keep them firmly in place.

Satisfied at last with his efforts he turned round, pulled his dangling braces up and over his shoulders and lowered himself carefully into the chair behind his desk. "OK, Johnny. What do you want? I always take a little nap before the club opens, as you know. If I don't have my nap I get quite tetchy, see. So tell me something to cheer me up and forget that you were the one that ruined my nap."

Morgan pulled over a chair and faced the quivering jowls of his mother's favourite brother. "Sorry, but I haven't got anything particularly jolly to tell you. I just thought you might like to know a little about what's been going on at the Ambassador's place?"

Folds of flesh in Owen's neck rippled as he reached to scratch his chin. "Can't say that's a very good reason to disturb my beauty sleep, Johnny boy. You got yourself into some trouble there or something? I wouldn't like to hear that you're in trouble after all the effort I put in to get you that job."

"I'm not in trouble. It's just that the police are taking an interest in the Ambassador's staff and are poking around like. I thought I'd better let you know."

"The police are poking around, are they? Why's that then?"

Morgan sighed. "A girl who worked at the Embassy, Joan, was found dead. So they're just sort of investigating about that."

"Joan, eh? Dead is she? Nice looking girl. That's sad but what's it to us?"

"Nothing, Uncle. Just thought you'd like to know. Because Joan and I, you know…"

Beads of sweat running from the top of Owen's head made their tortuous way down the valleys and crevices of his face.

Morgan shifted uneasily in his chair.

"Look, Johnny. I know you love the girls and I know they love you. You have a talent, a talent which, as you know, I am prepared to back."

"Yes, Uncle."

"And you like them particularly sweet and innocent don't you, just like many of our other friends and clients." Owen stared into the distance for a moment then looked back gloomily at his nephew. "I don't want any more detail. Just keep your head down and keep the police out of my affairs. You're a bright enough boy to manage that, I think."

"Just thought you'd like to know what was going on."

"Indeed, Johnny. And I thank you. And all you need to tell the boys in blue is that you had nothing to do with the girl, isn't that right?"

"Yes, Uncle. But they're going to be talking to others. And what about Norton? They'll be talking to him."

"Don't you worry about Norton. He's a diplomat. Doesn't have to answer any questions if he don't want to, does he? You just make sure nothing gets back to me, alright?" With surprising agility, Owen shot out an arm, grabbed his nephew's lapels and pulled him close. "'Cos if it does," he shouted "I shall be a very unhappy uncle, understand me?"

* * *

Arthur Norton was not feeling at his best. The interview with the two schmucks from Scotland Yard had unsettled his equilibrium. As he tetchily completed his toilette, his temper was further aggravated when he noticed a red spot next to his left nostril. He applied a fingernail to the offending item and removed the head. The eruption of pus splashed against the bathroom mirror. Grabbing a handkerchief from his dresser he removed the stain. What the hell was he doing having spots at the age of forty-six? The police had unsettled his physical equilibrium as well as his mental equilibrium. He must calm down and maintain a level head.

He was meeting Freddie Douglas at the Café Royal. Douglas had promised that he would be making an important introduction tonight.

In normal circumstances it would be a twenty minute walk for him to the Café Royal. In the blackout and with the pavements and roads iced over, it would be longer. He stood around for a few minutes hoping that a taxi might emerge from the darkness. Eventually he gave up waiting and headed off in the direction of Piccadilly. In Berkeley Square a voice from a doorway made him jump. "Fancy a bit of fun, dear?"

A woman emerged from the dark, a torch pointing up at her heavily made-up face. As street prostitutes go, Norton thought, she wasn't so bad-looking. The lipstick and foundation plastered on to her face couldn't conceal the fact that she was younger than most.

"No thanks, honey. Not tonight."

"Where you from then? You a Yank dearie? I love Yanks. Come on. Don't be a spoilsport. I'm very reasonable. Give me a couple of quid and I'll make it worth your while." The woman moved closer and put a hand on his shoulder. Her other hand brushed against the front of his trousers and remained there briefly before starting to move slowly up and down. Norton couldn't help himself and stiffened. This girl was good at her job. His eyes closed.

"You alright, sir?"

Norton opened his eyes to see the outline of a helmet lit by the prostitute's torch. The policeman had a torch of his own which he shone into their faces. The girl broke away. The men listened to the sound of her heels clattering on the icy pavement.

Running the light beam over him, the policemen took note of Norton's expensive astrakhan coat. "You ought to be very careful out here in the blackout, sir. These conditions is paradise for the dregs of society. Some of these girls will pull a knife and rob you as quick as you can say 'Jack Robinson'."

"Thank you, Constable. She just came at me out of the dark and grabbed me. I'm so pleased you came along."

"You be careful now. We don't want to see any of our brethren from over the Pond murdered on the streets of London. Can I guide you anywhere?"

"I'm going to the Café Royal, constable. It's not far now. I think I can find the way."

"Alright, but you watch out, sir."

Norton mentally thanked the constable for helping him to keep his evening on track. She was a sexy tart though. He would look out for her on another, more convenient night.

The Café Royal was throbbing with life. Norton ploughed his way, with some difficulty, through the crush. He caught sight of Douglas talking animatedly to two other men at the bar. Ducking his head down again he struggled towards them.

"It's goddamed crowded tonight, Freddie."

"Arthur. Glad you could make it."

Douglas sported a bright red bow tie with his evening wear and was smoking a pungent black cigarette. "You know Vivian, don't you?" Vivian Pemberton smiled a languid greeting.

"And of course my colleague, Edward Fraser." A portly man with an unruly mop of curly brown hair and a small upturned nose reached over to shake Norton's hand. "I think we need some more drink. Krug alright for you, Arthur?" Fraser waved at one of the barmen.

"Have you noticed that ladies seem to greatly outnumber gentlemen in this establishment?" Douglas wafted his cigarette at the melée.

"I'd say that's a trend that is going to be further exaggerated if this silly war carries on."

"Now, now, Vivian. I don't think it's wise to use words like 'silly' about the war in public, do you?"

Two bottles of champagne arrived in a large ice bucket.

"Cheers. Here's to it." Fraser raised his glass and the others followed suit.

"I think it is a silly war and the sooner Mr Chamberlain settles it peaceably the better."

"I can see you're in a combative mood tonight, Vivian. I think we'd better get a table."

A waiter was called, a note was passed, and they were swiftly seated at a corner table as private as could be obtained. Two pretty young girls giggled and simpered at two much older men on the nearest table.

"Tell me, Freddie, we've known each other a while but the subject's never come up, is there a Mrs Douglas somewhere?"

"Not yet, Arthur. I am spoken for though. Lovely girl. She's in Shropshire at present. Probably going to stay there for the duration. Her father thinks London's too dangerous. Still, leaves me some room for adventure." Douglas smiled across at Pemberton who winked mischievously. "Before you arrived, Vivian was telling us about his new job at the Ministry of Information."

"Oh, yes. You mentioned that the other night."

Pemberton yawned. "It's a bloody bore, Norton. Can't really tell you much about it but I shall die of tedium if my current project doesn't get completed soon. Every idea I have goes off for review by some committee of philistines who wouldn't know art from a lump of coal. It's very frustrating. All I can say is that if the military decision making of our war machine is subject to the same sort of bureaucratic delay and dithering as are my modest little propaganda film efforts, then

I should be surprised if this fine establishment hasn't been turned into a bierkeller by March."

"Vivian, please." Douglas glanced carefully around him. A white-haired gentleman on a nearby table gazed sternly at the group for a while before returning to his brown Windsor soup.

Douglas suggested ordering food and as the party muttered its approval of this idea, he put his hand on Fraser's shoulder. "What's wrong with you tonight, Edward? You've hardly said a word."

"Oh, nothing, Freddie, nothing at all."

"Well, buck up and get a bloody waiter over here will you? We're all starving."

Just as the main course was being delivered, the table was approached by a tall man with olive skin, dark eyes and a small goatee beard. Douglas rose in greeting.

"Count. Good to see you." The newcomer clicked his heels and bowed. "A pleasure to see you again also, Signor Douglas."

The Count smiled engagingly at the party, revealing a set of immaculate teeth which almost matched his white dinner jacket.

"Arthur, may I introduce Count Ricardo Giambelli."

"Delighted to meet you, Count." The Italian's teeth flashed out again from beneath his appropriately Roman nose.

A waiter brought over a chair and Giambelli seated himself between Douglas and Norton, declining the offer of food. A fresh glass of champagne was poured.

"The Count is chef de cabinet at the Italian Embassy."

"So you are Arthur Norton?" The Count flourished a black handkerchief with which he mopped his brow. "I have heard of you from my Ambassador, who is a good friend of your admirable Mr Kennedy."

"I know that Mr Kennedy was highly appreciative of all the help your embassy gave him when he travelled with his family to the Pope's Coronation."

"Ah, yes. Your Ambassador is a good Catholic man with good Catholic views. Good political views I believe, as well."

"I am sure they are well known to you and your embassy."

"And are his views also your views?"

"The Ambassador and I are as one in our political outlook, Count." Norton's features assumed a steadfast appearance.

"Indeed, Mr Norton. That is good to hear. Signor Douglas mentioned something of this to me already."

Douglas nodded, leaned forward and lowered his voice. "We are in close touch with the Count's department at present. Some interesting ideas are being put forward by his Excellency and his colleagues. I think that Mr Kennedy would be keen to hear them."

"I'd be delighted to learn about them whenever you think appropriate but…"

The house orchestra struck up "The Lambeth Walk" while a statuesque blonde squeezed past their table and attracted everyone's attention. The Count laughed. "I think, my friends, we should concentrate on pleasure tonight. But I would be happy to meet at any time which is convenient. I have taken up golf. Do you play golf, Mr Norton?"

"I play a little."

"Well, I am sure you are much better than me but perhaps we might play a round this weekend. I am a member of a club in Surrey. What do you say?"

"It would be a pleasure."

"Bene. I shall look forward to it."

"Good. That's fixed then." Douglas patted Norton on the back. "Now, gentlemen. Any ideas about the rest of the evening? Shall we stay here or try somewhere else? I thought we might go on. Arthur and I know one or two good places, don't we, my friend?"

* * *

Morgan shivered as he put his latchkey in the lock of the

outside door. His condition was not solely due to the freezing night air. He might be flesh and blood and he might have done his nephew several good turns but Morrie Owen gave him the creeps. When he looked at Uncle Morrie's bloated features he found it hard to believe that his mother was in any way related to him, let alone his only sister. Megan Morgan was a short, trim woman, with the remnants of what everyone in the village said had been a very pretty face. His nan and gramp were small too. There was no accounting for it. There was one thing they had in common though. Brains. His mum was bright and Morrie was as sharp as a razor. What were the words he'd heard some of the Americans use about the Ambassador? A very sharp cookie. That was Uncle Morrie too. Hard as nails as well, but smooth, oh so smooth, when he wanted to be. He did not want to get on the wrong side of his uncle, that was for sure.

The mechanism was stiff as always and he had to rattle the key in the lock a few times before the door gave. He'd spent the evening losing money steadily at the snooker hall. It was late and someone had diligently turned off all the lights. He groped his way through the hallway, up the stairs, and along the warren of corridors to the bedroom. All he could hear was his own footsteps and the whistling of the wind outside. He rummaged in his trouser pockets for the other key. There'd been a bit of a rumpus when he'd insisted on having a lock on the bedroom door. No one else did and some of the others had complained vigorously. Miss Edgar had a sweet spot for him though and she'd turned a blind eye. He needed security. Thanks to his uncle he was a busy man and he couldn't afford any slips. What if he forgot and left something dodgy in the room? Priestley, for one, was always nosing everywhere. The thought of his uncle's reaction if he compromised him in any way made him shudder. The key slid smoothly into the lock and he entered the room. He switched on the light, hurried over to the fire and dropped a coin into the meter. After ten minutes the room had warmed up enough for him to take his coat off. Sitting down on the bed, he remembered with pleasure what he'd been doing at roughly the same time the previous night. What a body that girl had! And a sweet face – such a sweet face. Perhaps he could engineer a return engagement next week? Provided his uncle didn't keep him too busy. Slowly the circulation returned to his fingers and toes and he bent down to untie his shoe laces.

The agreeable images of Kathleen faded as his mind turned again to his uncle. Much as he feared him he had decided he wasn't going to do any more of that other stuff. No matter that Uncle Morrie paid him double-whack. There was a limit.

He rose from the bed, removed his tie, collar and studs and walked over to the basin. The wind was now howling rather than whistling but this didn't stop him hearing the floorboards creaking outside. He can't have been the last one in after all. The cold tap was running and he splashed his face a few times before giving his teeth a good clean. Outside the creaking had stopped but he walked to the door, which he hadn't yet locked, and poked his head out into the corridor. Seeing nothing, he closed the door and looked on the bed for his key. He found it, turned and walked straight into a fist. He felt something in his nose crack before he was hit again. Blood was streaming into his eyes and he swung his own fist weakly into empty air. Two sickening blows to his stomach were followed by another to his face. He was vaguely aware of the loosening of teeth. Struggling to breathe he flailed uselessly with his arms before he felt his legs being kicked from underneath him. One eye was completely closed but through the bloody haze of the other he saw something glinting. He was pushed flat on the floor. Was there one shape above him or two? He couldn't tell. A boot landed in his groin and he doubled up. He would have cried out but he didn't have the strength.

CHAPTER 5

Thursday February 1st

The inhabitants of Hammersmith were just awakening to their morning cuppas when the two policemen arrived at Joan Harris' lodgings.

"I'll leave it to you to knock on the door, Sergeant. I think I'd prefer to get a more distanced view of Mrs Bowen at this early hour of the morning."

"Right you are, sir. Better take off the hat. It's so smart she might jump on you when she sees it."

Bridges rapped the door knocker sharply once, then once again. The door opened a crack and they could hear whispering. A hesitant female voice spoke out. Merlin thought he detected a hint of West Country in the accent. "I am afraid Mrs Bowen is out. She said she'd be back from the shops within the hour."

"Would that be Miss Simpson or Miss Foster? I'm Detective Chief Inspector Merlin. It's you we've come to see. Did Mrs Bowen not tell you?"

The whispering continued behind the door.

In due course the door opened to reveal two elderly ladies. One was tall and thin with a grey bun and spectacles. The other was short and round with saucer eyes and a tight perm of dyed-brown hair. The taller woman inclined her head. "Please come in."

In the hallway Merlin shook hands, took off his hat and pointed it in the direction of Mrs Bowen's front parlour. When they were all seated, the taller lady introduced herself as Eleanor Simpson and her companion as Emily Foster.

"I presume Mrs Bowen has informed you of the tragedy which occurred while you were away."

Miss Simpson removed her spectacles and started cleaning them with her handkerchief. "Mrs Bowen told us about what happened to the poor girl when we got back from Malmesbury yesterday. She did mention that you might need to speak to us, but we didn't know that you would be here to do that today." Miss Simpson spoke in the clear ringing tone of one who had been born to command obedience. Merlin wondered what unhappy events had led her to these second-rate lodgings in a dingy quarter of Hammersmith. Her companion smiled nervously and wrung her hands. "Yes, yes, so sad. Such a lovely girl."

"I'm sorry to catch you unawares but we got a message last night that you had returned and thought we'd better get round here first thing to see you. I'm afraid we haven't got an awful lot of background information on Miss Harris and we need every scrap we can get."

"Of course, Chief Inspector. How can Emily and I help you?"

"Perhaps you could both give us your impressions of Miss Harris?"

Miss Foster looked anxiously at her friend. "I'll start, shall I?"

"Yes, Eleanor, go ahead; you are so much more observant than me."

"I doubt that we'll have much of interest to tell you. We occasionally encountered the poor girl on the staircase and once or twice had tea together. She seemed a bright young thing. Pretty with it too. Generally, she kept herself very much to herself. She seemed kind. I do remember once when Emily fell on the stairs, Miss Harris was most attentive and offered to go out to the chemist for bandages etcetera. Do you remember, dear?"

"Oh, yes, very kind, a very kind young girl." Miss Foster's eyes watered and she caught her breath.

"I understand Mrs Bowen runs something of a tight ship here. Lock-up at 10.30pm, I believe. Do you know if that ever inconvenienced Miss Harris?"

"You mean did she ever stay out past her allotted curfew?"

"Yes."

"It has not been our habit while staying in Miss Bowen's establishment to spy on other lodgers."

"Oh no, not at all." Miss Foster's cheeks quivered as she shook her head to and fro.

"I wouldn't suggest such a thing, ladies. I was just wondering what you might have observed in the normal course of events."

Miss Foster shook her friend's arm and whispered something behind her hand.

"Yes, well tell them, dear."

Miss Foster cleared her throat. "I was saying that there was an occasion when Miss Harris did arrive home after curfew. I know because she threw some pebbles at my window to attract attention."

"And what did you do?"

"I opened my window of course. Joan asked me if I could slip down stairs and open the door to let her in." She removed a green handkerchief from a sleeve and delicately blew her nose.

"You let her in?"

"Of course. I couldn't let the girl freeze outside."

"Was she on her own?"

"She came in on her own."

"But did you see anyone outside who'd brought her home?"

"Oh." Miss Foster looked into the distance somewhere above Bridges' head. "I did hear another voice, I think."

"A man's voice or a woman's voice?"

"I don't know if I can rightly say. It might have been a woman's. You know, her friend's."

"Which friend is that?"

"You know, her friend from work. I don't know her name. A sweet thing with red hair. She came here a few times with Joan. But then again, it was very late. I'm not sure. It could have been a man's voice. They were whispering, you see."

"Any sign of an accent?"

"I don't know that I can remember, Inspector. Oh dear, I'm not being much help, am I?"

"On the contrary, Miss Foster. Apart from this red-headed friend from work, did either of you ever see Miss Harris with other friends or acquaintances?"

The ladies both shook their heads.

"Did you notice her going out in the evening very often?"

"I suppose we did see her go out in evening wear a few times. That sort of thing stays in the memory, doesn't it, dear?"

"Yes, Eleanor. And very nice she looked too, I must say. Reminded me of you in Watley Court, so many years ago. Do you remember the Hunt Ball, when was it, just after the Jubilee when…"

"Did either of you ever feel that there was something worrying Miss Harris? Did she ever seem preoccupied in any way?"

"No, but…"

"Yes?"

"It's just an impression and it might be my imagination, but when she first came here she seemed very cheerful. More recently, if I think about it, her demeanour was, well, less happy. She didn't seem quite as full of the joys of spring as before, shall we say. Don't you agree, Emily?"

"Oh yes. I think I do. She seemed to be frowning a lot recently and there was one time when she seemed very flustered. Not so long ago either. Just after New Year I think. I came in here and she was reading a letter. When I entered, she put the letter back in its envelope and ran to her room. There was something odd. She smiled at me as she passed but then I am sure I heard her sobbing as she ran up the stairs."

"She never talked to you about what had upset her?"

"Oh, no, no."

"Is there anything else you can tell us?"

As the ladies again shook their heads, some strands of hair

dislodged themselves from Eleanor Simpson's tight bun and for a moment Merlin glimpsed the pretty young girl of the Hunt Ball long ago.

"Thank you, ladies."

"I hope Emily and I have been of some assistance, gentlemen."

As the front door closed behind them, Merlin caught sight of Mrs Bowen's bosom heaving violently as she strode purposefully along the pavement towards them.

"Get in the car, Sergeant. And make it snappy."

* * *

Merlin was reading about the British Expeditionary Force when the A.C. breezed into his office. Charlie Merlin was a Lieutenant in the BEF and was somewhere in France. *The Times* was, not surprisingly, unenlightening about troop movements on the Continent and he put the newspaper down none the wiser. Charlie's wife Bea had heard nothing from her husband since Christmas and was naturally getting agitated. Merlin would have to make time in the next few days to go and see her and little Paul.

"Well done, Frank." The A.C. beamed at him.

Merlin returned a disconcerted look. "For what are you congratulating me, sir?"

"Solving the Birdcage Walk hit and run, of course."

"Oh, right."

The previous night there had been a note on his desk from Johnson – he had a positive identification on the driver of the car. There were further details but he hadn't read them.

"I gather Johnson's going off to pick the chap up later today?"

"Er, yes, sir."

"Good officer, Johnson."

"Yes, very good."

"Reminds me of you when you were younger."

"Does he?"

"Yes." The Assistant Commissioner scratched his neck and gazed out of the window at a nearby barrage balloon. His temporary mood of jollity passed. "Any progress on the Barnes case?"

"We have been carrying out our interviews at the Ambassador's residence."

"Haven't upset anyone I hope?"

"I don't think so." Norton's angry face briefly materialised in front of him.

"Learned anything useful?"

"There are some interesting characters but I don't really have any clear leads. I'm going to investigate one of the embassy chauffeurs. We seem to have caught him out in a lie – said he'd never been close to the victim, but one of the other chauffeurs says he saw them together at lunch just before the girl disappeared."

"A lover's tiff that went wrong?"

"Perhaps. This fellow's a bit of a ladies' man. The girl was pretty and the initial evidence points to her having a reasonably active social life. That's about all I've got at present."

The A.C. clasped his hands together and flexed them above the desk. "Any mileage in the security aspect?"

"The girl had sight of confidential embassy information. She was obviously aware of the political outlook of the Ambassador and his staff but that's pretty much common knowledge. No doubt there's plenty of sensitive information that she was privy to which is not common knowledge and which might provide a lead, but I can't see the Embassy helping me with that."

"I suppose not." The windowpanes rattled loudly. "I think you're barking up the right tree by pursuing her personal life. I'm sure that's where the answer lies."

Clouds were being chased rapidly past the window by the strong wind that had suddenly got up. The barrage balloon was now straining hard at its tethers.

"When is this bloody war going to get going, eh, Frank?"

* * *

At lunchtime Merlin shared some cheese sandwiches with Bridges at his desk.

"Any apologies about the food by the way?"

"No. Iris said I was upset because I drank too much beer with the meal. She's going to have a go at another Indian recipe next week."

"She'll have to reckon with me if she does."

"I'll tell her."

The klaxon of a passing barge boomed out as Merlin licked his fingers.

"Want me to follow up anything the old ladies told us, sir?"

"They didn't really tell us much, did they? I wonder what bad luck brought them to Mrs Bowen's fine establishment."

Merlin swung his feet onto the desk. Bridges wondered again whether he should tell the Chief Inspector about the hole in his shoe. "How'd you mean?"

"Mrs Simpson was clearly brought up in circumstances of position and wealth. How did she end up in those dreary lodgings? Miss Foster seemed of a different class, though. Perhaps she was her maid once. Well that's doubtlessly irrelevant. The only thing I think we need to follow up is the story about the late return home. Better check with the Irish girl, that it was her seeing Miss Harris home. And it would be interesting to see what was in that letter." Merlin looked at his watch, ran a hand through his hair and lowered his legs to the floor. "Let's get over to Kensington."

As they came out of the office, they bumped into a slight young man with a small black moustache and a well Brylcreemed short back and sides.

"I understand from the man upstairs that you've sorted out the hit and run, Peter. Well done."

"I don't know about that, sir, but I have got a suspect." Johnson was a Geordie and Merlin instinctively liked him. One of his father's suppliers had been a Geordie and he'd always had a kind word and a toffee for young Frank.

"Haven't had a chance to read the note you left me yet. I should be back around five. You can tell me everything then."

Johnson shifted uncomfortably on his heels. "I was hoping that you could give me some advice, sir. The situation is a little delicate."

"Can it wait a bit?"

"I suppose it can if it has to." Johnson turned reluctantly and disappeared down the corridor.

"The A.C. says Johnson reminds him of myself when younger. Can't see it myself but he's a good copper. He'll have to do something about that moustache, though."

* * *

Miss Edgar was supervising the installation of some additions to the lobby's floral display.

"I'm sorry gentlemen, it's Morgan's day off and I have no idea where he is. No not there, you silly girl. Over here beneath Mr Adams."

"How about Miss Donovan? We'd like a chat with her if possible."

"Kathleen has called in sick. Someone dropped a note off to say she had the flu and wouldn't be in today."

"Ah." Merlin couldn't restrain himself from raising an eyebrow at Bridges.

"Have I said something amusing, gentlemen?"

"Certainly not Miss Edgar. Could you tell us where Mr Morgan lives?"

"He shares lodgings with some of the other servants in an adjacent building. I suppose you might find him there at this hour. Ah, Priestley." Morgan's colleague scurried through the front door.

"Have you seen Morgan?"

"Not since yesterday, miss."

"Any idea where he is?"

"No. I've been running an errand for Mr Zarb."

"Well, perhaps you could show these officers to the lodgings. He might be in his room. No Mary, not there, put the flowers beneath the second Mr Adams not the first."

Priestley shrugged his shoulders and stepped back through the door. He turned right at the bottom of the steps. Clumps of snow had been shovelled up against the railings and the pavement was dotted with icy puddles. Merlin walked straight into one and grimaced as the freezing water seeped through the hole in his shoe. They followed Priestley around a corner and halted outside a bright red door.

"This is the staff annexe." Priestley pushed at the unlocked door and as they entered, the clatter of pans and smell of boiled cabbage told Merlin that they were not far from the Ambassador's kitchens. The chauffeur led the way through a warren of corridors, up a narrow staircase and finally to a door which was slightly ajar. He knocked politely. "Johnny. Are you there? I've brought the coppers to see you."

There was no reply and Priestley looked enquiringly at the policemen.

"Let's go in."

It was dark and a sickly smell filled the room. "Sergeant, open a window for God's sake. Where's the light?"

Bridges went to the far side of the bed to pull back the curtains and open the window latch, while Priestley scrabbled around for a switch.

The light he eventually switched on revealed an overturned chair, a bed and beside the bed a body. Morgan's bulging eyes gazed lifelessly at the ceiling, his handsome features grotesquely distorted. Stained and broken teeth snarled out from his twisted, gaping mouth. Bright flecks of blood were spattered over heavily-bruised cheeks. His right hand rigidly grasped his neck. Above the hand was a big red gash from which a bloody mess had evidently poured onto the carpet.

Priestley groaned, staggered, retched and ran out of the room.

"Madre de Dios! Open the window, Sergeant." Merlin took a couple of deep breaths before kneeling down and examining the dead man's wounds. A medical qualification was not essential for diagnosis of what had happened to Johnny Morgan – "His throat's been cut."

"Quite a thorough job too, sir."

"Look at the bruising, Sam, and his nose is broken and there are a couple of teeth missing – he took a good walloping beforehand. A hard death. Any sign of a weapon?"

Bridges searched under the bed and around the room while Merlin continued to look closely at the body.

"There's a razor here in the washbowl. It looks clean though."

"Don't touch it. We'll leave it for forensics." Merlin rose to his feet with a grunt. Morgan's battered, lifeless face smiled bizarrely up at him. "Better find a phone and get the usual crew here."

"This must be connected with Miss Harris, don't you think, sir?"

"Two of the Ambassador's employees dead within a week. Does seem a bit of a coincidence, doesn't it?"

* * *

By the time Morgan's room had been thoroughly searched, the body removed, all relevant items bagged, the fingerprinting work done and the residence staff questioned about their last sighting of Morgan, it was late. Various people at the residence had seen Morgan when he went off duty at around 6pm the previous evening but no one had seen him later. To Merlin's annoyance, no one had heard, or would admit to hearing, any noise in Morgan's room. The arrangements in the servant's quarters were such that Morgan's room was in something of a cul-de-sac, quite a way from other rooms, but the commotion from such a violent attack should have been noticed by someone. No one had seen any strangers in the corridors. No one had been seen asking after Morgan. The knife had yielded no clues. The police doctor had given his view that death had occurred very late in the evening or very early in the morning. Apart from that he and Bridges had pretty much drawn a blank.

Worried that Kathleen Donovan might somehow be at risk, Bridges had sent a constable around to her lodgings but there was no sign of her, and her landlady hadn't seen her since the morning of the previous day. Merlin had got back to the Yard too late for Johnson. He'd have to deal with that tomorrow.

He was in no mood for another long walk home and grabbed a car from the pool. He was dead beat and as he pulled into his street all he could think about was his bed. When he got out of the car and heard a loud shout he realised that this was not yet to be.

"Hola, Frank, you old dago. Where've you been? I've been waiting here for ages."

"No fires to put out then, Jack?"

"You know there aren't any bloody fires, clever dick. This phoney war is a pain in the arse! Anyway, I'm off duty now and I've tomorrow off. I thought it would be rude not to start a day's leave with a major hangover so I popped round here to see if you were up for one yourself." Jack Stewart had a rumbling Scottish brogue which was one of many things about him that women seemed to find attractive.

"You know you never get hangovers-it's the poor sods who drink with you who get the hangovers."

Stewart laughed, "Come on then. It'll only take five minutes to get to The Surprise."

Merlin sighed wearily. "A couple of drinks and a pie, Jack, but that's it. I've got far too much on to allow myself a binge. So I'll come if you promise to be a good boy and let me go early."

"Spoilsport. Alright then. Let's be off. You can tell Uncle Jack all your troubles and I'll make sure you're back in beddy-byes in good time."

He sat down at a table at the back of the pub and smiled to himself. Jack Stewart could be annoying sometimes but more often he was a laugh. They were opposites in many ways. Stewart was a muscular, gregarious, handsome charmer with the gift of the gab and a Rabelaisian hunger for pleasure. Merlin was a loner, perhaps more of one now than he'd ever been. They'd met through football, on opposite sides. Stewart had marked him out of the game for eighty minutes before Merlin had slipped a tackle and scored the winning goal. Stewart had insisted on dragging him on a pub crawl as retribution and he'd been around ever since. He could be coarse and blunt but his charm somehow made that excusable, and Merlin always bore in mind the deprived childhood Stewart had had in the slums of Glasgow. Rather like Merlin's father, despite an almost complete lack of formal education, Stewart was exceptionally well-read, fiercely intelligent and great company. And, of course, he'd come up trumps when Alice had gone.

Merlin leaned back and surveyed the scene. Two blowsy women who had clearly had more than enough to drink were in his immediate sightline. One of them, whose face was not totally unattractive, gave him a lopsided grin. "Alright, darling? Aren't you drinking then?"

"My drink's on the way."

"Have you got a nice friend with you then?"

Stewart emerged from the scrum at the bar with two pints of Courage and his usual whisky chaser.

"You have got a nice friend, haven't you?" The two women cackled to each other.

"Aren't you going to offer us a little drinkie then?"

He sighed, took out his CID badge and waved it in front of them. "Sorry ladies but I'm engaged on official police business.

My friend there is Sherlock Holmes' nephew and I'm about to seek his advice about a murderer who's copying Jack the Ripper and cutting up ladies he meets in pubs around this part of London. Perhaps you could excuse us just this once."

A look of hurt shock mingled with elements of fear and disbelief registered on the ladies' faces. "Sorry, I'm sure," said the plainer of the two as they picked up their handbags and scurried off.

"That wasn't very nice of you, Frank."

"An early night I said, Jack, and an early night it's going to be. You can go and find them when I leave if you're so keen."

"One of them wasnae half bad. Didn't think much of yours though." Merlin shrugged and took a sip of his beer. "Crowded tonight again."

"'Morituri te salutant' – those who are about to die salute you." Stewart looked quizzically up at the ceiling. "No that's not it.What's the phrase I'm looking for?"

"'Drink, drink and be merry for tomorrow you may die'?"

"Something like that. A misery at the station was pontificating today that the government expects 100,000 deaths per night in London when the bombing starts. I calculate that would mean the entire population of London would be wiped out within three months if they kept it up every night. If that's really the case, no wonder everyone's keen to drink or fuck themselves into a stupor before the curtain comes down."

Merlin laughed. "Which particular stupor are you focusing on?"

"I don't see any reason why I can't do both, do you?"

"None at all. I don't think I've got time for either."

Merlin leaned back in his chair and began to relax as the alcohol had its effect.

"Come on then, feel free to unburden yourself to Uncle Jack. You'll be better for it."

Merlin trusted his friend implicitly and had respect for the insights Stewart occasionally brought to bear on his cases. He explained the latest developments in the Barnes case. He had told Stewart about the first murder on their previous night out. When he'd finished, Stewart rose. "Another beer is needed, I think."

"I haven't finished this one yet."

"You will have by the time I emerge from this jungle."

"It's my shout now, anyway."

"Och, don't worry about it. You can pay next time when we go out for a proper drink." Jack tapped his nose. "I'm no mug, you know."

Stewart returned with meat pies as well as drinks and Merlin bit into his hungrily.

"And your next line of enquiry?"

"I have to find Kathleen Donovan. We need to know that she's safe and perhaps she knows who Morgan was seeing last night."

"No sign of her in her lodgings then?"

"No. I've put a high priority search order out but with the administrative chaos here at the moment, I'm not very optimistic. They could put Will Hay in charge of running London these days and he'd do a better job."

Stewart moved his chair into the table as a portly Chelsea pensioner in full regalia squeezed past him. "I know that you're not making much progress in this case, and that's frustrating, but you seem more concerned than usual – or is it just that you've been eating too many of those awful sweeties and your facial muscles have collapsed?"

"Ha, ha." Merlin leaned forward and lowered his voice. "It's the political angle. Two messy murders of US Embassy personnel – low level personnel but nevertheless Embassy people. We're undermanned and overworked and I've got my boss on my back. I've already had warnings about not upsetting the Americans in my investigations, given the delicate nature of our relations with the US and our potential reliance on them in the future. I've got two nasty murders to solve, the country's up against the wall and at present I can't really see the wood for the trees." Merlin sat back.

"There I go, mixing my metaphors again."

"I see." Stewart gulped down his chaser and sucked his lips. "Apart from recommending a substantial intake of alcohol, I'm not sure I can give you much help." Merlin sat up and shook his head. "Let's forget all that. Tell me what you've been up to. Any news on the romantic front?"

"Och, I've had a bit of a disaster there. I think I told you I met a nice Polish girl who lived round the corner from the station. Gorgeous girl. Lovely red-brown hair. I took her out for a drink a couple of times, then dinner. I was getting quite sweet on her. Anyway, a couple of nights ago I'd just got off duty and was having a bite to eat with a friend in some place just off Shaftesbury Avenue. As we were leaving, the light from the restaurant door picked out someone passing and I thought it was my Polish friend. I called her name but there was no reply. I said so long to my mate and went off in pursuit. Not easy, of course, in the dark but I managed to pick out the girl and tried to catch up. She kept moving at quite a lick and before I could catch her up, she'd turned into a side street and I thought I'd lost her. There was a door and I looked at it with my torch. It was a nightclub of some sort. The girl had disappeared so abruptly that it occurred to me that she might have gone into the club." Stewart paused to swill more beer. "So, I went down the stairs of this place and went through a door guarded by a grim-looking doorman and all of a sudden, out of the murk in the room I entered, I was surrounded by girls. It was a bloody clip joint! I glanced around and sure enough, in a far corner at the bar I could see the lovely Sonia taking her coat off. A bloody clip joint and I was getting sweet on a tart, for God's sake! So I cleared off. Women, eh!"

Merlin smiled in commiseration. "Plenty more sardines in the can, Jack. I wouldn't worry about it."

Stewart lit up a cigarette. "Maybe I shouldn't be so choosy. From what I saw of them, the other girls looked quite smart. Maybe we should go there tonight. That'd certainly help you get your mind off work."

"I don't think so, thank you."

"Here you are. Just for future reference. I picked these up there. The name and address are on the back. You never know, Francisco."

Merlin picked up the blue book of matches and read the words on the cover – The Blue Angel. Stewart blew a smoke ring. "Not very original, is it?"

CHAPTER 6

Friday February 2nd

Kathleen Donovan sat mute and pale-faced in one of Miss Edgar's straight-backed and rather uncomfortable chairs, her eyes fixed firmly on the floor. They had been telephoned first thing at the Yard and informed that she was back at work. Bridges looked across at his boss who was looking a little the worse for wear. He was aware that Merlin didn't have much of a head for booze and also that his intake had increased substantially since his wife had died. He was protective of his boss who had been almost like a father to him and worried if he should say something about the drink as well as about the hole in the shoe. Then again perhaps not – the Chief Inspector's sense of humour had certainly reappeared since the New Year, and he was making some effort with his appearance – look at that flashy hat he had just put down on the table.

"Has Miss Donovan said anything to you about her whereabouts yesterday, Miss Edgar?"

"Not yet, Chief Inspector. She came in and apologised saying she had a bit of flu yesterday. I was going to ask her some questions but then thought you'd prefer to do that. I couldn't see how I couldn't tell her about Johnny though."

"Of course."

Kathleen whimpered then blew her nose. Bridges moved towards her and placed his hands gently on her shoulder.

"Come on now, love. We need to ask you a few questions."

She slowly shook her head.

Merlin took Miss Edgar to one side.

"What did she say when you told her about Johnny Morgan?"

"She didn't say anything. She just burst into tears and has been like this ever since."

"Perhaps it's best if we speak to Miss Donovan in private."

She gazed rather unsympathetically at the young girl.

"Good luck to you." She picked up a file from her desk and left, muttering something under her breath.

"I know this is very upsetting, Miss Donovan, but we have a duty to Joan and Johnny to find the people who killed them. We've only got a few questions. Why don't you come over here and sit in a bit more comfort?"

Kathleen remained motionless for a short while then abruptly rose and moved across the room to join him on the sofa. Bridges parked himself in the vacated chair. Her face assumed a resigned look as her fingers kneaded the yellow handkerchief she was holding.

"Good. Now can you tell us what happened to you yesterday and the day before?"

"I wasn't feeling very well so I took yesterday off."

"So we understand. You had the flu?"

She nodded.

"Can you let us know why you weren't at home yesterday, because we sent someone round to your lodgings to find you and your landlady said she hadn't seen you at all since the day before?"

"I went to stay with some relatives."

"And who would they be?"

A little colour returned to her cheeks. "Why do you need to know that? I don't want them being bothered. What have they got to do with anything?"

"You were a friend of two people who have been violently murdered. It is our job to know your whereabouts and movements."

Her eyes opened wide. "Are you saying I'm some sort of suspect or something?"

"We have to explore every avenue. No one's saying you're a suspect but we have to make certain that everyone's telling the truth. We will need to know who you were staying with."

She looked up at the ceiling and sighed. "I was staying with my brother's family."

"And your brother's name?"

"Cormac. Cormac Donovan. He's been over here for a couple of years. He's in the building trade. He lives in Kilburn. He's got a wife and a lovely little daughter. Kathleen she is. Named after me." Bridges noted a flicker of family pride passing over the girl's face. He was the proud uncle of a nephew and two nieces himself.

"We'll need their address."

"If you must." She darted a glance at Bridges who waved his notebook in such a way as to indicate he'd take it down later.

"When exactly did you go to your brother's?"

"That would have been the night before last. Wednesday night."

"And when was the last time you saw Johnny Morgan?"

"I think I saw him at some time during that Wednesday."

"In the Ambassador's residence or outside?"

"Oh, in the residence. Just in passing. In the lobby I think." Bridges sensed the girl tensing as her shoulders tightened.

"In the morning or afternoon?"

"I think it was in the morning. I bumped into him in the lobby.

"You weren't so very well that morning, were you?"

Kathleen blushed and cast her eyes back down to the floor. "I suppose the flu was just starting then."

"Can you remember the last time you saw Mr Morgan before you saw him on Wednesday morning?"

She stared hard at the floral carpet beneath her. She put her crumpled handkerchief to her nose. "Oh, I don't know. I suppose I must have seen him around the day before."

"In the residence you mean?"

"I suppose."

"You don't think you might have seen him in a pub on Tuesday night?"

She dropped her handkerchief and bent quickly with a shaking hand to pick it up before Bridges had a chance to do it for her. "What do you mean? No… I…" She darted an anxious look at Bridges.

"Mr Merlin and I thought you might have had a friendly drink with Mr Morgan on Tuesday. Now think hard, Miss. Perhaps you're confusing dates in your mind."

She took a moment to compose herself.

"Yes, I remember now, I did have a drink with Johnny on Tuesday night. I must have been thinking of the night before."

"And when was it on Tuesday that you met up?"

She closed her eyes. Merlin fidgeted impatiently with his tie.

"Come on now. Best to tell us everything."

Her green eyes reappeared, watery but still beautiful. "I remember now that we went for a drink together after work."

"Where did you go?"

"To the pub around the corner. It's called The Prince of Wales, I think."

"How long were you there?"

"We spent quite a while there. I was upset about Joan's death and all the questioning."

"Did you have a lot to drink?"

"I suppose we both did. Drowning our sorrows, so to speak."

"Did Johnny say anything in particular about Joan?"

A teardrop slowly trickled down Kathleen's cheek and briefly sparkled as it was caught by a beam of winter sunshine which had found its way into the room. "He was worried whether I'd told you that he'd been out with Joan."

"And had he?"

"One of the other chauffeurs thought he'd seen him out on the Thursday before she disappeared, but he denied it."

"Had he been out with Joan on other occasions?"

"He said that he had met up with her out of the office.

Apparently she'd asked him advice on occasions. Something about getting new lodgings, although she never mentioned that to me."

"An attractive man, Johnny Morgan, wasn't he? And Miss Harris was a pretty girl. It's quite easy to imagine them having a fling, isn't it?"

"He said there was no fling, so – "

"Did you find Johnny attractive?"

She pursed her lips. "I don't see that that's got anything to do with things."

"Where did you go after your drink? Home to your lodgings?"

"No." Her voice rose. "If you must know I went back with Johnny to his place. I'm not really that sort of girl, you know, but Johnny had got me drunk. I don't know how many drinks I had, but I've never had that many before."

"You say you went back to his place. When you got there, what happened?"

Kathleen flushed. Bridges wondered whether Merlin was not being a little too hard on her but bit his tongue.

"Did you have any more to drink?"

"No. He offered me a whisky but I don't like whisky and anyway I'd had enough."

"Then what – did he, did he take advantage of you?"

She rubbed her forehead slowly before glaring at Merlin. "How do you know all of this? Have you had spies on me or something?"

Bridges rose abruptly from his chair, looked earnestly over at his boss and pointed towards the door. Merlin hesitated a moment before getting to his feet and following the sergeant out of the room.

"Don't you think we're being a bit heavy-handed, sir? Perhaps we should speak to her later, when she's a bit calmer."

Merlin dabbed some perspiration away from above his right eye and drew in his breath. "You think so, Sergeant? I don't know." He drew in his breath again. "No, we need to get on with it. In the light of what happened to Morgan, the events of Tuesday night now loom large. And what about the visitor who arrived just before I left? Who the hell was he? We've got to get her story out in full. If you think I'm doing it too roughly, why don't you have a go?"

They went back in. Kathleen had curled up, her legs tucked beneath her, at the end of the sofa.

Merlin went over to the window and stared out at the traffic and the park. A bus covered in a colourful advertisement for Ovaltine passed by. It had snowed again during the night and a large and impressive snowman had been constructed directly opposite.

"Now, Miss, we know you went back with Johnny to his room – I'm sorry but there's no delicate way of saying this – you went to bed with Johnny?" Bridges himself blushed as he put his question.

She buried her head in her hands.

"Did you sleep with Morgan?"

"Yes. Yes."

"With consent or did Morgan force you?"

"I can't really remember much of what happened. I was very drunk. I remember Johnny soaking me with whisky when he dropped the glasses he was holding, then I remember suddenly finding myself in bed. Then I remember pain. Then sleep and I remember waking up with a terrible headache. When I woke up it was light but I was alone."

"And, sorry Miss, the pain was?"

Her voice hardened. "What do you think it was? He had his way with me didn't he? Got me drunk and had his fun. I was a – I'd never done it before."

Merlin moved over from the window, sat down by her side and patted her hand. "I'm sorry to put you through this, dear. Is there anything else?"

"Isn't that enough?"

"I was wondering whether Johnny had any visitors while you were there?"

"The whole night after we got to Johnny's room is like a dream – no a nightmare – to me. I can't remember any details. I had a lot to drink and I think Johnny might have given me some pills as well." She shuddered at the memory.

"When did he give you pills?"

"No idea. I just seem to remember taking some pills or medicine at some point."

"What type of pills?"

"I don't know. I just remember being in pain and Johnny telling me that he had something which would make me feel better."

"And you can't remember anything else? A man coming to give something or take something from Johnny, perhaps?"

"No. I can't remember, I can't remember. Please stop asking your questions!" She shook her head rapidly back and forth before becoming calm again.

"Just one more, dear. You said that you went back with Morgan to his place. Was it your impression that the room he took you to was his own?"

"When he asked me back first, I said I didn't want to go back to the Ambassador's residence. I didn't want anyone gossiping you know. But he said he had another place nearby. I remember saying how nice it was when we got there and asking about it but he just shrugged."

"Alright. That's it, Miss Donovan. I know it's been difficult. Thank you."

She dabbed her eyes with her handkerchief as she rose unsteadily to her feet.

"I'll be getting on then."

* * *

Merlin found Johnson hovering outside his door.

"Ten minutes please, Peter. I've got a couple of things to do then you can come and tell me all about it."

Johnson nodded and withdrew reluctantly.

Merlin sat down heavily at his desk and in the process knocked his Eiffel Tower paperweight to the floor. He knelt down under the desk to retrieve it, grateful to find it all in one piece. As he surfaced, he was confronted by a familiar pair of pinstripe trousers.

"Not trying to hide from me are you, Chief Inspector?"

"Heaven forfend, sir. Just saving a Parisian landmark."

The A.C. smiled bleakly before sitting down. "This is getting very worrying indeed, Frank. Two Embassy murders now. I know they're not very important people but I'm going to have to put the Foreign Office in the picture. I filled in the Home Secretary this morning. He looked like he was chewing a particularly sharp lemon when I told him. Didn't say much though. Just said to be careful not to tread on any important toes, as I've already told you, and said that Halifax wouldn't be very happy." The A.C. gave his own impression of someone chewing a particularly sharp lemon. "Any ideas on this second murder?"

"The fellow whose throat was shredded, Morgan, was the chauffeur I was telling you about. It seems a distinct possibility that he was involved with Miss Harris in some way. We spent the morning interviewing another Embassy girl who Morgan went after."

The A.C. drummed his fingers on the arms of his chair. "Do you think the murders were committed by the same person?"

"Too early to say. I am inclined to think that the victims were both mixed up together in something unsavoury – something unsavoury which might explain their deaths."

"Perhaps this chauffeur killed Joan Harris and someone has taken his revenge?"

"A possibility. I'm trying to keep an open mind about all possibilities."

The A.C.'s cheeks flushed crimson.

"It seems to me that you'd better begin narrowing the possibilities down pretty quickly. This could become a bloody mess if you don't get to the bottom of it soon. Who knows where this might lead with our American friends, eh?"

He jerked to his feet and stalked to the door, behind which he found a waiting Johnson.

"Come in, come in." The A.C. paused and stood back briefly. "Good God man, in this light you look like Adolf Hitler. Shave that thing off, will you?"

The door banged and Johnson sat down in a mild state of shock.

"Was he being serious, sir?"

"I rather think he was."

"My girl really likes this moustache. She was the one who asked me to grow it. Thinks it makes me look like Ronald Coleman."

"We all have to make sacrifices in this war, Inspector. The loss of your moustache will have to be one of hers. Let's hope it's the biggest sacrifice she has to make, eh?"

Johnson managed a weak smile.

"So what's the story, Peter? Who's your suspect for the hit and run?"

"Have you read my report yet, sir?"

Merlin shuffled his papers and eventually found Johnson's note.

"Sorry, what with everything that's been happening, I still haven't had a chance. You'd better tell me everything."

Johnson rummaged in his jacket for his Woodbines.

"May I?"

Merlin nodded and declined the offered cigarette.

"I'd better start off by saying that although I think I've made some progress, the case is far from open and shut."

"Why then, is the man upstairs under the impression that we can pretty much close the file?"

"Well, sir, he cornered me in the corridor yesterday morning first thing. He asked me rather aggressively how I was getting on in this case and I told him that I had just identified a suspect. I attempted to give him some of the detail but he didn't listen to me, slapped my back and asked when I was going to pick the suspect up. I told him I was hoping to do that yesterday afternoon."

"And did you?"

"No."

"Why not?"

"Because I wanted to speak to you first. There is some delicacy in the situation."

"How so?"

Johnson smoothed his slick hair and sighed. "The suspect is a diplomat at the Foreign Office. Also, as I think you know, the victim was some sort of weaponry expert at the War Office. In the circumstances, I was a little nervous about how to approach the suspect. I wanted your advice as to how to handle it."

"I see…" Merlin swivelled in his chair. Across the river he could see tiny figures scurrying around on the roof of the LCC building. Probably strengthening the gunnery up there, he thought.

"Does the A.C. know who your suspect is?"

"No. As I said, I attempted to give him some more detail but he wasn't listening. I suppose he was just very keen to latch on to some good news so he…"

"Jumped the gun."

"Sir."

The haze of cigarette smoke rising above Johnson's head made odd swirling shapes in the weak sunshine filtering into the office.

"Let's forget about the A.C. for now. Just tell me who your man is, how you identified him and what you propose to do."

Bridges appeared at the door and Merlin waved him in.

"As so often, it's routine stuff with a bit of luck thrown in. I contacted all the garages in Westminster and Central London to enquire as to whether any cars had been put in for a repair which might match the details of the accident as we estimate them. As you will recall, the victim, a Mr Emmanuel Goldberg, was found in the gutter on the park side of Birdcage Walk. Our one witness, an office cleaner called Mrs Bancroft, who was strolling further up Birdcage Walk near the barracks, thinks the car must have collided with Mr Goldberg on the front left side from the way she saw him fall from her viewpoint. This would seem the likely conclusion also from where we found Mr Goldberg. I put out a general enquiry for any cars coming in with damage to any part of the front of the vehicle but have kept a particular lookout for cars with damage to the left of the grille or the left headlamp."

"Couldn't this Mrs Bancroft help with a description of the vehicle?"

"Not really, sir. The accident happened at about 7pm so it was pitch dark. To be frank, in the circumstances, I was surprised she had anything useful at all to tell me. She does say that after the collision she thinks she heard a car door open and shut, though she couldn't see whether anyone got out, and then the car drove off at speed, towards Parliament Square."

"I see. Carry on."

The inspector toyed briefly with his doomed moustache. "Over the two weeks or so since the accident I kept in close touch with the various garages. Strangely enough, given the increased accident rate since the blackout, nothing close to a match was reported for almost two weeks. There were some cars damaged in the front but all very minor compared with the damage likely from hitting a person at high speed. I followed up all instances of damage, even if minor, but none appeared to fit. Then I got a call two days ago from a garage in Pimlico. They had an Austin car with a lot of damage to the front left headlight and the front bonnet. The funny thing was that they said they normally wouldn't get this repair to do. They were doing a favour for a friend working at the Foreign Office motor pool, who passed on several cars for repair because there was some security work going on which was taking up their own garage space."

"So, the owner or driver of that car would have reasonably expected to have the car repaired in the privacy of a government department rather than in a public garage."

"Exactly. And if it were not for the Foreign Office garage having to sub-contract out some of its own work temporarily, the damage would never have come to my attention. That was my bit of luck."

"And are you sure the car's the right one?"

"Our scientists have had a good look at it, sir. The damaged area has obviously been cleaned but there appear to be minute traces of cloth there. The scientists believe there is a match to Mr Goldberg's suit."

"Those material matches can prove tricky at trial. What else have you got?"

"Naturally I've asked them to see whether they can find any traces of blood. Nothing found as yet."

Bridges stuck an enquiring hand in the air. "So who is the owner of the car, sir?"

"I went along to the Foreign Office car pool and spoke to a couple of the mechanics. One of them checked his paperwork and said the car had been put in for repair by a civil servant at the Foreign Office called Edward Fraser. The other mechanic then remembered someone from the Foreign Office dropping the car off and saying it had been in collision with a deer somewhere in the country."

Johnson finished his cigarette and stubbed it out in the brass ashtray in front of him. Merlin leaned forward. "It's not a bad story for a diplomat, Peter. They're off having country weekends hunting, shooting and fishing all the time. Unless you get some clear scientific back-up or of course a confession, you're still some way short of the finishing line."

"I know."

"You'd better get off and see him."

"Is there any particular advice you can give me, given the fact that the man's a diplomat? Should I ring ahead and inform his superiors that I need to interview him?"

"To avoid any awkwardness between the Home Office and the Foreign Office, you mean?"

"Well yes."

"No, I don't think you need to give Mr Fraser any advance warning. You're a sensible fellow, with or without a 'tache. You're not going to behave like a bull in a china shop, are you?"

"You mean you'd like me to go easy on him?"

Merlin shook his head and grinned. "Not at all, Peter. I know you can be a tough interrogator, and I expect you to be. Just use your common sense. If Mr Fraser whinges to his superiors, I'll back you up, don't worry. Of course, if you prefer I can go with you, although my time is a bit tight."

"No thanks, sir. I'll handle it. I'll take Sergeant Windsor with me." Johnson stood and looked to Merlin more like his usual confident self.

"Before you go, Peter, remind me one more time about the background of the victim?"

"He was a Jewish gentleman. Originally from Vienna but escaped to England in 1938. From what I understand, a very clever chap and very useful at the War Office, but I haven't been able to find out much more than that. Naturally they're pretty cagey at the Ministry."

"Chances are he was valuable to the war effort. The A.C. said there was some concern as to whether he might have been run over intentionally."

"I am bearing that in mind."

"Good."

Johnson stroked his moustache again, this time a little apprehensively, before disappearing through the door.

"Diplomats on all fronts for us at the moment, eh, Sergeant? Fancy a little walk?"

They walked in silence across Parliament Square, past the sandbagged Parliament buildings and the Abbey. Cutting through the back streets behind Victoria Street, they came out into Birdcage Walk.

A gust of wind disturbed a pile of leaves in front of them as they entered St James' Park. A little old lady in threadbare clothes was standing by the lake feeding the birds with stale crusts of bread. Two men in bowler hats and British warm coats strode along the path, debating some issue vehemently. Big Ben struck two o'clock.

Merlin nodded in the direction of an empty park bench overlooking the lake and they sat down, avoiding the bird deposits at one end. "In the midst of all the tears and the story of her night with Morgan, we forgot to ask Kathleen about what the two old ladies told us."

"Joan Harris' late night, you mean?"

"Yes. We'll raise it when we see her next. Hopefully she'll be a little calmer. I'd also like to have another go about the late visitor. She must be able to remember something even if she was drugged up. Did you get her brother's address?"

"Sorry, not yet."

"No matter. We can get it from Miss Edgar when we need it."

Merlin shivered as an icy current of air blew into them from the lake. "We'll need to visit the place where Morgan took Kathleen. I think I'll be able to find it. There must be a key in Johnny's possessions – they've been sent over, haven't they?"

"They have."

"And when do we get the full forensic report on Morgan?"

"Monday, sir."

"That's a pity. I'd like to have read it over the weekend."

Merlin picked up a pebble and threw it into the water. It made a satisfying plopping sound. "Johnny Morgan's background, Sergeant. Remind me again how he got his job."

"He came up from Wales and his uncle helped him get a driving licence and then the job with the Ambassador."

"Must be a man of some substance, this uncle, to get him a job like that. Have we got a name for him?"

Bridges took out his notebook and skimmed over the pages. He shrugged apologetically.

"You'll be able to get that from Miss Edgar as well. Give her a call when we get back."

Merlin bent down to tie a loose shoelace. "I found out where that nightclub is, Sergeant."

"Sir?"

"You know, The Blue Angel. Remember the matches I found in Miss Harris' room? The nightclub which I must presume she visited. It's a clip joint. A friend of mine discovered it by accident."

"Which friend would that be?"

Bridges knew Jack Stewart and laughed as his boss told the story. "And you believe he went there by accident?"

"He's a good looking bloke and I doubt he's ever had to pay for it. Anyway, I don't care. Now we know where The Blue Angel is and I think we should pay a little incognito visit. If we go along as coppers I doubt we'll find out much, but if we go along as punters we might pick up something useful."

"Expensive places, aren't they?"

"You can bet the A.C. will kick up a fuss about the expenses but what the hell."

"When?"

"Let's see how we get on looking for Morgan's alternative accommodation, but we could go tonight. Friday night should be a busy night. We might not stick out too much. Better send a message to Iris that you'll be late."

"She's got a sewing circle tonight. She won't miss me."

The little old lady who had been feeding the birds turned away from her task and walked past the two policemen. She smiled a grinning toothless smile at them. Merlin and Bridges touched their hats.

"Pretty birds. I love my birds you know. I've given them their lunch. They're happy now. Pretty birds."

The old lady wandered happily away round a corner, the sound of her prattling slowly fading away in the wind.

"My mother liked birds."

"Did she, sir?"

110

"Kept a canary once. And a cockatoo. Very messy creatures. I hated them and so did my dad. 'Ninos d'inferno' he called them. 'Children of hell'. Never a man for understatement, my father."

"More of a dog man myself."

"In fact my dad hated all animals. Must have been something to do with looking after those sheep when he was young."

They got up and walked across the park into Birdcage Walk.

"I suppose Johnson's hit and run happened somewhere around here." Merlin kept his eyes trained on the gutter as they walked along.

"Can't see any signs of the accident, can you?"

"Well it is a few weeks ago now."

"So it is. I wonder how Johnson's getting on."

Passing the Westminster tube station they heard the hum of an aeroplane. Some passers-by looked up with anxious faces. A small, officious looking man wearing a bowler hat shouted out loudly, "Everyone keep calm! It's one of ours."

* * *

"It's alright, dear. It's not a German bomber so don't panic."

Miss Edgar looked severely over her spectacles at the taxi driver, a large man whose stare hung heavily on his sallow face. "I never panic, driver." She paid out the exact two shillings fare, with no tip. The driver looked at her with disgust and the words "mean" and "cow" floated in the air as the taxi drove off. Despite wearing her warmest fur-lined coat she still shivered in the freezing fog which was now settling on the London afternoon. She stepped gingerly over the sand which had leaked from the bags outside the Embassy and ran as briskly as her high-heeled shoes would allow her, up the steps and through the main doors.

At the reception desk she announced that she had an appointment with Secretary Zarb. A handsome young officer in US Marine uniform looked down at a list on his desk.

"You're new here, aren't you, Lieutenant?"

"Yes, ma'am."

The officer called through to Zarb's office. "Yes, Miss Edgar. He is expecting you. Follow me please."

She followed the lieutenant up the wide marble staircase, then through a maze of corridors, eventually arriving at an open pair of large, white double-doors.

Herman Zarb was a small, neat man. His brilliantined dark hair was combed across his head in a largely unsuccessful attempt to cover his growing baldness. He had piercing eyes, flaring nostrils and a small, thin-lipped mouth. His smile was wide and vaguely menacing.

Zarb sat at a large desk which commanded a panoramic view of the square. "Philippa! Thanks for coming over at such short notice." He rose, extended both arms then grasped his guest's right hand in his. "Thank you, Lieutenant."

"You're looking wonderful today. Sit down. Take the weight off your pegs. Isn't that the phrase?"

"Yes, Herman. You'll make a cockney yet!"

"I doubt it. Anyway, to get straight to business, Philippa, I'd like to talk to you about what's been going on."

"What would you like to know?"

"Know?" Zarb gave one of his sinister smiles. "I think I know most of what I need to know. It's got very messy, hasn't it?"

"I take it you are referring to the murders, and yes it's very messy indeed. It's also very frightening but I don't know that there's much I can do about it. The police are investigating carefully."

Zarb stared briefly out of the window into the foggy square. "I took a call from the Ambassador on the subject today. I don't know how he had heard about it, do you?"

"I haven't spoken to the Ambassador since he went back to America."

"I suppose I would have been telling him myself shortly. The death of the secretary outside the residence probably didn't merit his being bothered, but the death of his favourite chauffeur on the premises – on that I think I would have made a report. In any event, he was very upset. Said it had ruined a beautiful day. Apparently the sun is blazing down in Palm Beach and the golfing conditions are perfect. The Ambassador said he wouldn't be surprised if he wasn't heavily beaten today in light of this disturbing news."

Miss Edgar pursed her lips.

"Hard to sympathise with him looking out at this freezing pea-souper, isn't it, my dear?"

He leaned forward and pulled a piece of paper across the desk. His eyes skimmed over it. "I had a letter sent over from the Foreign Office this afternoon. A polite letter from Lord Halifax's office, saying they had asked the police to be as discreet as possible in their enquiries. They are apologising for any inconvenience caused and say they've issued instructions to expedite the investigation. Very nice of the Foreign Office, I'm sure."

Zarb removed a packet of chewing gum from his pocket, and waved it across the desk. Miss Edgar twitched her nose in distaste and declined. He noisily unwrapped the packet and popped a piece in his mouth. "Any idea what the police are thinking, Philippa?"

"Not really. They've interviewed pretty much everyone as you know. Did you glean anything from your own interview?"

"No, it was very perfunctory. A few questions about Joan Harris and the work she did. Asked whether she had done any secret work. I'm not sure how far they're likely to pursue that line."

"They spent a lot of time with Mr Norton, who, as you know, particularly liked Miss Harris to do his typing. I don't know if he gave them any assistance in that area. He seemed pretty bothered when his interview finished. I saw him storming out of the residence in a temper."

"Yeh. Arthur had a little moan to me about that. Said he was going to complain to the higher-ups in the Yard. I told him not to be so stupid. Anyway, if there's some security angle involved, I can see at a stretch how Miss Harris might be embroiled, but how can there be any security angle with Morgan?"

"I don't know, Herman."

"Any other lengthy interviews?"

"The policemen spent a lot of time this morning with one of my girls."

"Yes?"

"We have an Irish girl, I think you know her, Kathleen Donovan."

"Pretty girl. Looks a bit like that film star, what's her name?" Zarb screwed up his eyes and concentrated. "O'Sullivan, O'Hara, something like that."

Miss Edgar provided no assistance.

"What's the story with her?"

"She was friendly with both of the victims. She has also been behaving rather oddly the past few days. Obviously she was upset at Joan's death, but she was off work the day Morgan's death was discovered and the day before she was in a bit of a state."

"Do you think the police are going to concentrate on her?"

"She had a long interview. There were a lot of tears I understand. She wouldn't tell me what the police were asking, but…"

"Was she in some kind of relationship with the chauffeur?"

"Possibly. I don't encourage relationships between workers at the residence, as I'm sure you know."

"Hmm. Well, let's wait and see what the police come up with. If it all turns out to be a messy domestic affair which embroiled these three poor young people, that's probably for the best, isn't it? With a bit of luck the police will solve this before the Ambassador returns." Zarb stroked his thinning hair and sighed.

"Any news on the Ambassador's return, Herman?"

"He's coming some time next month. He was pretty vague and if I were a betting man I'd say nearer the end than the beginning. I mean, what would you choose, Philippa? A sunny, warm, war-free Florida or a cold, dark London, waiting for the Luftwaffe? A London which the Ambassador believes won't survive more than a few weeks of war."

She started to say something but thought better of it and bit her lip before asking "Do you have any instructions for me?"

He rose from his chair, removed the gum from his mouth and threw it in his desk-side bin. "Just let me know as much as you can of how the police are proceeding and what lines of enquiry they're taking." He moved around his desk and accompanied Miss Edgar to the door. As he opened it he held her by the elbow. "An odd fish, Norton, don't you think?"

She had a couple of inches on Zarb and looked down at him. "He's not the usual type of diplomat, I suppose, but, as a close and trusted advisor of Mr Kennedy, I give him my full respect."

"Yes, yes. But don't you think he's a bit strange?"

"It's not my place to make such observations, Herman."

Zarb chuckled. "Alright, dear, we'll leave it at that. But I'd like you to keep a particular eye out for him. I'd like to know what he gets up to away from here."

After he'd shown his guest out, Zarb returned to his desk. He looked out at the darkening square and switched his desk-lamp on. He picked up the Foreign Office letter and read it again. The name of the fellow who had signed it was familiar. A high-flyer he had heard. He spoke the name out loud: "Mr F. R. Douglas."

* * *

Bridges pulled the car over to the kerb. Merlin looked up from the IRA case report he had been immersed in during their short journey. They were a few hundred yards from the Ambassador's residence. "I managed to speak to Miss Edgar concerning Morgan's employment, sir. She told me that he was put up for his job by Mr Norton. A reference was also provided by a Mr M. Owen, who described himself in his letter as being a restaurant owner. He apparently used Johnny as a driver and commented favourably on his driving skills."

"The uncle?"

"I would guess so. Miss Edgar gave me an address for Mr Owen in Earl's Court."

"We'll pay him a visit tomorrow. First things first."

Merlin got out and led Bridges down a narrow alley into a cobbled mews street. "This is it. I'm sure."

Merlin strode ahead and stopped next to a garage door. He turned with his back to the garage and flashed his torch at the facing house. "Number 15, Sergeant."

Bridges handed over the bunch of keys which had been found in Morgan's jacket. The front door was successfully opened and their footsteps echoed over the linoleum of the small hallway and up the uncarpeted stairs. They unlocked and went through the second door and Merlin swore in Spanish as his knee connected with something solid. He hopped up and down as Bridges switched on the lamp on the solid oak table and looked sympathetic. Merlin's pain eased and the two men silently took in the room before them. "Looks like he'd come into some money, Sergeant. Must be three times the size of the other place."

Bridges crossed the opulently furnished bed-sitting room and entered the only other room in the flat. "Nice bathroom as well, sir."

Merlin limped over to him. "Doesn't feel very lived-in this place, does it? It's like a service flat."

Bridges nodded. "Shall we have a poke around?" The two men spent the best part of an hour looking around the rooms. They found no clothes, no personal items and no correspondence, not even bills. Everything was neat and clean and there was little sign of human habitation.

Merlin sat on the bed. "Nothing much to help us here. It's as bare as Clem Attlee's bonce. All we can do is check out the ownership of this property and see where that leads us."

"The drink's been cleaned up."

"What, Sam?"

"You know. Kathleen said that Johnny spilled the whisky over her. No sign of that on the carpet, nor of any drinking come to that."

Merlin looked at the carpet and then at a full bottle of whisky standing on a drinks cabinet by the bathroom door. "You're right. Someone tidied up after them." He rose stiffly to his feet. "Come on. We've got a long evening ahead of us."

* * *

It was just after 10.30 when they arrived in the small side street behind Shaftesbury Avenue.

Bridges' torchlight revealed letters to the right of the door. "'BA Club'. BA short for Blue Angel we hope, Sam, rather than Bugger All. I think it's best that we go in separately. If we're together and start asking questions and someone gets suspicious, then we'll both hit a brick wall. If we are asking them separately we'll have better odds and a better chance of getting information."

"Fine by me."

"I got some cash out of the kitty. Here's a couple of tenners. Probably a ten to one shot against you having any change left when we get out."

"Who's first then, sir, you or me?"

"I'll dive in first. Give me ten minutes then follow me down." It was dark behind the door but there was a glimmer of light when he reached the bottom of the stairs. Further along a narrow corridor a dirty, bare bulb shone onto a black door, to the right of which was a small printed card with the design of Joan Harris' matchbook and the words 'The Blue Angel'. As his eyes became accustomed to the weak light, Merlin saw another corridor on his right. A stale, fatty smell wafted towards him from that direction.

He took a deep breath and pressed the doorbell beneath the card. An elderly evening-suited man, with the ears of a small African elephant, appeared immediately. His jacket appeared to have been tailored for a larger body and hung down baggily from his hunched shoulders. There was a red curtain behind the doorman and Merlin could hear music, chatter and the clink of glasses.

"May I 'elp you, sir?" A black wart nestling under the doorman's battered nose moved around disconcertingly as he spoke, while his flapping ears created a nice breeze.

"A friend of mine told me that this was a good place for a drink."

"That it is, sir, but was it just a drink you were looking for?"

"He said you offered good company as well."

"May I know the name of this friend, sir?"

"Name of Jack. Met him in a pub tonight. We had a few drinks together and I asked him if he could recommend some clubs. I'm in town on business. Staying the night and thought I'd like to have some fun. He gave me a few names but said your club was the nearest and the best."

The gloomy doorman gave him a bleak smile. "Very well. Please come in. I hope you have a good time."

As the red curtain parted, Merlin's nostrils were assaulted by a wave of cheap perfume. The room was bathed in a subdued red light. The walls were decorated with a garish purple paper and a number of flesh-filled paintings in the style of Toulouse-Lautrec. He saw a bar in the distance, and several table booths scattered around the edges of the room. In the middle of the room was a small dance floor, where a few couples were dancing to the music of a three-piece band playing from a raised dais next to the bar. The musicians were, for some reason, dressed in Mexican outfits with Zorro hats, tight leather trousers, and frilly shirts.

"Can I show you to a table, sir, or would you prefer a drink at the bar?"

"The bar, please."

As he made his way past the dancing couples, he was conscious of a host of eyes giving him the once-over. When he reached the bar three girls bore down on him.

"Hello, dear, buy us a drink will you?" said a Mae West look-alike wearing a tight silvery dress, out of which her bust was bursting.

"I saw him first, Carol. You're going to buy me a drink first, aren't you ducks?" The second girl was older than the first. Her dark hair was long and fell in curls round her neck and over a less monumental bust than that of her companion. She wore a particularly pungent cheap perfume.

A third girl, the youngest and prettiest of the three, sidled up to Merlin along the bar and put her hand on his.

He smiled at the three women.

"Hang on a sec, ladies. All this beauty has taken my breath away. I'll need a while to recover so if you don't mind, I'll just settle in and get myself a drink for now. I'll try and catch up with you later."

The buxom blonde and the brunette melted swiftly into the pink gloom. The third girl, a petite girl with wavy fair hair and bow lips, withdrew to a chair further along the bar. She took a long drag from her cigarette. "Take your time, dear, there's no rush."

He struggled to get the attention of the barman, who was chatting to a plump man at the other end of the bar. Eventually the barman dragged himself away from his companion. "A beer, please."

"Run a tab sir, or pay as you go?" The barman was Irish, a short, fair-haired man with a cast in one eye.

"I'll pay as I go, thanks."

The barman delivered the drink and passed a bill across

the counter. Merlin frowned and handed over ten shillings. "Busy tonight?"

"Pretty normal for a Friday. It'll probably get a lot busier after midnight."

In a bowl on the counter were some loose cigarettes. He'd just have the one to steady his nerves. The barman threw some matches over.

"Thanks." Merlin looked at the familiar design and lettering. "I live out of town but I've been to plenty of London clubs over the years. Never heard of this one before. Apart from in that Marlene Dietrich film that is. Been in business long?"

The barman looked suspiciously at Merlin with his good eye. "I've only been working here a couple of months. I think the club's been here for a while but they change the name from time to time."

The man at the other end of the bar shouted for attention and the barman moved away. Merlin sipped his beer and had a good look around the room. The curtain by the entrance was being pulled back with some regularity and the club was filling up. The band was playing a romantic tune with a Latin American beat. The kind of music his father would have loved.

As he trawled the recesses of his memory to try and remember the title of the song, he saw Bridges being ushered into the club by the lugubrious doorman. Bridges stood for a few moments by the door before heading to the opposite end of the bar. He was also quickly surrounded, in his case by a gaggle of four women. Looking a little perplexed and glancing briefly in Merlin's direction, he sent three of the girls packing and kept the fourth, a dark-haired, foreign-looking woman. Then he ordered himself a beer and the girl a glass of wine.

"Friend of yours, is he?"

Merlin turned with a start to face the pretty girl perched along the bar. "Not at all. Why do you say that?" He wondered briefly whether the girl had arrived at the club just after them and seen them at the street door. But no, the girl had been well established at the bar when he'd arrived.

"Just seems that you're taking a great interest in him, that's all."

He puffed at his cigarette. "I just like watching what goes on. I'm a curious sort of person. These places are very interesting."

The girl finished her drink. "Don't you find me interesting, dear?"

"Of course I do, I'm just taking my time. Didn't you say there was plenty of time?"

The girl rose from her stool and moved along the bar. She placed her arm around Merlin's shoulder and leaned her chest against his arm. "There's plenty of time, dear, but the place is getting busy and you might miss your chance. That would be a pity as I think you're rather nice. Tall, dark and handsome, just as I like them. How about you getting us a nice bottle of wine and we can go over and sit at one of those cosy tables."

Before entering the club he had naively envisaged a strategy of flitting from girl to girl, speaking to as many people as he could as if he were at a drinks party. Clearly that wasn't going to be possible and he decided he might as well sit down for now with one girl and see what he could get out of her.

The drinks menu was brought and he ordered the cheapest wine he could find. The barman nodded and indicated that he would bring the bottle and glasses over to the table. He followed the girl to a secluded corner booth. As they sat down the band struck up a jolly rendition of 'A Nightingale Sang in Berkeley Square'.

"My name's Eve, dear. What's yours?"

Merlin told her as he tried to make himself comfortable in the rather cramped seat.

Eve giggled sweetly. "And where are you from, Frankie boy?"

"Brighton. Just up in London on business."

"Oh, I love Brighton. Ever been to the races there? Someone

took me last year." Eve sounded like she'd taken an elocution lesson or two, though with limited success.

"I've been to the races, of course. There are quicker ways of losing money, though not many. This place probably ranks up there."

"Like a bit of a flutter then do you, dear?" Eve reached out and squeezed his leg just as the barman arrived. "Come on darling, pour the drinks. I've got a dreadful thirst."

Merlin poured out the wine. He clinked glasses with Eve and drank. He winced. Eve swallowed half the glass. "It's better if you drink this stuff in big gulps. Of course, you can always buy a better bottle when this one's finished." Eve finished off the glass. "How about a dance, darling?"

While his father's vocal talent had not been passed down to him, Merlin had inherited a sense of rhythm and was no bad dancer. He had cut a fine figure as a young man on the dance floors of East London and had once won a prize for his pasa doble. He realised immediately, however, that Eve's style of dancing required little reciprocal skill in her partner. Whatever the pace or beat of the song, Eve's steps consisted of a relentless grinding of her upper and lower body into his. Eve had large blue eyes, a button nose, a small round mouth and hair cut short but with an abundance of wavy curls. Her features would be better displayed in about a third of the make-up she was wearing but the overall effect was nevertheless very pleasing. She was a little over five feet tall and had a good figure.

Bridges soon made his own appearance on the dance floor. He appeared to be enjoying himself and Merlin hoped that he wouldn't have to explain any disastrous consequences of this adventure to Iris.

He managed to drag Eve off the dance floor after four songs. As soon as they sat down, she placed her hand on his stomach and began to move it slowly downwards. "We don't have to hang around here all night if you like. I can come back to your hotel whenever you want."

"Won't your bosses here be unhappy if you leave?"

Eve tossed her hair back and took another big swig of wine. He realised she was getting tipsy.

"You'll have to make a little donation to the house, that's all. Shouldn't be a problem to a rich, handsome bloke like you, should it?" Her hand now moved up and down Merlin's inside leg.

"And who is the house, exactly?"

She rested her head on his neck and whispered. "See that fella over there in the far corner? That big fat bloke, sitting on his own?"

He peered through the cigarette smoke swirling in blue trails above the dance floor and found a very large, bald head. He guessed that the substantial head was attached to a substantial body. "What's his name?"

"Morrie. Morrie the Lorry we call him. He can be smooth as silk with the customers but he's a bastard to us. A fat bastard and a mean one too. Anyway. If you want me to come with you now, you just have to drop Morrie a few quid."

"Maybe after a couple more drinks. I like to get to know a girl a bit."

Eve finished her glass. A girl in a spangly leotard stopped at the table.

"Cigarettes, madam?"

Eve looked sweetly at Merlin. "Would you, Frank?"

He forked out some more cash with a sigh. The barman wandered over to ask whether the gentleman would care to buy another bottle of wine and he nodded unhappily. He very much hoped that he was going to get some information out of Eve.

The barman deposited the second bottle on the table. Eve removed her hand from his groin and poured out two glasses. "Down the hatch, darling."

"Cheers."

She took a big gulp from her glass and then leant over to place her lips on his. He kissed back for a few seconds and then pulled away.

"Don't you like me, Frankie?" Eve asked in a little girl voice.

"I like you very much, sweetheart, but we can get down to this properly at my hotel, can't we?"

She rested her head on his neck again. "Alright, dear. As you like."

There was a pause in the music and they could hear loud laughter nearby. Merlin thought he heard a familiar voice. Eve leaned her head out of the booth, returning with a grimace.

"What?"

"That Yank prick is in again."

When Merlin carefully poked his head out he saw Arthur Norton sitting down at a booth in the far corner of the room, accompanied by the plump man he had seen earlier at the bar, another man and some girls. The party was boisterous and noisy.

He drew his head back sharply. He didn't think Norton had seen him.

"Friend of yours, Eve?"

Eve turned her mouth down and grunted with disgust. "Not bloody likely. He's a…" She struggled hard for the right word before settling with evident dissatisfaction on "swine."

"In what way?"

"And swine isn't the half of it but lets just say he's rude and rough and leave it at that."

"Come in here on his own, does he?"

"Sometimes. Or with his mates. That chubby one with him is here a lot. Don't know his name. Other fancy blokes sometimes. Anyway now, where were we?" She snuggled up to him again.

"You know, you can earn a little money from me without going back to the hotel."

She pulled away and shook her curls petulantly. "I knew you didn't want to take me out of here. It's not nice leading a girl on, you know." She removed a small mirror from her handbag and scrutinised herself carefully before adjusting a few hairs.

"Look dear, let's not argue. There's a couple of quid in it if you can tell me something. We can still talk about the hotel but first of all…" Merlin put an envelope on the table and opened it. "I was wondering whether you could tell me if you recognise this girl."

Eve primly pursed her lips and returned the mirror to her bag. "You a copper or something?"

"Never mind. If you can tell me whether or not you've seen this girl in here there's money in it for you."

Eve chewed on her lower lip, then pulled the photograph from Merlin's hand.

"It's the fair-haired girl in the middle."

She peered at the photograph. "I can't see anything in this light. Pull that candle over."

Merlin did as he was told.

Eve frowned with concentration. "Yeh. I've seen her in here."

"Work here, did she?"

"Give me another quid and I'll tell you."

"Another ten bob, Eve. Fifty bob in total but that's it."

"I've seen her in here with that Yank and his mates."

"Often?"

She shook her head. "Not often but I remember her because I was in the party once. That fat bloke was there too and some others. Pretty little thing really. Didn't seem very happy."

Merlin was distracted a little by raised voices nearby but continued. "Is it common for men to bring women here?"

Eve lit a cigarette. "No. But it happens sometimes." She blew a smoke ring which floated briefly above them before disintegrating into the gloom.

"Why would a man do that?"

"Who knows, darling? Showing off or maybe a man likes to humiliate a girl. Who knows?"

"And did…"

The raised voices now became a loud commotion. The source was a booth on the other side of the dance floor. Merlin saw a man standing up with one of the girls haranguing him and hitting him with her hands. There was a lull in the music and he could hear her words quite clearly.

"You bastard. I'm not gonna answer any more of your questions. Get away from me!"

The man stepped back into the light and, with a jolt, Merlin recognised his sergeant.

Two burly waiters hurried over to the table followed by the owner. After a few more screeched words from the woman, Bridges was grabbed, punched and manhandled through the red curtain and pushed out of the door. He could hear the fading sound of his protests as he was taken up the stairs.

He had no option. He kissed Eve on the cheeks and put three notes in her hand. He left some money on the table and rose. "Thanks, sweetheart. You've been very helpful."

Eve tugged at Merlin's jacket. "Don't go, darling. I don't care if you are a copper. Stay a bit longer."

He pulled away with some difficulty and blew her a kiss, which she returned with a wistful smile.

Merlin wasn't sure if he'd left the right money, but no one stopped him as he raced through the door.

Out in the street he saw Bridges being held by one man from behind while the other pummelled him. Bridges managed to raise a leg and knee the man facing him but this only served to provoke a heavier onslaught. Merlin threw himself into the fray and pulled the attacker away, allowing Bridges to lean forward and pull the other waiter over his shoulder. Merlin threw a punch and connected cleanly with his man's jaw, putting him on the ground next to his partner. The waiters looked briefly at each other before rising groggily to their feet and limping towards the club.

"Alright, Sam?"

"Just a little winded."

Merlin sucked his knuckles. "Ouch! Haven't done that in quite a while. It really stings!"

CHAPTER 7

Saturday February 3rd

The sergeant arrived in Merlin's office just after nine, his right eye surrounded by a dark blue and black circle.

"That's come up nicely, hasn't it?"

Bridges smiled ruefully. "The missus wasn't too happy. She'd have been round to The Blue Angel last night if she'd had her way."

Bridges had explained in the taxi after the fight what had happened. He had not been getting very far with his questioning of Dolores, who claimed to be from Argentina. When he recognised Norton, he started asking about him and his companions and she became edgy. The blow-up had occurred however when he had realised that Dolores' wandering hands had extracted a tenner from his trouser pocket.

"Think Norton recognised us, sir?"

"I doubt it in that murk."

Bridges carefully felt his bruise.

"I told you last night, Sam, how my girl was quite helpful about Joan, Norton and the club. One thing she didn't know was the name of Norton's chubby friend. I suppose your girl didn't – ?"

"I asked but she clammed up on me."

Merlin leaned forward and rummaged through the papers on his desk. Eventually he found what he was looking for and read out an address in Earl's Court. "Come on then. Time to pay Mr Owen a visit. This should be enlightening."

Merlin looked at the boarded-up doors of The Tate Gallery and the sandbags piled outside. "They've taken all the pictures into the country."

"Sir?"

"I hear that the collections at The Tate, The National and so on have been taken out of London and put somewhere safe for the duration. Wales or somewhere, according to a friend of mine in Special Branch."

"Oh." Art appreciation was not one of Bridges' strong points.

"I met my wife in The Tate Gallery, Sergeant."

"Yes, sir."

"She slipped on some stairs and I helped her up."

Bridges knew the story well. As usual, he felt that reticence was the appropriate response when his boss mentioned his wife.

"It was a lovely summer's day and she was wearing a pink dress."

As they passed The Royal Hospital and Battersea Park on the other side of the river, Merlin remembered a happy picnic in the Park with Alice, Jack and Jack's girlfriend of the moment – what was her name – Rachel or Rebecca? A Jewish girl whose parents had escaped Hitler's Germany. What had happened to her, he wondered. Jack's turnover rate was high. She had been one of the better ones and she and Alice had got on like a house on fire. Happy days.

Merlin was jolted out of his reverie by a sudden recall of his resolution and a loud blast on the car horn. A couple of scruffy lads were crossing over to the river side of the road, carrying a sandbag between them. Bridges wound down his window. "Oi. Do you want to get killed? And where are you going with that?"

The boys grinned back and shouted something which Bridges couldn't quite make out but knew was rude. They turned and ran down a walkway towards the houseboats tethered to the Chelsea Embankment.

"Up to no good, I'm sure. Shall I chase them?"

"No, Sergeant. Bigger fish to fry today."

They arrived at a tall Edwardian block of mansion flats

just off the Earls Court Road and, the lift being out of order, climbed wearily up three steep flights of stairs. Bridges knocked four times at Number 32 before a woman's voice rasped from behind the door. "Who's there?"

"It's the police. We'd like to talk to Mr Owen."

A disgruntled male voice took over. "Whaddya want? I'm trying to get some sleep. Come back later, can't you?"

"Is that Mr Owen?"

"Yes it is, and I can't see you now. Come back after lunch."

"That's not possible, sir. We have some questions to ask you about a Mr Johnny Morgan. Your nephew, I believe."

There was a period of silence before the man spoke again. "Is the boy in trouble?"

"I'd rather do this in person, if you don't mind."

The door opened to reveal Morrie "The Lorry" Owen, wearing a tattered brown dressing gown under which a shabby white vest and long johns could occasionally be glimpsed. Merlin noticed the flicker of surprise on Bridges' face. Behind Owen, they could see a small, skinny woman, her hair set in paper curlers, holding a black cat. "What's the boy got up to then?" Morrie Owen asked. He made no attempt to move back from the doorway to allow the policemen entrance.

"May we discuss this inside please, sir?"

"We're not dressed yet, but I suppose you might as well come in. Go and get decent, Annie, and then pour me a glass of Tizer, will you? I'm parched." Owen shuffled back through a small hallway and into his lounge. He apparently had no worries about his own decency and, lowering himself into an outsize armchair, he waved his hand in the direction of the two chairs facing him and an unlit gas fire. "Annie. When you're dressed come and light this fire, will you? It's bloody freezing."

The room was large and well-furnished. A tall antique grandfather-clock stood in a corner and there were some attractive old prints on the walls. Everything was spick and span and Merlin guessed that Owen made sure his wife earned her keep. "What's this about Johnny then?"

"You obviously haven't heard, Mr Owen. There's really no easy way to say this but your nephew is dead. His body was found the day before yesterday. His throat was cut."

Owen's mouth turned down and his jowls sagged further into the folds of his neck. His pudgy hands gripped the arms of his chair tightly.

"I know this must be a bit of a shock, but we would like to ask you a few questions."

Owen's eyes moved slowly from Merlin to Bridges and back. "Got any suspects 'ave you? If you people can't find out who did it, I bloody well will. Bastards whoever they are. Does his mother know? She'll never recover, you know. Already lost one boy down the mines."

"I understand the Embassy were trying to notify the family in Wales yesterday, Mr Owen. They should know by now."

Owen sighed heavily and an expanse of hairy flesh emerged from under his nightwear. "What is it you want to know?"

"We understand that you helped Johnny to get his job at the American Embassy."

"I gave him a reference if that's what you mean. He was a good driver and I told them so."

"It was a little more than that, wasn't it? We understand you introduced Johnny to someone who works in a senior capacity at the Embassy, who then procured the job for him."

Owen scratched at one of the folds of his neck. "Same difference. The American Embassy needed a driver and I gave Johnny a reference."

"Did you learn about the job opening from a Mr Norton, a Mr Arthur Norton?"

"Norton? Is that his name? I'm not very good at names. If that's what you say his name is, I'm sure you're right."

"We understood that Mr Norton might be some sort of friend of yours."

"I don't know about that. Just heard about the job through

the grapevine really. Johnny had only been up in London for a short time. I didn't really need him as I already had a driver so I was just making work unnecessarily. Heard about the job and gave him a reference, as I said. What's all this got to do with his death anyway?"

Mrs Owen entered wearing a floral housecoat, with a handkerchief tied over her head to cover her curlers. She handed her husband his drink, knelt down a little creakily, lit the fire, then disappeared.

"Mr Owen, we need to investigate Johnny's background thoroughly to identify any possible enemies. It's also helpful to know who his friends were. Would we be right in thinking that Mr Norton was a good friend to Johnny?"

Owen shifted in his seat and some of the sticky liquid in his glass spilled on to the arm of his chair. He wiped the mess with the sleeve of his dressing gown and stared pugnaciously at the policemen. "Better ask Norton that, copper. I don't know."

Merlin decided to change tack. "Could you tell us a little about your business activities, Mr Owen? You're in the restaurant and entertainment business, aren't you?"

"Yes."

"Can you tell us about it?"

"What's to tell?" Owen said sourly. "I have some premises. Eating or drinking places with sometimes a bit of music. That's it."

"Would one of these premises be called The Blue Angel?"

Owen leaned forward in his seat and slopped more Tizer over the armchair. "Annie, come and clean this mess will you?" His eyes became more alert and he looked carefully at the policemen. "Thought I'd seen you before." He peered under the brim of Bridges' hat. "Nice shiner you've got there. You upset some of my staff last night, didn't you? Were you there too, Merlin? Yes, I think you were. What were you doing skulking around like that in my club? And why all these games? Yes, alright, I do own The Blue Angel. What of it?

Perfectly proper club it is. What's it got to do with Johnny?"

"Was Norton one of your customers last night?"

"Might have been. I have lots of customers you know. Don't know all of them."

Merlin felt himself becoming impatient of Owen's limited acquaintance with the truth. "Come on. Norton's a customer who was friendly enough to find a cushy opening for your Johnny in the American Embassy. Perhaps he owed you a favour, perhaps you owed him a favour. Which is it?"

Owen's face became flushed. He kicked out with his right foot at his wife, who had reappeared as commanded and was on her knees mopping away at the stains. "Get out of it, woman. That's tidy enough." She picked up the cat which had followed her into the room and scuttled away.

"Alright. He's a customer. A friendly customer. What of it? He mentioned where he worked one night and I asked him to bear Johnny in mind if there were any jobs going. Simple as that. I have lots of friendly relationships with customers like that. This one worked out well for Johnny. That's all. I don't like to talk about my customers, see, as they expect discretion. Without discretion I'd be out of business, wouldn't I?"

Merlin put his hand inside his jacket pocket. "Have you ever seen this girl before?"

Owen snapped open a glasses case on his side-table and examined the Harris family photograph through thick-rimmed spectacles. "No. Never."

"Are you sure?"

Owen removed his glasses and snapped the case closed. "Don't recognise her, copper. What more can I say?"

"We believe she visited your club."

"Lots of girls visit. Can't expect me to recognise them all, can you?"

"This one was called Joan. We think she visited the club in December with Norton."

"No. Rings no bells."

Merlin could feel his blood pressure building. "If your

bells peal out at any time soon, please let us know, won't you? You see, if you care about us finding your nephew's killer, information about this girl might help us. Her full name is Joan Harris, does that mean anything to you?"

"Nothing at all."

Merlin rose abruptly to his feet and stepped forward, placing his hands on the arms of Owen's chair. He leaned down. "Nothing at all? Well, Miss Harris was also employed by the American Embassy and, like Johnny, recently met a violent death. Johnny knew her, Norton knew her and they are both linked to you. We will be digging deep, Mr Owen, and it would be best if you were honest with us. If you're not then we may be bound to make life a little difficult for you, do you understand me?"

Owen's chins shuddered. "That's no way to speak to a recently bereaved man. Here I am in mourning for my nephew and you're threatening me. Shame on you, copper!"

"Come on, Sergeant."

At the bottom of the stairs they passed the Owens' cat, which had a mouse in its jaws. It glared at them with a lack of warmth matching that of its owners.

"You might have mentioned that you thought he'd be the club owner, sir."

"I wasn't sure it would be him, Sam. Just had a hunch after the girl told me his first name and then Norton turned up. I didn't know for sure till he opened the door."

"Hmm."

"Got Miss Donovan's brother's address yet?"

"No, sir."

"I think we can leave it for the weekend. We'll see her on Monday. She should be fully recovered by then."

* * *

At the Yard, on their way up to the office, a heavily-built man in a trilby hat rushed down the stairs towards them. They were climbing two abreast and the man twitched his small nose furiously at them as he waited for one of them to move aside and let him past. Bridges obliged and the man hurried on.

When he reached his floor Merlin turned, looking puzzled.

"Did that man look familiar to you?"

"Can't say he did, sir. I didn't really get much of a look at him."

Inspector Johnson appeared at the other end of the corridor and joined them. He had shaved off his moustache as ordered.

"How goes it, Peter?"

"I've just had my suspect in. He was here because I missed him at the Foreign Office yesterday. If I'd known you were going to be here now I'd have held on to him."

"Hmm." Merlin stroked his forehead thoughtfully. "Would I be right in thinking that Edward Fraser is a portly gentleman with a snub nose?"

"You would. Did you see him on his way out?"

"He barged past the Sergeant and me on the stairs. A rude fellow."

"'Arrogant' and 'bumptious' are the words that come most immediately to my mind."

They went through into Merlin's office and sat around the desk.

"How far did you get with him?"

"He persisted with his story about hitting a deer. He was very upset that I'd been to look for him at the Foreign Office. Said it looked really bad for him. Interesting line in swearwords he has. Must have had a few years in the army before joining the diplomatic corps."

"Find any chinks in his armour?"

"Not really. He gave me chapter and verse about where he'd been on his country weekend – some place in Surrey owned by a Lord and Lady Pelham. Said he hit the deer somewhere in the country near their estate as he was driving up for the weekend. Didn't think he'd killed it. He was on his own in the car and there was no one about, so no witnesses to the accident, although he said that several people at the house party could vouch that the car was damaged when it arrived at the Pelhams' place."

Merlin picked up a pencil and tapped out a tune on his front teeth. "Did he give the location of this accident?"

"A rough idea, but I don't think a hunt for an injured deer in order to check his story is really on."

"No, of course not. So, he's given you a just-about plausible story without third-party confirmation. He could just as well have killed Mr Goldberg and driven to the Pelhams and told everyone the story of the deer to give himself some credibility. Have the scientists got any further?"

Johnson stroked his bare upper lip wistfully. "Not really. They've told me that the cloth they're examining is extremely common, so even if there's a match with Mr Goldberg's suit, Fraser could say that the cloth could have got there in other ways – someone else might have leaned against the car. It's circumstantial and weak."

They were interrupted by clanging noises. There was still some sort of activity going on on the roof of County Hall, but Merlin couldn't tell exactly what they were up to. "I'm sorry. Still some distance for you to cover."

Johnson shrugged and looked more carefully at Bridges.

"That's a beauty you've got there, Sergeant."

"Looks worse than it is. I got a little roughly handled by the staff of The Blue Angel. I gave as good as I got though."

"You see, Peter, I try to introduce the Sergeant to smart London night life and he shows me up. Can't take him anywhere!"

Bridges shrugged his shoulders with a smile.

"Our outing was not wasted though. We learned that Miss Harris visited the club with Arthur Norton, and that Johnny Morgan's uncle owns the club."

"That's interesting."

"I think so."

Merlin closed his eyes and kneaded his forehead, a mannerism which Bridges had noticed was becoming increasingly frequent, then chuckled to himself.

"And, I think we've learned one other interesting thing today."

"Oh?"

"I knew the chap looked familiar and now I've got it. Norton's chubby companion last night, Sergeant – it was Fraser, I'm sure! Your Mr Fraser, Peter, was at The Blue Angel with Norton. They're both diplomats and I suppose it's not surprising that they know each other but, nevertheless, a strange coincidence. And coincidences always worry me."

* * *

A sea of hands rose above the terraces as the ball thudded into the back of the net. Jack Stewart calmly lit a John Player to replace the one he was grinding into the concrete beneath. The half-time whistle blew.

"Sure you don't want a smoke?"

"You know I'm trying to cut down."

Stewart slapped Merlin hard on the shoulder.

"Come on, Frank. What's life without fags, beer and women? That's what it's all about, isn't it? You're already doing without one of the three. If you give up another there'll only be beer. I suppose there's football as well, but this is the first game you've been to in ages, and I don't think there'll be much more football to watch until we've got hold of old Adolf and shoved his head up his backside."

Merlin laughed. "That'll be hard I think. He must have one of the tightest arses in Europe. You can see that by the way he minces around on the newsreels with that permanently constipated expression." He pulled his scarf tighter around his neck. The relative mildness of the morning seemed to have disappeared, or maybe it was just the wind rattling through the draughty nooks and crannies of Stamford Bridge that was making him shiver.

"Good goal that last one, Jack? Chelsea played much better in the last fifteen minutes of the half."

Stewart stamped his feet on the ground and took a deep puff of his newly-lit cigarette. "I suppose they did a wee bit better. But they need to keep it up."

The two men fell silent and enjoyed listening to the banter of the crowd. Merlin had sent Bridges off to Iris for the rest of the weekend, telling him he deserved the break. They had agreed to go around to the Ambassador's residence first thing on Monday to tidy things up with Kathleen Donovan. Merlin felt he needed a little time to think. When he'd got back home after midday, he'd found a message. Chelsea were playing Fulham at home and Stewart would be in The Dog and Fox, round the corner from the Stamford Bridge ground, at half past one. He'd decided to forget work for a few hours. A break from the task in hand and a cleared mind usually made him think better. For the first half-hour of the game Merlin thought he'd regret his decision, as Fulham ran Chelsea ragged, but a late first-half goal offered the prospect of a good fight-back in the second half.

"I went to your nightclub, Jack. Quite a useful visit it was too."

"Glad to be of assistance to the constabulary. Meet any nice girls there?"

"Yes. Well, I met one girl who was quite helpful."

Stewart slipped down onto the lower step of the terrace, as a man behind him lost his balance under the weight of the child he was supporting on his shoulders.

"Sorry about that, mate. Come on, Bobby, give your old dad a bit of a rest. I'll put you back up there when the second half starts. He's getting a bit too big for me."

"Don't worry, pal." Stewart climbed back to his position and blew on his hands. "That's good if you found someone helpful."

"Pretty little piece she was. Speaking of pieces, that's what

I've got to do. Piece a lot of loose ends together. The thing is – "
His voice was drowned as the crowd roared its welcome to
the teams retaking the field. Chelsea kicked-off and
immediately launched a move which resulted in a headed
goal by their thickset, young centre-forward. Stewart jumped
up and down and hugged his friend and the ebb and flow of
an exciting game again pushed Joan and Johnny out of Merlin's
thoughts for a while.

* * *

In The Dog and Fox the game, which had finally ended in a 3-
3 draw, had been fully dissected and a few pints had been
sunk. The bar was heaving and they were crushed against a
wall at the corner of the bar.

Stewart had ordered another round of drinks, which was
taking a long time to arrive. "I'm seeing that Polish girl tonight.
You know, Sonia."

"She who works at The Blue Angel? Why are you doing
that?"

"Oh, well. I bumped into her yesterday near the station.
She's a gorgeous looking girl, you know. We had a cup of tea
and she was flashing a lovely smile at me. I thought I might
give her the benefit of the doubt."

Merlin ran a finger around the rim of his empty glass.
"That's very good of you, and what exactly does this 'benefit
of the doubt' involve?"

"In some of these places, girls might just work for tips, you
know. Not every girl in these places sleeps with their
customers, do they?"

"I don't know. You're the man of the world, aren't you?
All I can say from my little experience of the club is that the
girl who was entertaining me was all over me about going
back to my place. Her supposed name wasn't Sonia, mind
you, nor was she Polish, so you might be right there, in giving
her the benefit of the doubt, I mean."

"Very droll. Anyway, I'm taking her out to dinner and I'll ask her what the situation is."

"And you'll believe what she says?"

Stewart swirled the dregs of beer around in his glass. "I'll see. I think I'm a good judge of women, don't you?"

"I'll reserve judgement on that. However, it does occur to me that I need some corroboration of what my girl said, so it would be useful if she could answer some questions for me. I'd like to show her my photo of Joan Harris. And one of my suspicious characters from the Embassy was at the club. She might know him and have some information on him."

Stewart grimaced. "Come on, Frank. That's not going to do me any good, is it? Taking the girl out with my friend the copper. 'Yes dear, we'll order shortly but first the policeman here would like to cross-examine you about your nightclub career.' Why don't you just go around to the club and pull some other girls?"

"I'm sure they'll all have been warned by now to keep their traps shut. Perhaps, away from the club your friend might help. Look, don't worry, I won't ruin your night out. Do you know where she lives?"

"Yes, I'm picking her up there tonight."

"Nothing to stop me visiting her on another occasion to ask some gentle questions, is there?"

"No, I suppose not, assuming I give you the address but… watch out!"

Merlin narrowly avoided a drunken supporter lurching towards him and spilling beer everywhere. He wiped his arm with a handkerchief.

"Thanks. Look I promise I won't do anything over the weekend. Just let me have it and I'll drop by some time next week. No need for her to know that you and I are in any way connected. I'll just say we got a tip-off she worked at The Blue Angel."

"Alright. I'll probably be off her by next week anyway. It's just off Baker Street. Got something to write with?"

The Count looked a little uncomfortable in his bright brown checked golfing attire, although his outfit was less jarring to the eye than the bright green plus-fours sported by Arthur Norton. Golf was little played in Italy but the Count had made a good fist of learning the basics since his arrival in England and had held his own with Norton who, although a regular player, was not much good. Norton's hangover affected him on the front nine, where he had played poorly, but he had recovered enough on the back nine to beat the Count on the eighteenth.

The wood fire in the drawing room of Norton's apartment crackled as he handed the Count a dry martini and poured out a dry sherry for Freddie Douglas. He poured a large slug of bourbon for himself out of an antique crystal decanter he had paid a fortune for a few days before at Mappin & Webb's. "Your health, gentlemen."

His guests raised their glasses as Douglas joined the Count on the couch by the fire. Norton sat in his window seat and stretched his legs.

"How was your game?"

The Count held his arms out towards the fire. "It was freezing, wasn't it, Arthur? I thought my hands and feet would fall off through frostbite."

"Oh, it wasn't that bad. I actually thought it was a little milder than it has been."

"For you, a sturdy New Englander, maybe it was a little milder, but I am from the Mediterranean. I can tell you, Freddie, it was freezing."

Douglas smiled sympathetically. "May I ask who won?"

"Arthur just 'pipped me at the post', is that how you say it? He won at the last hole."

Norton attempted a modest smile. "I'm sure the Count will beat me if we play in the summer."

"We shall see. Now, gentlemen..." The Count withdrew

an envelope from his jacket pocket and placed it on the table. "Shall we discuss our little bit of business?"

* * *

Jimmy Reardon shivered behind the wheel as his boss carefully levered himself out of the car. The light was rapidly fading. "You want a hand?"

"Of course I want a hand."

He moved around from the driver's seat to help Owen out.

"You're sure no-one followed us?"

"Look, boss, there's no traffic around today and I drove three times around Berkeley Square to make sure there ain't no tail. If there is one they're bloody invisible!"

"Alright, alright. Give me a pull, will you?"

Reardon's ears swayed back and forth as he tugged hard to extract Owen's rear-end from the car seat. Owen was wearing a navy overcoat whose buttons were straining at the leash. "What number does that Yankee bastard live in again?"

"Number 6, boss."

"Well go on then, open the door."

Reardon did as he was told. The two men stood in the lobby of a smart new residential block around the corner from the Dorchester Hotel. A young porter looked expectantly at them from behind a marble desk.

"Here to see Mr Norton, sonny. Important delivery for him. No need to call him." Owen slipped half a crown across the desk. "He'll enjoy the surprise."

As they crossed the lobby, a bell rang and the lift door on their right slowly opened. Freddie Douglas and Count Giambelli were engrossed in conversation as they moved towards the main door and didn't notice the other two men.

The sour expression which Owen habitually maintained in the presence of Reardon and his other employees was transformed into the warm and attentive one he presented to his customers. Reardon never ceased to be amazed at the rapidity and comprehensiveness of the change – Spencer Tracy in that Jekyll and Hyde film had nothing on Morrie Owen. "Hello Mr Douglas, sir. And how are you today?"

Douglas stared with surprise. "Ah, Owen. How are you? What are you…"

"Just here to see Mr Norton on a small matter of business, sir. And this would be the Italian gentleman who was in your party the other evening. Did you enjoy yourself, sir?"

Giambelli looked in confusion at Douglas.

"Mr Owen, Count, the proprietor of the nightclub we visited the other night."

"Ah, si. Thank you. Very nice. Very nice."

"Well, a pleasure to see you, Owen, but we must be off. Goodbye." Glancing disdainfully at Reardon, Douglas led the Italian out through the door.

In the blink of an eye, Owen's features metamorphosed. "Stuck-up sod. Well, we know all about Mr Douglas, don't we, Jimmy?" Owen tapped his nose and leered as they stepped into the lift. With difficulty, Reardon reached round his boss and pressed the button for the second floor.

"Wait outside for me, Jimmy. If I call for you, come in. If I don't and I'm not out in half-an-hour, come and get me."

The two men squeezed out of the lift and Reardon sat in a chair placed in an alcove on the left. He took a ragged copy of *Tit-Bits* from his coat pocket and started to read. At Number 6 the door opened to reveal Arthur Norton, mouth open in surprise. "Hey. Owen. What the hell are you doing here?"

"A delivery, Mr Norton. I'm delivering myself to you for a little chat. May I come in?" Owen produced a grim smile. His stomach was already over the threshold but Norton held the door against it.

"What the heck possessed you to come here? If you need to talk to me we could surely do that better at your club."

Owen pressed his stomach hard against the door. "What has possessed me to come here is firstly that my nephew is dead and secondly that the police are pestering me. I'd like to have a little word with you on both matters, alright?"

Norton stepped back, allowing the remainder of Owen to gain entry. "Johnny's dead. My God. How?"

"He had his throat slit on Thursday. How come you don't know about it and how come you didn't mention it to me last night?"

"I didn't know about it at all. I didn't go into the Embassy yesterday. I wasn't feeling so well."

"Feeling a bit rough after Thursday, eh?"

"No, I just wasn't feeling… anyway that's neither here nor there. Come on. You'd better come in." Norton led the way through to his drawing room.

"Good God, Johnny dead, eh? My condolences. Do they know who did it?"

Owen sank slowly into an armchair. "They haven't a clue. Do you?"

"Me? God, no. Why would I have a clue?" Norton went to his drinks cabinet and poured himself another whisky. He held a glass up to Owen who declined.

"You might have a clue because you did it. Perhaps you and Johnny fell out, eh? Had an argument over your little arrangements together. I know you've got quite a temper. Perhaps you lost it."

Norton shook his head vehemently before seating himself opposite Owen. "You know I'm not the sort to slit a man's throat, Owen. I did have some words with Johnny occasionally. He was a damn greedy fellow. Always asking for more money than I thought we'd agreed. But then you'd know all about that, wouldn't you?"

Owen grunted. "He had a lot of expenses to cover."

"Yes, well, still, I'm hardly likely to slit his throat over a few extra expenses, am I?"

Owen shifted in his seat and sighed, then pulled out a handkerchief and mopped his forehead. "Poor Johnny. Too big for his boots he was. Must have tried one of his tricks on the wrong customer. Silly bugger. Or perhaps it had something

143

to do with your friend Joan, eh? The police were pestering me about her too."

"You didn't tell them about me going to your club, did you?"

"Didn't need to tell them. They saw you there themselves. The two coppers on the case were there last night."

Norton stared gloomily into his glass.

"Look Mr Norton, I'd like to know who did Johnny in but I think I can make some enquiries of my own to do that. I'd appreciate any information you can provide. However, what I don't want is the police buzzing around my affairs and Johnny's affairs like flies, and I'm sure you don't either. Now, you've got some influential friends and I suggest you ask them to get the coppers to hold back. If you can't, then I've got some cards to play too but, well, I'd rather keep them in reserve."

"I'll speak to my friends. See what I can do. Meanwhile, I suggest you tell everyone at your club to keep their traps shut."

"Don't teach me to suck eggs, Mr Norton. All my people know what will happen if they go against me. I think you'd better worry more about your fancy friends." Owen managed, at his second attempt, to rise from his chair and moved to the corridor with Norton in tow.

"I saw your poncy buddy Freddie Douglas downstairs. With his spick friend."

"Yes, we had a little business to discuss."

"Very lucky fellow, Freddie Douglas. He's just about to inherit a fortune from his father, did you know?"

"Someone mentioned it, yes."

The door was opened and Owen squeezed through. "Oh, yes. I almost forgot. You'd better give me back the key."

"What key?"

"You know which key. It's not as if you'll have any use for it now. Wouldn't be very wise, would it?"

"Wait a minute."

He disappeared down the corridor and returned with a key on a piece of string.

Norton watched sulkily as Owen waddled away. "I'll, er, still be getting the latest package, won't I? I mean, when it's ready."

Owen rolled his eyes and snorted. "Yeh, you'll be getting it. Don't worry."

Reardon was snoring gently in his chair. Owen kicked him and he slowly came to life. "Come on, you decrepit old git, I've given Mr Norton a clean bill of health, for now."

CHAPTER 8

In the distance, church bells were ringing in the City. The sound always reminded him of his days as a choirboy in the small Catholic church in Limehouse. Merlin had not been a very good choirboy. Briefly he had had a reasonable treble voice but his voice had broken early and never really settled into anything else. Still his father had insisted, and his father's will was not to be brooked.

Last night he had dreamed about his father who was riding an ageing piebald through a bleak landscape like his hero Don Quixote. In the middle of a long poetic declamation, Harry Merlin had disappeared in a puff of smoke, rather like he had in real life. When the smoke had settled, he'd seen his brother Charlie emerging, bloodstained, from a muddy trench, asking for his help. His sister Maria had then appeared from somewhere, guiding him away from the battlefield to a room in which various uniformed men, including Hitler and Franco, had been playing cards. He had just been asked to join them when he'd awoken with a parched mouth.

He sat down at his desk and methodically laid out his own notebook, the notebook he'd taken from Bridges on Saturday morning, a clean sheet of paper and a pencil. He drew a straight line down the centre of the paper. At the top to the left of the line he wrote down Joan Harris' name, and at the top on the right Johnny Morgan's. He flicked through both notebooks then stared for a while at the ceiling before picking up his pencil. Under Joan's name he wrote: "Johnny Morgan, Kathleen Donovan, The Blue Angel, Arthur Norton". Glancing at his own notes, he looked at the inscription he'd found in Joan's copy of *Huckleberry Finn*. He turned back to his list and wrote in the Harris column, "Who is J (inscription)?" He skimmed through Bridges' notes again and wrote down, "Letter to Joan (upset/old ladies)". He sucked on his pencil. Turning to the right column he listed the same names and added that of Morrie Owen. Staring up at Van Gogh's cornfields he ran over his conversations with the Assistant Commissioner. Picking up his pencil again, he wrote across the central line, "Love/Sex?" and beneath that he wrote, "Secrets?"

Sitting back in his chair he stared at the paper for a while. He had an uncomfortable feeling that this case was driving him rather than as it should be, vice versa. He needed to assert greater control over the still somewhat amorphous set of facts and events. Leaning forward he turned the paper over and wrote with a flourish, "Action" at the top of the page. Under this he wrote:

Identify J (Johnny Morgan – unlikely – ask Kathleen Donovan)
Find letter (JH's belongings stored downstairs)
Speak to Vice about Morrie Owen

Merlin turned the paper over and stared at it again before adding to his 'Action' list:

Find out owner of Johnny's mews house.
Give Norton a wide berth for the moment but put tail on? (Tail on Morrie Owen?)

He heard the sound of marching boots outside and walked over to the window. A long line of khaki-clad soldiers were making their way in the crisp morning sun past Scotland Yard, heading towards Charing Cross and then, Merlin guessed, to France. He wondered how many of those boys would survive until the spring.

* * *

Just after noon he hopped on a bus and made his way to Fulham. He got off on the New King's Road, crossed over Eel Brook Common and turned down a side road, arriving promptly, as promised, at one o'clock at the end of terrace house. His sister-in-law smiled and gave him a warm embrace, while his nephew tugged excitedly at his trouser legs.

Lunch was, as always, excellent. Beatrice had somehow got hold of a huge leg of lamb and cooked it in the Spanish style, just as he and Charlie loved it. Unusually for his generation, their father had liked to cook and Aggie Merlin had been happy, at occasional Sunday lunches, to make way for him in the kitchen. Lamb was his father's speciality and Bea had learned well from Charlie how to replicate the recipe.

Afterwards Frank Merlin sat, stuffed, in Charlie's armchair with his four-year-old nephew on his lap. He'd promised to take him out onto Parson's Green with a football once he'd had his cup of tea. For now, thankfully, young Paul was dozing, his stomach also full of meat and rice pudding.

Bea emerged from the kitchen and removed her apron. "A glass of port wine for you?"

"No thanks, dear. A cup of tea will be fine. No rush though. Rest your feet for a moment."

She fell back into the other armchair in the front room of the spruce little house which Charlie had been able to buy after his promotion to Assistant Manager at the local Martin's Bank.

"I'm sure you'll hear something soon, Bea."

"Let's hope. It doesn't sound as if things are progressing very well over there, does it?"

"No. It doesn't."

Little of the anxiety she felt for her husband was reflected in her face which, pretty and serene as always, returned Merlin's sympathetic gaze stoically. "What will be, will be. Now what of you, Frank? Have you stirred your stumps yet?"

Paul quivered and whimpered softly as Merlin shifted uncomfortably in his seat. "How do you mean?"

"You know very well what I mean. It's time you got yourself out of those lodgings and into a proper place of your own. It's not as if you can't afford it."

Merlin attempted to loosen his trouser belt but was unable

to achieve this with the young boy on top of him. "I'm quite happy where I am, as you know."

"Nonsense. Time you put the past behind you and a new place of your own will help you do that. And, with no disrespect to Alice, time you found yourself a new woman too. I'm sure she wouldn't have wanted you to mope around in misery forever."

Merlin decided that it was best to say nothing. He'd already had this conversation with Bea several times. She was right of course and he'd already accepted the wisdom of her words but he was too stubborn to admit it to her face.

Bea ignored his silence. "Just look at how happy young Sam is now he's hooked up with Iris. And he was miserable too but he got up and did something about it."

Bea had a soft spot for Sam Bridges as she had been an orphan as well. They had both done well after dreadful beginnings.

Paul stretched out an arm and opened his eyes. Merlin grasped his opportunity. "Time for that game of football I think, eh, Paul? Hold the tea for the moment, Bea. Back in a while. I'll have that cup of tea then, please."

Paul trailed him happily out of the door, ball in hand, as his mother shook her head ruefully.

* * *

The Florida sun was high in the sky but there was a cool breeze and the Ambassador shivered a little. He put down the papers with irritation and stared briefly at the sea twinkling beyond the garden wall before raising his hand. A small, white-jacketed man emerged promptly from the house. "Bring me my tennis sweater, Manuel – and an orange juice. Oh, and get me Diedrickson on the phone – his home number's in the book on the hall table."

He noticed a new sunspot on the hand he had raised and made a mental note to fix a check-up with his dermatologist when he got back to Boston. Manuel re-emerged holding a telephone receiver which he plugged into a wall-socket by the marble table.

"The Señor is on the line, sir."

"Diedrickson. What are you doing to me? The account's down twenty per cent in three months. What's that? Well I'm sorry if I'm interrupting your lunch but I think servicing your most important client might perhaps feature higher in your priorities than knocking back Long Island Teas or whatever else you people drink in East Hampton. Oh, very well, you didn't do too badly for me last year so go ahead and have your lunch. Call me tomorrow, alright?"

"Something wrong, honey?" A small blonde head rose from its resting place on a lounger at the far end of the pool. The head was attached to a tanned body shown off to near perfection by a tight polka-dotted cream swimsuit.

"Just money, dear. Nothing to worry your pretty head about." Joseph Kennedy thirstily drank the juice that Manuel placed in front of him, got wearily to his feet and walked towards his companion. He bent down and touched her red-varnished toes, ran his hand over her feet, along her legs, over her belly and her breasts, eventually cupping her chin in his hand.

"That was nice, Mr Ambassador. Did you have anything else in mind?"

"After lunch, Rhoda. I've still got a little work to do." His glasses sparkled in the reflected light from the water as he leaned forward to kiss her on the lips.

"I can't wait. Hurry up with that work."

Rhoda, one of a string of perky contract actresses his people in Hollywood kept him supplied with, sat up and giggled cheekily at him before lighting a cigarette.

The Ambassador returned to the table and picked up another of his stock reports. This broker was doing a better job for him and he smiled. An hour later he had finished his reading. Diedrickson's account at J.P. Morgan was the only one which was down, and since his position there had doubled in 1939 he could cut the guy some slack. He hadn't gone over his foreign positions today but he knew he was doing very well there. Hitler would have done enough damage by the summer at the latest for him to close out all his short positions and provide a substantial top-up for the campaign fund. Then he'd show that stuck-up liberal cripple in the White House what was what.

A hummingbird fluttered by as he stood up and stretched his arms. He was still feeling a little stiff from yesterday's golf round. After lunch and some fun with Rhoda, he'd get that nice young girl from The Breakers Hotel to come over and give him a massage.

He went into the house and ran a hand over the ivories of the grand piano that was backed-up to the French windows. On top of the piano were scores of family and business photos. Pride of place went to a picture of his two eldest boys sailing in the waters off Cape Cod. Strong, bright, fine-looking boys who took after their father in so many ways. Or so he was doing his damnedest to arrange.

"Call from London, sir." Manuel appeared with another telephone receiver.

London, thousands of miles away and about to disappear in smoke if they didn't listen to him. Why should he spoil his Sunday by talking to London? Only depressing things happened in London. The winter months had been particularly miserable, which was why he'd high-tailed it back to America. Not so depressing and miserable as to cause him great anxiety though. He'd done all sorts of things in his life but he prided himself on his strong nerve. It took a lot to rattle him and events in London had not done that. But he was glad to be out of it, for the moment at least. "Tell them I'm out. They'll have to call me tomorrow."

"Sir."

CHAPTER 9

Monday February 5th

A blaring car horn somewhere below in Sloane Avenue woke him. Fraser pulled the bedclothes up over his head and wished the morning away. He'd called in sick on Friday and he thought he'd keep up the act for a few days more. For one thing, he'd be able to think things through. He'd given himself Sunday off from worrying but now he had to apply his mind calmly to the situation. Not many people would be able to do that, of course, to push such important matters away from the mind, but he'd just about managed with the assistance of a good supply of gin and Charles Dickens. In times of stress he'd always found Dickens a great comfort. He'd first read *The Pickwick Papers* when he was eight and it remained his favourite. The book lay on his bedside table now, open at the point of Mr Pickwick's entry into Newgate Gaol. He considered whether he should telephone his smug colleague to confirm that he continued to be indisposed? No doubt Douglas had another week of nefarious machinations in prospect in which he'd be looking for support. No. He decided to leave it for now. As for his problems, they could wait a little longer. He reached out for his book.

* * *

The cuckoo made one of its brief appearances outside its little house as Bridges went through the office door. He could see that his boss was looking in much better shape as he enquired about his weekend.

"I had a superb Sunday lunch yesterday, Sergeant, courtesy of my sister-in-law who only nagged me just a little bit for once. Then I had an early night and slept like a log. We're going to get somewhere this week on these murders. I'm determined. Now let's – "

Merlin paused as Johnson came through the door, fiddling nervously with his collar.

"I've just been upstairs to give the A.C. an update on the hit and run case, sir. He wasn't very happy. I don't think I've ever seen his face so red."

"Not to worry. That's a regular occurrence these days with the man upstairs. Let's put our heads together later and see what we can do with your Mr Fraser."

"I would appreciate that, but unfortunately the A.C. now wants to see you in his office."

"Hey, ho. When I get back, Sergeant, we'll go and see if we can find Miss Donovan. Oh, and can you try and find out where the Johnny Morgan forensic report is?"

As he entered, the A.C was on the telephone. "Yes, dear. I'll be sure to do that. No dear, of course. Yes, well you can tell your sister it's all in hand. I'll be speaking to Claire tomorrow. If she wants to she can. Yes. Now I really must go, dear."

Merlin had met Mrs Gatehouse several times. A formidable lady in a formidable body frame. The A.C. was a tall man but his wife was taller and much broader and expected to be deferred to by one and all, not least her husband.

The A.C. cleared his throat noisily, successfully expelling all recent traces of sweetness and docility. His face reacquired the rosy hue noted by Johnson. "I have two bones to pick with you, Chief Inspector?"

"Sir?"

"The first concerns Johnson's hit and run. I don't know why you and he led me to believe that the case was solved when it clearly isn't."

"I don't believe either of us told you that the case was solved, sir. You assumed that good progress was being made, which I believe was the case at the time you enquired. It still seems to me that we have a good suspect, but more work is necessary."

The A.C. screwed up his eyes and strode from the window to his desk. He drew a piece of paper towards him. "More importantly, I was telephoned this morning by a – " he consulted his notes, "a Mr Douglas from the Foreign Office. I told you to be careful in your dealings with these American diplomats but clearly you ignored me. Mr Douglas said that he had heard directly from the Ambassador himself, all the way from Florida indeed, that there was distinct dissatisfaction with, what were the words he used…?" He peered at the paper again, "'the heavy-handed and offensive way in which the investigating officers were dealing with these unfortunate incidents'. Mr Douglas said that the Foreign Office took a very dim view of the police behaviour and that it was clearly highly prejudicial to the good health of Anglo-American relations. That this should be occurring in connection with the demise of people who were little more than domestic servants he found particularly surprising." The A.C. pushed his piece of paper away with distaste. "What do you say to all that, eh?"

"As my father used, rather amusingly, to say, it's a load of bull and cock, sir."

"This is no occasion for levity, Chief Inspector. How so?"

"We have not been heavy-handed. In only one instance have feathers been ruffled and that was when one of the Ambassador's aides wouldn't answer our questions properly."

"Well, there you are. No doubt you could have been more diplomatic with this chap and he's complained to the Ambassador."

Merlin could feel his own cheeks reddening. "I am sure you are right that this gentleman is the source of the complaint, sir. I have to tell you that, short of not doing our job and refraining from questioning the gentleman at all, we could not have been more diplomatic. The truth is that this individual was offensive to us from the outset and is, in my view, a nasty piece of work. I would put money on him having some unpleasant involvement with both Joan Harris and Johnny Morgan and propose to investigate him thoroughly. In any event, although I am obviously not as politically in the know as our friends at the Foreign Office, given that the American Ambassador is already doing his level best to keep America out of the war, I cannot for the life of me see how getting up his nose or the nose of one of his cronies can prejudice our chances of getting the Americans into the war, which I take to be the prime sensible target of British foreign policy at present! As for the comment about domestic servants, I think that can be treated with the contempt that it deserves."

The A.C. twiddled a pencil in the fingers of his right hand. His face had regained its normal pallor. His eyebrows relaxed. He looked out of the window. "Looks like the weather's improving." He twiddled his pencil a little more. "Very well. I hear what you say. From all I'm told Kennedy's a lost cause to all but the appeasers, but there are plenty of those in the Foreign Office as you know. You carry on then, but be careful. And keep an eye on Johnson, will you? I may have been a bit rough on him."

"May I go now?"

The A.C. nodded. "Oh, and Frank?"

"Sir?"

"Just for peace's sake, pop in and speak to this Douglas chap at the F.O. Let him know everything's being done properly."

"It will be my pleasure, sir."

* * *

A small, impeccably dressed man was sitting with Miss Edgar when the policemen entered her office. Bridges nodded to the man. "This is Mr Herman Zarb, sir, the First Secretary at the Embassy. He and I spoke last week when you were otherwise engaged."

Zarb rose and shook hands. "Pleased to meet you, Chief

Inspector Merlin. This is all so terrible. Beyond understanding really. I hope everyone is being helpful. We must catch the criminals responsible."

"Everyone's been most accommodating, sir." He decided to pass over Norton's failings for the moment.

"Have you made any progress?"

"A little, but it's slow."

"If there's anything Miss Edgar or I can do, please let me know." He picked up his gloves. "I think we've covered everything, haven't we, Philippa? I'll be on my way. Good luck with your enquiries, gentlemen."

Zarb retrieved his overcoat and trilby from a stand in the corner and departed.

"We're keen, Miss Edgar, to have another word with Miss Donovan. Is she back at work?"

"I'm sorry, she's not here. The state she was in on Friday I did tell her that she was free to take today off if she hadn't fully recovered over the weekend. I think she has taken me at my word." A siren began to wail nearby. "Oh, dear. There it goes again. I'd better get everyone down to the basement." Miss Edgar reached down to a drawer in her desk and removed a brown box from which she pulled out a gas mask. "Will you be joining us, gentlemen?"

"No, thanks. We need to get on. Do you think Miss Donovan will be at her own lodgings or staying with her brother?"

Bridges leaned across to help Miss Edgar, who was struggling to close the box – it had an awkward latch mechanism. "Thank you, Sergeant. I should think she's with her brother. That's where she said she was going when she went off on Friday. The address is here in my address book."

As Bridges took down the details, Miss Edgar grabbed her mask and bustled out into the corridor. "Come on everyone! Down to the basement please. Hurry up. Let's have no stragglers."

It was raining heavily outside and the policemen paused

on the steps of the residence to watch the massed umbrellas race towards the shelters. A solitary plane moved in and out of the clouds above them.

* * *

"It's off on the left side of the Edgware Road, Sergeant, shortly after the road changes to Maida Vale." Merlin gazed blankly out at the sodden streets. "Zarb didn't seem unduly perturbed about how we are carrying out our investigations, did he?"

"No he didn't. Did you think he would, sir?"

"I didn't tell you before, but part of the bollocking I got from the A.C. concerned complaints from the US Embassy – supposedly the absent Ambassador himself. Apparently he told the Foreign Office that we were being heavy-handed and undiplomatic. But then Mr Zarb, the senior diplomat actually here on the spot, couldn't have been more charming to us just now."

"I'll bet you can put the complaints down to Norton."

"Quite so. In any event the A.C. wants us to have a soothing word with the chap at the Foreign Office who relayed the complaint."

"Something to look forward to then."

As they reached their destination, the all-clear sounded and the pavements rapidly filled with people. They pulled up outside one of a long row of Victorian terraced houses. The Donovans' house appeared to have been painted recently and stood out brightly in the otherwise shabby street.

A small, round-faced woman wearing a white apron opened the door. "Can I help you?"

Merlin displayed his police badge and asked for Kathleen Donovan.

The little woman's face flushed and her hands fluttered in the air. She had a decidedly broad Irish accent. "Oh, dear. The police. Kathleen's here alright. I'll let her know you'll be wanting to see her. Come on into the front room, if you please."

The policemen followed her into a small sitting room to the right of the hallway. The scent of pipe tobacco mingled with the appetising smells from a meat stew cooking somewhere at the back of the house.

Mrs Cormac Donovan flitted busily around the room with a feather duster. When she was satisfied she motioned for the policemen to take their seats and went to the bottom of the stairs. "Kathleen. Can you come down? It's the police to see you."

She arrived looking apprehensive, wearing a cream dress which highlighted the rich colour of her hair.

"Kathleen looks a little better but she's still not right. Cormac and I told her she should have another day's rest and that's what she's doing. If it causes problems at the Embassy, so be it. The girl needs to recover her health after the dreadful – "

"Yes alright, Marie. There's no need to go on." Kathleen smoothed her dress and perched nervously on the edge of an armchair.

Merlin declined the offer of tea and indicated that they required privacy with Kathleen.

"I see. Yes. I'll be in the kitchen if you need me."

Merlin waited till the door had closed. "Sorry to bother you again. There were one or two questions we forgot to ask you last time."

The girl tossed her hair in what Bridges thought was a rather beguiling manner. "I hope it's not anything more about the night I went out with Johnny."

"No, I haven't got any more questions about that except, that is, I wondered if any memories of the visitor had surfaced."

She shivered as if a strong draught had hit her. "Nothing."

"Very well. Joan Harris then. We know you occasionally did things together. Did you visit her lodgings?"

The interview proceeded slowly with answers being

extracted like teeth. Bridges realised that Merlin's previous untypically rough handling of the girl had left its mark. Gradually, however, and together the policemen made progress. Kathleen revealed that she had visited Joan several times at her lodgings, but never at night and never in a taxi. They'd done the normal sorts of things young girls in London did on their days off – the parks, the pictures, tea and cakes and so on. Joan had been very secretive about her social life otherwise, but Kathleen knew that she had been taken out to nice places like The Ritz and the Café de Paris. Naturally Kathleen had been interested in hearing more about these visits but Joan had clammed up about them as soon as any questions were asked.

"She was odd really – one minute she'd mention these places with excitement, and then she'd seem depressed about them. She was quite – oh, what's the word? – cynical sometimes. She used to tell me that men weren't all they were cracked up to be and I should watch out for myself."

Joan had never revealed who had accompanied her to these places, and Kathleen certainly couldn't think that one of the men might be Johnny Morgan, nor indeed anyone else at the residence or Embassy.

Notwithstanding, Merlin had listed a few names. Mention of Arthur Norton provoked a sharp intake of breath and the policemen leaned closer to her. She smelt of roses. Merlin assured her that she would not get into trouble by talking to them about her superiors. Her vivid green eyes appraised Merlin carefully. "I'll trust you then. Mr Norton is a vile man. He's always smarming up to the girls in the office. He thinks he's God's gift, and if you're passing him in a corridor or in an office, his hands always seem to…" She squirmed in her chair, "to be everywhere."

"And he would have been like that with Joan."

"Of course. He did it to anyone in a skirt and she was probably the prettiest. I would have assumed it even if she hadn't mentioned it to me.

"Did she…"

They were interrupted by the sound of voices in the hallway then the door opened to reveal a tall, middle-aged man with the same blazing red thatch of hair as Kathleen. The man had to bend to avoid the door lintel as he entered. He wore a long, brown jacket, and the bottom half of his trousers and his boots were caked in reddish-brown mud. Attached to his right hand was a little girl of seven or eight. "Who have we here then, Katy my sweet?"

The child looked up in confusion. "I don't know, Daddy."

"It's the police, Cormac. They've come to ask me a few more questions."

The man patted the little girl on the back and sent her off towards the kitchen. "Cormac Donovan." He held out his hand. "Pleased to meet you. I hope you haven't been upsetting Kathleen any more. She was in a terrible state when she got here on Friday after you had questioned her."

"It's alright. The two officers are only doing their job and I'm not in the least upset today."

"Glad to hear it, my dear."

Donovan's wife appeared, shaking her finger at him and complaining about his failure to remove his filthy boots. She sent him off down the corridor.

Merlin asked for a few words with the couple.

"Let me just go and give young Katy her stew and I'll bring Cormac back with me."

"You won't be needing me again, will you?" Kathleen rose to her feet.

"Not today, thank you. If we have any more questions will you be back at work tomorrow?"

"I'll be there." The scent of roses lingered after she disappeared behind the door.

Merlin walked over to the fireplace and examining the framed photographs lined up on the mantelpiece. An unsmiling, grey-haired woman dressed in black lace sat on a bench outside a whitewashed cottage, presumably somewhere in the depths of Ireland. Another photograph showed an old man with a shock of white hair dressed in a dark suit and white shirt without a tie, smoking a pipe in front of what seemed to be the same cottage.

"My parents, Chief Inspector." Cormac Donovan smiled as he came through the door. "At home in County Kerry a few years gone. My father's dead now, I'm afraid, but my mother's still going strong. Do you have parents living?"

"No. My father died some time ago. He was always an unlucky man. He was killed by a bomb in a Zeppelin raid in 1917. Not many died like that. He was so upset when I went off to the front. Thought I was bound to cop it and probably I should have, but I came home without a scratch and he got clobbered by a bomb down by the West India Docks. My mother never got over it and died a few years after."

"Sorry to hear that. My parents were a little luckier, though they had a hard time. They had a smallholding which they worked all their lives until my father died. Struggled to bring up a family of seven. But my father lived to see seventy and my mother's just turned sixty."

"Is Kathleen the youngest of your parents' children?"

Cormac Donovan pulled a pipe out of one of his trouser pockets, tobacco and matches from the other and sat down. He pressed the tobacco firmly into the pipe-bowl and lit up. "Yes. Kathleen is the youngest child by several years. Bit of a surprise to us all she was. She had a difficult birth as well. But everything worked out fine in the end."

Mrs Donovan reappeared. "Kathleen's keeping an eye on Katy but I hope you won't need us for too long, as Katy's got to get back to school." She wiped her hands on her apron and smiled nervously at her husband as she balanced herself on the arm of his chair.

"Only a few questions. Mr Donovan, I believe that you have some involvement in the building trade?"

Donovan took a long pull on his pipe and poked his chin in the air. He had a strong, weather-beaten face with large, grey-green eyes and a prominent, broad nose. "That's a very grand phrase, isn't it, 'some involvement in the building trade'? I'm a carpenter, and I work on building sites. Occasionally if there's no carpentry work on site, I turn my hand to other general labour." Donovan held his arms in front of him and flexed his muscles. "I'm a strong man, Chief Inspector, and strength has its uses. I'll turn my hand to anything to keep my family as comfortable as I can, and I do that alright, don't I Marie?"

"Oh, yes. Cormac's a good provider. A hard-working and good man, there's no one can say otherwise."

"How long have you been living in London?"

"It would be about five years this April, wouldn't it, Cormac?"

Donovan nodded.

"And Kathleen has been in London since – ?"

"She came over in the summer. May or June it was. She'd seen the advertisement for a job working for Mr Kennedy in an Irish paper, applied for it and came for an interview. She succeeded at the interview and was offered the job." Mrs Donovan glanced at her husband who patted her hand.

"They say old Joe Kennedy has an eye for the pretty Irish lasses, so that's probably why she got it."

"Oh, Cormac. She's a very bright girl!"

"She is that too, but I don't think her looks did her any harm."

Merlin's stomach rumbled as the smell of the lunchtime stew briefly broke through the pipe fumes. "How long did Miss Donovan stay with you until she moved to her own lodgings?"

"She stayed about a month. I told her that it would be much better if she stayed with us. A beautiful young girl like her on her own in London. Anything could happen. Look what did happen to her friend Joan. There are a lot of evil, godless men in this place and that's the truth. I've told her that Marie and I would be more than happy to have her here now."

"Is she going to move in with you?"

"She's got a mind of her own and we can't force her. She says she'll think about it."

"Did either of you ever meet Johnny Morgan?"

"No, Cormac and I never did."

"Did Kathleen tell you anything about him?"

"Only that he was a Welsh boy and that she liked him."

"What did she tell you, when she came to see you last week?" Donovan removed his pipe and placed it in an ashtray at the foot of his chair. He leaned forward and held a large, gnarled hand up to his wife. "Kathleen arrived here from work on Wednesday night. She was very pale and upset. She told us about her friend Joan's death. She also told us that she had had a little too much to drink on Tuesday, with a friend, because she was so upset. She said she felt like a rest and did we mind her staying with us. Of course we were happy to help her."

"She didn't say any more about the drinking episode, who she was drinking with or what they did?"

"She didn't give us any detail and we didn't press her for it either. She looked all in. We packed her off to bed with a hot drink and a hot water bottle. She rested on Thursday and went back to work on Friday. On Friday, as you know, she learned about Johnny's death, and you interviewed her. By the time she came back to us on Friday afternoon, she was in a bad way again. Marie put her straight to bed."

"Did she tell you that Johnny Morgan was the friend she'd been drinking with?"

"No, she didn't say anything about him except that he had been murdered."

Merlin nodded at his Sergeant. "Thank you both. Sorry to disturb your lunch."

Donovan clambered to his feet and gave Merlin a firm handshake. Out in the car, Merlin looked at his hand. A faint brownish-red stain covered his palm.

Ignoring the complaints of the secretaries in the outer office, Norton pushed through the door and strode into the room.

Zarb was at his desk sipping Coca-Cola from the bottle, a half-eaten ham sandwich in front of him.

"Nice lunch, Herman? What's the matter? Can't afford a glass?"

"What do you want, Arthur? If you need to see me, make an appointment like everyone else."

"I need to see you now. I've got vital information for the Ambassador and I've tried to contact him but can't get through."

Zarb slowly finished his sandwich. He turned in his chair to take in the view over Grosvenor Square, wiped his mouth with a napkin and swivelled back to look at his visitor. "It was indeed a nice lunch, until you barged in." He looked his visitor up and down. "Seems like you've had a good one too – several Martinis, I'd guess? You should bear in mind what that Hollywood friend of the Ambassador's – Cary Grant or Errol Flynn – I can't remember which, said – 'a good Martini is like a woman's breast: one is too few and three are too many'."

"Shut up, Herman." He pulled a white handkerchief out of his pocket and blew his nose loudly, before falling heavily into the chair facing Zarb.

"I have important stuff to pass on and I can't raise him on the phone."

Zarb's thin lips creased into a smile. "If it's serious, you'd better tell me and I'll make sure the Ambassador gets to hear it."

"Come on, Mr Secretary, you know that the Ambassador likes me to plough my own furrow. He gets his official information from you and your colleagues and his unofficial stuff from me. You know he doesn't like mixing them up."

Zarb leaned forwards, steepling his hands in front of his face. "I don't think there's much I can do to help you then."

Norton snorted angrily and a stale smell lingered in the air. "Look, tell me where the Ambassador is, will you? I rang Palm Beach. They said he wasn't there and refused to tell me where he was. Same thing when I rang Hyannisport. Said they'd let him know that I needed to talk to him urgently but I've heard nothing."

"Perhaps he's keeping some pleasant female company and doesn't want to be disturbed for a few days. Anyway, Arthur, if you've got something confidential to tell him, you shouldn't be discussing the matter over an open telephone line. Our friends in MI5 are all over the telephones at the moment. I'd use some other safer form of communication if it's something you don't want the British to know about."

"Depends which British."

"Pardon?"

Norton shrugged.

"And as for the Germans," Zarb continued, "our people and my friends in Whitehall tell me that there are spy-cells everywhere. Best to work on the assumption that the Post Office is not secure in either direction, I'd say."

Norton shifted impatiently in his seat.

"Of course, Arthur, you could put a message into cipher and we could wire it over to the Ambassador. I'm pretty sure the cipher hasn't been broken yet, but of course there are few absolute certainties in the world anymore."

"To put something into cipher I'd have to trust one of your cipher clerks, wouldn't I?"

"You would. You're not cleared for access to the cipher, despite your exalted status with the Ambassador. You'd either have to trust one of my cipher clerks, or just put whatever message you want into one of our diplomatic bags, which, as you know, will take a while to reach its destination. But isn't that perhaps the best method? Can this matter be so urgent?"

Norton rose stiffly and walked to the window. "Any idea when he's coming back?"

"I wouldn't be surprised if it's going to be a few weeks yet.

As you know there's talk of him taking soundings about a run for the Presidency, and then again the weather is so lovely in Florida at this time of year."

"I really would like to get this information to him as soon as possible."

"I can arrange for you to meet one of our cipher clerks this afternoon."

Norton mumbled his grudging thanks.

"I've got a few calls to make. Give me half an hour and I'll take you along to the Cipher Department myself – there's a reliable young man who I'm sure will be able to help."

* * *

A procession of military vehicles slowly made its way into Victoria Street heading for the Duke of York's barracks in Chelsea.

After the vehicles had passed, a crocodile of purple-blazered schoolboys processed across the pedestrian crossing and around their parked car.

"What now, sir?"

"I'd like to have a close look at Joan Harris' belongings. They're now boxed up somewhere in the Yard?"

"In one of the basement storage rooms."

"And you say we'll have the Morgan forensic report this afternoon?"

Bridges nodded.

"Good."

"Shouldn't we have another word with Norton, sir? Press him further about his dealings with Joan Harris?"

"Let's leave him for a little while. We know he's lied to us but if we push him now he'll just deny everything and kick up a further fuss with the powers that be. We'll bide our time for a day or two and see what else we can dig up." He looked at his watch. "Speaking of the powers that be, let's go and get an unpleasant task out of the way. We'll smooth this

166

Foreign Office chap out and buy ourselves a few more days of peace."

They made the short journey to the Foreign Office in no time. Police badges gained their car access to the inner courtyard and a prompt response from the uniformed porter at the front door. "Please make yourselves comfortable over there. I'll try and find Mr Douglas. Have you an appointment?"

"No, but it's very important." Merlin looked suitably grave.

"I see. Well, I think I saw him returning from lunch about ten minutes ago."

The porter wandered off out of sight behind some ornate pillars, leaving them alone in the vaulted lobby.

The high walls around them were hung in every direction with colourful paintings chronicling the history of the greatest empire the world had ever seen. Bridges was fascinated. History had been his favourite school subject. "Quite a place, isn't it, sir?"

"That it is." Merlin wondered bleakly how much of the glory of the empire would remain intact by the end of the year.

Puffing a little, the porter reappeared. "I've found him. He's prepared to see you in five minutes. I'll take you to one of the meeting rooms."

The policemen followed him up an elegant broad staircase and along a corridor whose canvases depicted memorable events in the history of the Raj. "If you'll just wait here a moment, I'm sure Mr Douglas will be with you shortly."

A long mahogany table filled the room. The one window revealed the dingy, grey back of another part of the building and let in a minimum amount of light. They sat down in the middle of the table, backs to the window.

"Should I take a note?"

"You'd better. Slippery customers these diplomats."

As he was looking with interest at a detailed depiction of a Crimean cavalry charge, a door at the far end of the room opened and Freddie Douglas drifted through. "Good afternoon. I understand you're from Scotland Yard. I'm Douglas. How can I help you?"

"A courtesy visit, Mr Douglas, at the request of the Assistant Metropolitan Commissioner. D.C.I. Merlin and this is D.S. Bridges. As you know, we are currently investigating the violent deaths of two employees of the American Ambassador."

"So you're the chaps who are handling that case, are you?"

"We are looking into the deaths of Miss Joan Harris and Mr Johnny Morgan. Both particularly unpleasant deaths and naturally, in the course of our enquiries, we are having to interview members of the Embassy staff. We understand that you have had complaints about our handling of the case?"

Douglas sat down opposite them and looked thoughtful. He was immaculately turned out and Merlin wondered at the perfection of his skin. No matter how carefully he shaved he always found a few specks of bristle lurking on his chin or under his lip during the course of the day. Douglas' face was as smooth as a billiard ball. "I have indeed received a complaint from the Ambassador himself. The charge is that you were unnecessarily harassing senior diplomatic staff."

"I can assure you, sir, that there has been no such harassment. We have approached our task with awareness of the diplomatic sensitivities and will continue to do so."

Douglas pursed his lips and shook his head sorrowfully. "Do you officers have any idea of what a perilous position this country is in? Within six months our country and empire may be utterly destroyed. Unless Mr Chamberlain can find a sensible, peaceful way out of this mess, our only hope is to see the United States join the war. In the circumstances it is essential that our relationship with the United States at all levels is kept as tranquil and regular as possible. We understand from the Ambassador that certain senior diplomats who have a key role to play in the nurturing of this relationship are being distracted and dismayed by your questioning concerning these grubby deaths. Surely you can see that it behoves you and your colleagues to tread very lightly and carefully in this area and I must insist that you do so. If we receive any further complaints, we shall be insisting on other, more sensitive officers, being given charge of the investigations."

Merlin stared hard at the polished grain of the table. He was conscious of a low bubbling noise which he thought might be his blood boiling.

"I hope I have made the Foreign Office's view clear. I think that will be all now gentlemen."

"May I ask, sir, if you were in direct touch with the American Ambassador about this matter?"

"All you need to know, Merlin, is that the Ambassador communicated his displeasure to us, and on the basis of that I contacted the Assistant Commissioner."

"Does that mean you spoke yourself to Mr Kennedy about the matter?"

"That is neither here nor there and I don't care for your tone. You're a foreigner, aren't you? So my contacts tell me. You should learn to do things the English way and know your place."

"I am British born as it happens, but that's certainly neither here nor there. Would I be right in thinking that the complaint you received was not made directly by the Ambassador but by a Mr Arthur Norton?"

Douglas flushed and patted the table.

"Do you know that gentleman, sir?"

"I know most of the senior diplomats at the American Embassy, that's part of my job."

"And would it have been Mr Norton who complained? You see he is the only person at the Embassy with whom we have had any difficulty. And we had that difficulty because he didn't want to answer our questions and was most unhelpful. We believe Mr Norton is hiding something which bears on the murders. And if we believe that, it is our job to investigate him further. And, in all the circumstances, I can't see that that is going to prejudice our national security in any way."

Douglas abruptly rose to his feet. "You're a fool, Inspector. What can a little plod like you understand of our national security? These victims you talk about were people of no importance. Their deaths are meaningless – a tart from the back of beyond and…" Douglas paused to remove a speck of something from his eye, "and an ignorant oik from the valleys. Hardly worth the effort, are they? You must have more important things to do. I really must advise you and Sergeant Bridges, for your own good if for nothing else, to leave Mr Norton alone."

Merlin counted to ten before lightly brushing the Sergeant's shoulders with his hand. "I think we've finished. Let's get along."

They followed Douglas into the corridor. "Thank you, sir. A pleasure to meet you."

"Tread carefully, Chief Inspector. That's my strong advice to you."

"I'll bear that in mind, sir, but it's my job to catch the murderers of these poor, unimportant people and do that job to the best of my ability for as long as I'm allowed to do so."

"Very well. Good day to you both." Douglas glided away but, as he was about to disappear around a corner, Merlin called out. Douglas' head turned. "Do you know a Mr Edward Fraser? Works here, I believe."

"He's a colleague of mine."

"Close colleague is he?"

"He's in my department. What the hell is it to you?"

"Perhaps nothing, sir. Thank you again."

* * *

Jimmy Reardon picked his way cautiously along Dean Street

towards Soho Square. Although a thaw seemed to have set in, there were still odd pockets of ice and snow on the pavements. Sure enough he slipped on an icy puddle and landed hard on his backside. He struggled to his feet and leaned against a lampost to catch his breath. His right hand had been grazed and he mopped up the blood with his handkerchief.

"Lucky there, Mr Reardon. You could have done yourself some real damage. Alright are you?" A fat face under a bowler hat a size or three too large peered up at him.

"Yeah," Reardon grunted. "I'm alright, ta."

"Good. Well I'll be seeing you soon, no doubt."

Reardon watched the little man waddle down the street carrying, with difficulty, a bulging briefcase almost half his size. Close to the corner, the man turned into a doorway and disappeared.

With a deep sigh, Reardon resumed his journey, crossing into Soho Square then turning right onto Oxford Street. Narrowly avoiding a taxi, he crossed over then went left onto Tottenham Court Road. A little way along, he turned into a narrow alleyway. Before reaching the alley's dead end, he halted outside a small shop window in which an easel and artists' palette were displayed. "Myerson's Artistic Supplies" was painted in fading black letters on the window.

He banged on the small black door next to the window, shuffling his feet impatiently until he heard the sound of bolts being unfastened. A crack of light spilled out over the cobbled pavement.

"Whaddya want? Who is it?"

"It's me – Jimmy. Morrie sent me round to pick up that stuff. Come on. I almost broke my neck to get here, so now I'm here, let me in."

The door opened slowly and a head appeared. It was covered with a thick thatch of dark black hair parted down the middle. Two small, black eyes peered out over a bulbous, red nose and a chin thick with grey stubble. "Ah, it's you. Sorry." Bernie Myerson's rasping voice still clearly revealed his Middle

European origins but the half a lifetime spent in London had also made its mark.

He opened the door wide and beckoned Reardon in. "I was just having a late lunch. Want some?"

The shop was dark and poky. A bulb at the far end lit a shop counter on which sat a half-empty bottle of Bell's Whisky, a glass and a plate of bread and cheese. On a wall was a poster advertising the virtues of a brand of paintbrushes against a backdrop of snow-topped mountains and woodland. Opposite were dusty shelves containing a variety of unmarked boxes.

Myerson led his guest to a tall stool at the counter. "Sorry to hear about Johnny. Such a nice young man. And talented too. Who could have done such a thing?" The two men shook their heads and shrugged their shoulders. "Do you want anything? Piece of cheese? Glass of whisky?" Myerson went behind the counter and poured himself a shot. "To Johnny. God rest him." He raised the glass and downed it. "I'm sure I've got another glass somewhere." He rummaged beneath him and produced another tumbler. "Eh, voilà. Fancy a bit of rat poison, my old friend, yes?"

A large measure was poured and as Reardon drank, he examined the cheese and noticed several green spots around the edges. "I'll pass on the cheese. I had a pie at the club before I left."

Myerson refilled his own glass and gulped it down again. Reardon glanced around at the empty shelves and shabby surroundings. "Business booming, I see."

Myerson took a large bite out of the slab of cheese and chewed it noisily. "The shop? The shop don't matter. You know that. I've got better ways of making money."

"Have you got the latest stuff?"

Myerson nodded as he was overcome by a coughing fit which he brought under control with another shot.

"Shouldn't you go a little easier on that stuff, Bernie?"

"It's like medicine to me, Jimmy, the booze. Don't do me any harm."

"If you say so. Where is the stuff then?" Reardon set his empty glass down.

"I was up till late finishing it off. Only got to bed at three. Another nice piece of work if I say so myself. I've got it downstairs. Hang on a tick." Myerson disappeared through a shabby brown curtain. Reardon heard his shoes clattering down the stairs and then heard him wheezing and coughing as he climbed back up. He re-emerged with a large brown envelope in his hand.

"Got the money?"

Reardon drew a bunch of shiny white fivers from his coat. Myerson's eyes lit up as he reached out. "Uh, uh." Reardon held the money above him.

"I'll check first, thank you."

"Be my guest."

Reardon opened the envelope, pulled out the contents and, after a quick glance, put them back in. "Looks satisfactory."

"Good. So give me my money."

The notes were placed in Myerson's clammy hand. "If I were you, Bernie, I wouldn't splash it all out on the booze. You're looking very pasty. All this time in the dark can't be good for you. Take a trip into the country. Get a bit of fresh air."

Myerson carefully counted the money. "It's very good of you to worry about my health but you're looking pretty pasty yourself. All that time in Morrie's dingy club can't be so good for you either. Perhaps we can make up a twosome. Have a weekend by the sea, somewhere. How about it? Brighton, Eastbourne, Margate?"

Reardon rose from his stool and smiled thinly. "Very funny. You take care of yourself. Morrie appreciates your talents, Bernie. I don't think he'd care to have to find someone else because your liver exploded, that's all."

"I'll do my best not to peg out. Wouldn't want Fat Morrie to be put out in any way, would I?"

"I'll probably be back for that other stuff tomorrow, alright?"

"It'll be here, don't worry." A dog barked in the distance as Myerson showed his visitor out.

* * *

Merlin had been back in his office for an hour, mulling over the meeting with Douglas. He'd met quite a few toffee-nosed twerps in his time but he thought Douglas took the prize. The office, which was normally under-heated, seemed stuffy today for some reason and he was struggling to open one of the windows.

"Can I help you with that?"

Merlin gave one last heave to the window and it juddered open a few inches. "No thanks, Sergeant. Now off you go and get the box containing Joan Harris' stuff from the basement."

As the door closed, Merlin fell back wearily into his chair, swung his legs up onto the desk and threw a couple of Fishermen's Friends between his lips. Whatever work had been going on at the top of County Hall had stopped. If new gun emplacements had been installed he couldn't see them from his position. Perhaps the camouflaging techniques employed by Civil Defence were improving at last.

He closed his eyes for a few seconds before reaching for his notes of the previous day. He took up a pen and added Freddie Douglas to his list of names. It was obvious that Arthur Norton had used his influence to get Douglas to complain to the Assistant Commissioner. Although he was a strange kind of non-career diplomat, he was still a diplomat and would naturally know people like Douglas. The coincidences were, however, piling up – Norton knew the two victims, Norton was a regular customer at Morrie's club, Norton knew Douglas who worked in the same office as Fraser who, while a suspect in a completely unrelated case, knew Norton and was a customer at Owen's club. It was Owen's club that Joan Harris had visited with Norton and it was for Morrie Owen that Morgan had worked before Owen got him the job with the Ambassador.

The conversation with Douglas replayed in his mind. He had been warned that 'a little plod' like him could have little understanding of 'our national security'. He couldn't see how upsetting an associate of the Ambassador was likely to have any negative impact on America's possible entrance into the war. The Ambassador was doing everything he could to keep America out of the war anyway. Was there something else? Was there some other issue of national security involved which Douglas couldn't spell out?

A disturbance in the corridor alerted him to the return of Bridges who entered, breathing heavily and perspiring, carrying a large cardboard box with the help of a young constable. The box landed heavily on the flooring in front of Merlin's desk.

"Thanks, Tommy." Bridges paused for breath. "You've been a great help."

The young man smiled nervously at Merlin as he went out of the door.

"You need to take a bit more exercise, Sergeant."

"Excuse me, sir. I am perfectly fit. We had to lug that box up five flights of stairs. I'd challenge anyone to do that without getting a bit puffed."

"The constable seemed to manage it."

"Tommy's a cross-country runner. Bit of a champion in Surrey he is."

"Is he now? Never mind. Let's see what we've got. The scientists didn't find much when they dusted for prints, as I recall?

"They did find a few partial prints, apart from Miss Harris' own prints that is. There's a list of what was found right here."

"Partials won't be much use to us unless we find a suspect."

The Sergeant's eyes skimmed down the forensic report. "Says here that they aren't very clear and it will be difficult to prove a match."

"We'll just have to rely on old-fashioned detective work

then. Let's get everything out. Is this the only box?"

"I left the box with her clothing downstairs."

"I see. We'll have a look at that later, although I think the main point of interest there is that some of it was very smart – a friend must have bought her some expensive outfits or given her the money to get them." Moments later, Merlin stood gazing sadly at the pile of objects set out on the floor, the pathetic remnants of a short life. There were the china cats and dogs which had been on her mantelpiece and the little clock which had been next to the modest book collection. Merlin reached over Joan's collection of toiletries to pick up her edition of *Huckleberry Finn*.

"Here's the inscription I mentioned to you."

"Beg pardon, sir. This is a bit of a bugger."

The Sergeant was struggling with the lock mechanism of a small black box which Merlin didn't recall seeing before.

"It's a book inscription to J, presumably Joan – it says 'To J. Hope you enjoy it as much as I do. Good luck with everything. Your friend J'."

Suddenly the black box snapped open and something shiny spilled out on to the carpet. Bridges picked it up and whistled as it caught the light – a delicate gold necklace on which hung a small pendant encasing a single pearl.

Merlin took it and held it up to the light. "I'm not an expert but I'd say this was a superior piece of workmanship. There's some fine design work here around the edge of the pendant. These swirling floral designs are quite special, I think. Quite unusual. No name on the box, I suppose?"

"No."

"Shouldn't be impossible to track down where this came from, given its quality and singular nature."

"No, sir."

Merlin carefully placed the necklace back in its box and sifted through various other unilluminating objects before coming at last to a small package of papers, wrapped in green ribbon.

There were four letters, a couple of bills, a theatre ticket stub and an advertisement for a book sale cut out from a newspaper. The ticket stub was for the performance of a revue at the St James' Theatre dated Friday November 17th 1939. "Jack Buchanan. One of your favourites, Sergeant." Merlin turned to the advertisement. "'A Hatchards sale. Classics at bargain prices'. Determined to improve herself, wasn't she?"

One of the bills was from a Dr Jones. Dated January 3rd 1940, it referred to services rendered by way of consultation and tests and was for the sum of five shillings and six pence. There was a signature at the bottom confirming receipt. The other was from the Grand Hotel, Brighton. It covered the cost of a double room for the night of Saturday 18th November 1939. The bill listed the room charge and various meals and drinks consumed. It was charged to a Mr and Mrs Brown. "Looks to me like she had a wonderful weekend. Theatre on Friday night followed by a champagne-filled weekend at Brighton's best hotel. Knocked someone back thirty quid."

"Wonder why she kept the bill?"

"A souvenir? The theatre ticket likewise?"

The first of the letters wasn't dated but the envelope was postmarked December 4th. The scrawl was not easily decipherable nor was the signature at the bottom. At first he thought that the signature was Joseph. On second thoughts, he thought it might be Janet. "What do you think?"

Bridges turned the letter sideways. "Looks more like Jumbo to me."

"Thank you. Most helpful. I don't think that the author of this scrawl was the author of the *Huckleberry Finn* inscription." He made a second attempt at reading the letter. "I think it's probably from a sister or brother – just a family letter updating Joan with developments in Gloucestershire."

The next letter was Joan's original letter of appointment from the Embassy. The terms and conditions warned that only the highest standards of behaviour would be acceptable in her employment. It was signed by Miss Edgar.

The third letter was in an unstamped plain envelope addressed simply to "Joan". Inside was a short undated note on plain notepaper. Merlin read it out: "'Will see you in Piccadilly (next to Eros) at 6pm. Looking forward to a wonderful time. J x'."

There was no envelope for the final letter which was crumpled and torn. Most of the top half was missing. "I think the signature's the same as on the doctor's receipt, Sergeant. And what's this – 'nancy test – negative'?" Merlin held the letter up to the light. "Looks like the bill for five and six was for a pregnancy test from this Dr Jones – a test that proved negative." He passed the letter to Bridges.

"Perhaps this was the letter Miss Foster saw her crying over?"

"You'd think a letter like this to an unmarried girl would be a source of relief rather than unhappiness." Merlin closed his eyes and rubbed his forehead. "But what if… what if Miss Harris had set her heart on someone – 'J' perhaps – and hoped she was pregnant as one way to catch and secure him?"

Bridges shrugged his shoulders. "Maybe."

Merlin rose slowly and stiffly to his feet. "We have to find out who 'J' is. I think this necklace might be our best bet. You'll need to check out all the major jewellers. And we must get on and identify this Dr Jones. There's no address on the invoice, which isn't very helpful. And we need to check out the hotel in Brighton." Merlin sucked in his breath, then exhaled slowly. "I wish to God we had some extra hands. We also need to get some background on Morrie Owen from Vice, assuming they've got any. We need to check out who owns the mews house where Johnny took Kathleen, and I'd like to put a tail on Owen and Norton. Then there's all the other stuff I'm meant to be keeping an eye on."

"Can't you speak to the A.C.?"

"I'll try. Meanwhile, let's start picking off the tasks. It's too late to start with the jewellery shops. You can start that tomorrow. Perhaps you can also check out how many Dr Joneses there are in West London. I'll have a chat with Jacko Niven in Vice. See what he knows about Owen. And where the hell is that Morgan forensic report? We're supposed to have it by now."

CHAPTER 10

Arthur Norton jerked awake. There was a banging sound somewhere. For a moment he thought it must be morning and he could hear the garbage collectors at work. He found his reading glasses and in the weak light of the bedside lamp saw from the alarm clock that it was a quarter to one. His senses gradually returned to him. A wave of pungent perfume rippled over him. He could see items of female clothing hanging from the bedposts and he remembered that he was not alone.

A pretty head poked itself around the bedroom door. "Got any milk, darling?"

"It's in the icebox."

"In the what?"

A petite naked body followed the head through the door.

"In the refrigerator. Next to the sink, Edie. It keeps things cold."

"Oh, I thought that was your boiler or something." Edie ran back out and reappeared with two glasses of milk. "I had a dreadful thirst. Must have been that champagne you poured into me. You had quite a bit too, so I thought you might fancy a glass."

"No, no milk for me thanks."

Edie shrugged and slid back into bed as Norton took a bottle of Johnny Walker from his bedside cabinet. "Fancy something to put a bit of zap in it?"

She grimaced and shook her head before drinking half of her milk. "Never seen one of those refriderators, or whatever you call them, before. Wonderful. The milk is lovely and cool."

Norton's left leg brushed against hers. "I was lucky to find you again. I thought the policeman might have scared you off that pitch."

"You'll find me most nights in the Square. Coppers ain't normally too fussy." She finished her drink and wiped her lips. "I'll be off now then. Ta very much." Norton rolled over and put his arm across her breasts.

"Don't go yet. How about some more fun?"

"Sorry darling. You've paid me a couple of quid and you've had a couple of quid's worth. I'm tired now and I want to get back home. It's been very nice but I'm off." She tried to get up but Norton tightened his grip.

"Sweetheart. Money's not a problem. If you want more I've got plenty. Come on. Don't be a spoilsport." His arm moved down her body and he stroked her left thigh. She sighed with resignation. "Alright then, lover boy. I'll stay another half-an-hour but it'll cost you another two quid."

His hand slid to the crinkly dark bush of hair between her legs.

"Hang on! Money first!"

"OK. OK." Norton withdrew his hand and got out of the bed. Staring down at his flabby chest, he became self-conscious and threw on his dressing gown. He went to his wardrobe and rummaged around in his clothing. As he did so he realised he was drunker than he had thought. He stumbled and fell clumsily to the floor. The wardrobe teetered, dislodging a pile of papers and a large cardboard box from its top.

"Are you alright, darling?"

Norton rubbed his knee and winced. "Yeah, I'll live."

Edie knelt down beside him, her breasts swinging freely beneath her as she leaned forward to pat his arm. "Let me give you a hand." She turned and reached out for some of the papers which had fluttered under the bed. She pulled back abruptly and screamed as something scurried out and disappeared under a chest of drawers behind them. "Mice! Fancy having mice in Mayfair, darling. I'd speak to your landlord if I was you." Edie recovered herself and settled back on her haunches, shivering. "I'm going back to bed. It's a bit parky here. I'm sure your maid can sort this lot out in the morning." As she rose she glanced at the cardboard box whose contents had spilled out over the carpet. She knelt down again to look more closely and giggled. "You naughty boy, what's this little box of tricks then?"

"It's nothing. Nothing. Now up you get." Norton stood and helped her to her feet before closing up the box and returning it to the top of the wardrobe.

"Don't worry darling. Your secret's safe with me. Got to have a broad mind in this business haven't I?"

Norton's dressing-gown cord had loosened in all the commotion and her eyes fell on his shrivelled manhood, poking out from a mound of greying hair. She giggled again and looked away.

"Come on, Edie. Here's a fiver. Back to business. For that we can have a really good time, can't we?"

"What did you have in mind?" She found her handbag and deposited the crisp white note.

He let his dressing-gown fall to the floor and pulled her on to the bed. "How about something a bit different?"

He turned her on to her front and slapped her backside hard.

"Oi. What are you up to? That hurt!"

"Pain is sometimes the same as pleasure, sweetheart. We've done the normal boring stuff. Now we're going to be a bit more adventurous."

"But..."

He clamped his hand over her mouth. "There now. Be a good girl. I've paid my money and now I want my fun."

* * *

A string of puffy white clouds sailed sedately over the L.C.C. offices, the sun peeping through and occasionally dappling the wintry river with its rays. This agreeable prospect failed to make much impression on Merlin. He had had a frustrating morning. His first port of call had been the residence of Stewart's Polish friend. After rising early to try and make sure that he caught the girl at home, he found only her flatmate, a dark-haired leggy girl with an impenetrable accent. As far as he could eventually understand, her name was Maria, she hadn't seen Sonia since the previous morning and she had no idea where she was. He had hung around at the end of the mews for a while hoping that Sonia might return, but no luck.

Back at the Yard, Merlin had sent up a request to the A.C. for additional manpower. This request had been refused in a brusque note within minutes of being submitted. Sergeant Bridges was out, perhaps for several more hours, checking jewellers. Merlin's friend, Chief Inspector Niven in Vice, had been seconded to the British Expeditionary Force on a special investigative mission and the Vice officer he had been able to speak to had not been helpful with information on Morrie Owen. On the plus side, the Morgan forensic report had at last arrived on his desk and Bridges had managed to identify several Dr Joneses practising in West London. He looked up and returned the crotchety gaze of Van Gogh's Dr Gachet, wondering whether he had any option but to work through the list himself.

Just after Merlin had finished the rather stale ham sandwich he'd bought himself for lunch, Bridges returned from his travels and collapsed wearily into the chair facing him.

"I didn't know there were so many jewellers' shops in London. I've been just about everywhere. No luck in Hatton Garden, in Bond Street, Regent Street, Oxford Street or in Chelsea. Finally I had a look in Kensington. Found a little jewellers about half-way up Kensington Church Street. Name of Baldwins." Bridges stretched out his legs and bent forward to rub his calves. "There was a nice young lady behind the counter. Pretty girl – looked a bit like Iris in fact. Anyway, this girl, Angela Goddard her name was, she recognised the necklace straight away. After some umming and aahing and talk about client confidentiality and all that, and after I'd told her this might be vital information in a murder case, she told me who bought it."

The torpor which often afflicted Merlin in the early afternoon suddenly lifted. "Who?"

"The necklace was bought on an account held by the American Embassy."

"On a general account or a named account?"

"On a named account, as it seems."

Merlin looked eagerly across the desk. "And?"

"It was in the name of the Ambassador himself."

Merlin stood up and walked around the desk. "Did Miss Morris deal directly with the Ambassador when she sold the necklace?"

"No. She explained that it was normal practice for an Embassy employee to visit the shop, pick out items of interest, take them back to the Embassy on approval and then confirm any purchases, or return any unwanted items, in person at the shop."

"How was the account settled?"

"Sometimes cash, sometimes by cheque, at the end of the month."

"And the account covering this necklace?"

"By cheque, sir."

"And the name on the cheque?"

"Joseph Kennedy."

Merlin returned to his chair and rubbed his forehead slowly.

"The employee. Was it the same employee every time?"

"Yes. She says he was dressed in a chauffeur's uniform and remembers his name as Mr Morgan."

A shiver went down Merlin's back. "This is some can of worms we are opening here."

There was a firm knock at the door and both men tensed. A young, uniformed officer stood at the threshold, his features looking vaguely familiar to Merlin.

"You remember Tommy, sir. Constable Cole. Helped me bring Miss Harris' boxes up yesterday."

"Ah. Yes. The cross-country runner. What can we do for you, Constable?"

Cole edged nervously into the room. "A.C. sent me, sir. He asked Sergeant Miller to find someone for you. Sergeant picked me. Said you were short-handed and needed some help with your murders."

Merlin's slightly startled expression swiftly gave way to a smile of pleasure. "Wonder of wonders. I don't know why Mr Gatehouse changed his mind so quickly but I'm not going to complain. Welcome."

Cole grasped Merlin's extended hand and gave him a lop-sided grin.

* * *

Daylight was fading rapidly as Johnson drove his car up the driveway of Pelham Court. He drew to a halt before two classical stone columns, beyond which stood the main doorway to the house. He got out of the car and filled his lungs with the crisp country air. He had read up a little on the Pelhams before his visit and knew from one of the books he'd got out of the library that Pelham Court dated from the late eighteenth century and had been designed by a protégé of John Adam's, although the architect's name now escaped him. Whatever his name, he'd done a good job. The grand and stylish building soared above him. To the right and left he could see the elegant wings of the house extending into the distance. Behind him to his right, acres of manicured lawns rolled away down towards the Thames.

He nervously stroked his bare upper lip as he scrunched his way over the gravel. A long, red rope dangled beneath a lamp to the side of the door and after a moment's hesitation he pulled it.

"Can I help you, sir?"

"Detective Inspector Johnson, to see Lord and Lady Pelham. I called earlier. I believe they are expecting me."

The short, fat, white-haired man in tails who had appeared at the door retreated a little and waved him in. "If you would be so kind as to wait here sir, I'll inform her ladyship that you have arrived."

The servant soon returned and ushered him across the vast, chequered, marble floor into a long wood-panelled drawing room. A blazing log fire crackled away at one end of the room. He was led to a chair close to the fire, and relieved of his overcoat. Darkness had now fallen and he could see his reflection in the French windows. He looked tired. Above the fire was a portrait of a fierce-looking man in a white wig. The subject, according to a plate at the bottom, was Henry, the first Lord Pelham 1651-1727. Johnson's eyes travelled down and over the intricate red and black geometric patterns of an antique rug. He was embarrassed to see that his shoes were dirty and scuffed. His collar itched with the sweat and dirt accumulated over what had been a long day. He felt grubby and out of place in the midst of all this luxury.

"Mr Johnson?" A handsome woman moved elegantly towards him. She held out her hand and smiled warmly before lowering herself gracefully into the other chair by the fire. "Some refreshment perhaps? I am sure you would appreciate something after your drive."

"No – thank you."

Her necklace and earrings sparkled in the firelight as she leaned forward. "So, how can I help you, Inspector?"

"Will Lord Pelham be joining us?"

"I'm sorry, my husband had to go up to town to deal with some urgent business."

"I had hoped to see him as well."

"He's a very busy man and I'm sure I shall be able to provide you with whatever you need."

"Very well. If you'll just bear with me." Johnson rummaged

in his jacket for his notebook and pencil.

"Goodness, Inspector, this is all very formal, isn't it? Whatever can we have done?"

"As I mentioned briefly on the telephone, your ladyship, we are investigating a hit and run case that took place in London just over two weeks ago."

"Indeed, so you said. I cannot for the life of me imagine how you think I can help you."

"Do you know a Mr Edward Fraser?"

"Indeed I do. I have known Edward since he was a child. His parents were good friends of my uncle."

"We have some grounds to think that Mr Fraser's motor car may have been involved in the hit and run."

Lady Pelham's back straightened. "You do surprise me. You are aware no doubt that Edward is a high-ranking diplomat at the Foreign Office."

"Of course."

"And you are suggesting that Edward was involved in this unsavoury incident?"

"There is some evidence, your ladyship."

"This is quite preposterous." The silk of her dress rustled as she leaned back in her chair. Absent-mindedly she toyed with the pearls of her necklace and looked away. "What is it you want to know about Edward?"

"The accident we are investigating took place on the evening of Thursday January 18th. Mr Fraser has told us that he came here to join a house party on the following day, Friday 19th. Can you confirm that?"

A gust of wind rattled the French windows. "You are talking about three weekends ago, I think. Yes, Edward was here then. We had a group of friends to stay. Lord Pelham took some of them out shooting on the Saturday. It was a very agreeable weekend."

"And may I know who was in the rest of the party?"

"Really, Inspector, I don't think that's on. My guests are entitled to their privacy."

"The information will be helpful in corroborating Mr Fraser's story, your ladyship. It could assist in exonerating him. I would be most grateful if you could."

She compressed her lips, shook her head, then sighed. "Very well. I will get Williams to prepare a list of the guests for you."

"Thank you. Could I ask you a little more about Mr Fraser? When he arrived for his weekend visit, can you remember if he said anything about his car?"

"Do you think I am in the habit of discussing motor vehicles with my friends?"

"I don't mean did you have a discussion regarding mechanics. I mean, did his car feature, in any way, in his conversation? Did he say anything about his journey from London?"

A brief flash of recognition crossed her face. "Ah, I see what you're getting at. Edward did mention that he had had an unfortunate accident on his way from town. He said he'd hit an animal of some sort on the road. A deer or a stag or something. Said he'd damaged the car a little."

"Did you see his vehicle, your ladyship?"

"Why on earth would I look at his vehicle?"

"I just wondered."

"Inspector, if Edward says he had an accident and hit an animal, then I'm sure that was the case. And if, somehow or other, in ways I cannot imagine, this accident has somehow got confused with your unfortunate hit and run, please believe me when I tell you that Edward Fraser is not your man. He's a man of utter integrity. Lord Halifax himself has spoken to me in the warmest tones about his talents and personality. You are barking up the wrong tree." She rose from her chair and rang a small bell on a side-table. Williams appeared instantly at the door. "The Inspector will be leaving now. Before he goes, please be so good as to give him a list of the guests invited to our weekend party three weeks ago."

As his car carefully crawled down the unlit drive, Johnson

tried hard to look on the bright side. He had a guest list in his pocket that might well shed further light on the case. The trouble was that the people on the list were powerful and looked after their own. Even if he could prove that Fraser was the guilty man, would the establishment really allow him to be pursued? The more he thought about it, the more pessimistic he became.

* * *

Bridges, having just sent Cole off on his first piece of detective work tailing Morrie Owen, had been summoned by Special Branch at the Houses of Parliament to help deal with some sort of security panic. After numerous interruptions, Merlin had finally settled to read the Morgan forensic report in his office. As he turned the second page, his door opened yet again.

"Ah, Merlin, you're here. Someone I'd like you to meet." A young lady in police uniform followed the A.C. through the door. "This is Chief Inspector Merlin, my dear. Frank, this is my niece Claire, or rather I should say, W.P.C. Robinson."

He recognised the girl from the picture on the A.C.'s desk. She was prettier in the flesh. Her blonde hair had been cut short and it suited her. She had full lips, a beauty spot just below her neat little nose and deep brown eyes. He held out his hand.

"Pleased to meet you, Chief Inspector." Claire Robinson enunciated her words with crystal clarity. She could have been a BBC newsreader had they allowed women to do the job.

"Claire has just finished at Hendon Police College. I wasn't expecting her to arrive so soon but she's here now, and as you are so pressed I thought you might appreciate another pair of hands. And it would be good experience for Claire of course."

"You've already sent me another pair of hands – Constable Cole."

"Yes, yes. I know that but then I had this idea about Claire. Surely you're not going to complain if I give you two additional officers for your team?"

Clearly he had no option. "Of course not. Glad to have you, Constable. Let me fill you in."

* * *

Tommy Cole shivered in a doorway over the road from The Blue Angel. He was wearing his one and only suit and a thin overcoat. He wished he had his uniform. Although of rough material, it was thick and warm, unlike his suit. He did have warmer casual clothes but Bridges had told him to dress as well as possible in case his surveillance duties required him to go anywhere smart. He wore his black tie, normally reserved for funeral use, as Bridges had rejected his only other neckwear, a salmon pink number which had been much appreciated by a girl he'd met at the Hammersmith Palais the weekend before.

He had been outside the club since four o'clock and had just heard Big Ben chiming seven in the distance. He was bored stiff. When Sergeant Miller had picked him out to help Merlin and Bridges he had been excited. He had always wanted to be in the CID. However, three hours of tedium in a freezing, dark, Soho street, following a couple of hours outside Morrie Owen's Earl's Court flat, had dampened his enthusiasm. As he understood it, the club wasn't likely to open for another three hours, so it would be ages before he would have anyone or anything to observe. He shuffled his feet to keep warm and began to feel pangs of hunger. Then someone came out of the club. Cole dithered for a moment before setting off in pursuit. He couldn't see much but he knew that the figure was not Owen. Having seen the clubowner in the light of day, it was clear to him that Owen didn't walk anywhere. When Owen had been picked up at his flat, the driver was a tall, thin man with hunched shoulders and big ears, a description which fitted the person he was following. If he was right, Owen clearly wasn't going anywhere and there could be little harm in following the driver on the off-chance that he went somewhere interesting. Apart from anything else, following this bloke would help his blood to circulate again.

A blaze of light briefly flashed out from one of the shops in Dean Street and provided solid confirmation of the identity of the man he was shadowing. Cole felt his heart pounding as he crossed Soho Square, a discreet distance behind Owen's sidekick.

*　*　*

Reardon turned off the Tottenham Court Road and walked to the end of the alley. There was no sign of life in 'Myerson's Artistic Supplies' but, as he knew, there was nothing unusual about that.

"You better come in." The stubble on Myerson's chin was a day thicker. He wore the same shabby clothes as before and held a full whisky bottle.

"Celebrating again, Bernie?"

"Just having my dinner, aren't I?" A large slab of cheese, this time looking reasonably fresh, lay on the counter.

"Do you ever have any grub other than cheese and whisky?"

Myerson picked his nose and chuckled, revealing stained teeth and rancid gums. "I vary my diet a lot, thank you, my friend. Some days I have cheese and gin, and on special occasions, like Hanukkah, I have cheese and brandy. It's very good for you, you know."

"I'll take your word for it. Have you got the other stuff?"

"Yeh. Gimme a sec." Myerson disappeared downstairs as before and returned with a large brown envelope. Reardon looked at the contents, grimaced, and handed over a wedge of notes.

"Quite artistic really, don't you think?"

"Very. They'll soon be comparing you with Michelangelo, no doubt."

Myerson snorted, spraying the counter with small specks of cheddar. "You're quite an educated man really, aren't you, Jimmy? Beats me why an educated man like you works for a pig like Morrie."

With a speed belying his years, Reardon reached over and grasped Myerson's shirt collar tightly. He pulled him spluttering and choking back across the counter. "It don't do to go calling my boss names. I may not like him much myself but whatever he is, he's my boss, and if you treat him without respect it's the same as treating me without respect." He relaxed his grip.

Myerson regained his footing, spat something green on to the floor and grasped his whisky bottle. "No need to resort to violence, you know. I was only wondering why an intelligent chap like you worked for Morrie, that's all. No offence intended."

"Let's just say I make a living out of it, and leave it at that."

"Fine, fine. No hard feelings." Myerson deposited the money in a drawer behind him.

Reardon straightened his tie, adjusted the buttons of his coat and, with a short wave, left Myerson to his meal.

"What you looking at, mate?" The drunk lay sprawled on his back, staring up at Reardon in the light of the open pub door where a brawny barman stood surveying his handiwork.

Reardon ignored him and hurried by. He crossed Soho Square and entered Dean Street. At the end he stopped at a shop door and rang the bell. A chubby little man wearing a white coat and an oversized bowler appeared, smiling weakly. "Come on in. You could've come a little earlier. The wife and I are just about to have something to eat."

"Have you got it?"

"Yes, come with me. Almost came a cropper on the ice,

didn't you, yesterday? Better take more care – we're none of us getting any younger." He led Reardon through the shop to a door at the back.

Reardon waited at the door and enjoyed the appetising smells of a roast dinner as the little man disappeared down a corridor. Reardon heard a woman's voice. He couldn't hear what she was saying but caught the peevish tone. The man returned with a white cloth bag tied with string. "Here you are."

"The usual quality, is it?"

The man removed his hat and scratched his bald head. "Good as ever. Got the dosh?"

Reardon held the bag to his nose, then handed over some notes. The little man counted them carefully before stuffing them into his coat pocket.

"Bloody peanuts. Hardly covers my expenses." The man looked sourly at Reardon, who shrugged his shoulders. "If you don't mind, I'm going to eat my supper now. Nice doing business with you, as always."

* * *

The bar of the Carlton Club was beginning to clear as people made their way into dinner. Douglas was sitting at a corner table reading *The Times* when Norton hurried over to him. "Sorry, Freddie. I got tied up with something at the Embassy."

Freddie Douglas cast a languid eye over Norton's flushed face. "Glad you could make it, Arthur. I'm sure whatever delayed you was important."

Norton sat down and mopped his glistening forehead with a handkerchief. "Yes, yes. It was. What's that you're drinking?"

Douglas swirled the amber liquid in his glass. "This, my friend, is a fine twenty year old Balvenie. You should try it. It's a malt whisky as smooth and refined as Mr Chamberlain's frock coat."

Norton nodded and Douglas signalled to a waiter. "Late night again, Arthur?"

"No, not really. I think I've got a touch of flu or something."

Douglas raised an eyebrow.

"No, really, I think I do have a bug of some sort."

The waiter returned with Norton's drink. "Well, here's to your rapid recovery." The men chinked their glasses.

"All fine at the Embassy?"

"Yes, I think so."

"And did you manage to pass on that little message?"

"I did."

"What did the Ambassador say?"

"Well, I haven't actually spoken to the Ambassador myself."

Douglas drew hard on his cigarette and blew the smoke fiercely out of his nostrils. "How did you pass the message then?"

"I couldn't get hold of the Ambassador at any of his residencies. I tried Palm Beach, I tried Hyannis, I tried New York, I tried Washington. Given the urgency I decided I should send him a cable."

Two elderly men nearby burst into laughter. Douglas glanced at them with distaste. "Wasn't that a little bit risky?"

"I sent the cable through official channels and had it encoded at the Embassy."

"Hmm. And who did the encoding for you, may I ask?"

"A guy called Kent, Tyler Kent. I insisted on everything being highly confidential, of course."

"Kent. I know of him. Should be alright. I understand he's a good friend of Major St. John." Douglas stubbed out his cigarette and lit a fresh one from a small, gold case. "When would you expect to get a message back from the Ambassador?"

"The message went off last night. I suppose I could get a response at any time. Then again, perhaps the Ambassador will simply act without acknowledging receipt of the message."

"That would not be terribly satisfactory as I'd like to be able to report back on developments."

"Don't worry. I'll keep on trying the telephone. I'm sure I'll get through to him eventually."

Douglas drained his glass. "Eventually isn't a very encouraging word, Arthur. However, you will let me know when you speak to him, won't you?"

"Of course, of course."

"Oh, and by the way."

"Yes?"

"I spoke to those jumped-up police officers. I think I got the message through. I doubt you'll be bothered by them again."

"Thank you kindly."

"I do think we should all give The Blue Angel a miss for a while though, don't you?"

"I suppose so. These policemen have got a damned nerve poking around as they have." They heard Douglas' name being called from across the room. "Ah, here's Vivian. We have a dinner engagement, Arthur. I'd better be off. Let me know as soon as there's any news."

Norton watched the two Englishmen leave the room, then asked the waiter for a glass of water. He pondered whether he should have a quiet night for once.

CHAPTER 11

Wednesday February 7th

Through the rising steam Merlin watched a small spider scurrying across the bathroom ceiling. He closed his eyes and slid further down into the water. He had always found the bath a good place to think. Something said the previous night, when the A.C. had cornered him on the stairs as he was heading home, had been playing on his mind. Gatehouse had advised Merlin that he felt he was concentrating too much on Joan Harris' case at the expense of Johnny Morgan's. Merlin had pointed out that the two cases had to be interconnected and that finding Joan Harris' murderer should lead him to Johnny Morgan's. But was this really so? Morgan was Morrie Owen's nephew and who knew what he'd got up to on Owen's behalf before joining the Embassy? Maybe he'd picked up some enemies who had nothing to do with the Harris case. His sympathy was naturally more engaged with the innocent young girl than the lady-killing spiv. He dipped his head under the water and concluded that he should keep a more open mind. If there were parts of Morgan's life which needed to be exposed and sifted, however, he felt they were most likely to emerge from a close scrutiny of Morrie Owen and his activities. He must try and re-read all the paperwork on the cases as well. He had almost fallen asleep at the Yard reading the forensics on Morgan and he hadn't taken it all in. He was sure that there was something he'd come across which had struck him as odd and significant but, when he'd woken up, for the life of him he couldn't dredge it from his memory. He'd have another look at the Harris forensics too. Something might appear in a new light.

His mind floated off briefly and he guiltily conjured up an

image of his family, gathered around the kitchen table, his father pontificating on some literary matter while his mother bustled away at the oven. He could see his twelve-year old self, serious and thoughtful, listening diligently to his father's words while his brother and sister squabbled over the last piece of bread and jam. He thought with a shiver about his brother Charlie fighting in France, and then with a sigh about the family members killed on both sides of the recent conflict in Spain. In Tuesday's post he'd found a letter from his sister Mary who, on a visit to Spain eight years before, had met and married a second cousin, Jorge, and had settled down to raise a family in Galicia. She had lived through all the horrors of the Civil War and had amazingly come through it with her immediate family intact. It was through her that he had learned of the fortunes of his never seen paternal relatives. Mary, or Maria as she had inevitably reverted to in her new life, had recently settled down with her husband to run a small café in a village just outside Corunna. All was apparently well but she was naturally concerned about England's prospects and had written several times to try and encourage Frank to join her in Spain. "We're in Franco's homeland here, the safest part of the country, and there won't be any war here now. Come out and bring Beatrice and Paul. We are not rich but we can get by," she had written again in her latest letter. If only things were so simple, he thought.

He put the flannel over his face. So now he had two new recruits. He had been annoyed at first when the A.C. foisted his niece on him. Having to baby her along was more likely to hinder his investigation than to help it, he'd thought. However, after chatting to her a little, his irritation had faded. She appeared to be a forthright and sensible girl. She'd passed out top of her year at the College and had made a point of saying she expected no special favours because of who her uncle was. She had volunteered and emphasised that she wouldn't be discussing any of her work for Merlin with her uncle. He'd set her on to sifting the Dr Joneses. She certainly was a pretty thing and brightened up the office. And Cole was undoubtedly enthusiastic.

Reluctantly he pulled himself out of the bath. He picked up his watch. It was half past seven. Time to have another go at the Polish girl.

* * *

It was just after eight when he turned the car off Baker Street and parked outside the mews. He walked over the cobbles to the little pink house and rang the bell. This time he was in luck. A pale face peeped nervously out of the door.

He could see why Jack Stewart was impressed. Saucer-like blue eyes stared out at Merlin over a perfectly designed nose and full lips. A few brown freckles were scattered evenly over both cheeks. The girl was wearing a towel over her head but a few wisps of tawny auburn hair peeked out and trailed down over her ears.

"Can I help you?" The accent was strong but not impenetrable like her flatmate's.

"Sorry to bother you so early. Detective Chief Inspector Merlin. I was hoping you might be able to answer a few questions for me." He waved his identity card in front of her.

The girl tensed. "I have done nothing wrong."

"I'm sure you haven't but I have reason to believe you might be able to help us in connection with a case which we are investigating. It's quite straightforward, I assure you."

"Very well. Come in. I am afraid I am not dressed yet." She tugged on the belt of a white dressing gown which closely hugged the contours of her body.

He followed her into a cramped living room. A small kitchen area led off to the right and he could see piles of dirty dishes spilling out from the sink. The girl disappeared up some stairs at the back and Merlin sat down in a small, white armchair and leafed through an old magazine he found on the bamboo table in front of him.

The girl re-emerged wearing a bright blue dress. Her thick, coppery hair tumbled down attractively over her shoulders. She removed a lipstick from a small bag on the table and carefully applied it in front of a small mirror. Finally, satisfied with her work, she sat down, placing a cigarette between her now deep red lips. "Sorry. Would you like one?"

Merlin declined.

"I am useless without my morning cigarette." She shrugged and flicked her hair out of her eyes.

"I won't take up too much of your time. Could you tell me your name and how long you have been in England?" Merlin had a brief, enticing glimpse of black suspender as she leaned back in her chair. He felt a part of him which had been dormant for some time exhibit a spark of life. "My name is Sonia Sieczko. I have been in England for just over a year." Merlin looked puzzled. "That's S.I.E.C.Z.K.O, Sieczko."

He wrote the name down. "And what brought you to England?"

"Huh! What brought me here? What do you think? Mr Hitler brought me here."

"I'm sorry?"

"I am Jewish, or to be strictly accurate, half-Jewish, although that makes no difference to them. Poland has never been a good place for Jews at the best of times. With that maniac Hitler rattling his, how do you say, swords at Poland – "

She pronounced the "w" in "swords", rather charmingly, Merlin thought. "I think the word would be sabres."

"Yes, well, with Hitler rattling his sabres at Poland, I thought I would not like to stay for his war."

"May I ask on what basis you, er…?"

"I have a proper visa, you want to look at it? I have relatives here. They live in Manchester. I had no problems. They arranged it all."

"And what brought you to London from Manchester?"

She leaned forward to flick ash into a heavy, black ashtray.

"Money brought me to London. Isn't it money which brings everyone to London?"

"Not necessarily, Miss Seeshko."

"It's pronounced with a 'Ch' not a 'Sh' – Seechko, you see." Sonia laughed and threw her hair back.

Merlin shrugged apologetically. "Do you have a job?"

"I work in a shop. Swan and Edgar. You know it I am sure. In Picca …"

"dilly, yes, I know it."

"I work in the ladies clothing department."

"Does it pay well?"

"Well enough."

"Do you have any other jobs?"

"What do you mean?"

"Our information is that you work in a club at night – a club in Soho called The Blue Angel."

Sonia looked coolly at Merlin. Her eyes narrowed. "And who has given you such information?"

"I'm afraid I can't reveal our sources. That information is correct, though, isn't it?"

She stubbed out her cigarette and glanced at her nails. "What of it? I am a poor Polish girl and must do what I can to survive."

"I'm really not concerned with how you make your living. I just need to ask you about someone who may have been in the club. It is The Blue Angel, isn't it?"

"Yes. I have worked there for a few months. Only one or two nights a week. I have drinks with the men, I get tips."

Despite himself, his right eyebrow rose and she glared back at him. "I don't get big tips for what you are thinking, Mister Policeman. I get good tips for being good company and that's all. I am not a whore, if that's what whoever gave you this information told you. I laugh, I chat, I drink, I go home. And I go home here, alone. Sometimes men ask but I always say no. You can ask any of the other girls there!"

Merlin raised his hands defensively.

"You can ask the owner. That fat man is always asking me to go off with customers and I refuse. It is because of this I haven't been for the past week. You ask him, that animal." She bit her lip and seemed close to tears.

"I'm sure that what you tell me is correct and I never had any intention of insulting you. To be frank, however, what you get up to at The Blue Angel is not really my concern."

Her temper cooled and she relaxed back into her chair.

"Anyway. To get to the real point of my visit." He produced the crumpled Harris family photograph and passed it to her.

"If you could look at the rather pretty girl in the middle of this group, I would be interested to know if you ever saw her in the club."

Sonia's face became a picture of concentration. She held the picture close. "Yes, I think I have seen this girl."

"You have?"

"Perhaps three or four times."

"At the club?"

"At the club and elsewhere."

"And elsewhere? Hmm. Please tell me first about the club."

"She came every time in a party of men. I don't know if she was working when she was with the party, if you understand me, but I only ever saw her with such a party."

"And who was in the party?"

"I do not think it was exactly the same group every time but one of the men was the same each time. He is an American who has been in the club many times when I have been there. He is a loud, pompous man who drinks too much and is rude to all the girls."

"Did you catch his name?"

She closed her eyes. "Arthur, I think. Yes, Arthur. I sat with his party once but I could tell he was a pig and left. The owner was very unhappy but I said I would only sit with people who were, how do you say it, polite and who were gentlemen. For this reason also I was not very popular with the fat man."

"Do you remember any other names?"

"I can remember two or three English men who were very well-groomed, is that the right word? I cannot remember their names. And there was a large one who was nervous and laughed too loudly. I'm sorry but apart from that I can't remember anything."

"Can you remember anything particular about the girl?"

"Not much. She was very pretty and did not say a lot. She did not look happy when she visited the club. She did look happy the other time I saw her, though."

"When was that?"

"I think that would have been at Quaglino's. I was taken for dinner there in, I think, November or December. She sat at a table near us. I only noticed her because I recognised her from the club."

"Do you remember who she was with?"

She shook her head.

"Was she with this fellow Arthur from the club?"

"Possibly. But I do not think so."

"Perhaps another older man?"

"I couldn't really see the man. He was just out of sight behind a pillar. It might have been an older man. I can't really say. What I can remember is that she was laughing and happy."

"And you're certain you can remember nothing about her companion?"

She smiled at Merlin. "I was more interested in the man I was with, Inspector."

"Of course. Do you mind telling me who that was?"

"A friend called Jack Stewart." She rummaged in her make-up bag. "Here is his card. I don't know whether he noticed more than me."

"I'll be sure to follow that up. I think that's all for now. Thank you."

"You British police are so much nicer than our Polish ones. I am so glad I came here."

He returned her smile and held out his hand.

Out in the street a milkman was making his deliveries from a rickety old cart. Merlin walked past the ancient carthorse and got into his car. As the engine juddered into life, he heard a shout and saw Sonia running towards him. "Sorry, Mr Merlin. I was thinking as you walked away. You asked me if I thought the man with your Miss Harris was this Arthur fellow and I said not. One reason I thought not was that I couldn't imagine Miss Harris passing a happy time with such a man. But then I think it could have been him because I heard him calling out to a waiter, and he did have an American accent. I am not very good at such things but I know that there are many different American accents and the one I heard was similar to this Arthur's. You know, it was very much, how do you say, an accent from the nose."

"Arthur Norton is from New England. It's in the north-east of the United States."

"Oh?"

"They speak like that in New England, Miss Sieczko. I think what you're telling me is that the man with Miss Harris had a New England accent."

"Yes, then I believe I am." They made way for the milkman who had finished his deliveries to the mews. As the cart passed, the horse looked at them curiously before noisily evacuating his bowels. As they jumped back, Sonia made a face at him and they both burst out laughing.

When their laughter had subsided, Sonia pointed a finger at Merlin. "Something tells me you do not smile enough, Mister Policeman. You should you know. You have a lovely smile."

* * *

"Earth hath not anything to show more fair." Merlin felt rather jolly after his meeting with the beautiful Polish girl and the opening lines of Wordsworth's 'Composed Upon

Westminster Bridge' sprang unbidden to his mind as he looked down on that very bridge. Motor traffic on it was sparse this morning, but crowds of pedestrians swarmed across, heading to their offices and desks. He still found it hard to believe that business life continued almost normally with the spectre of war, death and destruction looming larger every day, but it did. The Stock Market was as active as ever, while cargoes of oil, minerals, rubber and tea, moving largely without interference as yet over the oceans of the world, were traded freely in the commodity markets of the City. Cars, machines and pots and pans continued to be engineered in the factories of the Midlands. Cinemas, having been briefly closed at the outbreak of war, had reopened. Tea and cakes were still freely available at Lyons Corner Houses and cafés everywhere. People were dying natural deaths and being buried, marriages were being celebrated and, with or without benefit of the latter, babies were still being conceived. And, as he knew well, ordinary people continued to commit ordinary crimes, regardless of the latest news from Poland or France.

He returned to his desk and read a note sent to all senior detectives by the A.C. It summarised the increased incidence of various categories of crime since September 1939 and contained an exhortation to increase effort and improve detection. Hey ho. He pushed the note to one side. There was a knock at his door. "Ah, Cole, come on in."

Feeling much more comfortable back in his uniform, Cole led Bridges into the room.

"The Sergeant tells me you had an interesting time last night."

"Did he tell you what happened, sir?"

"No. I wanted to hear it from you. Sit down."

Cole did as he was told, produced his notebook and cleared his throat. "As instructed, I attended Mr Morrie Owen's flat at 32 Palace Gardens, Earl's Court at 3pm. At approximately 3.15 a car arrived and picked Mr Owen up. I followed the car in my own vehicle to its destination just off Shaftesbury Avenue in

Soho. The driver of the car and Mr Owen entered a doorway, which I believe is the entrance to The Blue Angel nightclub. I waited outside the club for three hours and no unusual activity was noted." Cole felt a bead of sweat sliding slowly down the back of his neck.

"At approximately 7pm, Mr Owen's driver came out of the club. I understand from Sergeant Bridges that Mr Owen's driver and general right-hand man is one Jimmy Reardon, so I shall now refer to the driver as Mr Reardon.

"Thinking it unlikely that Mr Owen would go anywhere without his driver, I decided to follow Mr Reardon to his destination. Mr Reardon's first port of call was a closed shop just off the Tottenham Court Road. I couldn't see the name of the shop in the blackout."

"No torch with you?"

"No, sir."

"Remember to carry one with you in future."

"In any event, before reporting in this morning, I went down to Tottenham Court Road to get the shop name – it was called 'Myerson's Artistic Supplies'."

"Well done. That name rings a bell, doesn't it, Sergeant?"

"Bernie Myerson. We had dealings with him a couple of years ago, if you remember."

"Involved with that Italian mob, the Sabinis, wasn't he?"

"He provided us with some useful information."

"I remember."

Cole looked down at his notebook and cleared his throat again.

"Continue, Constable, continue."

"When Mr Reardon came out of Myerson's Artistic Supplies, although it was difficult to make out, it seemed to me that he was carrying something. I can't be sure; if he was, he put it in his pocket very quickly. He then headed off back in the direction of the nightclub."

"What do you think it was?"

"Perhaps a small package or envelope. On his way back to

The Blue Angel, Mr Reardon paid one more call at another closed shop, this time in Dean Street. On this occasion, thanks to the light from the opening door, I was able to make out its name, which was 'Evergreen Chemists'. As previously, Mr Reardon spent about ten minutes in the shop and when he re-emerged he was certainly carrying a small package, which he put inside his coat. I did not have an opportunity to see the person he was visiting..." Cole paused and turned his notebook a page back. "... nor did I have an opportunity to see the person Mr Reardon visited first. Mr Reardon then returned to the club. I waited outside the club until approximately 3am, at which time Mr Owen emerged from the club with Mr Reardon. Prior to 10pm I saw approximately thirty women enter the club and after 10pm I saw approximately twenty-five men enter the club. I think I saw two women enter the club with men, but I saw approximately fifteen women leave the club with men. The features of the men and women were hidden in the darkness but..."

"Don't worry about that, Constable, it's Owen and his people we're interested in for now."

"Well, I could recognise Mr Owen when he left as his physique is, um, unusual."

"That's a good word for it I suppose." Merlin smirked at Bridges.

"Mr Reardon brought the car round and drove Mr Owen back home, where he arrived at around 3.30. Mr Reardon drove off and I made my own way home."

Merlin leaned back in his chair and raised his arms behind his head. "I suppose Reardon might have innocently been picking up a prescription from the chemist out of hours, but we should check it out. As for Bernie Myerson, he's quite a piece of work. I wonder what he's up to. Anyway, Cole, well done. You must be dog-tired, although I have to say you don't look it. You have my permission to take a few hours off to get your energy back if you want."

"I'm alright, sir."

"No. Off you go. Better if you're fresh. I…"

There was another knock at the door.

"Come in."

"Ah. Yes. Hello there." Merlin stood up automatically and cleared his throat. "Gentlemen, I didn't have a chance to tell you before, but the Assistant Commissioner has given us yet more assistance in the form of W.P.C. Robinson, his niece as a matter of fact."

"Not that that's of any importance, is it sir?"

"No, no, of course not, Constable."

Merlin introduced his colleagues.

"Robinson has been working on the Dr Joneses. Any luck yet?"

"No, sir. I've dealt with those in Fulham, Chelsea and Earl's Court. Nothing there. Now I'm going to deal with one in Kensington and after that I'll see the one in Hammersmith."

"Hard to credit there are so many, but I suppose it's a common name. Carry on then. You too Cole. Go and have a nap."

"I'd rather not, sir."

"If you really insist then we can find you something to do. Sergeant, before we go off to see Myerson, set Cole on to the land registry details for Johnny's love nest."

* * *

Douglas sat back and smiled with satisfaction. He had cleared his in-tray with ruthless efficiency today in less than two hours. The final item had been a memo from Halifax, congratulating him on a paper he'd drafted for the Cabinet on the Italian political situation. He rose, tightened his braces and put on his jacket. Feeling in his inside pocket he found the letter received that morning from his mother, imploring him to make a final visit to his father in the country hospital where he was dying. He fished it out and with a sniff deposited it in the wastepaper basket. He'd done enough crawling to his father for one lifetime. The will had been sorted and the old boy was comatose. What was the point of a long and tedious journey just for appearance's sake? As he returned to his desk, the door burst open.

Edward Fraser's mop of unruly hair looked even more out of control than usual, while two livid gashes on his chin indicated a hurried encounter with a razor.

"God, you look a mess. Where the hell have you been?"

"Didn't you get my message? Haven't been feeling too well."

Douglas finished tidying up his papers and placed them in a neat pile to the right of the lamp on his desk. "I got a message at the end of last week that you were sick. Not too sick, as I understand it, to miss a night on the town with our friend Norton on Friday night, but nevertheless, today is Wednesday. I've had to cover with several people who asked for you, ranging from Scotland Yard to Lord Halifax himself."

Fraser sat down and lit himself a cigarette.

"Ah, yes. Scotland Yard. Sorry about that. I've dealt with it now. I saw the chap on Saturday. Some misunderstanding about an accident. You remember, don't you, that weekend at the Pelhams, when I bashed into a deer? Through some mix-up they thought my car might have been involved in a hit and run at around that time. Complete rubbish of course, as I've now made clear to the police. As to Norton, well that's work, isn't it?"

"Not necessarily, but I'm glad that the police story is wrong. Anyway, I hope you're ready to get back to work properly."

"Yes, yes." Fraser blew a smoke ring. "What did Halifax want?"

"Don't worry. I dealt with it. He's on his way back from the War Council in Paris today."

"And how's the Italian business coming along?"

"I saw Norton last night. He says he's passed the message on but has had no reply. I've had Giambelli on my back for the past few days wanting to know what he can say to his people. It doesn't help that Norton has been distracted by these goings-on at the Embassy."

"What goings-on?"

"Hasn't he told you? One of those Embassy girls that Norton used to have on his arm – Joan, you remember – was found dead in the river. Soon after that they found that good-looking chauffeur, Morrie Owen's nephew, with his throat cut."

"Good God!"

"Yes, the police seem to have taken a dislike to Norton, so I had to lean on them a bit. I want him to remain focused on our work."

"Of course. Well I'd better go and check what's on my desk."

"By the way, Edward. I think it would be wise if you stayed away from Norton's sleazier clubbing haunts for the while, don't you? With these policemen sniffing around everywhere it might be… you get my drift?"

"I do."

* * *

Bridges parked their car around the corner from Bernie Myerson's alleyway. As he turned the engine off a lorry with a partly detached bumper clattered past them. Merlin didn't appear to hear it. "Do you think I should tell the A.C. about the Ambassador's involvement?"

"I doubt it'll help our investigation much, sir."

A strong wind was blowing in from the East and it had become very cold again. Merlin doodled with his finger on the passenger window, which had been steamed up by their breath. "It won't help our investigation, but it might help to protect our rears."

"You've never been much of a one for that, have you?"

Merlin drew a large J on the window. "No, but this is the

first case I've had where someone as important as the Ambassador of the United States appears to have been mixed up in a murder. If the gentleman dining with Joan at Quaglino's was not Arthur Norton, then with the necklace and Sonia's identification of the accent, the odds on it being the Ambassador himself seem pretty strong. I hope to God there's an innocent explanation but clearly, in normal circumstances, we should be questioning him about his involvement with Miss Harris."

"It's hard to believe that Mr Kennedy could have been involved with her death."

Merlin wiped the window clear with the palm of his hand. A sheepishly attempted smile briefly reflected itself back to him before he turned to Bridges. "As I understand it, the Ambassador has been in the United States for several weeks and wasn't here at the time of her murder, so he can't be directly in the frame. However, there are plenty of questions to be asked if he was having some sort of relationship with her and using our other murder victim as a go-between. And he's a very powerful man. He can arrange things."

Bridges leaned forward to open his door.

"Did you check Brighton out yet?"

"I spoke to someone down there, sir. They were going to send an officer round but they haven't called me back yet."

A dog barked frantically in the distance. Merlin shrugged and ran a hand through his hair. "Shall we go and renew our acquaintance with the charming Mr Myerson?"

"Alright, alright, what's the racket for? Is Hitler driving up Oxford Street or something?" Bernie Myerson looked carefully out through the doorway.

"Here. I know you two, don't I?"

"How are you, Bernie?"

Myerson groaned. "Rozzers. What the blinking hell do you want?"

Merlin edged his foot into the small gap Bernie had allowed

when opening the door. "We've a few questions to ask you. Won't take long."

"Ain't you got better things to do than to bother an old Jew like me? Don't you know there's a war on? Why don't you go and find yourselves a few German spies and leave me alone?"

Merlin added the pressure of his hand to that of his foot on the door and, after a few more squeaks of complaint, Bernie fell back and the policemen pushed through into the shop.

In the dim light which filtered through the grimy window, Merlin could see that their host was still in his dressing gown and pyjamas, although it was now almost midday. The brown dressing gown was mottled with a variety of stains on whose origins he preferred not to speculate. "Like your evening attire, Bernie. Who's your model, Noel Coward or Cole Porter?"

Myerson bared his decaying teeth at the policemen. "Merlin, ain't it? The dago copper. And your sidekick, what's his name, Vauxhall Bridge or something? Got a warrant have you? Barging into my property like this. Who do you think you are? You're no better than Hitler's Gestapo, you lot."

"You better watch out, Bernie, or I might have to remember that you're an enemy alien. Where is it you're from? Austria, isn't it? That's part of Germany now, so I think you might pose a threat to the security of the realm. With your expert photographic skills, you'd be a prime candidate for processing secret documents and the like. I think I'd better get on to the Home Office straight away."

Myerson stepped away and coughed violently. Dark flecks of spit now added themselves to the other stains on his dressing gown.

"You'd better sit down, Bernie. I wouldn't care for you to die before we've questioned you." Merlin pulled over a rickety wooden chair from a corner of the shop and pushed Myerson onto it. The chair creaked. Myerson extracted a filthy handkerchief from his pocket and blew his nose. Bridges picked up a glass of what he took to be water from the counter and handed it to Myerson, who drank it down and passed the glass back. Bridges flinched as the gin fumes hit him.

"Hungary!"

"What's that, Bernie?"

"Hungary is where I'm from, not Austria."

"But when you came over here – correct me if I'm wrong – thirty years or so ago, wasn't it all the same thing? The Austro-Hungarian Empire, God rest its soul."

"Yes, but I'm from the Hungarian bit, not the Austrian bit."

Merlin stroked his chin. "Sorry, but at times of national emergency, these fine details tend to get lost. To the people who decide these things, I'm afraid, it's all the same. Austria, Hungary, Germany who cares, best to bang you up for the duration just to be on the safe side."

Myerson stood up and Merlin pushed him back down. The chair groaned again. "But I'm not a bloody foreigner. I've been a British citizen since 1920!"

"I don't think being a British citizen is going to save someone like Oswald Mosley from the lock-up, so if that's the case, why should it save a shady old crook like you?"

Myerson sighed with resignation. "What is it you want to know?"

"Any other chairs in this hole, Bernie? There's a lot of walking in this job and our feet tend to get a little sore."

Myerson rose and reached behind the counter, producing two chairs as rickety as his own. The policemen seated themselves carefully and Merlin undid his coat buttons. "Still got that nice line in dirty pictures going?"

Wiping his nose with the sleeve of his dressing gown, Myerson leaned down to brush a fly from his slipper. "I still do a little artistic work, if that's what you're asking."

"Dirty pictures, Bernie. We almost nicked you for that, didn't we? But we didn't. Seeing as you were so helpful about the Sabinis and their gambling rackets."

Myerson shifted edgily in his chair. "Dunno what you mean."

"I remember you gave us some very handy information about all those goings on down at Brighton, didn't you? Helped us to identify some of the culprits in the race-fixing."

"Just gave you a bit of background colour, that's all I did. Don't know why you're going on about it so."

"Very well. Forget the subtlety. We just wanted to remind you that you've got some potential enemies out there who might be upset at some of the things the Sergeant and I could tell them about the past."

Myerson got up again and shuffled over to the counter. He eyed his half-bottle of Gordon's before picking up the packet of Senior Service cigarettes and Swan Vesta matches next to the bottle. He looked back morosely at the policemen and lit up. "Look, Merlin. I've got the message. You're a wizard and you can do nasty things to me if I don't answer your questions. Why dontch'a just get on with it and ask away."

"Morrie Owen. Know him?"

Myerson sucked intently on his cigarette. "Yeh, I've heard of Morrie Owen. Runs a club or two in Soho and the West End."

"Had any dealings with him?"

"Not that I can remember."

"Bad answer, Bernie."

"Alright, copper, I might have helped him out a little in the past. You know, he needs girls for his clubs. He's had a bunch of clubs over the years. Always looking for girls to work at them. When I was more active in the artistic side of my business, occasionally I'd have, er, models, who were looking to earn money and I'd refer them to Morrie."

Bridges looked up from his notebook. "You mean you supplied prostitutes to Morrie Owen for his clip joints?"

Myerson narrowed his eyes. "I introduced girls to a potential employer, that's what I did, sonny."

"Is that all?"

"What?"

"Is that all you do for Owen? Find him girls?"

"I told you, Merlin. I did that in the past when I was still in the artistic business. I ain't doing that no more."

"What are your present dealings with Owen?"

"How do you mean?"

"Come on. We know you have something going with him."

"I don't know what you're on about."

"We know that Morrie's sidekick Jimmy Reardon has been to see you. What did you give him?"

Myerson squirmed in his chair and spat violently on the floor.

"Maybe Morrie has been returning a favour and sending girls to you as models. Perhaps you've revived your artistic endeavours. Is that what you've been up to and Jimmy's been coming round to pick up the pictures?"

Myerson leaned from his chair to reach for the gin bottle on the counter. He took a long swig and wiped his mouth on his arm. "And what if I have? What's it to you?"

"What it is to us, Bernie, is that there have been a couple of murders, one of Morrie's nephew and one of a girl who we know visited Morrie's club. We need to know what Owen is up to so we can see if he's involved somehow. I'm not going to book you for producing pornography, provided you co-operate with us. But we need to know what you gave Reardon. If it's irrelevant to what we're investigating, we'll move on to our next line of enquiry. Alright?"

"Well, what if I have been taking a few pictures for Morrie? Can't see how that's got anything to do with any murders or anything."

"Let us be the judge of that. Got any examples of what you've been doing for him?"

"Obviously I ain't got what I gave Jimmy the other night."

"No negatives, Bernie? Come on."

"I give him everything I had. Honest."

"You won't mind us having a look in your studio, if that's what you call it, will you?"

Myerson hugged the gin bottle to him. "Dontch'a need a warrant for that sort of thing?"

Merlin shook his head at Bridges and laughed. "Do you really want to get up my nose by asking me to get a warrant?"

Myerson's eyes flickered as he drained the last dregs of gin. "'Ang on a moment then." He scurried behind the counter and disappeared from sight. The policemen followed. A narrow staircase behind the counter led down to a grubby, ill-lit room. Bernie was rummaging around by a box in a far corner of the room.

"What are you doing?"

"Just tidying up a little. It's a real mess down here."

"What's in there?"

"You want to see some of my work, don't you? You did say you're not going to go after me for anything in these photos, didn't you?"

"Any agreement is dependent on you behaving yourself. Come on, bring it over here."

Myerson dropped the box on to the floor and dragged it over to the policemen. It was overflowing with black and white photographs. Merlin picked up the photo at the top of the pile and held it out to Bridges. "I don't think Iris would be happy if she knew you were looking at this sort of stuff."

"No, sir. Very athletic." The photograph displayed a naked woman, with long, flowing, dark hair, lying on a chaise-longue. She faced the camera with a pouting look and her legs splayed wide.

With his eyes now a little more accustomed to the light, Merlin looked around the room. Up against the wall he recognised the chaise-longue from the picture. On a chair nearby were draped various items of female underwear or nightwear. On the other side of the room a black curtain on rails closed off an area of space. Merlin could hear a tap dripping from behind the curtain. "So you snap the girls over here, Bernie, and then develop the pictures over there. Very efficient set-up, if I may say so. Rather like a Ford production line."

Myerson shrugged and sat down on the chaise-longue.

Merlin left Bridges to plough through the pictures in the box and walked over to the curtain. He pulled it back and saw a grimy metal sink. Next to the sink were a collection of tins and some clothes pegs. There was no work in progress and he pulled the curtain back.

"See anyone we know, Sergeant?"

"I don't think so. Some of these could be girls we saw at the club, but it's so dark in those places, I'd be hard pressed to be certain."

"Hmm." Merlin's stroll around the room had brought him to the corner from which Myerson had brought the box. "Any negatives there?"

"Plenty here in folders and envelopes at the bottom of the box."

"You won't mind if we take the negatives and pictures with us, will you, Bernie? Just so we can make sure we've not missed anything."

"I suppose I can't stop you, can I?"

"I don't think you can."

"Mind if I just go through the photos so I've got a reference list of what you've got? It's like my stock-in-trade isn't it? I need to have a record, see." He crept over to the box but Merlin shook his head and Bridges pushed him away. Swearing under his breath, the photographer fell back onto the chaise-longue.

Underneath the table on which the box of pictures had originally been resting, Merlin found a pile of old books. He leaned down and blew dust off the topmost volume. "What are these then?"

"Just photographic text books. Nothing important."

Myerson stood up and limped over to Bridges. "Can I help you carry the box upstairs, Sergeant, if that's all now?"

The large book on top of the pile was entitled *The Works of the Great Victorians*.

"Come on, Merlin, I'll help your young chap with the box. I think you've seen everything there is to see."

Merlin pulled the book out and opened it to a random page. An austere Victorian paterfamilias with his family stared back at him. "This is interesting stuff, Bernie."

Myerson dropped the corner of the box he had just lifted from the floor and hurried over. "Yes, well, Mr Merlin, I have learned a lot about photographs in my time, but I don't think there's anything of interest to you there." Myerson took hold of the book and attempted to close it but Merlin kept his hand on the page. "Hold your horses. I just want to look at some of the photographs. A little beauty will hopefully remove from my mind the ugliness of your own collection." He turned the page and found a sepia tinted landscape of hills and trees, in the middle of which sat a turreted house. "Scotland, Bernie, or perhaps Austria, your homeland."

"It's Hungary, Mr Merlin, as you know. Now let me put the book back and you can get on with your business." Myerson tugged again at the book, Merlin resisted and it fell to the floor. On impact something fell from its pages and fluttered under the table. Myerson bent down and put the book on the table. "Alright, alright. Look at the book if you want."

"Look's like you've lost a page there, Bernie. Don't you want to pick it up?"

"Oh, it's only a page marker. It ain't important. Can I turn the light out now?" Myerson reached over to the light switch, turned if off and went up the stairs. Merlin bent down and felt around in the dark for the page marker. He found it but, as he straightened, banged his head on the bottom of the table. Rubbing the growing bump on his head with irritation, he made his way up the stairs. Back in the shop Bernie had got hold of another bottle of liquor, this time whisky, and was thirstily drinking.

Merlin set the 'page marker' on the counter. It was another photograph. He picked it up, moved to the door and stepped outside into the light. After a while he came back into the shop. "Very interesting, Bernie. Unusual sort of stuff for you

I'd have thought. Diversifying a little I suppose. A good thing to cater to a broad range of markets."

Myerson's bloodshot eyes stared balefully back at Merlin. He said nothing.

"Can I have a look, sir?"

"I don't know, Sergeant, I really do think you might be a bit too young for this one."

Bridges took the picture and inhaled sharply.

"There must be a good story behind this picture, Bernie, and you're going to tell the Sergeant and me all about it. Apart from the interest of the content alone, and the circumstance that it was this picture that you were clearly most anxious to hide from us, there's the surprising fact that one of the characters featured might be known to the Sergeant and me. Now, put that bottle away, sit down here and tell us everything."

* * *

Herman Zarb was relaxing at his desk with a cup of tea when the call came through. His junior secretary spoke to him in the reverential tone she always adopted when she picked up a connection from the States. She still found it hard to comprehend the miracle of science which enabled the human voice to be transferred three thousand miles along a piece of wire at the bottom of the ocean. "It's Mr Hull, sir, er, I mean Mr Secretary Hull." She had been admonished by the senior secretary for omitting Mr Hull's title last time he'd come on the line.

"Put him through."

A distant female voice spoke. "He will be with you momentarily, Mr Zarb." The phone made a variety of clicking and buzzing noises until Cordell Hull's Tennessee drawl came through reasonably clearly. "How are you, Zarb?"

"Well, sir. And you?"

"Not so good, to tell the truth."

Zarb nervously stirred his drink. "Anything I can do?"

"That's why I am calling. The President and I have had several telephone conversations with the Ambassador in the last couple of days."

"Yes, sir."

"He is, of course, his usual bullish self about the British war effort."

"Er, yes, sir."

"I'm being ironic, Zarb. You know 'irony', that thing the British say is alien to the American mind. Well anyway, we listened to the usual amount of defeatist bilge that the Ambassador had to spout about Great Britain's prospects and the apparent invincibility of the Nazi military. Very depressing it was too. I hope to God he's not right."

"As you know, Mr Secretary, I have made every effort to encourage him in a more balanced view of Britain's position."

"Yes, yes, Zarb. I know you have done your best but you have not been successful. Mr Kennedy's views on the British war outlook are as unbalanced as ever. Of course, I understand from my friends on Wall Street that Mr Kennedy has sold short so many British and French stocks and bonds that it would be counter to his economic interest to moderate his views."

"I am aware of the Ambassador's dealings, as are the British authorities, who take a rather dim view of his market activity while in his diplomatic post."

"Naturally, but I am afraid it is only the arrival of the Final Judgement which is going to stop Joe Kennedy from dealing. Being in charge of the Securities and Exchange Commission didn't stop him, so I hardly think being Ambassador to Great Britain is likely to."

"Sir."

"Anyway, coming to the point of this call – Norton, Arthur Norton, what's he up to at present?"

"Operating in his usual maverick way. As you know, the Ambassador doesn't like me to interfere with him, so I can't give you a definitive report on his activities."

"I know that, but you must have some idea of what he's been up to. Who he's been seeing and so on."

Zarb leaned forward and pulled a piece of paper across his desk. "He does have a rather broad range of contacts in diplomatic circles. I haven't got anything like a complete list but I have asked a few of my colleagues to keep an eye on him. Recently he seems to have developed a particular friendship with a fellow in the Foreign Office, an up-and-coming young diplomat close to Halifax, name of Freddie Douglas."

A loud crackle came over the line and the voice in Washington faded. "Sorry, I didn't quite catch that, sir."

Hull's voice came back strongly. "I said, do you know who his contacts at the Italian Embassy are?"

"No. Do you want me to find out?"

"Please, Zarb. Apparently the Ambassador has received some communication which, according to him, is of the utmost importance to the future of Europe. He said he was going to fly up to Washington from Palm Beach to tell us about it. When I asked him the source of this communication, he mumbled something about the Italians. Couldn't get any more out of him so he's bearing down on the President and me tonight. I knew that you couldn't have been in the loop on this as you would have been on to me straight away, would you not?"

"Of course. I know nothing about any Italian communications."

"Quite. So it occurred to me that the likely conduit of such information to the Ambassador might be Arthur Norton."

Zarb's cheek began to twitch, the only discernible sign of anger in a man who prided himself on his self-control. He spoke calmly into the black Bakelite telephone receiver. "Norton was in here the other day in something of a flap about not being able to get hold of the Ambassador. In the end I put him in touch with our cipher department and he sent some coded message over to the States. When I asked the cipher clerk who dealt with it to give me a decoded copy, he told me that he had been expressly forbidden to reveal the details to anyone by Norton. As the clerk was in a difficult position, I let it pass, on the basis that I would take it up in due course with Norton and the Ambassador himself."

Through the crackle and hissing again coming down the line, Zarb could just hear Secretary Hull sighing deeply. "This, Zarb, is the trouble you get when amateurs are given high-ranking diplomatic posts. Just because Joe Kennedy spent some of his ill-gotten bootlegging money backing the President years ago, we have an idiot like Arthur Norton running round London fancying himself as a latter-day Talleyrand."

"Is there anything you want me to do?"

"No, no. I'll see if I can track down the encoded message Norton sent to the Ambassador but, in any event, I'll know whatever it's about in a few hours when Kennedy arrives here from his extended vacation – sorry, I mean his sick leave – in the sun. Anything else of note I should know before I ring off?"

Zarb stroked his chin and looked at his reflection in the elegant eighteenth century mirror to the left of his desk. His cheek had stopped twitching. "Well, Mr Secretary, we've had a couple of local junior employees of the Embassy die. It's been rather distressing and…"

Hull cut in abruptly. "That's very sad, Zarb, but these things happen. Now I think…"

"Sorry to interrupt, Mr Secretary, but these employees didn't die of natural causes. They were violently murdered. I know it may be of no importance in the greater scheme of things, but I thought I'd mention it since my sources, such as Miss Edgar at the residence, inform me that the police are regarding Mr Norton with great suspicion."

There was silence at the end of the line. "Sir, are you still there?"

"Yes, sorry. You shocked me. Does the Ambassador know anything of this?"

"Yes, sir. He knows."

"Send me a note of the details. It's strange that Norton has come under suspicion."

"Mr Norton is a rather louche character and has a very lively social life. I do not like the man but I find it hard to imagine that he's involved in murder. He can be pompous and aggressive so my guess is that he probably just put the police officers' noses out of joint. Generally speaking, I don't think the police have made any real progress yet and, in these fraught times, one tends to wonder whether there is any greater meaning to the violent deaths even of a chauffeur and an office girl."

"Yes, indeed. Well, keep on eye on the investigation and on Norton. I'll be in touch after we've heard what Mr Kennedy has to tell us." The phone clicked and the line went dead.

Zarb finished his tea, stood up and walked over to the window. While he had been talking, a thick mist had descended on Grosvenor Square. Disembodied heads bobbed along the pavement nearest the Embassy. He enjoyed watching this odd spectacle for a while before returning to his desk. Pulling a thick file towards him, he attempted to put the Ambassador, Arthur Norton and the dead employees out of his mind by reading the latest batch of intelligence reports from the Continent.

One of the bobbing heads belonged to Kathleen Donovan, who was on an errand to bring some correspondence and files to Zarb's office. As she emerged from the fog of Grosvenor Square into the brightly-lit hallway of the Embassy, Arthur Norton was coming out of the gentlemen's toilets to the right of the reception area. He stood for a moment straightening his tie and doing up the buttons of his overcoat, then noticed her. Her back was to him as she walked towards the reception desk and he took the time to appreciate her glowing hair, her curves, her legs. He was a connoisseur of beauty and she figured high in the rankings, as had Joan. Poor Joan. He sighed. "Kathleen. How are you?"

She started and dropped one of the letters she was carrying.

"I'm so sorry. I didn't mean to surprise you. Let me get that." He bent down to get the letter but she reached it first. She looked up to find Norton's face inches from hers. He reeked of after-shave and she put her hand to her mouth. They rose slowly to their feet.

"How do you do, Mr Norton. You'll forgive me if I don't stop to chat, won't you, but I have some letters to deliver to Mr Zarb and Miss Edgar wants me back as soon as possible."

"Of course, dear girl, of course. Time and Miss Edgar wait for no man, or woman. Glad to see you're back on the job. I understand you weren't very well. And then there's that sad business with your friends. Such a nice girl Joan and poor Johnny. Who could have wished either of them any harm? It's so puzzling."

She bit her lip to forestall the tears she knew were close to the surface. "Yes, well. If you'll please excuse me." She turned and just managed to avoid Norton's hand on her rear as she hurried to the stairs.

Norton remained in the middle of the lobby enjoying the charming swing of her hips as she retreated. He smiled as he put on his gloves. He was in a good mood. He wasn't even feeling miffed that his hand had missed its target. So Miss Kathleen Donovan, you think you're so perfect. Too good for Arthur Norton, are you? Joan thought that too. We'll see, won't we? We'll see.

* * *

Back in his office, Merlin found out from Robinson that she'd identified the doctor who Joan Harris had visited. This Dr Jones, with a practice just off Brook Green, remembered the girl and, moreover, remembered her being accompanied by a man. A patient with an urgent condition had interrupted before the doctor could give her a description of the man, but in any event Robinson had arranged for a sketch artist to visit the surgery the following morning. From Cole he learned that the Land Registry showed ownership of the Kensington Mews residing with two companies whose background Cole would be investigating at Companies House the next day.

Merlin was sitting back in his chair with a feeling that the fog was slowly beginning to lift just a little, when Inspector Johnson appeared at the door.

"Sit down, Peter. Got anywhere with Fraser?"

Johnson shook his head. "I went out to the country yesterday to see Lady Pelham. She was the hostess of the weekend party to which he was driving when he supposedly ran into the deer. She remembered him mentioning such an accident."

"That doesn't prove much."

"No. Except that he's been consistent with this story from day one."

"And forensics?"

"No progress, sir. The only fresh information I've got is the names of the others at the party, who will no doubt confirm hearing Fraser's story. I'm wondering whether it's worthwhile speaking to them. I don't really like giving up but the A.C. thinks I should pack it in. Says he'd like me, with your approval, to move over to either the dock case or to our IRA investigations." Johnson's shoulders slumped with resignation.

"Anything more on the victim?"

"Not really. The Ministry have clammed up completely."

"Makes you wonder, doesn't it?" Merlin gazed up at the ceiling.

"Sir?"

"Whether there's something more to this. You know. Scientific boffin providing important advice to the MOD. Enemy activity perhaps?"

"Of course I've considered that but I really think Fraser's the man. Whether he had some sort of motive, rather than it being an accident – well there's little point worrying about that when we can't pin the physical facts on him."

"I don't like throwing in the towel either. I suggest you give it another forty-eight hours, Peter. See what turns up. I don't want to hamper your case but since your Mr Fraser is a friend of Norton's and was seen with him and Miss Harris, I might want a routine chat with him myself. See if he's got anything on Norton. Will that be alright?"

Johnson nodded and headed for the door.

"Hang on a minute, Peter. You might be interested in this." Merlin walked over to the box of Myerson's photos which Bridges and Cole had lugged up the stairs earlier and, after lifting the cover Bridges had taped onto it, removed a few photographs and passed them to his colleague.

Johnson caught his breath. "Strong stuff. Where are they from?"

"The work of someone called Bernie Myerson, a photographer who's in cahoots with Morrie Owen, the uncle of one of our victims."

"Are these pictures connected with your murders?"

"Perhaps. We'll just have to sift through the box and see. But these girly pictures aren't all. Take a look at this."

From his jacket pocket he produced another photograph of naked flesh.

Johnson's cheeks reddened slightly. "Anyone you know?"

Merlin held the picture up close and inspected the two entangled bodies.

"This chap here, with his arm up, is someone called Freddie Douglas. He's an official at the Foreign Office. A colleague of your Mr Fraser in fact. Quite high-ranking apparently. And this other one on his front, it's not so clear but I think I have an idea."

* * *

Merlin found Jack Stewart settled in a warm and cosy cubbyhole of The Surprise, his head buried in a newspaper. It was getting late and Merlin was thirsty. He had spent the remainder of the afternoon carefully going through Myerson's photographs. He had recognised none of the girls in the developed photographs and the negatives had been sent off to the police laboratories for processing. Johnson had given him Lady Pelham's guest list and he hadn't really been surprised to see the names of Norton and Douglas. However, the photograph of Douglas certainly opened a new range of possibilities.

Stewart looked up as his friend squeezed onto the bench.

"Francisco. Buenas noches. Let me get you a pint."

"No, I'll do it. The usual?"

Merlin returned from the bar with two pints of Courage.

"Not so crowded tonight, is it?"

"No, amigo. It'll fill up before closing time though. People need beer to lubricate their dreams and drown their fears."

"Very poetic."

Stewart struck a recitative pose, his head angled back and glistening eyes fixed on some distant object above the bar.

"'Such hilarious visions clamber
Through the chamber of my brain.
Quaintest thoughts, queerest fancies
Come to life and fade away.
What care I how time advances?
I am drinking ale today.'"

Merlin smiled and nodded with approval before closing his eyes in concentration. A moment later he banged his hand on the table. "Edgar Allan Poe! Am I right?" Stewart clapped his hands slowly and grimaced before looking expectantly at his friend. Merlin swilled his beer around in his glass before copying his friend's artistic pose.

"'Here, with my beer I sit,
While golden moments flit.
Alas they pass unheeded by
And, as they fly,
I, being dry,
Sit, idly sipping here
My beer.'"

Merlin relaxed as Stewart ummed and aahed for a couple of minutes before signalling defeat with a shrug.

"George Arnold."

"That is bloody obscure, Frank! Have you nothing from Cervantes? You've usually got something from him."

"Here's one for you. 'Cada uno es hijo de sus obras'."

"Enlighten me."

"'Every man is the son of his works'. Nothing to do with pubs but I think it covers you nicely."

"And not you?"

"No, I'm the son of my father. He's the one who drilled *Don Quixote* into me. And all that English poetry. 'My two heritages', as he kept on saying before the Zeppelin got him. Anything in the paper?"

"Nothing. Don't know why I'm bothering to read it. You'd think wee old Adolf would have the courtesy to advertise his plans, wouldn't you? We're going mad with boredom at the station. Cups of tea, biscuits, incredibly dull conversations with one's colleagues, more cups of tea. If only the Fuhrer would just put a neat little notice in the paper, you know: 'Herr Hitler requests the presence of your company at his bombing party which will commence at 7pm in the West End of London on Thursday, March 1st, helmets will be worn, etcetera,' well, that would give us all something to focus on, wouldn't it?"

Merlin smiled and took the froth off his beer.

"Gather you saw my Polish friend this morning."

"News travels fast."

"I saw her at lunchtime. Asked me if I had any coppers for friends."

"Did she?"

"I denied any such friendships."

"Naturally."

"Find out anything worthwhile?"

"From your perspective, she vehemently denied being on the game. Said she was just supplementing her meagre shop-girl's income with the tips she gets at Morrie's club. She was most indignant in pointing out that she never went home with customers."

"Think she's telling the truth?"

"You know, I think I do."

"That's nice of you, Frank." Stewart doffed an imaginary hat in appreciation. "Did she have anything to say which helped your case?"

"She recognised Joan Harris. Said she was in the club a few times with Arthur Norton. She also saw Joan Harris another time and I was hoping you might be able to help me there."

"Me. How so?"

"She says she was on a date at Quaglino's with, she thinks you, before Christmas, in November or December. She can't remember, and she saw Joan Harris at another table. Do you remember?"

"I have taken her to Quaglino's a couple of times. Once before Christmas and once a few weeks ago. How can I help?"

"She says she saw Joan Harris having dinner with a man she thinks had a New England accent. It could have been Norton, but as she herself pointed out, Norton is a pig and Joan was very happy with the man she was with, so the chances are that it was another man. Did you notice this couple? Apparently they were at a nearby table next to a pillar."

Stewart stared into his drink.

"Sorry, Frank. I have to say rather cornily that, whenever I've been with Sonia, I've only had eyes for her. Can't say I noticed any Americans or other beautiful young things. But maybe I can help a little. I'm quite friendly with the maitre d' at Quaglino's. Usually getting these types to give information is like trying to prise open an oyster with a toothpick. Ernesto owes me a few favours, though. I'll see if I can get him to open up his reservations records to me."

"Thanks, Jack, but I'd already thought that we could do that."

"Trust me. If you go as the police to see him you won't get any worthwhile information. Leave it to me please." Stewart rose and tapped their empty glasses.

Merlin stretched his legs under the table. "I should tell you something else."

Stewart paused, tankards in hand.

"If the American gentlemen in question was not Arthur Norton, I have an idea who it might have been, and if it was that person, I'm going to be in something of an awkward position."

"Oh?"

"Sergeant Bridges found a record of some very fine jewellery being bought for Joan Harris by a very well-known New Englander."

"I'm all ears."

"Joseph Kennedy."

Stewart sat back down and whistled. "Well, well. I heard he was a bit of a ladies' man from a reporter friend of mine. That could be difficult for you. Are you telling me that if Ernesto says that it was the American Ambassador dining with Joan Harris that night, you don't want to know?"

"No, no. I want to know who it was. I'm just telling you so that you know. And perhaps Ernesto will be even more circumspect than he would otherwise be in providing you with information."

Stewart rose to his feet again, chuckling. "Don't you worry Francisco – old Joe Kennedy, eh!"

Merlin looked around anxiously, a finger on his lips.

"Och, relax man. I'll get them in."

CHAPTER 12

Thursday February 8th

The lift was working now and they rode up to the third floor. They knocked and heard muttering behind the door to No. 32 which, after a clattering of chains and deadbolts, opened a few inches. Mrs Owen's head, covered with paper curlers as before, poked out. "He's fast asleep in bed. Works late hours you know. He won't like being disturbed. He'll kill me if I let you in without his say-so."

She raised a bony hand to her small red parrot nose and scratched it.

Merlin lost patience and pushed hard against the door. Mrs Owen squawked and retreated down the hallway. As she bent to pick up their cat, Merlin had the misfortune to spot a scrawny breast making an appearance from beneath her dressing gown. He walked towards her, eyes on the floor. "Will you have another attempt at waking your husband or shall we do it?"

"You might as well have a go. I'm in for trouble either way." She shrugged and stepped into the living room, making cooing noises to the animal in her arms.

They had little difficulty locating Owen. Loud snoring could be heard at the far end of the corridor off the living room. In his bedroom, Owen's vast stomach rose and fell under a bright red eiderdown. As Merlin leaned over the bed, Owen exhaled noisily. Flinching at the halitosis, Merlin almost knocked over a glass of water, which on closer examination contained a set of teeth. Some water from the glass slopped onto his jacket sleeve and he grimaced. Bridges couldn't contain himself.

"Yes, yes, Sergeant, very amusing I'm sure. Perhaps you'd like to have a go."

"We'll need an electric shock machine to wake him up."

"Go on."

Bridges took a firm grip of Owen's shoulders and shook them energetically "Morrie Owen. Wake up please. It's the police!"

Owen's eyes slowly opened. A pudgy arm emerged from the bedclothes, then another, and he attempted to lever his body into a sitting position. Surprisingly, the manoeuvre succeeded. "What the bloody hell's all this about then? Where is she? Annie!"

Owen's spouse stepped timidly into the room. "I couldn't stop them. They barged their way in. Honest."

"Shouldn't have opened the door, should you? Stupid woman. Bugger off and make me a cup of tea. And you two. Get out. Doesn't a man get any privacy in his own home? Can't I at least get dressed in peace?" Owen's jowls quivered with indignation.

"We'll wait for you in the living room. We have questions and we want the right answers this time."

Eventually, Owen emerged from his lair. For him, getting dressed had involved putting on a dressing gown and applying a dab of haircream to his few strands of hair. He hadn't bothered to shave but had had the grace to put his teeth in. "You may as well get on with it." He lowered himself into his armchair and his wife crept in nervously with his tea.

"Bernie Myerson. What can you tell us about him?"

Owen's hand twitched and some tea slopped into his saucer. "Never 'eard of him. Who is he. Some Jew-boy friend of yours?"

Merlin raised his eyes to the ceiling. "No games please. You know very well Myerson's a pornographer off the Tottenham Court Road who supplies your club with girls."

Owen looked out of the window and belched. "Oh, that Bernie Myerson. Yeh, I know Bernie. What of it?"

"I gather he's been doing a few errands for you recently?"

"Well, as you say. He sometimes introduces girls to us.

Girls who want to earn a bit of money in the club."

"And you sometimes introduce girls to him as I understand."

"I don't know about that. I can't stop the girls in my club doing other work. If one of my girls finds out from another girl that there's a bit of money to be made by having a few snaps taken, there's nothing I can do about it, is there?" Owen set down his cup and rested his hands on his stomach.

"We understand from Bernie that he's been doing some speciality work for you?"

"Speciality work? What's that when it's at home?"

"Bernie would probably call it 'classical male studies' but I suppose I'd call it dirty pictures of homosexual men."

Owen narrowed his eyes as Merlin showed him the photograph. "Seen this picture before?"

The fat man grudgingly removed his spectacle case from his dressing gown.

"Recognise anyone?"

Owen moved the picture back and fore in front of him. "Bit tangled up, aren't they? Hard to recognise anyone like that, but no. Never seen the picture and I don't know the men."

"I'm surprised. This chap here. This is Freddie Douglas. Works at the Foreign Office. He's a friend of your friend Arthur Norton. But you know that, don't you?"

Unpleasant rumbling noises sounded from Owen's stomach. A lick of hair slid down his forehead into his eyes and he picked it up and smoothed it back on the top of his head. "I don't know anything, copper."

"As for this other chap. Well, the picture's not so clear, is it? Myerson rather unconvincingly says he doesn't know. As far as I can see, Douglas' eyes are closed. Perhaps he's asleep or perhaps drugged. As for his friend, I can see one eye and that seems to be open. There's a glint in that eye which seems familiar, don't you think?"

Owen stared at him blankly.

"Myerson says that your sidekick Reardon drove him somewhere in Kensington, took him into a room and asked him to take pictures of these two lovebirds. No questions asked, as he said. Says he didn't know the men. Now I'm sure he hasn't told us everything but it's pretty easy to put two and two together. There's Douglas, successful chap at the Foreign Office. No doubt quite well off. Got unconventional sexual tastes. Set him up with a compliant male and then blackmail him."

"You've got a good imagination, copper. Myerson's hardly a reliable witness, is he? I've got nothing to do with this."

"And what about the compliant male, eh? Who do you think that is?"

"I don't know. Perhaps it's your boyfriend here." He sneered at Bridges who returned a look of disgust.

"I'm really shocked, Morrie. I thought you were a good family man. Fancy letting your sister down and letting her son in for this sort of activity. It's Johnny, isn't it?"

Owen's face suffused with blood. "You bastard. How dare you! You can both get the hell out of here. This is..."

Merlin placed his hands on the arms of Owen's chair and leaned down into his face. "Look, Morrie. My main interest is in finding your nephew's killer and the killer of Joan Harris. I find it hard to believe that you topped your own nephew but..."

"I wouldn't kill my own blood, would I?"

Merlin stepped back. "Who knows with a specimen like you? Spiders sometimes eat their young don't they? And what are you but a grubby grotesque money spider. All I can tell you is that things are opening up. If you want us to find Johnny's killer and if you want to protect your own skin, I'd think of coming clean sooner rather than later. I'll need to know how far your little blackmail plan went. And I want to know a lot more about Norton. I know he brought Joan to your club. I'm sure you can tell us more about that."

Owen scowled. "Look, copper, I don't know who killed

this Harris tart. Alright, maybe she did come to the club with Norton, but what of it? Norton's a grown-up. Speak to him about it. As to what Myerson says, well he doesn't put me in the picture, does he? You'd better speak to Jimmy, but as Myerson's a lying kike, I'm sure you'll get nowhere. Perhaps Bernie had some nice little sideline going. Who knows? You've got nothing on me and I don't recognise these buggers. As to Johnny's murder, I'll tell you something. I'll find the bastard who killed Johnny myself."

Merlin rubbed his brow and shook his head sorrowfully at Bridges.

"I thought you were more intelligent, Morrie. Have it your way but we'll be seeing you again. Sooner than you think too, the way things are going."

* * *

The wipers fought hard to make headway against the driving rain as they entered Parliament Square. The two men had been quiet with their thoughts on the way back from Owen's.

"Shouldn't we have taken him in, sir?"

Merlin closed his eyes and pinched his nose. "When we've got a little more hard information, Sergeant. I'd like to have our forensic people have a closer look at the pictures to confirm it's Morgan, and I'd like to see Myerson again and get him to be a little more forthcoming. We'll obviously need to speak to Reardon and Douglas."

A pedestrian abruptly loomed up in front of them and Bridges swerved to avoid him.

"Assuming we're alive to do that."

"Sorry. It's not easy driving in this stuff."

Back at the Yard they removed their sopping coats and threw them onto the radiator. "Go and see if Robinson and Cole are around and let's take stock."

When Bridges returned, he found Merlin warming himself next to the coats. "Both still out."

"Ah." He bent down and removed his shoes. "Excuse me, Sergeant. I need new ones. One of these has got a hole in it."

"Sir."

Merlin sat in his chair and rested his feet on the radiator, watching small clouds of steam drift upwards from his socks. "We're going to have to divvi up our tasks again."

"Douglas and Reardon?"

"No, not yet, Sam. There are a couple of other loose ends I'd like to deal with first. You haven't heard from Brighton?"

"Still no message. I rang but the officer in question was out."

"And we still haven't got Bernie's negatives back?"

Bridges shook his head.

"While we're waiting on those items, I think you should go and see this chemist Cole saw Reardon visiting. See what he can tell us about Owen."

Bridges nodded.

"And when my socks are dry, I am going to see if Jack can help me identify the mystery man at Quaglino's."

* * *

A blue light shone in the window of Evergreen Chemists, illuminating a display of soaps, cosmetics, toothpastes, bandages and surgical tissues artfully scattered against some low screens. Bridges pushed the shop door open and a bell rang. A stunted, bald, white-coated man appeared and smiled in greeting as he plucked a bowler hat from a hat-stand and planted it on his head. "Yes, sir. How can I help you?" The chemist's odd appearance was complemented by a squeaky, high-pitched voice and he reminded Bridges of an old comedy music-hall act his long-lost mother had liked, what was his name, Tommy Dakins, Deakins – something like that.

"Detective Sergeant Bridges. I'd like to ask a few questions."

The little man's smile vanished. "Police? What on earth can you want with me?"

Bridges motioned towards the door behind the counter. "Perhaps we could discuss this in a more private place. It might be wise to shut the shop while we have a chat."

The chemist puffed out his cheeks, nodded and went to lock the shop door. He reversed a white card hanging on the door to show that he was closed. Bridges could see that the man was agitated. He was muttering under his breath and shaking his head. The bowler hat was too large for him and was wobbling precariously. "Couldn't you have called on me outside shop hours? Things are difficult enough as they are with this war and everything. And what if someone has an emergency? I'm the only chemist open today in this part of London. Morton around the corner has had to go to the country for a funeral. Said he'd be away for a couple of…"

"If we just get on with it, sir, I'm sure you'll be back in place in a jiffy to deal with any crisis."

The chemist led the way behind the counter and through the door into a small living room. A tattered, green lamp cast a dull glow over a worn, brown three-piece suite. Bridges shivered as he sat down in an armchair facing a dying coal fire. Still shaking his head, the chemist sat down opposite him.

"Am I right in thinking that I am speaking to Mr Frederick Braithwaite?" Bridges had seen the name above the shop door.

"You are."

"Had this shop for long, have you?"

Braithwaite picked nervously at his fingernails. "Since 1935."

"Business good?"

"Not so bad."

"I thought you said that things were difficult with the war and so on."

Braithwaite flicked part of a nail into the fire. "Quite a few of my local customers skipped to the country when war was declared. Knocked business a bit but most of them seem to be coming back now seeing as how Hitler hasn't done anything yet, and they've got fed up of life in the sticks."

"So things are picking up?"

"A little – but look, I can't think that the business prospects of a small chemist in Soho are of interest to you. Perhaps you can get to the point of whatever it is you're here for."

"Patience, Mr Braithwaite. I am interested because I was wondering whether poor trading conditions had tempted you to open up any new lines of business to supplement the income from your shop?"

"I don't know what you mean. I'm a chemist, that's what I do."

"Do you know a Mr Jimmy Reardon?" Bridges thought he detected a nervous flicker of the eyes. "Reardon? I think he's a customer. Yes, Mr Reardon. Works locally at one of the clubs."

"And do you know his boss, Morrie Owen?"

"I know Mr Owen. Not a very well man, you know. Carrying all that weight, what do you expect?"

"May I ask you what products you have provided to Mr Reardon and Mr Owen?"

"I can't tell you that. Professional etiquette you know. These are confidential matters." Braithwaite rose and walked to the fireplace, where he picked up a poker and daintily riddled the fire.

"Come on. It's not like you're their doctor, is it?"

Having induced no discernible increase in heat, the chemist returned to his chair. "Very well – if you insist. Normal run of the mill, off-the-shelf stuff and occasional prescriptions – Mr Owen has an asthmatic condition, amongst other things."

"Does Mr Owen pick up his prescriptions himself?"

"No. He always sends Reardon."

"If Reardon always picks up, how have you met Owen?" A small carriage clock, which was the only adornment to the mantelpiece above the fire, pinged to indicate the half-hour. "On occasion, I've had to drop medicine off at his club round the corner."

"So you've been to The Blue Angel?" Braithwaite nodded. "Have you ever supplied illicit drugs to Reardon or Owen?"

"What do you mean, illicit drugs?"

"You know. Cocaine, opium, that sort of thing."

The chemist reddened. "Certainly not. How can you suggest such a thing. I never…" They heard a rattling noise.

"The front door. It might be an emergency. I'd better go and see who it is." As Braithwaite got to his feet, a well-dressed and heavily made-up middle-aged woman came through the door. Pink lipstick delineated a small aperture of a mouth, which began to move rapidly. "What on earth is going on, Fred? Why is the shop closed at this time of the day? And who is this? Lucky I had my key on me or I might have been stuck outside in the cold forever while you gassed here to your mate. And why haven't you kept the fire up? It's like the Arctic in here. Come along. Get your friend out and open the shop up. You haven't been having a little tipple in here, have you? You'll be in trouble if you have, believe me."

Mrs Braithwaite briefly paused for breath and examined Bridges more closely. "And who are you?"

"This is Sergeant Bridges, dear. He's a police officer come to ask a few questions."

Mrs Braithwaite's hands went to her mouth and then fluttered theatrically in the air. "A police officer? My God! I told you not to…" She collapsed into a chair gasping for breath.

"Now, dear, the policeman will soon…"

Tears began to run down the thick powder on Mrs Braithwaite's cheeks. Her breathing became more steady. She tried to say something but couldn't get the words out.

"I'll go and get you your pills, dear. Sergeant, my wife has a condition. She'll be alright once she has her medication but I'll have to tuck her up in bed. You've asked your questions and I've given my answers. Perhaps you could now leave us in peace.

"Alright, sir. But I'll be back."

Merlin pulled up at the restaurant and found Jack Stewart sheltering under an awning. It had started to bucket down again. "Nice weather for it, eh, Frank? Be careful you don't ruin your nice new hat."

"Nice weather for what? Answers let's hope, amigo."

"Just so. At any rate, contrary to my expectations, Ernesto was more than willing to be of assistance when I telephoned him but insisted on speaking to you in person."

"Good." A heavy gust of rain blew in their faces. Water trickled down Merlin's neck. "Can we get inside? I don't want to drown before I find out who your waiter saw."

The men entered a brightly-lit lobby. Beyond glass doors they could see that the restaurant was filling up. "Look, Frank." Stewart lowered his voice. "I think Ernesto is less reluctant than I expected to talk to you because he knows there's a good chance that Mussolini will side with Hitler in the war. No doubt if that happens we'll start interning Italian nationals. He's been in England for over ten years, tells me he hates the fascists and wants to bank some credit for being helpful to the authorities."

Merlin removed his hat and shook it. "I don't care about his reasons as long as I leave here knowing who was dining out with Joan Harris that night."

"Here he is." A small, neat, smiling man in tails approached. He had a receding hairline from which a glossy layer of jet black hair proceeded to a point halfway down his neck. "Mr Stewart. And this must be your friend from Scotland Yard. Ernesto Santangeli, sir, at your service."

"Pleased to meet you. I understand from Mr Stewart that you can help me with some enquiries I am making?"

"Yes, signor. Please come with me." Ernesto spoke sharply in Italian to a passing waiter before leading the way to his office in a corridor off the lobby. "My apologies, gentlemen. It is a little cramped in here, but unfortunately this is the only quiet place where we can talk."

The men seated themselves around a small desk. "Not a problem, sir. I'm sure you're very busy so let's get straight to the point. As Mr Stewart has no doubt told you, I am interested in knowing the identity of one of your customers. He was accompanying an unfortunate girl called Joan Harris who has since been murdered."

The maitre d' sighed sympathetically. "Mr Stewart has told me what you are seeking. Normally, of course, I treat matters like this with the discretion that my customers expect. We serve very many influential and wealthy people here, as I am sure you know. However, there can be no room for delicacy in such a tragic case. I have a great respect for the British police, Inspector, so very different from the police of my old homeland. I say 'old' homeland, because I am about to become a British citizen. My application should be approved any day now. I wish to be a good British citizen."

"Please be assured that your good citizenship in assisting us will be noted down for future reference, sir."

The Italian smiled unctuously. "You are very kind. Very well, I learned from Mr Stewart that the couple you are interested in dined here on the same night as Mr Stewart and one of his lady friends. So I check for Mr Stewart's reservations, but not the recent ones, those before Christmas, is that right?"

Merlin nodded and leaned forward.

"I found that Mr Stewart dined here on Tuesday November 14th. And I understand from Mr Stewart that you are looking for an American gentleman, someone from New England?"

"Yes."

"Quaglino's has many American customers, of course, but I did recognise the name of one of the regular customers who had a table for two on that same night. A customer who comes from Boston."

"And the name?"

"The name, Inspector, is that of a very powerfully-connected man. I hope that there will be no repercussions for me and the restaurant if…"

"The name, sir, please."

Ernesto's nose twitched as he straightened his cuffs. "The customer was a Mr Joseph Kennedy."

"I was right then. The American Ambassador."

Ernesto shook his head.

"No, Inspector, not the American Ambassador. He has dined here many times, but no, not him. No, his son, Joseph Kennedy; his eldest son, he has the same name. A very attractive young man. It was he who dined here that night, I presume with this unfortunate Miss Harris of yours."

* * *

A barrage balloon which had somehow come adrift from its moorings sailed away past his window towards the City. The rain had finally cleared over Scotland Yard to reveal a pale, watery sun sinking slowly behind the Houses of Parliament. Merlin heard the door open behind him.

"I finally got that call from Brighton, sir. Not much of a description but definitely a young man. Tall and handsome according to one of the maids, and an American accent according to the concierge."

"Have we got a photograph of the younger Mr Kennedy yet?"

"Got one coming over from the Press Association any minute now."

He sat down and finished his cold cup of tea. "And the negatives?"

"They're being brought over from the lab by motorcycle tonight."

"What's the story on Braithwaite?"

"I'm pretty sure he's trading drugs to Owen and Reardon, though he denies if of course. My interview was cut short but I spoke to a couple of his neighbours and apparently a year ago or so he was in dire financial straits. Tried to tap them for a loan, unsuccessfully, and then talked of selling up or going bankrupt. In the next few months his situation changed. His wife had some nice new outfits, he bought a car and so on. Claimed to the neighbours that he'd come into an inheritance but they didn't buy it. They noticed Reardon, and various other unsavoury characters who'd not been around before, visiting the pharmacy."

"So you think Owen bailed him out in return for a direct supply of products?"

"I do."

"Well, we'll have to see what we can make of that. We should pull the husband and wife in when we get a chance. Anything from the others yet?"

"Robinson had a problem. Dr Jones was away on a call when she went round with the sketch artist. She was going to try and see him this afternoon. There's no sign of Cole. I presume he is still trawling through the files at Companies House."

Merlin eased himself out of his chair, briefly returned Dr Gachet's sullen stare, then glanced meaningfully up at the ceiling. Bridges caught his drift and reached to open the door.

* * *

"My God, Frank. The Ambassador's son? You're surely not suggesting…?"

The A.C. irritatedly set down the small can with which he was watering the three pots of cardinal red geraniums which his wife had insisted he transfer from the greenhouse at home in Richmond to his office earlier in the week 'to make the place more welcoming for Claire.' He hated geraniums.

"I'm not suggesting anything, sir. I'm just bringing you up to date with the progress of my investigations. Clearly this is a little awkward…"

"Awkward is putting it a little mildly, I think. And then this, this photograph…" The A.C. wiped his hands before picking up Freddie Douglas' incriminating photograph and holding it in front of him as if it was a dead rat. "Halifax will have a fit when he sees this." He dropped it distastefully on to an outer corner of his desk.

"I wasn't proposing to show it to Lord Halifax just yet, sir."

The A.C. raised an eyebrow, sniffed, sneezed and sat down. "Bloody weather's given me a stinker of a cold."

"Care for one of these, sir? They're pretty good decongestants."

The A.C. rejected the proferred packet of lozenges with a grimace. "Well, Chief Inspector, what is your line of approach?"

"With your permission, I'll need to have a chat with the US Embassy. The First Secretary there seems a decent chap. Make some enquiries about Mr Kennedy Junior."

"Do we know where the younger Kennedy is?" The room resounded as the A.C. noisily blew his nose.

"No, sir. I'll be getting onto that now. I know next to nothing about him but, as you know, the old man has a somewhat chequered background. If the son is a chip off the old block, well…"

"What do you mean?" With painstaking care the A.C. folded his handkerchief once then twice and returned it to his pocket.

"I'm not sure, but I'd like to get all the facts. What we have at present suggests that the younger Kennedy took a shine to Miss Harris and showed her a good time. All this in the weeks leading up to Christmas. After Christmas Miss Harris had a pregnancy test, which proved to be negative. She appeared to be unhappy about this result."

"You're not suggesting that Kennedy arranged for something unpleasant to happen to Miss Harris, are you? Because she threatened him with her possible pregnancy?"

"It's one line of enquiry."

The A.C. cast a malevolent look at the offensive flowers. "Hmm. I hope to hell you're barking up the wrong tree there, but if you insist, I won't stop you speaking to the people at the Embassy about him. Be as discreet as you can, that's all I ask. And what are you going to do about Douglas?"

"I propose to confront him with the photograph and see what he says."

"Are you certain the other party is Morgan?"

"I am. The scientists blew up the photo and matched a small skin blemish on the subject's back to that of Morgan."

The A.C. stared up at the ceiling and twitched his lips. "I suppose this makes Mr Douglas a suspect for Morgan's death."

"If Owen's blackmail plan had been set in motion, then yes."

A look of disgust again descended on the photograph as the A.C. leaned forward. "No need to go easy on my account. Do what you must. Just keep me informed."

The clanging of a police car alarm sounded from somewhere across the river as Merlin got to his feet.

"What's happened with Norton? Is he out of the picture now?"

"Far from it, sir. I had been treating him with kid gloves, as you may recall…"

"Yes, yes. Well, you can take those off now. This is a messy business and the best thing to do is clear it up as quickly as possible."

"Sir."

* * *

The Wisemans were feeling happy with life. Things were on the up again. In the last couple of weeks their normal fare of street robbing had been supplemented by some choice paying jobs. Jimmy Burgess had passed on some protection work in Hackney, while his brother had given them a little enforcement job up West. Steady Eddie Duncan had tipped them off about a lucrative burglary in Wandsworth and, with these jobs and a good run of street hits, they were quids in. As long as there was no conflict between paymasters, they would take anything on. Jimmy B had tried again to get them fully on board with his crew but they had managed to remain free without acrimony. Independence suited them. Of course, they paid their dues to the main men. Not to do so would be madness.

They ducked under a shop awning to shelter from the sudden cloudburst. Stanley's stomach rumbled loudly. "Shall we grab a sandwich first?"

"Nah. Let's get on with it."

"He's an ugly tight git, Sid, but it's good to get back on his list again, eh?"

"I s'pose. Nice little earner for an easy job like this."

A double-decker raced past them, splashing through the puddles. They ran to the other side of the road where scaffolding outside a department store provided further shelter. "You've got the downpayment safe, have you?"

Sid patted his pocket and nodded. "Unlike him to hand over such a large wedge of cash like that. He was always a slow payer before."

"I'm not complaining. Keen to get the job done. Something to do with a family tragedy his sidekick told me when we were leaving."

"Whatever. If you're ready let's get on with it." A gust of wind almost removed Sid's hat. Holding on to it tightly, he lowered his head into the drizzle and followed his brother round the corner.

* * *

Merlin was deep in thought and failed for a moment to register the Sergeant's excited arrival. He had been thinking about the A.C.'s question about the younger Kennedy. Even if Joseph Kennedy had led Miss Harris on to get his way with her and left her embittered or just a nuisance, could a potential pregnancy really have provoked him to arrange her death? He knew that the Kennedys had been closely involved with gangsters in the prohibition era, but he felt pretty sure that they had smoother ways of dealing with awkward women than having them end up as corpses in the river. "Sorry, Sam. Miles away. What did you say?"

"I've got the developed negatives."

Bridges threw a pile of photographs onto the desk. "Look." He picked out two and pushed them across. They were similar to the other examples of Myerson's work they had seen. Sprawling limbs and naked young flesh. Two black and white photographs, two women, both beautiful in their different ways.

Merlin scrutinised each one carefully.

"Any more of these two girls?"

"A few, yes, similar poses." Bridges slid the other photographs across to Merlin.

"And the rest of the batch?"

"Different girls, same sort of stuff. None that I recognise."

Merlin kneaded his forehead for a moment before struggling to his feet. "Come on, then. I think it's time we pulled Bernie in."

Darkness had fallen on Tottenham Court Road. Merlin gazed at the reflection that stared back at him from the car side window. He thought of Sonia and essayed another sheepish smile.

"The background in those pictures seemed a little different from the others we saw, don't you think, sir?"

Merlin rubbed his eyes and looked at one of the photographs. "I can't see in this light. We'll have a closer look at the pictures inside."

"Or perhaps Bernie Myerson will tell us." The car pulled up at the end of the grubby alley.

There was no answer from the shop. "Come on, Bernie, we know you're in there." Merlin shone a torch through the shop window. He could see someone sitting in a chair in front of the shop counter and rapped at the window, but the figure remained immobile. "I think he's in the land of nod. We're going to have to force the door."

Bridges stood back, braced himself and ran at the door. There was a loud splintering noise but the lock held fast. He ran at the door again and this time it gave way. They were hit by an overpowering stench. Bridges reached the chair first. The seated man's head lolled on to his chest as Bridges shook his shoulders. "Come on, Bernie. Rise and shine."

Merlin found the light switch and as the dismal décor of the shop revealed itself, Myerson slipped from Bridges' grip and slumped to the floor.

Merlin bent down and rolled the photographer's body face up. He recoiled as vomit spilled onto him. Bridges produced a clean white handkerchief. "Thanks, Sergeant. I'll buy you a new one." Grimacing, Merlin hurriedly wiped his coat before feeling for Myerson's pulse. After trying a few times he shook his head, took a deep breath and walked over to the counter, where he found four empty bottles of whisky and one of gin. "I made a mistake. We should have brought him in for his own protection."

"Wasn't this an accident waiting to happen?"

"Strange how he finally succeeds in drinking himself to death the very day I tell someone about the information he's given us." He knelt down again and ran his torch over the body. "Look, Sam. On his wrist. See that red mark. And there's one on the other wrist. Not as professional a job as they thought. This was no accident – his hands were tied and the booze poured down his throat."

"Owen, sir?"

"If not, who?"

"Someone else connected with these photographs?"

"We'll see." He stood up. "You'd better make the usual calls."

Bridges looked unsuccessfully around the shop for a telephone before going outside to find a police box. Merlin sighed and shone his torch down on Myerson's face. "No need now to worry about being interned, Bernie. No need to worry about anything at all."

★ ★ ★

At last they got away, leaving three other officers, the police doctor and a couple of forensic people at the scene.

"The Yard, sir?"

"Not yet. It's late but let's see if we can find Douglas. I've got that other photograph in my pocket."

They drove through Soho and Piccadilly towards Whitehall, where they drew to a halt outside the Foreign Office.

Bridges entered the building and returned with the information that Douglas had left a short while ago. "Porter suggested we try the Carlton Club. He usually goes there for a tipple when he knocks off."

Five minutes later, standing outside the grand façade of Douglas' club, Merlin pondered briefly why so many men liked to spend so much of their free time in these all-male mausoleums. Something to do with single-sex public school education, he supposed.

In the lobby an elderly man in a frock coat bedecked with medals approached them. "I'm afraid the club is open to members only, gentlemen."

"We are from Scotland Yard, chum. We'd like to speak to one of your members. You can get him out quietly or we can go in noisily. It's up to you."

The man's bushy grey eyebrows jumped. "Who is it you want to see?"

"Mr Freddie Douglas."

"He's at the bar, I think. Please wait here and I'll inform him of your presence." The porter muttered something to a younger colleague before disappearing down a corridor.

"Seeing some fancy places these days, aren't we, sir?"

Merlin looked up at the rows of portraits of former Prime

Ministers and other Tory worthies lining the walls. "We certainly are. Here's our friend."

A purple-faced Douglas was hurrying from the far side of the lobby. "What on earth do you mean by this, Merlin? How dare you call on me at my club. This is quite unacceptable. I am now going to withdraw. Kindly arrange an appointment with me at my office in the normal way!" Douglas turned on his heels.

"I wouldn't do that if I were you, sir."

Douglas looked back over his shoulder, eyes glaring. "Dammit, Merlin. Clear off."

"Not before I've shown you something. Something involving you."

Douglas turned round to face the policemen properly. A flicker of interest registered in his eyes. "What is it?"

"A photograph, sir. A rather embarrassing photograph. We can look at it here if you like, or we can find somewhere more private."

After a moment's thought, Douglas looked at the porter. "Can you suggest an appropriate place for me to talk in private to these gentlemen, Randall?"

"I believe the billiard room is empty, sir."

"Thank you. Come on then. Let's get on with it."

The cherry-red leather armchairs were unoccupied. The green baize table displayed evidence of an uncompleted snooker game. The brightly-coloured balls sparkled in the glow of the overhead lamp. Bridges pulled three chairs together in the corner of the room furthest from the door.

Merlin produced the photograph and slid it across the arm of his chair to Douglas, who went very pale as he stared at it with an open mouth.

"Have you seen this photograph before, sir?"

"No." The word came out in a hoarse whisper.

"Have you any idea how it came to be taken?"

He shook his head slowly.

"Just for the record, sir, could you tell us who the other gentleman is?"

Douglas again shook his head.

"Happen a lot, does it? You getting into bed with other young men, that is. Too many to remember? Never mind, we know who it is, don't we Sergeant? It's the recently deceased chauffeur at the American Embassy. You remember, don't you? Johnny Morgan. That was the investigation you wanted me to go easy on. Perhaps you'd like to tell us about the circumstances in which this photograph was taken."

Douglas' deep-set eyes retreated further into their sockets before he closed them and lowered his head.

A waiter came in and waved. "Can I get you anything, gentlemen?"

Merlin looked at Douglas' shaking hands. "Nothing for us, thanks, but bring a brandy for this gentleman."

* * *

Zarb was just leaving the office when the phone rang. He had had a long and tiresome day and was looking forward to a late supper at The Connaught with his wife. He briefly considered ignoring it, then sat back down at his desk with a sigh. The time difference was so much more convenient if you were the person at home calling Europe, rather than being the person in Europe called from home. This job would be the ruin of his marriage, he thought as he picked up the receiver. "Secretary Hull on the line."

"Put him through."

"Can you hear me, Zarb?" The receiver crackled.

"Just about, sir. It's a poor line again."

"I thought I'd better bring you up to date with our conversation with the Ambassador."

"Yes, sir." Zarb leaned back into his chair and looked over at the wall to his right and the portrait of the powerful Southern gentleman to whom he was talking.

"After listening to the usual harangue about the pathetic state of Britain's defences, and the inevitability of a Hitler walkover in the event of hostilities really getting going, the nub of what he had to talk about was some story about the Germans wanting to float terms for a settlement with Britain by us, so that we can then exert pressure on Chamberlain and Halifax to get a deal sewn up before England goes down the plughole – I think the Ambassador used slightly more colourful language. Apparently, his idiot sidekick Norton has been having discussions on this with the Italian embassy, who are acting as a conduit for the passage of this message from the Fuhrer. Kennedy says that he thinks there is likely to be a receptive attitude to these terms among several senior British government members – Halifax he regards in particular as a pragmatic man. Apparently, Norton has been talking to some senior Foreign Office officials who have fingers in this pie and who have been encouraging the Ambassador's involvement. That fellow called Douglas you mentioned is involved. Is this all news to you?"

Zarb felt one of his migraines coming on. "As I said before, Norton doesn't keep me informed about his activities. That said, I don't find the story of terms being floated so surprising. As you are aware, the Ambassador is not alone in his pessimistic outlook. There are many members of the Establishment who talk in private perhaps, but quite freely in some cases, about the need for an accommodation with Hitler. You know the sort of stuff. He's got nothing against us. Just wants a free hand with Europe. No designs on our empire. Oh well, yes, perhaps we can give him an African colony or two. And as for the Jews. Well, he's not so wrong about them is he? That sort of thing. And I wouldn't be surprised if the terms being floated, if they are genuine, aren't far from that assessment."

"You're right, Zarb. More detailed of course, but you've got the gist of them. And aside from the fact that the Ambassador trusts an idiot like Norton to be a go-between on them, the President and I are inclined to view them as genuine, bearing in mind all the information we've been collecting at the State Department."

Zarb dipped his purple handkerchief in a jug of water on his desk and applied it to his forehead. "Do you want me to take any action?"

"No. After we got shot of the Ambassador, the President and I had a long chat. First of all, the President said, it is apparent from his track record that any proposal or undertaking from Hitler will not be worth the paper it's written on. Any vacillation while peace is negotiated might slow up Britain's rearmament programme. Secondly, the President wants us to stay as well-removed from the scene as we can at present. Despite the strength of the isolationists in the American heartland these days, the President can see no value, electoral or otherwise, in setting ourselves up as some kind of honest broker between the home of parliamentary democracy and a thuggish dictatorship. Above all else, it would stick in the President's craw to do anything significant at the behest of Joe Kennedy – you know he's plotting to go after the party nomination against the President later this year, don't you?"

"Yes, sir."

"In any event, I wanted to keep you informed. You're not required to do anything at present, oh, except one thing. I'd like you to get Norton on the next ship home. He's a liability. It's bad enough having the Ambassador sporting his defeatist appeasement views to all and sundry – and that's not going to go on much longer, I can assure you – but to have his shady crony hanging around with English diplomats who might be regarded as teetering on the edge of treason – it's too much. Get him back here please."

"Does the Ambassador know that Norton's being sent home?"

"No, and I don't give a damn."

Zarb felt his migraine lifting. "Very good, sir."

* * *

The car was held up behind a bus just before the crossing on the corner of Sloane Square. A group of drunken sailors on leave were clumsily making their way from one pub to another. Bridges tapped the steering wheel impatiently.

"Do you believe him, sir?"

"His story has the virtue of simplicity." Merlin stifled a yawn and shivered. "Let's sleep on it. It's going to be another busy day tomorrow. You can drop me here. I'll walk the last bit. It'll warm me up. Can you pick me up from home at eight-thirty?"

"Where are we going first?"

"Resolving the Kennedy issue is the next priority, so let's go and see Zarb. Seems an accommodating sort of fellow so I'm sure he'll see us without an appointment."

"Tomorrow then."

Merlin blew on his hands, pulled his coat collar close around his neck and disappeared into the darkness.

CHAPTER 13

The Stars and Stripes flapped noisily on its flagpole in the stiff morning breeze as the policemen climbed the Embassy steps. They were swiftly ushered through the labyrinth towards Herman Zarb's white doors.

"Good of you to see us, sir, at short notice. I know you're a very busy man."

"Not at all, Chief Inspector. Please sit down. Can I offer you refreshments? No? So what can I do for you?"

"There have been some developments in our investigations. I thought it would be prudent to keep you informed."

Zarb smiled appreciatively.

"Taking the case of Miss Harris first, we have discovered some rather surprising things. One is a little delicate from a diplomatic viewpoint."

"Oh, how so?"

"Were you aware, Mr Zarb, that Miss Harris was involved in some sort of relationship with the Ambassador's eldest son, Mr Joseph Kennedy Junior?"

Zarb's cheek twitched. "No. I was not. Are you sure about this?"

Merlin paused as a large ornate clock in the corner struck the hour. "Pretty sure. Probably over the last three months of last year."

"Is there any suggestion that the Ambassador's son had anything to do with Miss Harris' death?"

"Not at present, but it would be very helpful if you could give us details of his movements over the past few months."

"I'll have to check with Miss Edgar. I'll speak to her and get a schedule of his movements sent over. They're all out of the country now, you know." He briefly closed his eyes. "Well, this is disconcerting. Most disconcerting."

"In any event, sir, her involvement with Mr Kennedy and its likely abrupt termination does appear to have contributed to a deterioration in her mental and emotional outlook."

"What makes you say that?"

"We are trying to explain to ourselves another surprising discovery."

Zarb raised his eyebrows.

"We found some compromising photographs of her."

"What exactly do you mean by compromising, Chief Inspector?"

Merlin struggled momentarily for the appropriate words.

"Naked, sir." Bridges chipped in. "There are pictures of her with nothing on, taken by a shady character we've just found dead in his shop."

Zarb's look of curiosity resolved itself rapidly into one of perplexity.

"We are trying to piece together the circumstances which led to these pictures being taken. What is apparent to the Sergeant and me is that, somehow or other, Miss Harris fell in with a disreputable bunch of people and we think this somehow led to her death."

Zarb leaned back in his chair and mopped his forehead with his handkerchief. The sound of an angry car horn outside briefly filled the room. "This is all very worrying. If I can speak in confidence…" Zarb cleared his throat. "I am not surprised about your information about the young Mr Kennedy. I know I shouldn't say it, but 'like father, like son' is the phrase. Joe Junior certainly has an eye for the girls, as does his brother Jack, but that said, I cannot believe that he is implicated in any way in this poor girl's death. As to the photographs, well… What could have possibly led her to…?" He looked away and shook his head gravely. "And where are you, Chief Inspector, as regards Morgan?"

"We know that Mr Morgan was involved with the

disreputable people I mentioned. His uncle is a crook who runs a nightclub where Miss Harris was seen. We suspect that the uncle may have been responsible for the photographer's death. We've also now discovered some compromising pictures of Mr Morgan."

"You're losing me."

"I'd prefer not to go into every detail at the moment. I would say that we now have an idea as to where these photographs might have been taken and that may take us closer to the truth."

"Is there anything you need from me apart from Joe Junior's schedule?"

"No thanks, but you should know that we are quite certain that Arthur Norton was also involved in some way in all of this and we plan to question him further. We may not be able to go as easily on him as we did last time. As you know, I think, Mr Norton got the Foreign Office on our back the last time."

"That was nothing to do with me."

"So we guessed. Anyway, we think it unlikely that the Foreign Office will come riding to the rescue again as the official involved last time is himself a little compromised with Mr Norton in these affairs."

"Not a fellow called Douglas, by any chance?"

A thin smile played across Merlin's lips. "That's the one, sir. You know him too?"

"I know of him."

"In any event, Douglas has provided us with further information and we're going to speak again to Norton. I just wanted to make sure that I wasn't treading on your toes by doing so."

"Not at all. I should just mention two things. First is that as an accredited servant of this Embassy, he does have the benefit of diplomatic immunity. The second is that I have just been requested by Washington to return him home. I was planning to speak to him this morning to tell him to get on the first available ship, so I should see him sooner rather than later if I were you."

★ ★ ★

Norton was nursing a cup of coffee when the telephone rang. He'd had another lively night, though this time not at The Blue Angel. He had decided to be sensible and follow everyone's advice by giving the club a wide berth for a while. He had not, however, given Berkeley Square a wide berth and Edie's friend Lucy, who was very adventurous for one so young, had only just left the flat. Norton was lying back thinking of little except the strange new rash around his groin. He was hoping it wasn't something he was going to have to see someone about when the sound of the phone in the hall gave him a start. He eased himself out of bed and padded to the hall. "Mayfair 468."

"Norton, is that you?"

"Yes, who's that?"

"It's Douglas."

"Morning, Freddie. What's wrong? You don't sound yourself. I've got some news by the way. The Ambassador had an appointment to see the…"

"Not on the phone, Arthur."

"No, of course. You sound terrible."

"Yes, well, something's come up. I think we should let this matter between us rest for the moment."

"But, I thought…"

"Look. I've decided I need to keep my head down. And if I were you, I would do the same."

"But what about when I get an answer back? I'll need to let the Count…"

"All that's up to you now. All I can say is that I'm dropping out of the picture. I've got other problems to worry about."

"But…"

"But nothing. And by the way, I'd watch out for those

policemen if I were you. I won't be able to keep them off your back from now on. And your friend Morrie Owen is a viper, so watch out for him too."

"What do you…"

"Must be off."

The phone clicked. Norton sat down and looked at his blotched face in the hall mirror. In the silence he could hear his heart beating loudly.

* * *

Merlin was pacing up and down the cobbled mews impatiently when they heard a clattering noise, then saw P.C. Cole appear around the corner. "What took you so long?"

"Couldn't find a car, sir, or a taxi. I had to come on my bike." Cole dismounted hurriedly and slipped as his boots hit the cobbles.

"Careful, careful. Here, put the bike up against the wall and give me the doorkeys."

Merlin opened the outer door to Morgan's mews flat and led the way up the stairs and through the second door. They stood at the foot of the bed looking at a soothing picture of a yacht sailing into a sunlit bay.

"The photographs of the girls, please, Sergeant." Bridges set the pictures down on the bed and Merlin studied them intensely before clapping his hands. "Look, you can just see the edge of the frame of that picture in these photographs. Ah… and here's what looks like the shadow of that chest of drawers on the wall. It's a different bedcover and there's nothing to really distinguish the bed but I'd put money on these photos having been taken here."

"It's a match, sir."

"Let's have a look at the Douglas picture. This is a little more close in so it's harder but, ah, yes, do you see? Behind Morgan's head. There are two small plugholes on the wall and if we… yes look, here they are."

Cole politely enquired as to the nature of the pictures.

"Sorry, Constable. I forgot that you were out of the loop on these. I'll let Bridges explain in a minute but, first, can you tell us whether you've got an answer on the ownership of this place?"

"It's quite a complicated situation, sir. Do you want all the detail?"

Merlin sat down on the bed and took his hat off.

"No. Just tell me the final name."

"I went through a long chain of companies and I finally arrived at a person, the name of that person being Mr Harold Parsons."

"That's not who I was expecting. Did you find out who he is?"

"When I got back to the Yard late yesterday – you were both out – someone from Vice dropped by and asked me to give you a file of Morrie Owen's previous convictions. Said you'd asked for it a few days ago and sorry for the delay. I hope you don't mind, sir, but I had a quick leaf through the file. First thing I noticed was a case made against Morrie Owen in 1933 for living off immoral earnings. He got off, by the way, and at the bottom of the page I noticed the very same name."

"The same name as who?"

"Parsons, sir. Harold Parsons was Morrie Owen's solicitor."

★ ★ ★

The wind was whistling hard against the windows when Merlin returned to his office. He found a note on his desk from Robinson saying that she had gone to get the forensic report on Myerson. There was nothing from Zarb as yet. He grabbed a pen and a piece of paper, paused for a moment's thought, then started to write:

"Owen, through his lawyer, owns Kensington Mews flat. In flat Myerson takes nude pictures of Harris and Donovan.

Assume photo of Donovan taken on night I followed her and Morgan back. Myerson must have been person I saw going in."

He stopped writing and stared hard at his words. Then he got up, walked to his open office door and shouted. "Sergeant, bring me the photos."

When Bridges had laid the pictures on his desk, Merlin took a magnifying glass out of one of his filing cabinets and stood poring over the images of the girls and Douglas. Eventually he sat down with a satisfied look.

"This is what I think happened, Sergeant, with the same method of operation for both girls. Morgan, a good-looking chap, attracts both girls – he takes them out, plies them with drink, gets them back to Owen's flat and gets them to bed. In the photographs we have, the eyes of both girls are closed. Once he's had his way, the girls, already very drunk, are knocked out by some sleeping draught, at which point our friend Bernie, waiting outside by prior arrangement, nips in and points his camera."

Bridges nodded his agreement, then held up his hand. "But why?"

"That's what we have to find out. Now with Douglas, I think things are clearer. Same method of operation but with a motive: Someone – Morrie Owen – knows Douglas' tendencies. Johnny Morgan is a flexible sort of person. He'll do anything if there's money in it. Somehow or other he's set up with Douglas. Pictures are taken in the flat of the two men, when Douglas has been knocked out with something as, again, his eyes are closed. The pictures are to be used to blackmail Douglas at the appropriate time."

"How does Kennedy fit into all this?"

"I don't know but I think we'd better pay Owen another visit."

The telephone rang as they stood up. "Thanks. We'll see you later." He listened and nodded.

He replaced the phone in its cradle.

"Robinson. The forensic people confirmed that Bernie died of alcoholic poisoning and that his hands has been tied shortly before his death. She's picking up the artist's sketch later."

* * *

After a wasted journey to Earl's Court where they were told by Annie Owen that Morrie had gone early to work, Merlin was feeling distinctly edgy. He led the way down the stairs to the club, and at the bottom they heard voices which didn't seem to be coming from behind the main entrance but from somewhere down the corridor. He saw a door at the end on the right and nodded to the others.

Owen and Reardon were sitting on opposite sides of a desk covered in bank notes.

"Robbed the Bank of England, Morrie?"

"Very funny, copper. Just counting our legitimate takings. What do you want?"

"I came to offer you my sympathy, Morrie. A close friend of yours has died. Bernie Myerson."

Morrie Owen, his hands reaching out protectively to the pile of cash in front of him, just about achieved a look of surprise. Reardon's gaunt features remained impassive. "That's sad. Painful death, was it?" Morrie pulled some of the cash towards him.

"Someone poured a few too many bottles of booze down him. Not a very nice way to go."

"From what I understand of Bernie's habits, it would probably have been his preference, eh, Jimmy?" Owen snorted.

"Strange, isn't it, how so soon after Bernie gave us a little information about you, he ended up dead?"

"I've got nothing to do with it, copper."

"Really? I find that a little hard to believe."

"Got any evidence? You need evidence if you're going to start making allegations."

"Don't worry. We'll find some."

Owen picked up a leather bag from behind his chair and started shovelling in the cash. "You're full of shit, copper. Why don't you just bugger off and leave me in peace?" Owen moved his chair back from the desk to relieve the pressure on his stomach.

Merlin reached over the desk and poked his finger hard into Owen's gut. "And another thing, Morrie. Know anything about drugs, do you? Perhaps that's where this cash comes from? Are those the weekly takings from your cocaine run?"

Owen glanced nervously at his inscrutable sidekick.

"Name of Braithwaite mean anything to you? A chemist round the corner. Jimmy here knows him, don't you? In and out of the place like a regular little hypochondriac. Another of my officers has gone to pinch the gentleman and his lady wife. Apparently he's come into a lot of money over the past year and we think we know the source. Good supplier, is he?"

"Don't know what you're talking about." Owen rubbed his stomach with a pained look.

"That's alright, because I haven't cautioned you yet. We'll have a longer chat when we get you back to the Yard. And I've got some other questions to ask about the little pad you own in Kensington. Sergeant, can you…" There was a sudden blur of motion on Merlin's right as Reardon jumped to his feet and bolted for the door. His old legs had surprisingly carried him almost to the top of the stairs by the time Cole hauled him down.

When Merlin and Bridges reached the street, with Owen puffing and wheezing between them, Reardon was spread-eagled face down on the pavement, his hands cuffed behind his back.

"A nifty turn of speed there, Jimmy. If you were a bit darker I might have thought you were related to Jesse Owens. Well done, Constable. Let's get them back to the Yard. We've got a lot to talk about, Morrie. And, we've got some more pictures to show you."

* * *

Arthur Norton was very angry and very drunk. His day had started badly with a rebuff from Nancy Swinton, with whom he had belatedly decided he might start to put his love-life on a more regular footing. She wasn't his ideal but he felt he had to put the whores behind him, and there was no doubt she had a certain style. Infuriatingly, however, she had declined his luncheon invitation because, as she put it in her fancy English way, she had it on recent good authority that 'not only was he an appeaser of the first rank but also a frequent habitué of the sleaziest of London nightclubs.' Then, following his upsetting conversation with Zarb, he had tried to track down the Ambassador. It took him an hour to get a connection. Eventually he had reached Hyannis Port but had been told that they thought the Ambassador was in Washington. Then, after another delay, he had got through to the Ambassador's New York office to be told that he had gone down to Florida overnight. Finally he got through to Palm Beach to be told that the Ambassador had just gone out on the golf course and had given instructions that he wanted no interruptions during his game. By this time it was past five and he had turned his attention to Jack Daniels.

He was due at a reception in the Italian Embassy at six-thirty. Before Zarb's call he had been dithering as to whether to send his regrets to the Embassy in light of Douglas' morning message. In his fury with Zarb he had then forgotten all about the reception. Now slumped in his chair and, emptying another shot of bourbon into his glass, he remembered. He blundered into his bedroom, pulled a clean shirt out of his chest of drawers and took down his tails, which were hanging on the outside of his wardrobe. "Damn them all," he muttered. He could do what the hell he liked and didn't care what Douglas, Zarb or anyone told him. He would go to the reception tonight and later he'd have some fun. Maybe he'd pick up someone new – or perhaps he'd search out Edie's friend. She was game!

Tomorrow he'd speak to the Ambassador and sort out this stupid business about returning to the States. He didn't want to go and he wasn't going to, at least not until he thought the bombs were about to fall and that was probably a few months away yet, even if the British government was idiotic enough not to pursue the terms he knew were on offer from Berlin.

He went into the bathroom and shaved. His hand was unsteady and he cut his chin. He swore loudly before mopping the blood away with his facecloth and applying a piece of cotton wool.

He was going to be late. He went back into the bedroom and, as he was dressing, he glanced up at the box on top of the cupboard. After he'd pulled on his trousers, he reached up – he wanted to look at the latest addition again. He was seated on his bed examining it with immense pleasure when the doorbell sounded.

* * *

They made sure that the Braithwaites had a good view of the handcuffed Owen and Reardon being bundled into the cells as they themselves were led into their interrogation room. Bridges left them on their own for an hour before starting and by then, as he anticipated, Mrs Braithwaite's nerves had been strung so taut that it took little time for the full story of her husband's sideline to come out. They made slower progress with the professionals. Confronted with the photographs of the two girls, Owen shrugged and said they were nothing to do with him. Confronted with the ownership details of the flat, he shrugged again and said that if a solicitor he used occasionally wanted to invest in property, what was it to him? When Merlin in due course told him that the Braithwaites had given sworn statements describing the drugs racket with Owen, he simply said he knew nothing about it and, furthermore, wasn't going to discuss anything further without his lawyer being present. Reardon, meanwhile, looked uncomfortable but just shook his head and said he was saying nothing.

When they had finished, Merlin suggested putting the two men in the same cell. "Perhaps being stuck with Morrie for a while will loosen Jimmy's tongue."

Bridges led them into the holding cell opposite the interview room and within seconds Owen was whining and swearing at his cell mate.

* * *

The wind had dropped finally but it had started to rain when they arrived outside Norton's apartment block. They waved their cards at the porter, who smiled nervously back at them and gave them the flat number. In the lift, Bridges smiled at his boss. "Think we'll get a warm welcome?" Merlin winked back.

"What the hell do you want? I can't see you now. I have an important engagement. I've got nothing to tell you anyway."

"Let us in please, Mr Norton. It is important that we see you."

"I don't think the Foreign Office will be very happy with you when I tell them that you've been harassing me again."

"If you're talking about Mr Douglas, sir, things have moved on a little. He's got other things on his mind now."

"I'm a senior diplomat, you can't speak to me if I don't want you to."

"That's bollocks now, isn't it? We know that you are being sent home to America in disgrace. We need to talk before you go."

The door opened wide. Norton stared at them wildly. A drop of blood fell from his chin on to his white shirt.

"Goddamit." Norton picked with a fingernail at the mark on his shirt and succeeded in expanding the size of the smudge. "Look. I'm not going home. It's all a misunderstanding, which the Ambassador will sort out shortly. That bastard Zarb is jealous of the relationship the Ambassador and I have. He'll…"

"We're not here to listen to your petty grievances against Mr Zarb. May we come in?"

"If you must."

He opened the door and they followed him into the drawing room. "Wait here a minute while I change my shirt." He lurched unsteadily down the corridor.

When he emerged he made directly for the drinks cabinet. "Like one, would you?"

"What we would like is for you to sit down and answer our questions."

Norton poured himself a drink, then wandered unsteadily towards a chair by the window. "Eighteenth century."

"Pardon?"

"Eighteenth century French chairs. Louis XV. The chairs you're sitting in, got them for peanuts on my last trip to Paris before the war started. Very fine, aren't they?"

"So they are. Perhaps we can get down to business."

"Ah yes, business. And what is that?"

"The murders of Joan Harris and Johnny Morgan."

"I've told you before that I hardly know these people and that I know nothing about their deaths."

"If you'll just hold your horses, there are some specific things we are not clear about. Sergeant, please." Bridges held out a photograph.

"This is a picture of Joan Harris. Not very edifying, but there it is. Have you ever seen a photograph of her like this?" Norton glanced briefly at the photograph and snorted. Then he started to rise but Merlin reached across and kept him in his chair.

"Answer the question."

"I want another drink."

"By the smell of you, I'd say you'd got the annual production of a medium-sized distillery inside you, so forget the drink. Does this photograph ring any bells?"

"The bells it rings, Inspector, are to remind me that Miss Harris was a pretty girl and that it's a pity that she's dead."

"Do you recognise anything particular about the picture?"

Norton's lips spread in a leering smile. "Which parts in particular of Miss Harris would you like me to recognise?"

Merlin just managed to avoid putting his fist into Norton's smug face. "Look chum, I don't like you very much and every second I spend in your company makes me like you less and less. Answer the question. Do you recognise the location where this picture was taken?"

Norton shook his head.

"Did you ever take Miss Harris out?"

"Would a man in my position do such a thing?"

"Why not? I understand there are others of exalted status in the Embassy who don't mind putting it about a bit – how about the Ambassador's sons, perhaps, or even the Ambassador himself?"

Norton shrugged his shoulders and looked warily at the policemen.

"We have reports that you were seen with Miss Harris in a nightclub."

"Not me."

"We understand you were responsible for recruiting Johnny Morgan for the Ambassador's residence."

"I don't know who told you that."

"Johnny Morgan was recommended to you for a chauffeur's job by Morrie Owen, a nightclub owner – he owns a club called The Blue Angel, which you denied knowing and where you were seen by more than one witness with Joan – and you put in a word at the Embassy. We have the records. Please don't waste our time by denying it."

Norton's mouth turned down. His hand trembled as he stroked his empty glass.

"The same Morrie Owen owns the flat where this photograph was taken. We've got Owen in a cell at the Yard, by the way. Helping us with enquiries he is, as they say. Not being very cooperative but he will be. Amongst other things, we found out about his drug business."

Norton swirled the glass around as if to dislodge any remaining dregs.

"Be more surprising if someone like Fat Morrie wasn't providing drugs, I suppose. In any event, the thing is, we have solid evidence about his racket. He's going to realise shortly that he's facing a long stretch on that alone and that none of his fancy friends are going to be able to save him."

"What's your point, Merlin?"

"My point is that I would expect to have all the details of Owen's involvement with you and your diplomatic friends and Miss Harris sooner rather than later. You associated with Owen and with both murder victims. You have lied to us throughout about everything. You seemed to have something going with Johnny Morgan, which you have been unforthcoming about. As they say in your country, you are right in the frame. If I were you and I were innocent, I think I'd decide to tell the truth, however dirty that truth might be."

"You can't scare me. You forget that I have diplomatic immunity."

"Dear, dear, Mr Norton. Is that the best you can come up with? We know that you're not very popular with your own Embassy at present. You say this is all going to be ironed out but who knows? Perhaps your friend the Ambassador hasn't got as much clout as he used to. And of course he's not on the spot. Now, if I wander round to Mr Zarb and tell him that the only conclusion I can form from your failure to provide us with honest answers to our questions is that you killed Miss Harris and probably Mr Morgan too, what do you think he's going to do, since he's such a great fan of yours? I don't know quite how these things work but if you've been recalled and overstay your welcome here, presumably your status ceases. Or given the potential for unpleasant repercussions arising from the Embassy's having employed and then protected a murderer, who's to say that the powers that be might not cut a little deal under which you are thrown to the wolves?"

"Alright, alright." Norton undid his bow tie and removed

the stud from his collar. He was sweating profusely. "Damn thing's choking me to death."

"Make yourself as comfortable as you like – provided it helps you to tell us the truth at last."

Norton wiped his face with a handkerchief, gave the policeman a look of deep loathing, then sighed in resignation. "Johnny Morgan was referred to the Embassy through me. I was introduced to The Blue Angel by some other diplomat, I can't remember who. I went there several times and Owen was always very attentive. At some point he mentioned that he had a nephew looking for a position as a driver, could I help? I met the boy. He was very presentable and had a cheeky sort of charm. I thought the Ambassador might like him. Not Irish of course but close to, being Welsh I mean."

"Go on."

"Well, I noticed that Morgan had a way with the ladies." He toyed nervously with the collar stud. "One evening I bumped into him at the pub. He was with a pretty young girl. He was rather drunk. We were all rather drunk in fact. And he… he asked me at the end of the evening whether I'd like to come back with him and watch."

"You mean watch him and the girl making love?"

"Yes. So we went to a flat…"

"This flat."

Merlin pointed at the picture. Norton nodded.

"Didn't the girl object?"

"Only for a short time. She was drunk when we got to the flat and he had some pills or drugs he gave her. She didn't really know where she was."

"Did Morgan require anything of you for this show he put on?"

"He asked for some money. I gave him a fiver that time, I think."

"And how does this bear on the story of Miss Harris?"

Norton closed his eyes. "Morgan invited me to watch

several other times but on one occasion the girl got very upset and it didn't work out. The invitations stopped but a while later he started offering me pictures. Said he knew someone who had a nice line in nude pictures and so on. I bought a few pictures from him. Then towards the end of last year I noticed that he was very friendly with Miss Harris. I thought she was very attractive and I suggested that I'd pay him well for a good picture of her. He said he thought he could manage it."

"So Johnny Morgan seduced Joan Harris?"

"I think he found it easier than he expected as she was on the rebound from someone."

"This would have been when?"

"Late November, early December."

"I can't think she would willingly submit herself to a photographer?"

"He drugged her for the pictures, same way he drugged the first girl I watched him with."

"So this is one of the photographs taken on that occasion?"

"I should think so."

"And you paid Johnny Morgan for this?"

"I gave him £20 for Miss Harris' pictures."

"And following this you started taking Miss Harris out?"

"Yes."

"Why did she agree to go out with you? I understand she didn't particularly like you."

"I showed her a photograph."

"You threatened her with exposure of the photograph and possible loss of her job unless she did what you wanted?"

Norton lowered his eyes.

"And so you took her to The Blue Angel and other places?"

"Yes."

"Did you sleep with her?"

Norton nodded. He felt nauseous.

Merlin felt nauseous. He walked to the window and looked out at the wet street below. "After you'd had your way with her, Mr Norton, what happened next?"

"After Christmas I decided that it wasn't so wise to see her so I…"

"You dropped her?"

"Yes."

"Or at least that's what you'd like us to think."

Norton staggered to his feet, his sweat-soaked hair plastered untidily to his forehead. "No, no, it's the truth. I told her to forget all about it."

"What did she say to that?"

"Look, she couldn't stand me. She was pleased that I lost interest. She was a bitch but…"

"But what?"

"She was very unhappy."

"And?"

"Are you sure this wasn't just a suicide?"

"We are, although if it had been a suicide it's pretty clear from what you've told us that you would be one of the main causes."

Norton shook his head.

"And Morgan. Did you do away with him so that none of this would emerge?"

"No, no. I didn't kill anyone. In fact, he was…"

"He was what?"

"Nothing."

"Sergeant. The other one, please."

Bridges showed Norton the second photograph.

"I presume you're trying to tell me Johnny was still working on getting you more pictures. Is that right?"

Norton stared at Kathleen Donovan's sinuous naked body and nodded, slowly.

"Same routine, no doubt. You fancied Miss Donovan, weren't getting anywhere, asked Morgan to seduce her and he got pictures taken when she was drugged up. Have you had a chance yet to practise your blackmail on her?"

"No, I haven't done anything to Kathleen. I swear."

"Only a matter of time though, wasn't it? I'll have that

photograph back, please, and before we go I'd be grateful if you'd give your full collection of photographs to the Sergeant."

In the bedroom, Norton retrieved the box from under the bed where he had hurriedly pushed it when the policemen had arrived.

"There's no need for anyone else to know about this is there, Sergeant?"

"You must be joking, sir."

"It's got nothing to do with Miss Harris' death."

"That remains to be seen. And who's to say that these photos had nothing to do with Johnny Morgan's death?"

Norton swore loudly then collapsed heavily onto his bed as Merlin joined them.

"One last question for now: Do you know if Miss Harris was seeing anyone in particular apart from you before or after Christmas?"

"No. Except for what Johnny said about her being on the rebound, and if that was true I don't know who she was on the rebound from."

"And do you know anything about her thinking she was pregnant?"

"Good God, no. She wasn't pregnant, was she?"

"No, sir, she wasn't. Come on, Sergeant. I need some fresh air. Please don't contemplate leaving London yet, Mr Norton."

* * *

A few yards along the corridor from Merlin's office, adjacent to one of the meeting rooms, was a little alcove used for brewing up. Four decrepit chairs surrounded a small, round table above which a grimy window looked out onto blackened brickwork. Cole was hurriedly shovelling tea leaves into the pot. He'd not had a chance to eat or drink anything all day and he was discovering that detective work was thirsty work. He was excited too and for some reason that always made his mouth dry. Ten minutes earlier he had been called down to the cells where Reardon had asked for a private word. After moving to the interview room, against a background of foul Morrie Owen invective, Reardon had informed him that he was ready to talk on certain conditions, which would have to be discussed with Merlin. Cole had arranged for Reardon to be deposited in another cell on his own, and was waiting anxiously for his boss to return.

Rummaging in the back of a cupboard he found a packet of just about edible digestive biscuits and settled down to his tea, with an ear cocked for the sound of life outside Merlin's office. He had just poured himself a second cup when he heard steps and stuck his head out into the corridor.

"Oh. It's you."

"No need to sound so disappointed. Any more in there?"

Claire Robinson squeezed past Cole to get herself a mug and sat down with a sigh of relief.

"A hard grind this isn't it, Tommy? I may call you Tommy, mayn't I?"

Cole shrugged. For some reason he felt a little nervous. He glanced at the door then sneaked a look at his companion out of the corner of his eye. She was an attractive girl, no doubt. Tommy Cole wasn't normally the type to get tongue-tied with a pretty girl. An only son, with four sisters, he knew how to handle women – but this one intimidated him for some reason. Robinson smiled across at him – when she smiled her nose crinkled appealingly and the little beauty spot beneath her nose disappeared from sight.

"You can call me Claire if you like. What are you up to?"

She spoke differently to the women he knew. Very posh but not too stuck-up. That's how it seemed anyway. And, of course, the A.C. was her uncle – a little disturbing that. He turned to face her full-on and attempted to gather his composure.

"It looks like Reardon's going to squeal. Wants to see the Chief Inspector as soon as he's back."

"Golly, that's good."

"And you, er, Claire? How is your side of things going?"

With difficulty in the confined space, Robinson managed to cross her legs, affording Cole the pleasing view of a finely-turned calf. "I'm just waiting for that damned sketch artist to give me his drawing. He said I'd have it by now."

There was a moment's silence as they both awkwardly contemplated their mugs.

"Mr Merlin seems a nice chap. Rather charming in an old-fashioned sort of way."

Cole nodded.

"Clever too, of course, as you'd expect."

Cole nodded again.

"And Mr Bridges is very pleasant. A cheery soul."

"Yes, he is."

Robinson uncrossed her legs and reached out for a biscuit.

"I understand you're a bit of a sportsman, Tommy. A cross-country champion, isn't that right?"

"I've had a few lucky runs."

"Modest with it too. I played hockey myself, at the Police College and school before that of course. I like taking exercise. I'm told there's some sort of gymnasium downstairs. Perhaps some time we might…"

The sound of a door banging down the corridor interrupted her. Cole jumped to his feet, cast her an apologetic smile and hurried out. Robinson shook her head thoughtfully before washing the mugs in the sink.

* * *

Merlin, Bridges and Cole sat facing Reardon as he made himself as comfortable as he could on the small, white, wooden chair at the end of the table.

"I understand you'd like to talk to us, so talk away." Merlin stared at Reardon's oversized aural equipment and couldn't help himself. "We're all ears."

Reardon obliviously tugged at his right earlobe. "If I tell

you coppers what I know, I expects something in return."

"I don't know that I can make any promises. Tell us what you know and we'll see what we can do."

A low gravelly sound, which Merlin took to be a laugh, emerged from Reardon's mouth. "You must take me for a mug. If I give you Morrie Owen on a plate, I expect to be looked after, alright?"

"And how are you going to give him to us on a plate?"

Reardon leaned across the table and spoke softly. "You want to know who did for Bernie? Ask away, but I want to know that I'll be protected and looked after. You can do it 'cos I know it's done all the time. You even looked after Bernie when he helped you out with the Sabinis, didn't you?"

"You knew about that, then." Merlin glanced across at Bridges. "Look Jimmy, we've already got Morrie for drug dealing, and you for that matter. Why do I need to cut deals?"

Reardon ground out another laugh. "Come on, copper. So you got a statement from Braithwaite and his old bag, eh? What makes you think they'll stick to their statements? Think Morrie can't get to them before the trial whether they're in or out of prison? Come on. He may be a fat slob but he's a powerful man. Why do you think he's banging away there telling me to keep my trap shut, eh? He knows he can sort out the Braithwaites."

"Why did you do a runner? And why are you telling me all this now?"

"Panicked, didn't I? Getting too old for this lark. Didn't think it through. Little spell in the tank allowed me to think."

"So, why not keep quiet and let Morrie Owen warn the Braithwaites off? That would save your bacon too, wouldn't it?"

"Nah. Thought about it, but I've had enough of Morrie Owen. I think he's had enough of me too. Heard 'im say to someone the other day that I was past it and that he was thinking of sacking me. In this business, sacking isn't just a matter of giving people their cards and a retirement clock –

it's a little more like the way Bernie was moved on." Merlin stared down at his hands and thought for a moment.

"Very well. If you turn King's Evidence we'll look after you. But we'll want everything, mind. We'll gratefully start with Bernie's death but I'll want to know all about Owen's other scams. And I'll want to know about his involvement with Joan Harris and Johnny Morgan. And the details of the Douglas blackmail. And be careful because we know plenty already."

"Whatever you want. As long as you keep your end of the bargain." He raised a hand to his nose and sniffed the nicotine stains on his fingers enthusiastically. "Couldn't get one of your boys to get me a fag, could you? I'm gasping."

CHAPTER 14

Saturday February 10th

The rising winter sun cast a feeble glow of light over the City of London and the river. In due course its muted beams reached Scotland Yard and a few delicate rays found their way to Merlin's desk, picking out the latticework of the Eiffel Tower paperweight before moving across the surface to touch his crumpled face. Faint as it was, the light imparted some warmth and his left eyelid cracked open. His right slowly followed.

The interview with Reardon had finished after midnight. Merlin had sent the others home and gone into his office to have a quiet think before making his way to Chelsea. Instead he had fallen asleep at his desk.

He rubbed his neck, which had a crick in it, and stretched his arms and legs. His wristwatch showed that it was just after eight.

In one of the bottom drawers of his desk he found a small wash bag, which he kept in the office for occasions such as this, and walked down the corridor to the washroom.

When he got back to his office he felt much fresher. He realised that he hadn't eaten anything the night before and was ravenous. A quick trip to Tony's was feasible. Bridges probably wouldn't be in for another half-hour and he set off down the stairs. Unfortunately, at the bottom, he walked straight into the A.C.

"Frank. Just the man. I was trying to get hold of you all of yesterday. Come and tell me what's going on."

"I was just nipping out for a quick bite to eat, sir."

"I'll make you a cup of tea in my room."

The A.C. bounded up the stairs energetically. For a man

who was stiff and rigid in most aspects of his life, he was surprisingly loose-limbed. Merlin knew that he had been a keen beagler for many years, chasing foxes madly around the Surrey countryside on foot with other like-minded country types. The A.C. had given up this hobby only the previous year. As a consequence, his weekends were now spent entirely in the company of Mrs Gatehouse, to which circumstance Merlin largely attributed the A.C.'s recent enhanced level of irascibility.

The A.C. pushed through his door, glared briefly at the offensive geraniums, then offered refreshment. And so Merlin sat listening to his stomach rumble with one of the A.C.'s notoriously weak cups of tea cradled in his hands. He had given a quick rundown of his progress, after which the A.C. found it difficult to remain still. Gatehouse got up, walked to the window, opened his mouth to speak, thought better of it then returned to his desk. His right hand strayed to an ink bottle which he twirled round for a few seconds. Eventually it appeared that what he had been told had settled in his mind. "Let me see if I've got this straight. The story now seems to be as follows. This swine Norton meets Johnny Morgan through the good offices of Morrie Owen, the owner of a sleazy club which Norton and various diplomatic friends of his frequent. Mr Norton procures Morgan a job at the Ambassador's residence. Morgan, no doubt a sharp boy, plays on Norton's weaknesses to extract money from him. Initially he allows him to watch him having relations with women in Owen's Kensington flat. Then he arranges to have pictures taken for his perverted edification. At Norton's prompting, he seduces Miss Harris, a pretty girl at the office who has rebuffed Norton's own advances. This occurs around the time that Miss Harris herself has been rebuffed by the Ambassador's son. Photographs are taken, which Norton uses to blackmail Miss Harris into having relations with him. Norton in due course tires of Miss Harris."

"That's about it."

"Miss Harris later attends a doctor for a pregnancy test

which proves negative, in the company of a man. You are waiting on a sketch of this man. It may be the Ambassador's son."

"That's right. I am awaiting confirmation as to his movements over the past two months. I'll be seeing the sketch this morning."

"In addition – thanks to Mr Reardon, is it?"

Merlin nodded.

"In addition, thanks to Mr Reardon's turning King's Evidence and your other enquiries, you have pieced together a picture of Mr Owen's criminal activities which overlap to a certain extent with the sad tale of Miss Harris."

"Yes, sir."

"This puts Mr Owen at the centre of a range of illicit activities including drug-running, prostitution, loan-sharking and blackmail. In the course of these activities he employed Mr Bernie Myerson, the man who took Morgan's lewd photographs, Owen taking a cut of Morgan's earnings for so doing. Myerson, also with the assistance of Morgan, took the photographs of Mr Douglas engaged in sodomy for Owen's blackmail purposes. Your discovery of Mr Myerson's involvement prompted Mr Owen to arrange for him to be murdered by some of his underworld connections, and Mr Reardon will give evidence to this effect?"

"Yes, sir."

The A.C. steepled his hands in front of his face.

"It's all terribly seedy, isn't it?"

"Very."

"However, while you've got a large cast of villains, it seems you still don't know who actually committed the murders."

"I think we're getting close."

"Yes. Well, you'd better get on."

Merlin smiled wearily.

"You haven't notified Douglas' superiors yet about the photographs, have you?"

"Not yet, no, sir."

"Well, I suppose I'd better. Halifax isn't going to be very happy."

"I'd rather you wait a little. Until I've finished my enquiries."

"If you prefer, but try and make it snappy."

* * *

The wind had got up again and raindrops the size of marbles were battering the windowpanes in his office. On the other side of Merlin's desk sat a cheerful Johnson, who had hurried into the office to convey the happy news that he had nailed Edward Fraser.

"The forensic people have matched a print from the victim's briefcase. At the time of the accident they lifted a partial print from the case but said they wouldn't be able to match it. But there's a new chap in there. Brought some new methods over from the States where he's been on secondment. He says he can make a match."

"I hadn't realised you'd got Fraser to provide fingerprints, Peter."

Johnson, his arms waving around with unusual excitement, explained how he had become friendly with a Special Branch officer the previous year, on a case he had worked when a Scottish communist had taken a pot shot at the Dominion Secretary. "I got in touch with him and asked if he could pull Fraser's security vetting file. He did, and on the file, of course, were Fraser's fingerprints. That's how we got the match." Johnson stood up. "I'm off to see him now."

"That's good work. Once you've brought him in I wouldn't mind a word to see what he's got to say about Norton. If…"

The door banged open and Bridges walked in with the two constables.

"Robinson's got the sketch, sir."

Robinson passed the drawing across the desk to Merlin

who stared hard at it before eventually grunting with disappointment. "No. It's certainly not Kennedy. I can't say who… something's stirring at the back of my brain but I can't pin it down. You've had a look, Sergeant?"

Bridges felt there was something familiar about the face but couldn't say more than that. Cole also couldn't help.

Merlin stood up with a sigh and walked to the window, leaving the sketch on the desk. "That's a bit of a let-down then."

"Mind if I have a look?"

Johnson, who had remained when the others entered, picked up the drawing, looked at it carefully then smiled. "The nose is a little wrong, and the hair isn't quite right, but…"

"You know the man, Peter?"

"Best put your coat on, sir."

* * *

It had snowed heavily overnight and was snowing still on the Wilhelmstrasse. As Giambelli emerged from the car, two men hurried out from behind a small truck to clear his pathway to the entrance of the building. He had not visited the German Foreign Office for a few years and on his last visit the sun had been shining on a sweltering July day. Today's contrastingly bleak weather better matched his mood. He had been enjoying a champagne cocktail at Friday's Italian Embassy reception when Rossetti had crept up to him in that irritatingly supercilious way that he had and pointed to the nearest exit. An urgent message from Rome had apparently just been decrypted. His ultimate superior, Count Ciano, had been asked by Berlin for a report on the progress of Giambelli's initiative with the British and the Americans. Apparently they would prefer a report in person. Transport had been laid on and so now, after a boneshaking journey via Stockholm in a freezing old Italian cargo plane, Giambelli stood unhappily in the austere marbled lobby of the German Foreign Ministry. It was not only the disruption of his evening and the travails of the journey which lay behind his sombre mood – he had come all this way with little significant progress to report. But then, he mused as he rubbed his eyes, that wasn't exactly his fault and was he not seeing an old drinking friend again? The Reichsminister had been Ambassador in London for a couple of years prior to the war. Giambelli's mood lightened a little, and lightened further when, on entering the Reichsminister's palatial office, he was met with a beaming smile and a glass of Sekt.

"Some champagne for you, my friend, to revive you after your, no doubt, tedious journey. It's one of my own." Ten years earlier, Joachim von Ribbentrop had been a champagne salesman. He had been a very good salesman and had married the daughter of his boss, the owner of the country's largest producer of Sekt, the champagne of the Rhine. Shortly thereafter he had met his idol, Adolf Hitler, and had begun his dizzying rise to the highest echelons of the Nazi command.

Giambelli grasped the proffered glass and returned Ribbentrop's smile, his face briefly registering surprise that his host was in uniform. "Ah, yes. The outfit. I'm sorry but Himmler has one of his patriotic teambuilding get-togethers this weekend – Wagner, Goethe and all that – and has asked me to attend and make a speech. I'm a member of the S.S. now, you know, Ricardo. What do you think? Quite smart is it not?"

"Very. It beats what Il Duce gets us to wear sometimes, I'll say that."

Ribbentrop slapped Giambelli on the back, then guided him to a sitting area to the right of a gigantic partners desk. "It is good to see you again, my friend."

"Likewise, Joachim."

They were speaking in English, their one common language.

"And how is London these days?"

"Surprisingly jolly. Much fun is still had despite the dark clouds hovering above."

"Ah, yes. The English and their famous sangfroid. I had a bellyful of that when I was there."

Ribbentrop shook his head, dislodging a thin lock from above his receding forehead. He smoothed his hair back then sneered. "We shall see how stiff their upper lips remain under the torrent of metal the Luftwaffe will soon be raining on them." He threw the remains of his drink down his throat and poured out another glass for himself and his guest. His features resettled into their original cast of benign equanimity. "Forgive me, Ricardo. There I go again. The thought of the English often makes me lose my temper."

He adjusted one of the medals on his jacket. "Now to business. Perhaps you are about to tell me that there will, after all, be no need for the Luftwaffe to cross the Channel and blitz the English. What news have you for me?"

"Not much, I'm afraid. We have had little communication and my sources tell me that our contacts may be in some difficulty."

"Difficulty. You mean they have been found out?"

"No. They have other problems."

The Reichsminister twirled his glass in the air and sighed. "Was a message ever passed to the Americans?"

"I believe so, but the conduit we used has not reported back to us. I should note that our people in Washington have observed that Ambassador Kennedy has met with the President recently."

"Ah!"

"Our people in Washington have also observed to me that Mr Kennedy is not currently in the best of favour at the White House."

Ribbentrop crossed his legs, causing his leather boots to squeak and creak. "I know. I know. The Ambassador is a powerful, isolationist voice it is true, but I tried to tell the Fuhrer that Kennedy was not the best channel to use. However, he insisted – he was sure that his would be the most persuasive voice to use on Roosevelt."

Giambelli sipped his champagne while declining a top-up.

"So we don't have any response from your people? What are the 'difficulties' you mention?"

"We have been using senior people in Halifax's office and a long-serving aide of Kennedy. I do not have the full picture but there seems to have been some unpleasant, unrelated events in which one or two of them may be implicated. The net result of this has been that my principal British contact has been avoiding me and my American contact's only recent conversation with me was a drunken babble in which he cried off from an engagement last night and said he couldn't talk to me anymore."

"I see."

"I am sorry, Joachim."

Ribbentrop stood up and wandered over to his desk, where he toyed idly with a small sculpture of his own head. "No need to be, my friend. I was against this approach all along. As you know, for years the Fuhrer has harboured delusions about establishing a grand alliance with our Anglo-Saxon cousins. I laboured tirelessly on his behalf to promote this idea during my time in London and was rebuffed at every turn. When Chamberlain used Poland as the basis for a declaration of war, I told him the game was up, and I thought he was persuaded – but still, in some small corner of that great mind, he keeps a door open. Even if this particular approach were to fail, as seems likely, he will probably persist. He will persist that is, of course, until the die is cast – a moment not so very far away now."

"Do you wish the Italian government to do anything further, if we hear no more from our contacts?"

"No. If the Fuhrer wants to try again, I shall use a different route to the American President. I also understand that there is a good prospect of Lord Halifax succeeding Chamberlain in the near future. A more sensitive approach to Roosevelt together with a new, more sensible Prime Minister, may yet pull the English out of the fire, though I doubt it. No Ricardo," he put his arm around Giambelli's shoulders, "all we require of Italy is that it finally gets off the fence and commits wholeheartedly to its destiny in full partnership with the Third Reich!"

Ribbentrop insisted on refilling his guest's glass and they clinked glasses. "Prost, my friend. To the Fuhrer and his, and our, glorious futures."

* * *

Edward Fraser was oblivious to the screech of brakes outside his apartment building. He turned to the final page of his book, read, then closed the book with a satisfied sigh. He set down Mr Pickwick, then toyed with the two other books which had been resting on his side-table. Nickleby or Dorrit – which shall it be? He plumped for Nickleby. He'd read it before of course, more than once, but he needed to continue with his comfort reading at this difficult time. He rose, tossed his chosen book into the open suitcase at his feet and stretched his arms. There was a knock at his door. He felt the hairs on the back of his neck prickle.

Merlin followed Johnson and Bridges into the room as Fraser retreated hesitantly to an armchair by the window. Merlin saw that Fraser seemed dressed for travel and noticed the suitcase next to his chair. The decoration of the room followed the style of the building. Merlin liked art deco and he particularly liked the lamp on the desk in the corner. A languid young female draped in scanty robes holding a globe aloft.

"I suppose you're still pestering me about that accident. As I've told you several times, I had nothing to do with it. My car hit a deer. That's the truth. Anyway, couldn't this wait till Monday. I'm just off to the country."

Johnson glanced at Merlin, who was examining the lamp with interest. "It's your show, Peter, but perhaps before you get to your business, I could ask Mr Fraser a couple of questions."

"Of course."

"I'm Detective Chief Inspector Merlin. These other gentlemen are Detective Sergeant Bridges and Constable Cole. Inspector Johnson you already know."

"A hell of a lot of policemen for a little case like this."

"That's as may be. As it happens, I want to ask you about something other than the case you've been discussing with the Inspector here."

"Oh, Christ. What now?" He waved his arms in frustration and sat down.

"Do you, or rather did you, know a Miss Joan Harris?"

Fraser muttered something to himself and ran his right hand rapidly through his hair. "Yes, I knew Joan. Friend of a friend. Nice girl. Heard she died. A great pity."

"Were you particularly friendly with her, sir?"

"I wouldn't say particularly friendly. She was friendly with a chap called Arthur Norton. I saw her with him."

"Never on your own, sir?"

"No, I don't believe so."

"You never accompanied her on a doctor's visit, for example?" Merlin thought he detected a slight colouring of Fraser's cheeks and a tremor in his hands.

"No."

"That's strange, sir, because we have an identification of you from a Dr Jones. He says he remembers you accompanying Miss Harris at his surgery on January 3rd."

Fraser's mouth moved but no words came out. Eventually he found his voice. "Sorry. I remember now. I went with her just the once. Norton had stopped seeing her. She was worried about something."

"About being pregnant?"

"Well, yes. She was in a bit of a state and asked me to accompany her. As a gentleman I didn't like to refuse."

"So, this was just a gentlemanly favour, sir?"

"Yes."

"You didn't have a relationship with Miss Harris?"

"No. No, I didn't."

"You work with Mr Freddie Douglas, don't you?"

"I do."

Merlin thought for a moment and then nodded at Johnson.

"The Inspector has something to say to you. I'll have some more questions to ask you later."

Fraser gave a slight inclination of his head.

"Mr Fraser, we have found proof of your involvement in the hit and run case…"

"What proof?" Fraser's eyes roamed around the room, avoiding eye contact with any of the policemen.

"We have fingerprint evidence which was found on the victim's briefcase. Conclusive against your…"

Fraser jumped to his feet and pointed a finger angrily at Johnson. "But you haven't got my fingerprints."

"We have received copies from the Foreign Office."

"That can't be right. How could you…?" Fraser walked to the window and leant his head against the glass.

"Now, sir, I am going to place you under arrest and caution you that…"

Fraser turned and walked back towards them, running his hand again through his hair. "Alright. I understand. Anything I say may be taken down in evidence. Look. I'm dying for a pee, so do you mind if I…" He waved behind him.

"Alright, but hurry up."

"As quick as I can, old boy." He disappeared through the door behind him.

Merlin found a small sculpture of a naked lady to admire. "Lovely, isn't it, Sergeant?"

"Not really my sort of thing, sir."

Merlin walked over to a bookshelf and inspected its contents while Bridges and Johnson stared out of the window at a party of children flying kites in Cadogan Gardens. A minute or so passed and Johnson turned and shouted out. "Come on, Mr Fraser. Time to go."

There was no reply. Merlin put a first edition Conrad

down. "El Diablo! Oldest trick in the game." He ran into Fraser's bedroom. Opposite the bed was a locked door and he made way for Cole to make a run at it. In the empty bathroom there was a horizontal window above the washbasin, just large enough for a man to squeeze through. The window was off its latch. Merlin climbed up and looked out. The weather had cleared for now and he could see a narrow ledge extended ten or so yards to the right of the window. He could see the top of a ladder attached to the ledge at the end. "What idiots we are. There's a fire escape here. Come on, Constable. You're the fit one. You go."

Cole squeezed through the window and made for the ladder. "I can see him, sir. He's getting close to the ground."

"Off you go then. Be careful. It will be slippery. Sergeant, you follow Cole. Johnson and I'll take the lift."

"I'll go down the ladder, sir. I think I'm a little nimbler than the Sergeant."

"Alright, Peter."

Bridges nodded his thanks as Johnson clambered out of the window.

They found the lift waiting for them. When they reached the street Johnson was almost at the bottom of the ladder. He turned and shouted. "Sloane Square!"

Merlin spotted Cole weaving his way through some pedestrians halfway down Sloane Avenue. "Start the car, Sergeant." Johnson jumped in and the tyres screamed as Bridges floored the accelerator. A delivery van swerved on to the pavement by the Cadogan Hotel as the car cut across the road. In Sloane Square they saw Cole running across the road and into a large crowd milling outside the Peter Jones department store. "There he is." Merlin followed Johnson's finger and saw Fraser's head bobbing up and down on the far side of the Square. "To the station, Sergeant. That's where he's heading."

Bridges pulled up at the pavement outside the Tube and they all jumped out. Fraser reached the opposite kerb and looked across, meeting Merlin's eyes. A large party of giggling uniformed girls suddenly emerged from the tube station and swarmed around the policemen. A penetrating female voice rang out.

"Now, children, we are turning left here. The Royal Hospital is not far away. Follow me. Single file if you please. Miss Davies, please take up the rear. Patricia, behave yourself or you'll not be coming on another outing like this again."

Cole had got within yards of Fraser but had tripped and was on the ground. Fraser saw him, thought for a second, then ran to his right down Sloane Gardens. Cole got to his feet as Merlin and the other two policemen struggled to extricate themselves from the school party. Merlin waved Cole towards Sloane Gardens.

Fraser had gained a hundred yards or so. He rounded a corner and ran towards the next road junction. In the distance, on the far side of Lower Sloane Street, he saw a taxi pull up. He was exhausted but somehow managed to pick up his pace. A passenger was getting out of the taxi. He reached the junction and shouted. "Stop. Taxi."

The taxi driver heard him and waited. Fraser looked behind him and saw Cole round the corner. He turned and ran into the road. He was almost safe, he thought. He'd get to Paddington and somehow… There was a flash of red, then a sickening thud and he felt a searing pain. As he fell to the ground, all he could see was the taxi driver's face. He could see lips moving. Then everything went dark.

* * *

Merlin paced back and forth in his office, chewing anxiously on a Fisherman's Friend. He was worried that Fraser would die on him before he'd got to the bottom of everything. They'd followed the ambulance to the hospital where, after something of a wait, they'd been told that Fraser was unconscious and fighting for his life. Merlin had arranged for Robinson to maintain a vigil in the hospital, so that he would know immediately of any improvement or deterioration in Fraser's condition. Then he'd sent Johnson, Bridges and Cole back to Fraser's flat to conduct a thorough search.

The telephone rang.

"Yes. Hello. Beatrice. A letter from Charlie? That's wonderful! Where is he? Oh, yes of course he can't tell you that. He's in good shape? Yes. Let's keep our fingers crossed that he stays that way. He was always a tough lad. Yes. If I can I'll be over for lunch tomorrow. As always, there's a case on but I'll let you know for certain later on. Love to Paul."

Thank God for that, he thought. Charlie was a survivor. He'd made it so far. The telephone rang again. "Yes, Robinson. He's awake is he? I'll be right there."

As he reached for his coat, the telephone rang a third time. "You've found what, Peter? Look I'm just heading off to the hospital. Fraser's just woken up. Bring what you've found and meet me there. Bridges and Cole? Well if they want to carry on searching, let them. See you shortly."

★ ★ ★

Having despatched Robinson back to the Yard, they waited impatiently in a narrow corridor of the Westminster Hospital. The antiseptic smells Merlin so hated were everywhere. Despite his best efforts, images of Alice and that awful leukaemia ward in St. Mary's inevitably floated through his mind. A short, barrel-chested man in a white coat eventually arrived. "The name's Lewis. Pleased to meet you. Now this chap has had a very bad knock. The bus bashed his head quite severely and he's broken a few bones."

"Will he live?"

"Touch and go. I understand this accident occurred when he was running away from you?"

"He was. Inspector Johnson and I are investigating a number of violent deaths. Fraser appears to have been responsible for one and was helping us with our enquiries about another."

"Serious stuff then?"

Merlin nodded.

"And you'll be wanting to speak to him now that he's conscious?"

"Naturally."

The doctor's nose twitched. "In normal circumstances I wouldn't allow it, but since these are such important matters…" He sucked his breath. "Very well. Not too long though."

He turned and called down the corridor. A nurse appeared and was instructed to take the policemen to Fraser. She led them down a long corridor, then turned right into another long corridor at the end of which was his room. The patient was lying on his side and was heavily bandaged. A small tuft of hair, one eye and half a mouth could be seen emerging from the dressing on his head. The eye was closed and he was breathing heavily but regularly. The nurse pointed to a small desk in the corridor and then stepped out.

They closed the door and sat down on opposite sides of the bed. "Mr Fraser." There was no response. Merlin gently nudged Fraser's arm. He leaned closer to Fraser's face. "We'd like to speak to you. It's the police."

The visible eye suddenly popped open. Fraser's breathing became irregular and his eyelid fluttered. He coughed twice and his eye closed to register the pain. He slowly cleared his throat. "Who is it?"

"It's Merlin and Johnson. We came to see you at your flat today and you ran away from us."

A noise faintly resembling a laugh emerged from the bed. "Gave you a good run for your money, didn't I? Not bad for a fatty. Bet that young Constable thought he could catch me but I outran him, didn't I?"

"Yes, you did."

Fraser appeared to smile. His eye moved from Merlin to Johnson. "You're the one trying to bag me for that hit and run."

"As I told you, we have got solid evidence…"

"Couldn't get me some water, could you? I'm parched."

Johnson took a jug from the bedside table, filled a glass and held it to the available portion of Fraser's mouth. Half of the water trickled down his chin. "Thanks." He licked his lips. "Hit him hard. Saw that he was a goner. Panicked. Should have stopped. Shouldn't have panicked. She told me. Just an accident. Happening all the time she…" Fraser drifted off.

"Mr Fraser… Mr Fraser."

The nurse reappeared briefly to wave her finger in the air and shake her head disapprovingly at Merlin's raised voice.

The eye reopened.

"You mentioned someone telling you not to panic. A lady. Could you tell us who that was?"

"You couldn't let me have a little water again, could you?"

Johnson poured out another glass.

"Who was the lady, Mr Fraser? Who told you not to panic?"

His cracked lips broke into a faint smile again. "Oh, no one. Sorry, drifting a bit. No lady. Just me. Stupid accident. Should have owned up of course. That's the public school way, isn't it?"

"Mr Fraser. Will you have a look at this? We found it in your flat. Can you tell us why it was there?" Merlin held up a bright red dress which Bridges had found crumpled in a corner of one of Fraser's closets, underneath a pile of bedding.

Fraser struggled to raise his head then fell back. "Ah. A dress."

"Chances are, Mr Fraser, that we shall find someone able to identify the owner of this dress. Why don't you save us the bother?

"The public school way, something I doubt you gentlemen know much about, eh? Own up to your mistakes, one and all." His chest produced an unpleasant gurgling sound. "Very well. I'll tell you about my other mistake as well. In for a penny, in for a pound." With some difficulty he cleared his throat again. "Joan Harris. Lovely girl. Messed around by that bastard

Norton. But I messed her around even more, didn't I?"

Merlin pulled his chair closer. "How so?"

Fraser took a tortured breath then croaked out a long sigh. "Miss Harris was with me on the night of my accident. We'd been out for a spin in the car. I was trying to help her. Cheer her up. After all she went through with Kennedy and then Norton, she'd had to put up with Johnny Morgan pestering her again. After what he'd done to her with Norton, he wanted to have a re-run with her. Pulling the same trick as Norton with the pictures. What a bastard. He'd taken her out for lunch. Said she'd have to go with him to that flat or she'd be in big trouble. Poor girl didn't know what had hit her."

His voice gained a little strength.

"And I didn't have anything to do with those pictures by the way. All Norton's doing. Filthy bastard. I only played along with the chap because of Douglas. Halifax told me to work closely with Douglas who said I should help him with his little plan. Said we needed to get Norton on side. So I cosied up to Norton, the Italian and so on. Thought they could be helpful in finding a peaceful solution to the country's problems. But you know what? See through them now. All this appeasement talk is a waste of time. Hitler's never going to make peace with us. Got to be faced up to. Full of cowards you know, the Foreign Office.

He patted the bed weakly with his right hand to emphasise his point.

"I felt so sorry for Joan, the way Norton abused her. And before that she was led up the garden path by young Kennedy. She thought she might be pregnant by Kennedy and she was pleased! Can you imagine? I went with her to the doctor to hold her hand. I pointed out to her that, even if she was pregnant, Kennedy wouldn't want the baby, but she was convinced that somehow this would help her get him back. It even occurred to me that the baby, if there was one, might be Morgan's or Norton's, but she said that was impossible. I don't know, she was an intelligent girl but... Perhaps she went a little mad because of what they all put her through. I…"

Fraser's eye closed as his words were brought to a halt by a violent coughing fit. The nurse scurried in and held her hand to his forehead, looking accusingly again at the policemen. "You gentlemen will have to leave now."

The racking noise ceased and the eye reopened. "No, Sister. It's alright. Got to get something off my chest apart from all that phlegm. Please let them stay."

Reluctantly, she returned to her desk.

"Thing is, Joan, she was with me when I hit that poor old chap. She wanted me to stop and report the accident. I was a little drunk, got in a flap and we drove off towards the Embankment. I parked the car somewhere. Joan and I walked along the pavement by the side of the river. It was pitch dark. She was a bit hysterical anyway, given all that had happened to her. She was shouting, trying to persuade me to go back to the scene of the accident. I'm afraid I got very het up. There were some people nearby and I was worried that they would hear us. She was trying to pull me back towards the car. I just…"

Fraser's head twisted around and his lips trembled. "I just lost it. I pushed her away. She fell and hit her head on a stone pillar. I didn't mean to hurt her. I didn't mean it. It was just another stupid bloody accident. I'm sorry. I'm so sorry."

Merlin's voice fell to almost a whisper. "And after she hit the pillar…"

"She was dead. Dead. I couldn't believe it."

"What happened then?"

"I, I went to get the car. I put her in the car. I wasn't thinking very straight. I drove in the direction of her lodgings. I don't know what I was thinking. Perhaps that I'd put her in her room. Anyway, as I drove I realised that that was not on. I reached Hammersmith and just realised I'd have to get rid of her body. I drove over Hammersmith Bridge and along the river. Stopped near Kew Bridge. There was no one around and it was pitch dark. It was high tide, and I, I threw her into the river."

"Miss Harris was in her underwear when her body was found."

Fraser's hand found Merlin's arm and squeezed it with surprising strength. "Yes. She was wearing a red dress and a red coat. That dress. Very bright as you can see. I thought she might be more easily spotted in the river, in her clothes I mean, so I took her clothes off. I burned the coat but, for some reason, couldn't bring myself to burn the dress. Smelt so much of her. I liked to smell her fragrance still…"

Something bubbled again in his chest. "She was a beautiful girl."

Dr Lewis appeared at the door as his patient dozed off again. "I'm afraid you chaps will have to come back another time. Nurse here thinks you're rather overdoing it."

* * *

Back at the Yard, the phone rang as he was reading the letter from Zarb confirming that the younger Mr Joseph Kennedy had been out of England since the beginning of December.

"Merlin here. I see. Thank you for calling."

He leaned back in his chair and stared up at his cuckoo clock.

"That was the hospital. Fraser took a turn for the worse. Died about twenty minutes ago."

Bridges looked up unhappily from his paperwork, scratching his head.

"Bugger it. And we hadn't a chance to talk to him about Morgan. He might have had something to do with his death. You know, him having a thing for Miss Harris and seeing her mistreated. Perhaps relieving his guilt at killing her by killing Morgan."

"If he wanted to do that, Sam, he'd have had more grounds to finish off Norton. But it's hard to see Fraser as a knight in shining armour. That stuff about removing her clothes grates. What's that you've got?"

"I was just going over the forensic report on Johnny Morgan."

"You know, I didn't really have as thorough a read of that as I wanted when it finally came in. Let me have a look when you've finished."

"You can have it now, sir. I've got to go and check out some more details on Owen with Jimmy Reardon."

"I think we should go and have another word with Kathleen Donovan."

"Probably best if I meet you at Donovan's place, sir – at 12.30 say?"

"Fine, Sergeant. And bring the pictures."

He settled down to read the report. An hour later he closed the folder, realising that he'd been too tired when he'd read it before. He realised what he'd missed and that it was important.

* * *

Kathleen looked pale and nervous as she opened the door to her brother-in-law's house. She managed a weak smile of welcome then led the way into the front room. There were no enticing smells wafting from the kitchen this time, and the house was quiet.

"On your own, are you?"

"My brother and his family have gone away."

"Ah." They sat down. "You'll be pleased to know that we have discovered what happened to Joan."

Kathleen hunched her shoulders and stared intently at Merlin as he told her about Fraser and Joan, the hit and run and Joan's fall. Her eyes welled with tears. "Poor Joan. I never knew anything about this Mr Fraser."

There was a brief silence, broken only by the sound of a ticking clock. Merlin withdrew a photograph from his coat pocket. "I wish I didn't have to do this but I need to show you something. You'll need to compose yourself."

Kathleen looked confusedly back at Merlin, then took the

photograph from him. She shook as she stared unbelieving at the image. "But… how could… Joan… how could she have posed for such a picture?"

Bridges explained about Norton's arrangement with Johnny Morgan. Kathleen's hand began to tremble and she dropped the photograph. "In certain cases Miss, Johnny appears to have drugged his partner, and the lady was unaware of the photographs being taken. We assume that Joan was unaware of her photographs until…"

"Oh, my God, do you mean…?" Her breathing began to come in short, sharp bursts.

Reluctantly, Merlin reached into his coat pocket again. "I'm afraid we have discovered photographs of you, similar to this one of Joan. It is with a heavy heart that I do this, but…" He placed a second photograph in her lap, blushing on her behalf. For a moment, face frozen with horror, she stared down at her naked self. Then, with a distraught cry, she flung the picture violently away from her, jumped up and ran out of the room.

The policemen waited silently for several minutes until she reappeared, her face pale and drawn, and resumed her seat. Merlin awkwardly extended then withdrew a hand. "I'm sorry I had to do that. We understand in the case of Joan that Norton, having obtained the photographs from Johnny, for remuneration of course, showed them to Joan, frightened her with the threat of their exposure to her employers, and thereby got what he wanted from her. He then tired of her. She turned to Fraser for help. He claims she died in an accidental fall during an argument with him. Whether Fraser's explanation is completely accurate we are unlikely to know, as he died today following an accident while he was trying to evade us."

Kathleen bowed her head.

"We naturally surmise that the photographs of you were taken with the same motive in mind. Mr Norton would no doubt have been attempting to take advantage of you in…"

"Yes, yes, I understand."

They could hear children laughing in the street.

"Can I ask where your brother has gone?"

"Back to Ireland."

"With his family?"

"Yes."

"For a holiday?"

"No. He's gone back for good."

"That's rather sudden, isn't it?"

"I suppose it is."

"What with his being fully employed, his little girl settled in school, and you here, having been through an unpleasant circumstance."

"He said with the war and everything he thought it was safer to go back home, even if work was less plentiful. He's paid the rent up here for a couple of months. Said I could stay if I wanted."

"Did he want you to go with him?"

"Yes he did. He was very keen on it, in fact."

"But you said you'd rather carry on here working for the Ambassador?"

"Yes." The clock on the mantelpiece struck the hour.

"Kathleen, what exactly did you tell your brother about what happened to you?"

Her knuckles whitened as she clasped her hands tightly together. "How do you mean?"

"You were not well at all after your night out with Johnny. Did you tell your brother the real reason why you weren't well?"

"I, I told him that Johnny had not been very nice to me." A tear appeared on her cheek.

"Did you elaborate on what that meant?"

She wiped her eyes with a hand, looked down and whispered. "I told him that Johnny raped me." After a moment's silence, her voice rose. "That's what he did, didn't he? Got me drunk, drugged me, raped me and to top it all took these awful pictures. And I thought he was a nice boy, didn't I? Says a lot for my judgement. I didn't want to tell Cormac or anyone but he was very persistent. He's a sweet talker. He's always been able to get me to tell him everything, has Cormac. He wanted to know what had made me upset and ill. He was concerned about the amount I'd had to drink. He knew I hardly ever drank. He kept on till he wheedled it out of me."

"And what did he do after you told him?"

"He went out."

"Was he in a temper?"

"What do you think?"

"And when did you next see him?"

"I saw him the following day when he came home from work. I spent the day in bed, remember?"

"And did he say anything about Morgan?"

"Nothing. He never mentioned the subject again. Just kept on asking me how I was, that was all."

"Was there anything unusual about him when you saw him?"

"No. Just his usual self."

Merlin folded his arms and leaned forward.

"Kathleen. Do you think Cormac killed Johnny Morgan?"

"No, I don't. But if he did, I don't think I could blame him for it."

He raised an eyebrow at Bridges and got to his feet.

"We'll be going now. At some stage I think you'll have to come to the Yard to make a full, formal statement. We're going to have to see if we can find where your brother is, so we can have a word with him."

"Chief Inspector?" Kathleen's voice was barely audible again. "What will happen to the photographs of me?"

"They are evidence. Joan's murder has been resolved without the need for a trial, but in the case of Johnny Morgan, the photographs might be needed – but I'll do my best to see if we can avoid that."

She stood up, her whole body shaking.

"Very well. I… I'll rely on your best then."

* * *

Merlin's feet were up on his desk again. Bridges noted that somehow or other his boss had found the time to have the hole repaired.

"You're sure that the brother did for Morgan, are you, sir?"

Bridges had just got off the phone to Dublin where the Garda had agreed to track down Cormac Donovan as a matter of urgent priority.

Merlin rubbed his forehead. "It fits, doesn't it? He's a big ox of a man. Despatching Morgan as efficiently as he was despatched would be child's play for Donovan. And when I saw what I'd missed before in the forensic report, the traces of red earth they found under Morgan's fingernails, I thought back to Donovan coming into that front room with red mud all over his boots. Morgan was a ladies' man, a fastidious man. I don't think he'd have allowed himself to have dirty fingernails. Even if Donovan had bathed after work, I'd bet the dirt from the building sites would be engrained in him. If Morgan had to fight Donovan off, red dirt could easily have got under his fingernails. Donovan had motive and opportunity and now he's skipped the country. Yes, I do think Cormac did it. An act of honourable revenge, I suppose. I don't know that I can blame him really, but the law will."

Bridges sucked in his breath and stirred his tea angrily. "Can't we do something about Norton? He's the one at the heart of this mess. If it weren't for him none of it might have happened."

Merlin closed his eyes. One of his favourite tunes played in his mind – 'C'est à Capri'. A lovely summery song. The version by Tino Rossi was the best. He wondered whether Sonia appreciated French music like that. Bridges coughed and Merlin returned to reality. "Of course I'd love to put

Norton away, but what for? Blackmail? A bit thin and anyway, I'm sure the A.C. and Mr Zarb would be encouraging us to hold off and sweep the whole business under the carpet. No. Unfortunately with Norton all we need is to dot some i's and cross some t's and then send him packing."

"It sticks in my gullet, that's all."

Johnson came in, followed by Cole and Robinson. Merlin removed his feet from the desk. "Good! Here's our team. Let me bring you all up to date."

* * *

Over a crackling line, a voice with a surprisingly refined English accent announced itself as Inspector Elwood from the Garda. It was almost midnight and Merlin had just finished writing his report. "We've found the Donovan family, but there's no sign of the man of the house. His wife says he's gone off in search of work. Says she doesn't know where and doesn't expect him back for a couple of days. We've put a description out across the country. We'll let you know when he turns up. I'm sure he will."

EPILOGUE

Arthur Norton looked out of the porthole of his upsettingly spartan cabin. It was dusk and the ship was slowly steaming out of Cork harbour. He'd been lucky to find passage on the MV Winchester at such short notice. Zarb had pulled a few strings and got him on its voyage from Portsmouth to Boston via Cork. His reluctance to leave England had melted away after his latest encounters with the British police. He had given up trying to get through to the Ambassador, who had no doubt succumbed to advice to keep him at a distance. He would have to remind him of what he knew about the seamier side of Kennedy business dealings when he next saw him.

He poured himself a glass of Bushmills and brooded. Those British bobbies would get what was coming to them when Hitler crossed the Channel. How would they like it when the Gestapo were doing their jobs? He thought of Joan's beautiful body. He'd had some fun in England. Pity about what happened to her but c'est la vie. Pity too that he hadn't been able to follow through with Kathleen. His blood pressure rose again. He'd teach that smarmy Irish crook a lesson. He'd make sure Joe Kennedy knew his worth.

After a second drink, he decided to get a bit of fresh air. Up on deck he noticed that the small complement of passengers at Portsmouth had been joined by a few newcomers. Everyone was leaning against the ship-railing, watching Cork recede slowly into the distance. He spotted a pretty brunette and squeezed into a space between her and a tall man. As soon as he got into position, the brunette turned away and walked to the other side of the ship. He sighed and gazed at the waves foaming around the vessel's prow.

"On your way home, are ye?" Norton turned to look at the sturdy red face of the powerfully-built man next to him.

"Yes. Home to Boston. At last."

"Been away a long time?"

"A couple of years in London, yes." The tall man stared hard at the fading lights of the town. "That's my home. Ireland that is, not Cork. Don't know when I'll see it again."

The man's brawny frame shuddered with what Norton took to be emotion.

"Headed for Boston, are you?"

"Yes, I've got some relations there. Hoping to get set up and have my family join me."

The man turned his head and looked closely at Norton. "I lived in England for a while. In north London, in fact." He held out his hand. "Cormac... er... Reilly is the name."

Saturday 17th February

THE TIMES : Losses at Sea

The Admiralty announced with regret last night the loss of three merchant vessels to German U-boat attacks in the North Atlantic. The Merchant Vessels Aurora, Darwin and Winchester were lost on Thursday and Friday.

Monday 19th February

BOSTON GLOBE : Prominent American Diplomat Lost in U-Boat Sinking

Mr Arthur Norton, a senior diplomat at the US Embassy in London for the past two years and a long-time associate of the Ambassador, Mr Joseph Kennedy, was one of the passengers feared drowned after the sinking of the MV Winchester just south of Greenland on Friday last. Mr Norton was believed to be returning for a leave of absence after a successful spell of service in London under Mr Kennedy. All crew and passengers are feared lost after the U-boat attack. Mr Norton was a bachelor and leaves no family.

DAILY MAIL : Knightsbridge Death

A Foreign Office civil servant was yesterday found dead in his house in Hans Place. It is understood from police sources that Mr Frederick Douglas appeared to have hanged himself. Mr Douglas was the only son of the recently-deceased Sir Matthew Douglas, the wealthy industrialist, landowner and former High Sheriff of Cheshire.

Wednesday 21st February

"How's your Polish friend, Jack?"

It was another packed evening in The Surprise. "Dropped me. Figured out that I put you on to her and won't have anything to do with me. Said she didn't like being bothered by policemen, even if they were as nice as you."

Merlin nodded his head in commiseration, while feeling his heart pound a little faster.

"Och, the sacrifices I make. I put you on to my pretty Polish friend to try and help you solve your case. I lose the friend and then hear from you that what she had to tell you wasn't crucial to the case in the end. I think you owe me, Frank. Now let's see. Say, when some nice, pretty female needs a bit of protection, you know who to pass the job on to. Better still, when a film star needs a security escort to a film premiere, I'm your man. Margaret Lockwood or Joan Fontaine will do nicely. You'll bear that in mind, won't you?"

"I will. And sorry about Sonia. Give her a bit of time and perhaps she'll have you back."

"No, no. Moved on to pastures new. There's a smart little

redhead working in an office near my post. Taking her out tomorrow. Muriel her name is. Could be in for some fun there." Stewart belched. "All your loose ends tied up nicely then?"

"Not quite. We still haven't tracked down Cormac Donovan. He seems to have disappeared off the face of the earth. Although our relations with the Irish police are not the best, I truly believe they've tried their hardest for us. I think he's skipped the country."

"Where to, d'you think?"

"America would be the logical choice. I'll have another chat with the Garda tomorrow and ask for his description to be circulated over there. To be honest, I don't really mind if we lose him completely. I'm pretty satisfied that he's guilty of Morgan's murder. If there's a trial, poor Kathleen Donovan will be dragged through the mill and I'd rather avoid that."

"Not like you to be so easy on a murderer."

"Maybe I'm getting soft in my old age. But you know we didn't have a bad result. Apart from Donovan, most of the culprits have ended up paying the penalty one way or another."

"I thought there was just one other culprit. The chap who was run down by the bus."

"Yes, and he may have been the least bad of the bunch. We got Morrie Owen closed down and charged with the Myerson killing, together with his hired hands, the Wisemans. Then there's Morgan, who suffered the Irishman's revenge. Not to mention Norton. Not sure if he wasn't the guiltiest of the lot."

"What happened to him?"

"He went down in a ship on his way back to America. I got the news at the weekend. Another U-boat attack. Terrible tragedy, but in his case, some good came of it."

The two men fell silent. Merlin stared into his beer and shuddered as he wondered what it would be like to drown.

"Is that a new suit you've got there, Frank? Very smart. Boss give you a raise or something?"

"You must be kidding."

"He must be very happy with you though?"

"He was very happy for about one minute. I thought in the brief afterglow of this case I'd try him one more time on the subject of my joining up but he blew me out of the water again. Then he started banging on about the IRA and what a terrible time the Home Secretary was giving him. Then he had a good nag about the fingerprint report I hadn't submitted to him. Finally, to cap it all, he had a go at me about his niece, the one he seconded to my team, because he'd heard she'd gone to the pictures with Tommy Cole, the Constable we had helping us. Said I should have kept a closer eye on her, and it was my fault if he had hell to pay with his wife!" Stewart attempted to look sympathetic but failed. He waved his empty glass in the air and Merlin wandered off to the bar. Rummaging in his pocket for change, he felt that sense of anticlimax he always felt when a case was solved. Alcohol was not the answer, though. He ordered a beer and whisky chaser for his friend and a lemonade shandy for himself. Tomorrow he had to interview an intriguing foreigner who'd been picked up acting suspiciously in Liverpool Street Station. He wanted to have a clear head for that.

Back at the table, the Scotsman frowned. "A chaser for me but not for you? That's not fair."

"Don't worry amigo, Salud. Cheers!"

Stewart laughed. The smile on his face widened almost into a leer. "By the way, Frank, despite her comment about policemen, I think Sonia took a fancy to you. She was intrigued when I told her about your family background. Looks like she might have a thing for dark, brooding, Latin men. You should pop around sometime to say hola."

Merlin looked up at the smoke-covered ceiling. The image of Sonia's captivating face, giggling uncontrollably at the milkman's incontinent carthorse, sparkled in his mind's eye. You know, Jack, he thought to himself, I might just do that – I might just do that!